WONDERFUL AND WILD

Hurt her? She'd never been this excited in her entire life. Her heart was tripping over itself, and she was convinced that if he pressed his mouth against her again, like that, it would explode. "Uh, no," she said lamely. "It's just that . . . I want you here, so I can see your face."

He smiled indulgently. "Okay. I'll stay up here, then. I want to see yours, too." His face was so kind, the last of her jitters were melting—almost.

She had to ask for one final assurance. "You won't hurt me, will you, Darius?"

He pulled her against the length of his body. "Of course not. Not like whoever hurt you before did. I promise."

BOOK YOUR PLACE ON OUR WEBSITE AND MAKE THE ARABESQUE ROMANCE CONNECTION!

We've created a customized website just for our very special Arabesque readers, where you can get the inside scoop on everything that's going on with Arabesque romance novels.

When you come online, you'll have the exciting opportunity to:

- View covers of upcoming books

- Learn about our future publishing schedule (listed by publication month and author)

- Find out when your favorite authors will be visiting a city near you

- Search for and order backlist books

- Check out author bios and background information

- Send e-mail to your favorite authors

- Join us in weekly chats with authors, readers and other guests

- Get writing guidelines

- AND MUCH MORE!

Visit our website at
http://www.arabesquebooks.com

Wonderful and Wild

Simona Taylor

BET Publications, LLC
http://www.bet.com
http://www.arabesquebooks.com

For my son, Riley Simon, born May 16, 2003. If I didn't know what love really was before I met you, I certainly do now. God bless you, sweetheart, now and always.

And for the real *Simona, my wonderful and wild feline friend who lent me her name, and who died in June 2003 at the age of 8, before my son had the opportunity to pull her tail even once. Thanks for killing all those creepy-crawlies, my angel, and for the many nights you kept my feet warm while I wrote.*

One

"Werewolves, huh?"

"Yeah."

"You're kidding, right?"

"Nope." Darius Grant squinted a little under the full blast of his brother's smoke. Darius didn't touch the stuff, wasn't a big one for drinking, either; but Phillip puffed like a steam train, and had had an entire room in his beautiful southern California ranch converted into a wine and spirits cellar. To add insult to injury, he didn't settle for plain old cigarettes: he favored slender cigars—the imported, Caribbean kind, the kind that could get a man into very deep trouble with customs officials, to put it discreetly. Phillip insisted that he smoked not because he craved the dubious benefits of tobacco, but because women loved it.

Darius didn't doubt him. Women seemed to love just about everything that Phillip did, said, wore, drove, and yes, smoked. At forty-two, he seemed to be a lodestone for success, both financial and romantic, although *romantic* might not be the most apt of words. From the stories of his conquests, Darius could deduce that Phillip's cravings lay a lot further south than his heart.

Nobody watching the two men seated at the small table in the upscale Los Angeles airport restaurant would have pegged them for brothers. Cousins, maybe, if you really pressed the issue, but the casual observer would have been content to let them pass for old friends, catching up on stories during a stopover.

Phillip took after their father. Dark, smoothly handsome, with his head meticulously shaved and his beard carefully cropped—he had it trimmed twice a week at a salon so exclusive you needed references to get your first appointment—he looked every inch the ladies' man that he was. He wasn't much more than medium height, but made up for it in breadth. His wide chest made the beautifully fitted linen suit work for its keep, and his biceps screamed personal trainer.

On the other hand, Darius, the last child of Estelle Grant's clutch of seven, favored her closely. He was one or two shades lighter than Phillip, and had inherited Estelle's clear, inquisitive, laughing brown eyes. His unruly hair was perhaps an inch or two too long, but somehow, to look at him, you would find the mess charming rather than unkempt. He was as noticeably tall as Phillip was broad, and slender to the point of being lanky.

Darius was always kidding his brother about his daily workouts, telling him that designer gyms were for people who no longer had to work for their living, and had nothing better to do with their time but pick up a piece of metal and move it from one place to the next—twenty times. For himself, he preferred to keep in shape by running ten miles when the spirit moved him. When the spirit did not, he did his best to undo his good work by stuffing his face with large helpings of anything he could get his hands on, although he always left others guessing as to where all that food went. Darius hadn't gained an ounce since he was twenty.

Darius's sartorial tastes ran to the casual. He wore a blue-and-gray-checked shirt, its sleeves unbuttoned and rolled up at the wrist, and faded blue jeans. Unlike the trendy youths that peopled the restaurant, however, Darius hadn't bought his jeans fashionably prefaded. He preferred to spend much less on the ordinary unstressed variety and then wear them to death. A fleece-lined denim jacket was tossed over the back of his chair, and a small pile of luggage waited at his elbow: suitcase, duffel, and laptop.

Replete, Darius finished the last of his cake and set his fork down. Peanut butter crunch cake, sprinkled with almonds and half suffocated in whipped cream. Maybe he hadn't had a favorite dessert when he'd walked into the restaurant, but he had one now! He had to struggle not to be unduly impressed by his brother's style. Fine dining, even in an airport. Just another example of the many fringe benefits that came with being Phillip Grant. When he was on his own dime, Darius's eat-out dinners came on little Styrofoam trays, and the dessert certainly wasn't peanut butter crunch, not even without whipped cream.

Darius didn't envy his brother's good fortune for a second. For one thing, Phillip had a good fifteen years' head start on him in life. Darius figured that at twenty-seven, he was still entitled to be living on a wing and a prayer. Besides, Phillip had worked hard, played the stocks, and won, and that made Darius proud. It was good to see a black man succeed so assuredly in life. Inspiring, even. He was merely enjoying the fruits of his labors. The stock market might be an unpredictable mistress, but to those on whom she smiled, she was bountiful indeed.

This, apparently, was not the case with art. If there was such a thing as a graphic arts mistress, she was definitely giving Darius the cold shoulder. He was brilliant, even gifted, and could make lines and colors assume a life of their own on his computer screen, but so far he'd seemed doomed to suffer the tedium of ad agency life, freelancing his way through his clients' demands, which swung like a pendulum between the mundane and the ludicrous. He'd persevered, complying with requests for toilet brushes doing the cancan across a sparkling white bathroom floor, wasp-waisted, glossy-lipped Anime superheroines touting motor oil, and cockroach funerals. To be fair, his cockroach funeral campaign had won him an award for graphic art last year, but even that hadn't exactly brought the lucrative offers pouring in.

Until now.

Darius straightened in his chair. Phillip was sucking on his cigar, eyeing him contemplatively, and waiting for him to speak. Werewolves might sound a little bizarre, he had to admit, but Phillip didn't know the whole story. He hastened to explain. "It's a really big job, Phil. Really, really big."

"It would be. You wouldn't have flown in all the way from Detroit if it wasn't. Who's minding your apartment while you're gone?"

Darius brushed away the question. "Forget the apartment. I'm trying to tell you about Circe."

Phillip frowned. "What's a Circe?"

"Circe's not a what, it's a who. *She's* a who. My client." Further clarifications seemed wise, as Darius knew that Phillip's reading material was restricted to the *Wall Street Journal* and a handful of men's and business magazines. "The original Circe, the one she's named after, was a Greek goddess. She turned men into pigs."

"Pleasant." Phillip pursed his lips and examined his cigar's label.

Darius felt obliged to stand up for the mythical being that had given him many hours of reading pleasure. "Well, to be fair, she eventually turned them back again."

"Okay. I got you. And this client, this woman, she's Circe what?"

"Just Circe."

Phillip lifted his brow. "You're working for someone who only has one name?"

Darius tried not to sound exasperated. He wanted badly to have his brother's seal of approval on this huge new step in his life, but Phillip was being deliberately obtuse. "It's not her real name, Phil, and you know it. Who calls their baby Circe? It's her pen name. It's on the cover of her books, and it's the way she signs her autographs. But that's all. Get it?"

Phillip was smiling indulgently. "Got it. Go on."

"And I don't know her real name. Nobody does. She keeps a low profile. Doesn't even allow herself to be photographed. Doesn't do the talk shows, doesn't do appearances. I haven't spoken with her at all. Only her agent. He called me up and made a pitch. A very generous pitch. Sent me a contract and a plane ticket, and here I am. She didn't get involved in anything."

"So this lady runs around with the assumed name of some goddess, is scared of cameras, hides behind her agent, and believes in werewolves? She sounds like a flake."

"I never said she believes in them. I said she writes about them," Darius countered loyally. Maybe Phillip was too busy living it up to settle down with a good book, but if anyone could change his mind about the worthiness of contemporary horror, it was Circe. "She's unbelievable. Five years, five books, five times on the *New York Times* best-sellers' list. And I've read them all." He enumerated on his fingers. "*Wolfbane, Delta Wolf, Cry Wolf*—"

Phillip cut him off. "Good, huh?"

Just thinking about Circe made the fine hairs at the back of Darius's neck stand on end. "You don't read her work and then sleep with the lights off. She does something to you. Her words . . . like poetry. No—" He corrected himself. "Not that soft. Not that gentle. Sharp, burning. Like acid. Like fine claws, just scratching the surface of your skin. You read her, and she leaves you . . . marked."

Phillip guffawed. His handsome face was creased with amusement, dark skin around his black eyes crinkling. He reached across the table and punched Darius good-naturedly on the shoulder. "What, you're *marked* now? She raked her claws across your chest, and now you wake on a full-moon night, out in an open field, and don't know how you got there? That's silly, Dar."

Darius felt his face grow warm. Phillip didn't mean to be dismissive; he knew he didn't. That was just his big brother's way. But the decade and a half that separated them, and the five sisters in between, only made the younger yearn for the elder's affirmation all the more. "Not exactly," he said. "But you never look at the night sky, or at other human beings, the same way after, either. Besides, she's done something for our people in science fiction that very few have before. So far, black characters in mythical literature have been restricted to shamanism and voodoo, and bad caricatures of them as well. This woman has dragged them into mainstream Western horror, into this century, with dignity and style. Black werewolves, Phil. That probably has never been done before, not like this."

Phillip was momentarily distracted, as a waitress brought the check. Darius watched the familiar flare of interest in his brother's eyes as he took in the tautness of the young lady's blouse and the brevity of her skirt. Her tailor was evidently a miser when it came to cutting fabric. Rippling, corn-colored hair swept her cheek as she bent forward slightly. She was fully aware of her customer's examination, and didn't seem to mind one bit. Her fingers lingered against his as she accepted payment. Was it Darius's imagination, or did a small, off-white business card nestle among the tendered bills?

Smiles were exchanged, and the distraction left their table in a cloud of perfume. Phillip smoothed his tie and returned his gaze to Darius, who by now had begun to wonder if he had somehow slipped into invisibility within the past few moments. "And now this lady Bram Stoker wants you to do her next cover?"

Bram Stoker wrote about vampires, not werewolves, but Darius let that slide. "And now this lady wants me to do her *whole book*. Her other novels have been pure prose, but this time she's decided to do something different. She writes the story, I create the art. Two hundred pages, six panels per page, full color. Dust jacket, posters, and promotional material. All of it."

Ice tinkled in Phillip's scotch glass. "You came all this way to draw a *comic book?*"

Darius tried not to allow his exasperation to gain ground. "Not a comic book, Phil. A graphic novel. There's a difference." He added hastily, "Not that I have anything against comic books."

"You shouldn't. You own thousands of them." Phillip's mouth was wry.

Ouch, Darius thought. S*ubtle dig. Right between the ribs.* Every once in a while Phillip would give him hell about his passion for comic books, and the massive collection he'd accumulated since he'd bought his first *Spider-Man* in the fourth grade. Phillip dismissed them as an amusing, if rather infantile, hobby.

Darius knew better. Darius knew that for him, his book collection was not just about good triumphing over evil, issue after issue, not just about superheroes and *über*-villains, and men morphing into monsters. For him, the story, weak or powerful, thrilling or mediocre, was superseded by the hand of the artist. Line and color, texture and shadow. Modern art, no less than the old masters, who were disparaged in their time, too. Figments of the imagination, born at the nib of a pen, eternal. Immortal. Alive. When two dimensions became three, Darius's heartbeat raced.

His passion went beyond the usual American fare, which ranged from slick X-Men to cheaply produced underground social commentary. His search for the art that fueled his imagination was global. Over the years he'd also accumulated a small but precious collection of French *bandes dessinées,* Spanish *libros comicos,* and graphic art from Britain, Spain, Japan, West Africa, and a dozen other places. In some, he could decipher the words, relying on his smattering of foreign languages and the support of the drawings. In others, he remained baffled by the foreign script. It didn't matter. What he valued about them was the art. For those he could not understand, he was free to make up his own tales. Once those drawings opened a door in his mind, his imagination ran wild.

Yet another difference between these two men, who shared a common blood but little else. Phillip put his money into paintings he didn't even like, but which some adviser or the other assured him would appreciate over time. When things went well for Darius, he bought signed color plates, original panels created by men who had what he deemed the most noble of callings: to bring smiles to the faces of millions of children every month as they rushed to the newsstand or the drugstore shelf, to entertain and amuse while teaching them to discern right from wrong, the way only a comic book hero could.

And now he would be one of them. The chosen few. The entertainers. He was to be given the chance to translate the images that teemed in his brain, clamoring for his attention, into a series of tiny works of art so that other people would see them, too. The chance to create these images in partnership with a woman whom he'd never met, but whose words so closely matched and mated with the pictures that swarmed in his head that it was uncanny. He knew Circe's every scene, her every character, more intimately than he did any real place or person, because somehow, milliseconds before his eyes perceived them on the page, her words were already there, burning in his mind, either by precognition, or her otherworldly ability to leap across that space between writer and reader and fulfill his needs before he knew them himself. He knew her sequoia forests: ancient, observant. He knew her wolves: gray, sagacious. He knew the rictus etched upon the faces of her men-beasts as the silvery lunar light broke through the impassive clouds, and their transformation began.

He could do this. Between them both, they could make what was real for them real for others, too.

"Dar?" Phillip's voice was a million light-years away.

Darius frowned. Slipped away again. The artist's curse. To be grounded one moment, like everyone else, and then, the next, to have melted without forewarning into that inner landscape to which only he had access. He shook his head to clear it. "Sorry."

"Good to have you back. You have the attention span of a gnat, you know that?"

Darius found the thread of their conversation without much effort, and picked it up. "There are many differences between a comic book and a graphic novel," he tried to explain. "Length, for one. This is a full-scale novel, except what is usually described in narrative will be up to me to convey in images. It's aimed at older readers, not the bubblegum crowd. There are lots of other differences, but that's not the point. The point is, this is the biggest break of my career. Circe's name is good for a million copies in sales in the U.S., and she's usually translated into at least five or six languages abroad. Think about the royalties. The advance alone was more than I made last year. And scuttlebutt has it that there's a movie being planned."

He leaned closer to emphasize his words. "An *animated* movie, all computer generated, based on her words and my drawings. And if I do the art for the book, who do you think they'll call upon to do the art for the movie? And she chose me, out of all the big-name players out there. She chose *me*. This'll be my breakout job. I could live out my whole lifetime and never get another chance like this to get my foot in the door."

For a change, Phillip looked serious. "I'm real proud of you, man. I know you've wanted this for a long time. I've always believed you'd get it."

Darius couldn't stop the smile from spreading across his face. Critical acclaim was a good thing: that would come. Arts awards were wonderful: they said that others recognized your talent and dedication. But a big brother's pride was as good as gold. "Thanks."

Phillip raised his near-empty scotch glass. "To an end to dancing toilet brushes."

Darius lifted his Virgin Mary in response. "And no more cockroach funerals."

They drank to that.

Darius looked at his watch. It was well past two. "I have to get going, bro. I still have to pick up my rental. And Big Sur's many hours away yet. I'll have to drive as if there are hellions on my tail to make it there by nightfall."

"I still don't know why you don't just spend the rest of the day with me and then get a fresh start tomorrow. We can hit a few clubs tonight. Or if you like, we can just hang around at my place, have a few drinks, and catch up. What do you say?"

It was tempting, the prospect of being in his brother's company for a few more hours. The best they had been able to squeeze in was this too-brief meal after Phillip met his flight. And he wouldn't mind seeing a bit of Los Angeles again. This was where, like Phillip, he had been born and raised, but since he'd left eight years ago, he hadn't been back more than three or four times. But he was bound. He shook his head. "I'd love to. You know that. But she's expecting me today. I'd call and reschedule, but that feels like starting out on the wrong foot. I don't want her to think I'm unreliable."

Phillip looked at him for several seconds, and then nodded slowly. "That's one thing nobody could ever accuse you of. Okay, I understand."

"Can I catch you on the way back?"

"You'd better!"

Darius shouldered his duffel and his laptop, but Phillip snatched the suitcase from his grasp and led the way outside. Soon, the rental car, a sturdy-looking station wagon, was procured, and stood idling in the parking lot. It was time to say good-bye.

"Mom called before I left to come over here," Phillip ventured.

"She called me before I left home, too. What did she say?"

"She says to make sure you packed enough socks. She says Big Sur can be chilly in the wintertime."

Darius smiled. "Tell her I did."

"She says to *make sure* you did. You're not just saying that to make her happy, are you? Don't make me go home and lie to our mother, man!"

Darius gave an exaggerated sigh. "Tell her I bought two three-packs. Extra thick." He stuck his foot out and hiked up the leg of his jeans, revealing a peek of gray cotton. "See?" Then he pretended to undo his belt. "You want to make sure I have my Underoos, too?"

Phillip threw up his hands in surrender, laughing. "You're on your own there!"

They stood facing each other, grinning like the boys they once were. Then Phillip reached into his jacket and withdrew his wallet. "Do you need any help?"

Not again. Darius crammed his fists into the pockets of his jeans so that Phillip could see, in no uncertain terms, that he had no intention of accepting the proffered bills. His brother had put him through four years of art school, certainly. And for that, he would always be grateful. In the early days thereafter, he had sent him many a "loan" to get him through the postadolescent rigors of apartment- and job-hunting; but those days were long gone—except that Phillip didn't seem to notice that. Between them, the subject of money often came up. Phillip did the offering, and Darius did the refusing. "No," he responded. He hadn't meant to sound gruff, but he did.

Phillip's carapace was too thick to allow him to take offense. He didn't withdraw his hand. "Sure? Let me at least stand you the cost of the rental—"

"I said no, Phillip!" His face was warm again, even in the crisp January air. "And don't do that again."

There was a flicker of understanding in his brother's eyes, and slowly he put his money back where it belonged. "Darius, I'm sorry."

"You keep forgetting," he muttered. "That was a long, long time ago."

"I know. I do forget. I'm sorry."

Darius could have said more, but now was not the time. Instead, the two men put their arms around each other and hugged awkwardly, like bears. Phillip was the first to withdraw.

Darius opened the car door and stuck a foot inside. It was time to get going. He threw his brother one last look. "I love you, Phil."

The silence that followed was so long, it became awkward. "Okay," Phillip said.

Two

Hailie was cranky. She hadn't had much sleep the night before: the cats had seen to that. They'd thundered up and down the roof of her cabin for hours, banging and crashing into Lord-knew-what up there, and then, when they were done with that, they took their ruckus under her cabin, banging on the underside of her flooring much as they had done topside. It was amazing just how much noise could come out of packages that small. She'd lain in bed half the night listening to the unholy caterwauling, painfully aware of each hour as it dragged on in stingy increments. Then, at daybreak, she'd dragged herself bleary-eyed out of her too-comfortable bed to prepare herself. Today, her artist was coming.

She was eager to meet him. Her agent, Tony, seemed to think the man was the bee's knees. "It's a sure thing, Mahalia," he'd told her. "This guy just *sweats* talent. So far, he's only done a whole bunch of the usual commercial crap, commissioned stuff, you know. But he's got vision. I look at his work and I can see *Romulus* clear as day. If anybody can bring your words to life, he's the one. He draws like you write. You were made for each other."

That remains to be seen, Hailie had wanted to say, but she trusted Tony. He had been with her almost from the start. She'd found him just after her first sale, and since then he'd been there, helping shape and nurture her young career until it had exploded into something far greater than she had ever dreamed, back when she was just a knobby-kneed schoolgirl in south-central L.A., filling her notebooks with her daydreams instead of paying attention in her too-crowded classroom. In Tony's hands, her career had no limit. Tony could spin straw into gold.

And so, she'd relied on his judgment. She'd let him hire an unknown artist instead of going after the big guns. Hailie was fine with that: every star had its genesis, and being unknown was no crime. A few years ago, in the era she thought of as B.T. (Before Tony), *she* had been the unknown, schlepping her manuscript from agent to agent seeking representation, and from slush pile to slush pile, hoping and praying that some summer intern assigned to read her submission would like it enough to pass it on to an editor for a second read. Then, just when she thought she would never survive the arrival on her doorstep of another S.A.S.E. hastily stuffed with a photocopied rejection letter, she'd made her first sale.

Somebody had taken a chance on her. It was her responsibility, as someone who had made it through the salt mines and arrived at the gold mines, to do the same for somebody else. It was good karma. It was the right thing to do.

Deep down, she was even excited. *Romulus* was the novel of her heart, the kind every author secretly works on for years, rewriting and polishing even while writing others that earned commercial success but did not satisfy the soul. If this gentleman was everything Tony said he was, maybe he would know that without her having to tell him. Maybe he would know how important this book really was to her.

She'd spent all day getting prepared for him, trying to

decide where they would start, how she would convey to him what she saw in her writer's mind, hoping he would be able to see it, too. Writers thought in words. Artists thought in pictures. Would they find a nexus?

She stood on the ground outside her cabin, hands on her hips, sniffing the cool evening air. It was getting late; the tall pines that surrounded her were throwing long shadows, and the birds were getting raucous as they returned home for the night. The winter sun was watery, almost sullen, seeming glad to leave, having given up sharing its warmth even before it fell out of sight.

From where she stood, she couldn't even see the cabin nearest hers, and that was one of the things Hailie loved most about Casuarinas. The writers' and artists' colony took work seriously, and believed in the value of isolation. It was not one of those retreats that leaned toward the pretentious, existing to pander to the egos of its residents. There was no heated pool, no bar, and no souvenir shop, if you didn't count the black-and-white postcards depicting the colony that were on sale at the receptionist's desk. People came to Casuarinas to work, not to be seen.

It was well over a hundred years old, having been founded by an eccentric husband and wife duo, she a pianist, he a painter, neither of whom had ever become successful in their fields of endeavor, but who were independently wealthy nonetheless. Asserting that every creative mind needed a place to work unhindered by mundane concerns such as food, lodging, and employment, they created the Casuarinas Trust before their deaths. Today, it catered to as many as fifty artists of every stripe at any given time, housing them in single-occupancy cabins scattered over eighty acres of rough, pine-dotted hillside, cut through by paths that all inevitably led to rocky cliffs that plunged downward to the

ocean. Here, artists were granted fellowships by a noto-
riously persnickety selection board, and were allowed
residencies of anything from one week to two months.
At Casuarinas, meals were either catered in the oak-pan-
eled hall in the main building, or delivered to the cabin
door in wicker baskets, upon request. At Casuarinas, the
creative mind was allowed to work undisturbed.

"Except when the cats drop in," Hailie muttered.
Which brought her back to the mission at hand. She
dropped to her haunches and tilted her head to one
side, bringing her face as close to the ground as she
dared. She'd done an extensive search of the area
around her cabin before breakfast this morning, looking
for casualties of last night's cat war. She was convinced
that they were now seeking refuge in the only place she
hadn't yet searched.

The crawl space under her cabin was probably eighteen
inches high, if that much. If she managed to squeeze
under, that would be a miracle in itself, but if she was unable to wriggle her way back out, there was no telling when
she would be missed, and how long it would take someone
to come looking.

And what would she find under there anyway? A
wounded female cat, certainly, and any kittens that would
have survived. But there might also be spiders. . . . Hailie
shuddered. If there was one creature on God's earth that
she didn't like, it was . . . those things. Animals, she loved.
Bugs, she tolerated. But anything with more than six legs
just had *no reason* . . .

"Get a grip, Derwood," she chastised herself. "You've
done worse. It's not going to take all night; ninety seconds, and it's a done deal." She took a deep breath,
dropped onto her belly, and counted to three. "Go!"

The ground was cold. Even through her sweats, she
could feel it: damp and hard. She moved commando-style,

propelling herself forward on her elbows, and pushing against the ground with her sneakered toes. When she was halfway under, it occurred to her that a flashlight might not have been a bad idea. She squinted. Her vision was not the best, even despite her contacts. Spending six hours a day staring at a computer screen had made sure of that. The objects that loomed at face level were disconcertingly unidentifiable. At least they didn't move! In the Casuarinas library, a series of rooms in the main building that were crammed ceiling to floor with volumes, she remembered spotting a book on snakes. She wondered fleetingly if having thumbed through it one evening when she was at a loose end had been wise. Imaginary vipers and adders (was there a difference?) had a way of cropping up at times like these, especially when you had an excellent memory for anything you read once.

"Think like a werewolf," she muttered. "Think strong." That was her battle cry, one so silly that she had never dared to share it with anyone. Some people whistled a happy tune when they were afraid. Some people hummed. Hailie thought like a werewolf. More specifically, she tried to think like Veda, the she-wolf heroine of her last three novels, who didn't take flack from anyone, especially real spiders and imaginary snakes.

"Courage, courage, courage." Her mantra was barely audible, but it propelled her several yards forward into even more profound darkness. She giggled. Veda had impeccable night vision. She wouldn't have had any problem finding her way around down here!

Something moved. Hailie went as still as a rock. Was it the object of her rescue mission, or was it a sign that any moment now she would be the one needing to be rescued? "Meow?" she asked softly.

"Hello!"

Her startled body jerked, arms and legs going rigid,

head snapping up suddenly to smack against the underside of her cabin. "Ow!"

"Hello?" Closer still.

That was not the voice of a cat! Hailie had an overactive imagination, but she was not a raving loon. One hand massaged what would soon be a substantial bump on the crown of her head, while she struggled to twist in the direction of the sound. At the end of the tunnel that threatened to hold her prisoner was a glimmer of light, and that light was just enough to make visible a pair of legs clad in denim.

"Somebody there?" she asked, although it was a stupid question, as someone obviously was. What she meant to ask was: *who is it?* Next time, maybe when a dozen jackhammers weren't pounding away at her skull, she would be more precise.

The feet—and they were rather large feet—turned slightly, as if the man they were attached to was trying to determine the source of her voice. "Are you there? Miss . . . Circe?"

Damn. That could only be the artist. Two hours late, and then he chose the worst possible time to turn up. Wasn't that just like a man! Well, there was nothing she could do but reveal her rather embarrassing location. "Under here!"

"Ma'am?" A pair of knees appeared at the opening of the crawl space as the man dropped to them. "Are you okay?"

"Fine," she muttered. She tried to turn around, but space didn't allow her to. She had no choice: she had to back out. She began to wriggle out the way she had come, slowly, all thoughts of Veda gone from her mind. Like most writers' imaginings, her favorite she-wolf tended to evaporate in the presence of others.

Her interloper was persistent. "Do you need help?"

"No," she answered shortly. Being caught squashed into a narrow crack was humiliating enough. She didn't have to add insult to injury by allowing herself to be helped out of it.

Perhaps he was hard of hearing. Perhaps he simply didn't put much stock in what other people wanted and didn't want. Either way, once she had squirmed free of the opening, and found herself still embarrassingly prostrate, twisting a little to look up at him hunched inquiringly over her, he was holding out his hand to help her up.

Tall was the first thing that ran through her mind. *Very tall. And that's not just because I'm all the way down at snake-eye level.* The latter thought was enough motivation for her to get up off the ground, and fast. Grudgingly, she took the extended hand, and found herself being firmly lifted to her feet.

The evening's last gloaming, and the security light that had automatically switched on, gave her enough light by which to see him clearly. She was pretty sure she goggled. He was . . . gorgeous. She had not overestimated his height, in spite of her formerly biased perspective. The open collar of his jacket was at her eye level, and she'd never considered herself short.

She let her gaze rise from the exposed hollow below his Adam's apple, up along his throat—were those *moles?* Sprinkled like coarse brown sugar spilled by a careless cook was a trail . . . no, a constellation . . . of cinnamon flecks that stood in sharp contrast with tawny skin that glowed, even in the gathering shadows. In the south, they disappeared into his shirt. In the north, they forced her eyes upward, as her mind played connect-the-dots, until they led her to their pinnacle, their North Star, just on the curve of his full lower lip. He could do with a haircut, and his hair looked as if he'd just gotten out of bed.

Hailie heard her breath escape through her teeth.

His eyes were the color of caramel in an iron cauldron, moments before it reached boiling point and bubbled over. They were impossibly deep, impossibly bright. Twinkling. *You've got stars on the brain, you idiot,* she chided herself irritably, even as she tore her gaze away from those astounding eyes to seek out their rivals, now appearing in the darkening sky.

For his part, the man was no more abashed than she in his examination of her. Her body prickled as he began at her hair, which she kept in braids because nobody with an ounce of sense would allow hair that wild and thick to stay loose for more than a day, not unless they were prepared to have it shorn off the next, after it had wound itself into inextricable tangles. He took in the fine gold hoops at her ears: peasant earrings, her mother had disapprovingly called them. They were too wild for a nice girl, Mama used to say. Indiscreet.

At her face, he lingered.

Hailie squirmed. Her writer's ability to leap from her mind into another's allowed her to see exactly what he did, through those astounding eyes. What he would see was a grubby woman in old, gray UCLA sweats, covered in dirt and under-the-cabin grime. A perfectly *ordinary* woman, sad to say. She had no illusions about that. After the splendor of her hair, there was little left to comment upon. Her skin was an unremarkable shade of brown, her eyes an unremarkable size and color. Her height: average, weight: average—or at least, that was what she told herself whenever she yearned for a second helping of pie. Her dress size was not significantly larger or smaller than that of any other woman she knew; her bra size was always the first to be sold out at the department store. Walk down a crowded street, and she turned no more heads than any other woman. She was, she knew, neither here nor there, neither pretty nor plain.

And yet, this man was staring.

His gaze had returned to her face, and stayed there. In his inquisitive examination of her, which bordered on the impolite, he reminded her of a small boy whose curiosity made a mockery of social convention. Her artist looked very young indeed. She'd been expecting someone dedicated enough to devote the long, grueling hours that it would take to pull this project off, and mature enough to handle the criticisms and differences of opinion that inevitably came with working as a team. What she got was a boy with sparkly eyes.

"Great," she heard herself say. "I asked Tony for an artist. He sent me a kid." She slapped her hand over her mouth, too late to prevent her thoughts from becoming words.

The laugh that rolled out of him filled the space between them. "I *am* an artist," he said. "So don't fire Tony." His voice was rich and deep, a black coffee voice to go with his caramel syrup eyes and cinnamon sprinkle moles. Oh, she had a sweet tooth!

Still mortified by her faux pas, she stammered, "I'm sorry. I have this awful habit . . . I say the first thing that pops into my head."

"I noticed."

"Aquarius," she added lamely. She could feel the heat in her cheeks.

"That explains everything," he replied gravely. She was half sure he was making fun of her. Then, he added, "If it makes you feel any better, I'm older than I look. It's just that baby faces run in my family."

"They do?" Her curiosity piqued, she struggled against the urge to stare again, to deduce his age by visual examination alone. If only men were like trees, so that you could tell how old they are by counting the rings around . . . *Stop*, she ordered herself.

He was still talking. "They do. You should see my grandfather. He looks twelve."

Now it was her turn to burst out laughing.

He stuck his hand out once again. "I'm Darius Grant."

She clasped his hand. No, his hand swallowed hers. There was strength there, without crushing. Masculine grace. What did he draw with? she wondered. Pencil, mouse, stylus? Tony had said those hands were magic. Would they work their magic for her, too?

"Grant, huh?" she managed to say. She tilted her head to one side and scrutinized him.

"Yes."

"Detroit, right?"

"Yes." He looked puzzled. "Why?"

"Nothing." There was no need to get into *that*. Too personal. Too painful. She was relieved when he didn't push the issue.

"So, shall I call you Circe?"

Oh, right. He wouldn't know her name. It wasn't something she made public, preferring the relative anonymity of a nom de plume. "Mahalia Derwood." She struggled to retrieve her hand.

Sensing her resistance, he released her. "Mahalia," he repeated.

"Call me Hailie." Mahalia was so awfully old-fashioned. Only her mother and her three elderly aunts ever called her that.

He considered it for a moment, and then shook his head. "I like Mahalia better."

She wasn't sure whether to be affronted or amused by his assertion. *He* was going to decide what *she* was to be called? She thought it would be better not to answer, and instead contemplatively rubbed the rising bump on her head.

His face instantly became concerned. "You hurt your-self?"

She shook her head, unwilling to tell him that it had been his arrival that had startled her. "It's nothing."

He didn't look convinced. "Sure?"

"Yep." She frowned, her thoughts having been drawn back to the crawl space under her cabin, and the purpose for her original mission.

He seemed to read her mind. "What were you doing under there in the first place? You lose something? Want me to help you find it?"

She shook her head. "No, I haven't lost anything. But there's this cat—"

"Your cat?"

"No," she explained, "a feral cat. Lives in the woods, I guess. I've been feeding her these past few days, since I got here. Last night, a tom came over. I think he beat her up. She's been hiding under there all day. I think she's badly hurt. I was just trying to see if I could catch her, and get her some help."

"She's got kittens?"

Her eyes widened slightly. The presence of male kittens was the primary reason for a tomcat attack, but she was sure you had to have a cat, or love them, to be aware of that. Could Darius be a cat person? Her mouth curved slightly. Cat people were special in her eyes. Not as much as wolf people, but . . . "Yes, she does. Two, at least."

He thought silently for a while, then, "I'll get them out for you. Then we'll see how much damage has been done."

She held up her hand. "You don't have to. I can do it. I was doing it, till you came."

"Nonsense." He walked over to the station wagon that was parked a few feet from them and threw open the back, leaned over, and began rummaging around. "Supposed to be an emergency lamp in here somewhere. We'll need it if we're going to see anything under there." His voice was muffled.

Hailie realized as he bent forward that she was becoming a little too interested in how his jeans fit. She noticed how worn they were in places, and wondered idly how soft that rubbed-out denim would be. He was slim, yes, but far from scrawny. Not where it counted.

Stop, she had to tell herself, for the second time in sixty seconds. What was it with her? The man had come all the way across the country to work with her, to work *for* her, and there she was, salivating over him like a schoolgirl. She glanced involuntarily up into the darkened sky, half wondering if she'd fallen under the influence of the moon. . . . But that was stupid. That was fiction.

Light flooded the space between them, and Hailie had to shield her eyes.

"Sorry," he said. He tilted the light downward. "Brighter than I expected." He handed it over. "Here, you hold it."

"Are you really going under?" She was skeptical. He was more than a little larger than she, and if she'd had trouble making her way . . .

"Sure. I can make myself smaller if I need to. Flatten right down like a spider, you'll see."

The mention of her least-favorite creature made her shudder. "I wish you hadn't said that," she muttered.

"You don't like them?" He laughed wryly. "Did I make your flesh crawl?"

It was getting late, and late meant chilly. She hugged herself. If he was going to do it, he'd better get started. "Darius, look—"

He took his cue, and dropped flat onto his belly. "Gotcha." He began crawling under the edge of the cabin's floor, while she tried her best to hold the light steady just ahead of him. "Bet Veda could've done this without a light," he joked.

Hailie almost dropped the lamp. That was exactly what she'd been thinking, just moments before he'd turned up! Did that mean he'd read her books? "Veda would probably have eaten the cat, if she'd managed to find it," she joked back weakly.

"Nah." His voice was muffled. "The Veda I love would've saved her stuff for meatier prey. The two-legged kind."

The wind grew chillier. *The Veda he loved.* It was true, then. This man knew her books, and knew them well. She swung between embarrassment and pleasure. It was always a strange feeling to converse with someone who had read your work so closely. Writing was the process of making the innermost secrets of your soul visible, trapping them permanently in a thin layer of paper and ink. When people read your work, they walked away with a small part of you. Sometimes, the sensation was a little like being naked. Hailie wished she had worn a heavier coat.

"Bingo." His voice was soft.

"Found them?"

"Yes." There was something not right in his voice. "I'm coming out."

She felt her heart tighten in her chest. She knew without having to be told that she wouldn't like what he would have to show her. Silently, she waited, trying her best to hold the lamp steady. He eased himself backward, more slowly than he'd gone in, and soon he was clambering to his feet, a white bundle in his arms.

She tilted the beam of light onto it. White fur was matted with sticky blood. The thin, wild-eyed cat pulled her lips back in a snarl; hissing, defensive, even in her pain. One side of her face was a raw, bloody mess. "Her eye," Hailie gasped.

"Can't see how bad it is. We'll have to get her cleaned up first. Take her to a vet, maybe. Have you got a basket?"

"What?" The sight of blood left her disoriented, dull-witted.

"Anything to put her into. So we can take her to the vet." He was patient with her, even though she was sure he found her obtuse. The cat was weak, panting, having probably lain there in pain all day. Her mind searched. There was her picnic basket from her lunchtime food delivery, but she was sure that the Casuarinas management would not approve of their using it to transport a bleeding, feral animal. The cat squirmed in Darius's arms.

"Mahalia?" he probed gently.

An idea hit her. "Uh, there's the laundry hamper."

"Get it."

Pulling her wits together, she took the two steps leading into her cabin in a single bound, ran into her small room, and tossed her dirty laundry onto the floor. Then, on further reflection, she folded a large, fluffy towel on the bottom of it and joined Darius outside. Together, they managed to ease the animal into it, careful not to hurt her further, in spite of her feeble resistance.

Darius placed the basket on the backseat. She ran around to the passenger's side, assuming she was going with him.

"One minute," he said. He went to the back of his car again, withdrew a tire iron, took a few paces, and began to stab at the hard earth.

"What . . . ?" she began, and then she knew. She joined him, wishing she could help dig, too, but there was no suitable instrument available, and besides, her arms felt like rubber.

When the hole was about eight inches deep, Darius withdrew two small balls of fur from the pocket of his jacket. One was as white as its mother. The other was orange marmalade. Both were dead, small skulls crushed by a blow from a masculine paw. "Both males, I assume," he said.

They were so tiny. They hadn't even grown to the stage of opening their eyes. What a waste! A sadness overwhelmed her that was huge in proportion to the loss. "Oh, my Lord." She wished her body didn't ache so much. She wished her chest wasn't squeezing her last breath out of her lungs. . . .

Darius laid them gently in the hole and began scraping dirt over them with his hands. When he was finished, he looked up. It was only when his eyes widened that she realized that she was crying.

He placed his hands on both her shoulders. "Mahalia, I know it's sad, but it happens. The male comes along and kills off its competition. It doesn't want the encumbrance of other males growing up on its turf. . . ."

"Even if they're his own," she stated bitterly. The mere idea of it appalled her. Made her sick to her stomach.

"Even if they're his own," he repeated gently. "That's nature's way."

"Well, nature's way stinks, if you ask me." The tears were coming faster. She hadn't meant them to, but they were. Hot on her cold cheek. In the weak light, his eyes were fixed on hers: concerned, kind. She resented him for his kindness, and resented herself for being so grateful for it. She smelled the earth on his hands as he stroked the tears away.

"Come, now," he whispered. The hand slipped from her cheek to her shoulder, and she felt herself being pressed against his chest. The next thing she felt was the rough border where denim gave way to fleece. She smelled a mixture of cologne, earth, and manly warmth. She let this man, this complete stranger, hold her as she wept, but her need for consolation was greater than shame or caution.

"It probably didn't hurt them long," he said, trying to comfort her. "It was probably quick."

That's it, she thought. *Let him think I'm weeping for the kittens. Let him think I'm soft in the heart, soft in the head, whatever.* She'd known him half an hour, perhaps a little more. There was no reason to expose herself more than she had to. No reason for him to know that the tears she shed were tears of rising frustration and bitterness about her own situation, and the perpetual pain that awaited her back home. A mother's tears.

Darius didn't need to know she was crying for her son, and for the circumstances of his birth. He didn't need to know about the boy's father, that cold and distant shadow from her past, who also believed in "nature's way." Survival of the fittest. Fatherhood a threat, an inconvenience, not a blessing.

Her son was her problem, and no one else's.

Three

"Still sleeping?"

"Yes."

Darius watched Mahalia reemerge from her bedroom. They had fixed up a small box with the towel she had placed in the laundry hamper, and settled the cat down for the night. It had taken them an hour to find a vet open that late, and the surgery had taken three hours. Although the vet had done his best, the cat had, indeed, lost the eye, and Darius was glad that the anesthetic had not yet worn off. He'd feel better if the animal would sleep through until morning. Life would be hard enough for it as it was, once it was up and moving around again.

He was seated at her work desk in her study, the only other room in the cabin besides her bedroom and bathroom. Casuarinas only had the wherewithal to provide the barest of bones in their program. Each resident had a bathroom, a bed, and a place to work. Apart from that, if cabin fever struck, there was the great outdoors.

As she sat down again, he gathered up the remnants of their meal. The Casuarinas kitchen closed at eight, and Chinese food had been all they had succeeded in scaring up at that hour. This wasn't downtown Detroit; Big Sur didn't exactly have a huge nightlife, and, like most of the other stores, the restaurants closed at a decent time. Takeout had also been their only option: with the two of them looking as if they'd spent a day at boot camp crawling under barbed-wire fences on their bellies, no decent restaurant would have let them in anyway. He tied the empty cartons into the plastic bag they had come in, and went outside to discard them in the garbage can next to her step. He searched for and found a small rock with which to weigh down the cover. Raccoon-proofing.

When he returned, she was sitting with her elbows on the table, and her face propped up on both hands, eying him contemplatively. She seemed to be waiting for him to speak.

"I never got the opportunity to thank you for choosing me," he told her from the bottom of his heart. "There are artists out there who would be willing to trade two years of their natural life span for a chance like this."

She smiled for the first time in hours, and when she did so her face was transformed. The slender gold hoops that hung from her ears were parentheses around her lush mouth, and the effect was so startling he had to force himself to focus on the sounds coming out of it, rather than its shape. "You might end up doing just that," she warned. "I'm told I'm hell on wheels to work with." Then she added, "But to be honest, I didn't choose you. Tony did."

"But you must have thought we'd be good together," he insisted.

She shook her head, looking a little embarrassed. "Darius, I'm sorry, but I haven't seen any of your stuff."

Ouch, he thought. He was such a huge fan of her work; he was half hoping she'd like his, just a little. He forced air through his teeth, making a hissing sound, like a tire going soft. "That's the sound of my ego deflating," he joked.

Laughing outright now, she leaned forward, clamping

one hand over his mouth to stop the hissing. "Don't let it deflate all the way! Every artist needs a little ego. It's like gas in our tanks. Keeps us running when everything else fails."

Her fingers were so soft against his lips, he wanted to grasp her wrist and press his mouth harder against her palm. That fleeting urge shocked him. If he'd glanced at his watch, it would have told him that barely six or seven hours had passed since he'd met her. Yet her skin was brushing his and his body tingled. How the heck had that happened?

She tore her hand away, like a cat leaping off a hot stove, and that was enough to tell him that she felt it, too. Color deepened in her cheeks, and she let her lashes hide her eyes. The silence in the room was thick and awkward.

Should he say something? he wondered. But if he did, what would he say? What did you say to a woman you'd just met—who was your new boss, by the way—but a woman you found yourself drawn to for no discernible reason? Except for the fact that she had an insane mane of hair that she struggled to keep under control with braids that had a mind of their own, just as she was struggling to keep her breathing under control now, and failing? Except for the fact that her skin was the color of the peanut butter cake he'd had at lunch, and her eyes held secrets. Sad ones. This was a woman who wept for dead kittens. Dead kittens and something else, because when he'd held her, the pain that he'd absorbed through his skin as she'd wept was greater than that. Too huge for such a small tragedy. Her sobs had come up from a deep and frozen place below her surface. He yearned to ask what had caused them, but knew without having to be told that to do so would be akin to crushing robin's eggs in his hand, just to see what they were made of. Destructive, damaging curiosity that

would do neither of them any good. He willed himself
not to bring his fingers to his face, to touch himself
where she'd touched him. He swallowed hard.

"Tony told me something about . . . about cockroach
funerals." She tried weakly to keep their conversation
normal. Her floundering gave him courage; it meant
that he was doing to her what she was doing to him. That
was good. Disconcerting, but good.

He cut her some slack, and allowed her the breathing
space she was struggling for—conversationally, if not
physically. "Ah, yes," he said gravely. "The former high-
light of my career."

She rubbed her cheek, seeming disturbed by the
warmth that had gathered there. "I'm sorry. I feel like
such an idiot. I should have asked Tony to send me some
of your stuff. . . ."

He brushed away the suggestion. "No need."

"But you've read my books, haven't you?"

Two or three times, he wanted to say. *Each.* But that
sounded weird. Flaky, to use Phillip's expression. Instead, he told her, "*Cry Wolf* was my favorite."

She smiled. "The first time we got to meet Veda."

"Great woman, that Veda. The strongest female I've
ever encountered, of any species. Real or imagined."

"Just wait till she meets Romulus. Then you'll see
sparks fly."

He was glad for the chance to talk shop. It gave him
something to focus on, to take his mind off the loneliness in her voice and in her eyes. It helped stop his mad
urge to touch her again, right in its tracks. "Is Romulus
a werewolf, too?"

She nodded, gravely. "An old one. Been around for cen-
turies. Came from an ancient line that made their way out
of Egypt and over to the New World. It's been a while since
she met one of her own kind, and longer since she's met

a compatible male. One who's as strong as she is, and as smart as she is. Who won't see her as a . . . threat."

"Like that cat," he interpreted.

"Like that cat." A flicker of something crossed her face.

He saw the shadow pass, and sensed the pain behind it. Once again, the urge to delve to its source blindsided him. What could possibly darken the heart so suddenly, and so powerfully, that the pupils of those large brown eyes could constrict like the shutter on an old camera? And why should he so badly want to know? He tried to keep both their minds on the book conversation. That was safe. "Is it a love story, then?"

She closed her eyes and her face softened. Her body rocked slightly, almost imperceptibly. He recognized what was happening to her: he was sure he looked the same way when his imaginary world took over. When he was seeing things that were alive, flesh and blood, bone and marrow—and altogether not there. "It is. She's been alone too long. Romulus is everything she's ever wanted. He's her every longing made flesh. But even so, he'll have to fight for her. To win her over."

"A good she-wolf is worth the battle," he murmured.

"Is she?"

"She is." He leaned in closer, throwing caution to the wind. Knowing he was trespassing on dangerous ground but unable to stop himself. "How do werewolves make love?" he asked. "Carefully? Like porcupines?"

"No." She hadn't opened her eyes, but he knew she sensed him near. "With wild abandon. Savagely, exchanging heat for heat. They make love in their human form, so that their minds can partake of the sweet experience, unclouded by their baser brains. But even so, they bring their wolf instincts into their bed. Their love of scent. Their need for contact."

His face was closer still. *Open your eyes,* he willed her. *Open them, so you can see me.* "Do they . . . bite?"

Her long, curved lashes lifted, as if responding to his mind's request. Her eyes were focused on his mouth, inches away from hers, and all he wanted to do was stop, stop, stop, before this got out of hand. Before he made a fool of himself, and offended her in the bargain. Before he did something downright stupid . . .

"I guess they do," she managed to say. She swallowed hard, painfully. "I . . . hope they do."

Her mouth should have tasted like wonton soup, but it didn't. Instead he tasted strawberries, but that was stupid, because they hadn't *had* strawberries. Nor had they eaten cantaloupes, but her lips were like that moist, firm flesh. They had a melon's sweetness, the kind one smelled rather than tasted.

When she kissed him back, there was hunger in her kiss, yearning, as if she wanted him to fill some yawning void. Because of the table between them, only their lips made contact, and that simply wasn't good enough. He broke their kiss just long enough to stand, move around the obstacle, and lift her to him.

"Oh . . . my." She was half protesting, half awed, but not struggling. Pliant.

"Shush," he instructed her. He wound his hand into her hair, holding her prisoner. He felt her palm against his chest, stroking him from shoulder to hip, repeatedly. Under her touch, his nipple burned like an insect's sting. Farther down, his groin ached, like a bruise. As if he'd been kicked. He wanted to clasp her bottom in both hands and fit her to him, to tell her without words just how sharply and deeply she had aroused him, but he was almost embarrassed. She had him light-headed, like a teenager. If he pressed her against him, and made even clothed contact with the one place his arching body strained to be, then what was to stop him from dropping onto his knees, laying her down on the rough wooden cabin floor, and covering her?

It was lunacy. He didn't know her, but his body wanted more. Bodies had a way of doing that, with or without permission and concurrence from the mind. His brain knew he was being foolish, but his hands and tongue didn't care. His intellect told him he was leaping over boundaries that shouldn't be breached, not now, not so early in the game, but his spirit sensed her need, and his, and knew that touch was all it would take to assuage them both. The part of him that thought and reasoned knew he was being a fool, but the part of him that felt and sensed didn't care, and was willing to plow ahead, devil be damned. He had to put a stop to this, before he had a full-scale mutiny on his hands, with his body overthrowing his mind.

"Too fast," he puffed against her cheek. "Mahalia, wait. This is happening too fast." He wanted to pull away, but her thumb was making circles through the fabric of his shirt. That small, circling digit robbed him of his will. He groaned. "We've got to—"

". . . Stop," she finished for him. She pulled her hand away and looked down at it, staring inquiringly, as if she'd just discovered it at the end of her arm and had no idea why it was doing what she had caught it doing.

He took the opportunity to take a few steps away from her. Now that the magnetic pull that had held them fast was broken, now that, like a space capsule speeding skyward, he was free of her gravitational force, sanity returned, both for him and for her.

She looked perplexed and ashamed. "I'm sorry—"

He wasn't letting her take the blame. "My fault, not yours," he cut in hastily. "I was out of line."

She didn't seem to have heard him. "I shouldn't have . . ."

She trailed off, and stood there, looking so perplexed that his heart was moved.

"Don't, Mahalia. Don't beat yourself up."

They regarded each other solemnly, wondering what to do next. A mutual decision to pretend that nothing had happened, maybe. Or more apologies. Neither would work, as far as Darius could see. For one, something *had* happened. Her agitated breathing, and the tingle that still ran the length of his body, were evidence of that. For another, he wasn't that sure he *was* sorry.

Eventually, she was the one who decided. "It's getting late, Darius. Tomorrow, we start work."

He knew a cue when he heard one. He took it gracefully, headed for the door, opened it, and then looked back. He could have offered her his hand in farewell, but they had gone past handshakes. So instead, he simply bade her, "Good night, Mahalia."

"Night," she whispered. She didn't look at him as she spoke.

If there was one thing Hailie could give Darius credit for, it was his ability to set aside their stupid, embarrassing lapse in judgment and get down to work. The past few days had put an end to her initial anxiety that after that ill-advised first-night kiss, their working relationship would have been downhill from there. But he'd turned up the next morning, scrubbed and serious, not acting as if they hadn't done what they had—which relieved her, because that would have been an insult to her intelligence and an affront to his—but showing that he was willing to move on from there and do the job they'd come to do.

Now, five days later, he sat in her cabin work space, rocking back slightly in her wooden chair, sipping her coffee, and arguing spiritedly with her. "The first time Romulus and Veda meet," he was saying, "should be from her perspective, not his. She's the one with the most to lose. Remember the point-of-view rule—"

"I remember the rule," she argued back. "I just want to show how she affects him. He's the one we've been following for several pages now. He's the one who has been traveling so far, all the way from North Africa. And now he meets this woman, and senses, smells . . . *knows*, that she's a—"

"Exactly. We've been in his point of view for a while. But right at this moment, Veda's got more at stake. Think of how long she's been alone. She hasn't met another male werewolf since book three—Orson—and they hated each other. She killed him, in that scene, down on the bayou, after she found out that he'd set her up to be caught—"

"I know she killed him." She couldn't contain her amusement at his enthusiasm, and his uncanny ability to retain, regurgitate, and interpret every scene, every character, from any one of her five books. "I wrote that scene, remember?"

Darius put his coffee mug down, sweeping aside a pile of artist's paper as he did so, and drew his long, perpetually jean-clad legs from off her tabletop. He leaned closer to make his point. "I remember. But think of how long she's been alone. All her lovers for the past forty, maybe fifty years have been human. Those who don't grow old and die on her reject her when they realize what she really is. Those that don't do either just aren't good enough for her. They don't challenge her. She's all woman, and then some: smarter than they are, stronger, faster, and wiser. Half of them are afraid of her. The other half resent her for being better than they. She's alone, and lonely, and had half made up her mind that this is just the way it's got to be. And then what happens?"

He waved his hands in the air, and so help her, Hailie could have sworn she could see the faintest ghosts of Veda and Romulus in the trail of stardust left by his fingers. "They meet . . ." He slammed one fist into his palm. "And bam! Fireworks. One of her own kind, and a fine specimen at that. One from the Old World, from a culture even she doesn't understand. A massive, powerful, ancient, Nubian werewolf. No, Mahalia. I disagree. When they meet, it should be from her perspective, not his."

So endearing, his passion. So flattering. This man's imagination had no horizon. It stretched further even than hers, and if there was one thing she knew about herself, it was that her mind had no fences. He had this uncanny ability to draw her into him, and show her his mind-pictures, without riding roughshod over hers, or making them feel invalid.

She closed her eyes for a few moments and tried to visualize the scene, shifting from one perspective to the other, her idea to his, and damned if his didn't provide the most drama. Veda was the one with more at risk than Romulus, and she was the one more likely to make the reader feel the awesome magic of the moment. Once again, Darius was right. Once again, his pictures had informed her words, rather than the other way around. She twisted her lips in rueful surrender. "You drive me crazy, Darius Grant."

"Just returning the favor, my dear," was his reply.

When she opened her eyes, he was flapping a page before her. "Look, I sketched it out for you, last night. Both ways, so you can see which works better, and decide."

She waved it away without looking at it. "Go ahead. I don't need to see it. You've already put it . . ."—she tapped her temple—". . . up here."

He placed his sketch on the haphazard pile of others. There was no teasing in his voice. "Am I hijacking your project? Because if I am, please tell me."

"Of course not. You have your vision, and I have mine. If we're going to do this, we're going to have to find the happy medium. When more than one person works on something, it often takes a little battling before they can both settle on something." She reached out and lightly touched the back of his hand in encouragement, to show him there was no harm done. She was about to say, *You're not hijacking, you're helping me see it all clearer,* but she couldn't make a note.

Touched him, her mind realized.

Stupid.

She'd been willing to put up with the rush of warmth she felt whenever she looked around suddenly, or glanced up, and caught him staring at her. She'd been willing to ignore, or try to ignore, his habit of not spending a heck of a lot of time on his hair, and forget how good the unruly mess actually looked on him. Sometimes, when she happened to have a pen in her hand, and found herself staring at his face, and wondering idly whether, if she drew fine lines along his jaw, down his throat and chest, she could transform his scattered moles into Scorpio, Little Bear, or the Big Dipper, she'd put the pen hastily down and given herself a stern mental lecture. She'd been a good girl. She'd maintained tight control.

But now she'd gone and touched him, and his skin was so, so warm, with the texture and resilience of calf's leather. A second's contact, and her touch-starved skin had groaned. She wondered if she had, too, out loud, because his eyes were upon her face. She shoved her errant hand behind her back and looked away.

"Hungry, Mahalia?" he asked.

Starved, she could have said, but was too smart, or too chicken, to actually do so. *I'm hungry, hungry, hungry. For respite from the loneliness that bricks me in, like a life sentence in solitary confinement.* He had no idea what her life was like. He didn't know that, when she wasn't camped out at artists' colonies, or on a book tour, she was confined to her L.A. home, and almost every hour of her day belonged to her son, and his thousand special needs. How his demands on her life scared away any man who approached her; in fact, they scared *her* so much that she had long resisted any approach in the first place, just to spare herself the pain of the inevitable abandonment.

What she was hungry for didn't come in either of the towel-covered wicker baskets, delivered hours before, which sat side by side on a small table. Her needs were for solace, comfort, human contact, and yes, sexual release. This, she'd reminded herself several times a day since that foolish kiss, was the only reason her heart leaped when she heard his knock at her door. It was the only reason she flinched if he brushed past her, afraid that her face or body would reveal her dangerous reveries.

It was touch-starvation that was responsible for what he was doing to her by his mere presence, not the man himself. His every attribute was magnified, colored by her emotional burden. No man was that good-looking. No man smelled that good, or possessed a voice that sonorous. Not outside the pages of fiction, at least. She was a writer, and a writer's imagination always blurred the frontier between reality and fantasy. Half of what she experienced wasn't real. What he had, she'd embellished. What he lacked, she'd imagined. She'd practically made him up. It was the only rational explanation.

"Mahalia?"

She got up, hurried to the door, and threw it open, letting the cool air in. "I don't want anything."

His footfalls went *boom-boom-boom* on the wooden cabin floor, and then he was standing inches behind her. "We missed lunch hours ago. Did you have breakfast?"

"I'm pretty sure I did."

"Pretty sure isn't good enough. Come on. Eat something."

His insistence was irritating. She spun around, frowning. "That's good enough for me, Darius! If you're hungry, eat something, but I'm not. I don't need to be badgered into eating."

He touched her cheek, much as he had that first evening, when he'd dried her tears. "I wasn't badgering. Well . . . I was, maybe a little, but I meant well. You just look so . . . droopy, I guess."

Laughter took her by surprise. "*Droopy* isn't a word I'd advise you to use around females, Darius!"

"Oh." He grinned. "I get you. I take it back. Wilted, then. How's that?"

"Flattering," she said dryly.

"I don't flatter. I call 'em as I see 'em. And what I see is that you need a break. If you won't eat, at least take a walk with me. There's prime hiking forest around here, acres and acres of it, and we haven't seen an inch of it beyond the little stretch between my cabin and yours. Come on." His smile was too inviting to resist. "Live a little. I hear there's a spot you can climb to, where you can stand on this big rock and look out on a killer view. I hear it's a once-in-a-lifetime experience."

"Darius . . ." She tried to talk her way out of his invitation, but even as she did so, she was poking around for her boots. "You know I'm a patron of the Casuarinas Trust, don't you?"

"I heard the rumor. Somebody said the Casuarinas board squeezes a big fat endowment check out of you every year, too." His words were entirely without envy or malice. "Heard you were the one that hooked me up with this residency here too, so we could work together."

"And you know I've been here maybe eight times in the past four years or so?"

"Yeah. So, what's your point?"

"The point is"—she was glad for the opportunity to take a whack at his presumption—"I've seen the damn view."

He grabbed up her jacket from behind the door and tossed it at her. "But I haven't. Give me two seconds, and we're out of here."

He snatched a box of cat food and disappeared into her bedroom. The cat had recovered sufficiently to be taking food and water, but rarely came out to them. When it did, it didn't venture past the front door, perhaps afraid that its attacker was still lurking outside somewhere, preparing for a second assault. So she and Darius had taken turns caring for her, although he was more meticulous about it than she, checking up on it what seemed like every two hours, and even holding it in his lap while he sketched, because, as he put it, "Cats need lots of loving."

He returned, looking satisfied at its progress, and rooted around in their lunch baskets, retrieving two apples and two baggies full of carrot sticks, which arrived daily with their meals. The Casuarinas kitchen had an unshakeable belief that residents had to eat healthy, even if it killed them. Hailie liked vegetables well enough, but she sometimes feared that if she ate all the raw food she was being given here, she'd turn into one giant carrot stick. She hoped Darius wasn't planning on wheedling her into snacking on their walk. He never seemed to believe her when she said she didn't feel like eating. In that, he was as bad as her mother. She grimaced. He responded with a telling grin.

Once they were outside, Hailie shut the door. There were no locks: it was against the Casuarinas honor code. Residents simply had to trust and be trusted. Locks were an impediment to the free circulation of energy within the colony, she'd once heard someone say, and if there was anything the artists relied on as they did food and water, it was energy. As far as she knew, nobody had ever experienced a problem with the system: when you returned from wherever you'd been, your possessions were still waiting for you, untouched. If only things were like that in real life!

The Casuarinas forest had more or less been allowed to follow its own desires and spread out where it wanted. Sweet-smelling pines and ancient cedars towered overhead, successfully cutting off most of their light, even though it was only midafternoon. The hidden face of the sun denied them warmth, and the pathway was cool enough to make Hailie glad that Darius had made her take her jacket. Around them, unseen insects chirped, clicked, and sang to each other, happily industrious, teeming their way through their miniature world. In the breaks between the branches overhead, the occasional bird's silhouette appeared from time to time, accompanied by a raucous cawing.

They fell into step along the path, which twisted upward or sloped downward at whim. When they came to a divergence, Hailie would point the way, but for the most part they enjoyed a companionable silence, tempered only by their footfalls upon the hardened soil, muffled by dried leaves and pine needles that were scuff-deep everywhere.

After a while, Darius chose to speak. "She'll have a hard time, back in these woods."

"Who?"

"Veda Two." That was the name he'd insisted on giving the cat, even though Hailie had protested that, as it was, Veda was a canine, or, more precisely, lupine, rather than feline name. But Darius had insisted that any warrior valiant enough to risk her life defending her offspring deserved a heroine's name, and so he had prevailed. "She's going to have it rough if we release her back into the woods once she's all healed. With just one eye, her depth of vision will be shot. It'll be hard for her to hunt effectively. She'll probably starve. Worse, there are probably all kinds of creatures around, like owls or falcons, that wouldn't mind a cat dinner, and she'll be less equipped to spot them coming."

She'd been thinking of that, but now that he mentioned it, the cat's future looked bleak indeed. "What do you suggest?" she asked, although she half knew what was coming. She was only slightly out of breath: with his longer stride, he could easily outpace her, and although he was making a conscious effort not to leave her behind, it was hard work keeping up. If he shortened his stride any more, he'd be taking baby steps. Instead of throwing her pride out of the window and asking him to slow down, she stepped hard and fast, keeping shoulder to shoulder with him. She reveled in that small victory.

"One of us could take her with us when we go."

"And which one of us would be most suitable, d'you think?" Now she knew where he was headed, but she played along.

"Well, I'm pretty sure she'd hate to fly. . . ."

"Darius, you're suggesting I take the cat home with me?"

"Well, you like cats, don't you?"

"Love cats," she murmured dryly. "Them and all God's little creatures."

"Except spiders."

"Except them."

"So, have you got a cat?"

"Uh, no."

"A dog?"

She didn't have a dog. Her son was terrified of them, having once been leaped upon by an overeager spaniel. She'd assumed that his fear of four-footed creatures would run the gamut, and as such, hadn't tried any cat experiments with him. "No, no dogs."

"So think about it. All I'm asking is for you to think about it. We've got six weeks. We can keep an eye on Veda Two, and if she looks like she isn't hacking it, we can get her a traveling basket. A few hours' drive to L.A. would be a lot less traumatic than a flight to Detroit."

Maybe so, she thought. But would Veda Two be met by smiles and hugs or by a hysterically screaming boy? And would *that* be less traumatic than a flight to Detroit? "I don't know," she mumbled. She stopped walking abruptly, so Darius was forced to halt and backtrack to her side.

"Why?"

It was a simple question, but it had a complicated answer. "Long story."

"I'm all ears." His face was solemn, and his eyes were on her.

She lifted her eyes to the forest canopy above them, and to the pale sky beyond, seeking intervention, or buying time. This was how their conversations usually ran. Darius was insistent, even pushy. When he wanted information, or wanted to get his point across, he was relentless. But he was treading on deeply personal ground now, where any misstep could cause her pain. Her son was a private part of her; she kept him in her secret garden for his and her protection. Only she, those who took care of him, and her family knew of him. Her press agent and Tony. That was about it. She hated exposure, and had carefully ensured that not even her public knew these details of her life. Should she keep it that way?

She glanced across at Darius, and then looked away. He hadn't moved a muscle. She put her hands on her hips, and released her breath in a defeated gust. Darius was her partner, at least as long as their project lasted, and a decent man: that she knew. But then again, there was this attraction between them, which she'd certainly not wanted, but which had imposed itself upon them from the start. She liked him not only as a collaborator, but as a man. She wasn't kidding herself; there was something brewing between them that had not been put to rest; even though they hadn't made any mention of it or attempted a repeat of that first night, it was still there, waiting in the wings for an opportunity to enter stage right.

And so, if she desired this man who desired her, could she risk that frantic backpedaling, the sudden host of excuses, reasons to get away, that men always found when they heard about Will?

Darius moved slowly, reaching out, and taking her hand, turning it palm up so that it rested in his, and then placed his other hand upon it, facedown, so that it was sandwiched between both of them. The tips of her fingers tingled.

"Your hand's cold," he observed inconsequentially. He rubbed it, not vigorously, but lightly, and that was all he needed to do to bring the blood surging to her numb fingers—and a host of other places.

"I don't know if I can take Veda Two with me," she began. She hesitated, and then forged ahead. "Because she might scare my son."

His stroking of her hand was interrupted for less than a heartbeat, but then his rhythm resumed as if it had never been broken. "You have a son?" He wore a surprised smile.

"Yes. Will."

"Short for William?"

She shook her head. "Willard."

"Nice name," he said encouragingly.

She shook her head even harder. "Awful name. My mother made me call him that. There's been a Willard in every generation of my family for almost two hundred years, and since I'm the only child, she wasn't letting me off that easy. I didn't have a choice."

He nodded wisely. "Mothers are like that."

"Tell me about it!"

"And he's afraid of cats?"

She lifted her shoulders. "I honestly don't know. He doesn't like dogs, so I just thought . . ."

"He's an infant?"

"No. Willard's ten in the spring."

Darius frowned slightly, still not understanding. "So why don't you just ask him?"

Hailie snatched her hand away—his touch was far, far too soothing—and shoved it into her jacket pocket. She braced herself for the look that would cross his face next, the look that said *too much for me to handle, I'm backing off.* "I can't," she told him. "My son doesn't speak much. He's autistic."

Four

Hailie waited for the shutters to slam closed across his face, the way they usually did when people were confronted with the idea of the disabled. She was familiar with it. She saw it whenever she walked into the mall with Will at her side, went grocery shopping, or strolled with him in the park. People knew at once that he wasn't like the other children of his own size and age, who ran and shouted and begged their parents for the newest video game, scooter, or basketball shoe. They looked at the contained little face, devoid of expression, unwilling to make eye contact, and knew that something was . . . not . . . right.

And they didn't like it. It made them uncomfortable. Some stared. Some looked away. Most responded as if whatever he had was contagious, and herded their own children to themselves, giving Hailie and Will a wide berth.

So Hailie looked up into Darius's face and waited.

"Come," was all he said. He led her off the path a few yards, eyes searching out and finding a fallen log, and gently pressed her into a seated position before dropping down onto it beside her. "I'm sorry to hear that."

She splayed out her fingers expressively, acknowledging his commiseration, but dismissing it. "Thanks. But you don't need to be sorry. We do okay."

"I'm sure you do. I just wish . . ."

She bristled. Here it came. The broken record that every man she had ever been interested in immediately trotted out and played for her before beating a hasty retreat. *I just wish you hadn't told me,* or, *I just wish he wasn't, because I don't like to have to think about it. I like you, I'm attracted to you, but I can't deal with this. It's not what I bargained for.* "Just wish what?" There was more aggression in her voice than she intended.

"Just wish I knew more about autism. Then I could understand better what you're dealing with."

She was sure the surprise registered on her face. "You do?"

"Yes. Why? I'm not supposed to? Should I be minding my own business?"

She was quick to reassure him that that wasn't what she was thinking. "No, it's not that. It's just that I've never met anyone before who wants to know about him, or his condition. Usually, people backpedal so fast they practically fall over." She watched him hard, almost suspiciously. "So why do you want to know?"

The dark denim of his jacket rose and fell with his shoulders. His face said *silly question,* but his mouth said, "He's yours. He's a part of you. If I learn about him I learn about you. So tell me. Explain."

Her relief outweighed her surprise. Darius hadn't flinched. He hadn't backed off, or looked away. He was asking her for more. . . . She wasn't sure if any man had done that before. She wondered where to begin. She did so by taking a swipe at the most obvious misconception most people had about her son's condition. "Well, he's not *Rain Man,* that's for sure."

Darius smiled reassuringly. "I didn't think he would be. Hollywood isn't necessarily the best source of information on these matters." Then, he added, "So, he can't speak?"

"*Doesn't*, probably, rather than *can't*. He has a vocabulary of maybe ten words. We're pretty sure that he'll learn more over time. He has sessions with a child speech therapist twice a week. He lives a very regimented life, of his choosing. He loves order, and hates change. I'm pretty sure he can tell the time, although he never looks at the clock, but he has his meals at exactly the same time each day, takes his bath at the same time, gets up, goes to bed, goes to the bathroom, plays with his toys, takes his walk in the garden, all on some sort of schedule that he made up for himself, that I've had to learn and adapt to."

"Is he responsive to you?" He asked his question without any hint of hesitation or embarrassment. His brows were drawn in a little, focused on her mouth, as if lip-reading would enhance his understanding of what she was saying.

"Very. He's not shut off from the world, although to look at him you might think so, because his face doesn't transmit much emotion. But he's very loving, very affectionate. He loves to be held and hugged, loves to touch things, and experience different textures: flowers, carpet, cotton, fur, wood, stone." She finished by saying, with great emotion, "He's a beautiful child."

Darius put an arm around her shoulder. "I'm sure he is."

His reassurance, his absence of revulsion, comforted her so much that she almost drew her wallet from her jeans to pull out Will's photos, but she hated it when people whipped out their family photos to regale her with, so she kept her maternal pride and the snapshots to herself.

"And his father?"

That question, the one she dreaded, always came. Maybe one day she would have healed enough to be able to talk about Will's errant father without knives turning in her belly, but that day had not yet come. "You're looking at him," she said gruffly.

Darius wasn't about to let her obvious avoidance of the subject daunt him. "Is he alive?"

"So it seems," she answered bitterly. "His monthly payments turn up in Will's account on time, anyway. I'll say that much for him. He's meticulous about money."

"Do you still see him?"

"No."

"Does he see Will?"

She would have laughed, if the situation hadn't been so tragic. "Darius, listen. Will's father is a successful man, a perfect man, who doesn't want any imperfection in his life, and that includes a less-than-perfect little boy. Not to mention what Will could do to his social life and his precious self-image. I'd be curious to know what his society friends would say about *that* little skeleton in his closet. But he's ancient history. Bad history, understood?"

"Understood." She expected her rebuff to shut him up, but he still wanted information, only in a different vein. "Who's staying with him now?"

"We have a live-in nurse, Coretta. She takes care of him while I write, and when I travel. At first, for years, I couldn't leave him, not even for a few hours. He'd scream and scream . . . it was awful. But now, he's gotten used to it. He knows I'll be back. That's made it a little easier. . . ." There was so much tension in her spine, so much fatigue. She put her hand to the back of her neck to massage the stiff muscles there, but he beat her to it. Warmth spread downward through her at his first contact, and she could have protested, but didn't have the willpower to do so.

"But it's still hard on you," he observed. "Big commitment."

"Commitment, yes, but not a burden. He's my child, and I'm happy to give him anything he needs. It's just that sometimes . . ." Oh, his touch was so gentle. His hand was large and intuitive. When it slid between her shoulder blades, it sought and found all her knots of tension, those little repositories of stress and fatigue, and worked at them. With his touch, he brought them into submission.

"Just that sometimes, you get lonely?"

She could barely get the word past her lips: humiliation and embarrassment inflated it to the size of a jawbreaker. "Yes."

"Why? Between Will and your writing, all your time gets chewed up?"

"That, yes, and the fact that . . ." Oh, she wasn't going on. He didn't need to know how many times she had been rejected by men who showed an initial interest in her, but who, after two or three visits, and time spent in Will's company, decided they just weren't prepared to invest the time into a relationship with a woman who came with such a huge commitment into the bargain.

She didn't have to explain any further. Darius caught the idea deftly, and ran with it. "Your boyfriends back out because of Will?"

She nodded, not trusting herself to speak, and folded her arms across her chest. It hurt to be rejected, cast away like a millstone from around a man's neck, and she wasn't sure she was willing to show Darius that hurt.

"Gutless." He looked disgusted. "Stupid creeps. You're better off without them."

Maybe, she thought, but that was the kind of thing she had to keep telling herself late on Saturday nights, when everyone else in the world seemed to have someone.

"I wish I could apologize for them. I'm embarrassed for my gender. I'm sorry."

Sorry? She wrenched herself away from him and got up, despite the fact that her body roared in outrage at having his caresses interrupted. "Stop saying that! Why do you keep saying you're sorry? I don't need your pity, Darius!" She was back on the path before he could overcome his bewilderment and follow her, stalking back in the direction from which they had come. In her agitation, she had to remind herself that the path dipped and rose sharply at whim, and she would do well to watch her footing before she found herself the victim of a humiliating tumble.

"I didn't mean it that way. I was trying to say that I sympathize—" In spite of her head start, he caught up with her before she could put much space between them. He grabbed her elbow in an effort to halt her, but she yanked it from his grasp and kept on walking.

He was only making this worse. "I don't need your *sympathy,* either!"

"Empathy, then! I'm trying to say that I understand! Why won't you allow me to do even that?"

"Because you don't! You can't!" She broke into a run, following the path more by instinct than by vision, just wanting to get away from him. His clumsy efforts to understand were almost as bad as the dismissal she had anticipated in their stead. Further understanding would bring him even more dangerously close than he already was, and that would be more than she could handle right now.

He didn't even need to run to keep her in his sight; just a steady, long-legged stride was enough. Around her, the trees seemed to be closing in, getting in her way. Branches snapped at her face, reached out, and grabbed her flying hair. The forest was awakening, terrifyingly, like a nightmarish scene in one of her own books. In the knee-high brush on one side, something scurried, making the greenery sway, and almost scaring her out of her mind. She tried to tell herself that it was surely just a rabbit, or some small, frightened thing, but that was cold comfort. The forest had become creepy, and she longed to be out of it.

She was the prey, and the hunter was taking his time. Then, in answer to her fevered prayers, her cabin appeared almost unexpectedly around the next bend, and she lowered her body into a sprint, reached the door, and tore it open. He was in behind her before she could slam it shut.

"Mahalia! What's gotten into you?"

He wasn't even out of breath, but she had to prop her hands on her knees to catch her own wind. "What's gotten into me? You go on about how sorry you are that I'm so *lonely*, like I'm some pathetic old dowager queen. It's embarrassing. . . ."

"No shame in that. No shame in being lonely, sweet." He could have touched her then, approached her, making her feel even more cornered, but he didn't. He gave her ample room. Even so, she was overheated, by his earlier touch, and from her vigorous run. She tore her jacket off and threw it on the floor. Bending without effort, he retrieved it, turned it right side out, and hung it up behind the door. In a few moments, his joined hers. He waited until she was breathing normally before he said another word. "So what do you do with it?"

She feigned ignorance. "With what?"

"With your loneliness," he clarified patiently.

"I write," she threw at him defensively. "For hours and hours; all night, if I need to."

He wasn't buying it. "And I draw. For hours and hours." He used her own words, but without irony. "So I know it doesn't help. Not entirely. Not when you need to be touched, and held."

"My son and I lie on the couch and watch movies, and eat buttered popcorn. Sometimes I think he follows the show. Sometimes, he just snuggles next to me. He's warmer than any blanket. . . ."

Darius took one step closer, and her body leaped as he came within range of her radar. "You know that's not what I mean. I'm sure he comforts you. I know he does. But I'm talking about a man's touch, your need for it. Skin hunger." Even closer still, and her body's sensory instrument shrilled *beep-beep-beep.* "How do you feed it?"

"I don't need to," she lied. "I've taught myself that it doesn't matter. I don't need anything else. . . ."

"Bull. I've touched you." He pointed downward at the floor. "Right here, on this very spot, not so long ago. I kissed you, and you kissed me back. And every inch of you screamed *touch me, touch me, touch me.* Your mouth opened up for mine like it hadn't tasted another man's lips in . . . ages. I knocked with my tongue, and you let me in. If we hadn't called a halt—"

Hailie slapped her hands over her ears, but the effort was futile. His voice was going around and around in her head, hitting home truth after truth, and she didn't like it. "Stop it, Darius!"

"Why? Why should I stop? I'm speaking the truth. You're the one who's in denial. I'm just calling it like it is. And I know what I see, because I feel it myself. What it's like to feel alone, even in a crowd, because when you get home at night there's nobody there waiting for you. I look at you and I see . . . me."

How could that be? No man who looked like him would ever have to go without companionship for any length of time. "Don't be ridiculous. You've probably got women crawling all over you like bees on a honey pot."

Or toffee pot, she corrected herself silently, to be more faithful to the color of his eyes.

To her chagrin, he grinned, and in spite of herself her tension slipped a notch.

"I'll take that as a compliment," he said. "But no, actually, I don't. I think I've holed myself up with my sketch pad and computer too long. After a while, imaginary people become more of your world than real ones. Besides, I'm . . ."

His eyes were on her lips, with a stare so intense that it was almost physical contact, and she had to fight against the instinct to put her fingers to her mouth.

". . . picky," he finished. "The bars of Detroit, or any city, are filled with lonely women. I could slip out at night and have one back in my apartment within the hour, if I tried. But you know what? I've been there enough times to know I'll never go there again. Sex and anonymity make bad bedfellows. I deserve better. I know what I want, and I won't settle for less. And it's been a long, long time since I've seen what I want."

This was too much! *He* was too much. He had the forwardness of youth on his side, allowing him to plunge forth without mincing words. His message was coming in loud and clear. He'd moved progressively closer to her as he spoke, but now he stopped, at arm's length, and stood immobile. He'd thrown down the gauntlet, and was waiting for her to scoop it up and close the gap between them.

Oh, how she wanted to! He'd homed in on her need with uncanny accuracy. Skin hunger. The need for a man's ministrations, to be pleasured and touched, after such a long time that she relied more on her imagination than her memory to tell her what it felt like. And it wasn't as though either of them hadn't seen it coming. The last time they'd kissed there was no denying their attraction, and as cool as they had played it over the next few days, it had still been there, simmering. On hold, not deactivated.

But what about the risks? Awkwardness would be the least of them. Shame, maybe even self-loathing, or worse, further hurt, the kind that came from opening oneself to another human being in such an intimate way. If she caved in, and they both gave each other what they so badly needed, what would he be like afterward? Right now, he was patient, exerting no pressure, leaving the next move up to her, but when all was said and done, and their blood had cooled, would he become dismissive, cruel . . . contemptuous?

He seemed to read her fears in her face. "I'd be kind, Mahalia. I'd treat you how you need to be treated, the way you deserve to be. I'm clean, drug-free, and healthy, but I'll still protect us both. And we can take this as slow or as fast as you want. The ball's in your court. It's all up to you. If you say no, well, no hard feelings. We'll sit and have lunch, and then get back to work. If you say later, we can put this on the shelf, and you can take it down and open it up whenever you're ready. But if you want to say yes, all you have to do is step forward."

Betrayed by her feet! She found her leather-booted toes just inches away from Darius's sneakered ones, and even before she could say anything more, he was planting soft kisses all over her face, her brows, her eyelids, her high cheekbones, and the tips of her ears. Her logical mind grasped at straws before her body drowned. "You're too young for me," she protested.

He disregarded her silly objection, and the kisses persisted. "I'm twenty-seven. What's that mean, four, five years between us?"

"Six." Even to her, it sounded stupid.

"Oh," he mocked gently. "That's a chasm!" His hands

were on her waist, insinuating themselves into the waistband of her jeans, tugging at her shirt.

She tried again. "I'm your employer!"

"Fire me. Any more flimsy excuses?"

"None that I can think of." She gasped when his fingers encountered the bare flesh of her midriff. His short, light, dragonfly-wing kisses ceased when his mouth reached hers at last, and deepened into something more intense, more demanding. A sigh escaped her, but was never transmuted into sound, as his mouth covered hers and he received it into himself.

Now she wanted to touch him as he was touching her, but his shirt was in the way. She tugged at it impatiently; her bumbling fingers were having a hard time with the buttons.

"You tear those buttons off, you sew them back on again," he said, laughing, and removed his shirt for himself.

"Just get it off, Darius," she said gruffly. Her tension ebbed under his wonderful, wonderful touch. His shirt hit the floor, and hers covered it moments later. The sight of his bare chest left her bereft of any further words—any words, perhaps, except *splendid*. He was lean, hard, and so well toned that she could trace every line and curve of his chest and muscled abdomen with her fingertip. The mole constellation that had previously only been visible above the collar of his shirt was bare to her view, and now she knew that it extended downward until it curled around his nipple like a scorpion's tail. Unable to contain herself, she leaned forward slightly, to touch her tongue to its stinger.

Shock catapulted a breathless curse from his lips, and his body tautened against hers. "You have no idea . . ."

He was wrong. She had every idea what she was doing, and she was enjoying every second of it. She slashed at his nipple again with the hot underside of her tongue, and with that the balance of power shifted in her favor. He was weak, wanting only for her to touch him again, and again, until the torture proved too much, and he thrust her gently from him.

"Honey, either we adjourn to your room, or we hit the floor. You've got three seconds to decide."

Mutely, she pointed at the bedroom door, and before she could turn to it, she was in his arms. "I'm heavy!" she protested, but her arms locked around his neck.

"Don't make me laugh." He kicked open the door—and found Veda Two directly in his path, solemnly regarding them with her penetrating stare.

"Cat alert," he warned her. He didn't put her down, but instead returned the cat's inquisitive look with a dead-eyed stare of his own.

"Tell her to get out or lie low." Hailie wasn't welcoming any interruptions, not right now.

"Veda Two, your ma says you either git, or avert your gaze, because we're coming through." The cat took her own sweet time contemplating her choices, and, in typical cat fashion, opted for none of the above. She leaped onto the windowsill, made herself comfortable, and began licking her paws.

"Outnumbered by stubborn females," he grouched, and laid Hailie tenderly upon the large, old brass bed that dominated the room. It was a Casuarinas antique, probably owned by the original founders, and Hailie loved it so much that she always requested this particular cabin whenever she stayed here, even though the bed was so big that it left her with very little room to maneuver around it. Now, as she felt the firm, springy mattress yield under their combined weight, she was grateful for its size and its solidity. As slim as Darius was, he was heavy, all hard, solid muscle, and a smaller bed would have made him very uncomfortable indeed.

Deftly, he unhooked and removed her bra, and tossed it overboard. She tried to cover up her shyness at being bare with a joke. "The Harry Houdini of bras, huh! And with your *left* hand to boot!"

He didn't seem to have heard her. He was propped up over her, on his elbows, staring down, riveted by the sight of her bare breasts. He extended one hand toward her, gingerly, like a parched man reaching out to ascertain whether the pool of water before him was indeed real, or just a mirage. His intense examination both excited and scared her.

Without a response, he eased her out of her boots, socks, jeans, and cotton panties—why, oh, why hadn't she been wearing something pretty, satin or silk? But Darius looked as though he wouldn't have cared if she was wearing sackcloth and ashes. He was far less interested in what she had been wearing than in what waited beneath. Now, as she lay naked before him, stretched out like a banquet, he looked like a starved soul unsure of where to start. She whispered his name again, timidly, and this time he heard her.

"Sweet?" He struggled to lift his eyes to hers. "Something wrong?"

"No. It's just that I was wondering . . . what you were thinking. You've gone so quiet."

He smiled, and the lights danced in his eyes. "I was dumbstruck."

Dumbstruck? Over her? He had to be putting her on. She was so ordinary. . . .

He hoisted himself into a squatting position at her knees and began a guided tour of her body, passing his fingertips lightly along each stop as he spoke. "You've got such gorgeous hair. Wild and crazy hair, and so much of it. I wish you'd let it loose. I'd sit with pen and ink and draw each curl, and it would take me a lifetime to get them all. You've got almonds for eyes, perfect almonds, and your lashes are long and thick, like my sable brushes. And your mouth . . . I kiss you, and your mouth tastes like berries, but I've never seen you eat any. How the hell do you do that?"

She almost didn't believe him. To hear him speak, when he looked at her, what he saw was beautiful, even though she knew she wasn't. Her body squirmed with pleasure at his evaluation and his exploratory touch. He might be a very good liar, but at least, today, she was willing to pretend to believe him. "Go on," she encouraged.

"Your breasts are like big, crisp apples. I know that if I bite, they'll fill my mouth with juices. And soft . . ." He could have lingered there, but he didn't. His index finger slipped into her navel, up to the first joint. "Your navel is like a little well. One day, if you let me, I'll fill it up with liqueur and sip it from you. . . ."

One day. Future tense. He was talking more than this, more than just today. Could he be lying about that, too?

He dipped down, without warning, and she felt the tip of his tongue flicker into her belly button, like a hummingbird sipping nectar from a buttercup. The warmth of his breath against her belly and the wetness against her skin made her tremble, a startled squeak leaping from her lips. Her hand shot up and clutched his hair, and her knees fell apart of their own volition.

His curious gaze slid several inches lower, and his visual exploration affected her as acutely as his touch would have. "Oh," he breathed hoarsely.

Oh?

"You're like a pomegranate, overripe, bursting. Spilling open, dark red, juices everywhere. And I feel like I haven't eaten in a thousand years. . . ." When he pressed his lips against her, she screamed, unable to contain the sharp, stabbing pleasure that convulsed her. Her body twisted like a serpent on a hot pitch road. Instantly, he was catapulted upward, and they were face-to-face again. His eyes were huge, round, anxious. "You okay? Did I hurt you?"

Hurt her? She'd never been this excited in her entire life. Her heart was tripping over itself, and she was convinced that if he pressed his mouth against her again, like that, it would explode. "Uh, no," she said lamely. "It's just that . . . I want you here, so I can see your face."

He smiled indulgently. "Okay. I'll stay up here, then. I want to see yours, too." His face was so kind, the last of her jitters were melting—almost.

She had to ask for one final assurance. "You won't hurt me, will you, Darius?"

He pulled her against the length of his body. "Of course not. Not like whoever hurt you before did. I promise you."

She needed so much to hear that. If the men in her life had been a game of five-card draw, she'd been dealt lousy hand after lousy hand. She'd rejected the idea of love long, long ago: that had gone out the window with Will's father. But even when she cast aside her reservations and sought out a lover, if not for romance but at least to assuage her loneliness and physical hunger, that, too, always ended badly. With guilt and self-recrimination. A clumsy, careless, or selfish man could do damage that took years to repair. She hoped this would be different.

"Am I it?" he asked.

"What?"

"Sometimes, when the loneliness gets too much, you find someone. Not for love, but for comfort. Just to keep you going, and remind you that you're a woman. To keep you sane. And then after, you find out that you hurt more than you did before."

Unerringly, he had read her thoughts, the way he did when they worked on their book. He couldn't be that close to the mark. She felt her face grow hot, and couldn't think of a thing to say. Eventually, she managed to ask him, "How d'you know?"

"Because I've dug myself into the same hole, too many times. Enough to know right now that it doesn't really help, only makes things worse. And I want you to know that this time won't be like the others. I'm not going to get up when we're done, get dressed, and throw a 'thanks, babe' at you before I walk out the door. I'm not going anywhere. This isn't about physical need. It's about intimacy."

"You don't know me."

"I know you're awesome, and beautiful, and special, and sweet. I know your mind. I knew you the day I finished reading your first book. Now I just want to know you more. I want to experience your body and feed your soul. You'll let me do that?"

"Yes." She meant it sincerely.

"Because if all you want is to be held, we can do that. All you have to do is say."

"We've gone beyond that now, Darius." Her body was fed up with her mind's timidity. She wanted him, and she wanted him now. She held her arms open.

He didn't need another invitation. He popped his shoes off without undoing the laces, and wriggled out of his jeans and undershorts, and then he was smooth, naked, gleaming. Then it was her turn to gasp. "Oh!"

He smiled at her appreciation, unabashed, and then reached into his wallet for a condom. She took it from him, and he submitted to her ministrations as she gently eased it onto him. Then he was stretched out against her again, smothering her with more kisses: harder, more urgent ones than before.

"Ready?" he rasped.

"Ready," she assured him.

She was parched, drought-ravaged earth, and he was rain. She soaked him up.

Darius was convinced that if he felt any more euphoric, the cops would bust the joint looking for illegal narcotics. He was floating over the moon, positively high on good loving, and the feel and taste and smell of the beautiful woman who sat across the table from him. Mahalia was bundled up in a thick, burgundy bathrobe, having declined to put any clothes on after their shower. She glowed; a thousand watts radiated from her skin, and it made him proud to know that he was the one who had flicked the switch to "on." As she shoved her plate aside and stretched her arms overhead, looking every bit as satisfied as Veda Two did after a good meal and a few hours in the sunlit window, he thought, what a change from the defensive, closed-in woman whose barriers he'd tried so hard to breach just a few hours before!

They'd made love for so long that the sun had gone down on them, and now their abandoned lunch stood in the stead of an early dinner. He was replete in every sense, fulfilled, satiated, and yet, looking across at her, he wanted more. And more, and more. Idly, he wondered what the chances were of getting her back into bed with him, even if it was just to watch her fall asleep against his shoulder. Her state of mind was hard to predict right now; she'd welcomed his lovemaking, probably more motivated by need than by a desire for him, specifically. He supposed he could live with that. But now that those needs had been seen to, would she withdraw?

She was regarding him solemnly, almost suspiciously. He wasn't sure he liked that look. "What?" he asked.

She feigned ignorance. "What, what?"

"What's that look?"

"Oh, I was . . ." She dipped her head so that her braids tumbled down and veiled her face. "I was waiting for you to find an excuse to hightail it out of here. You know . . . pressing business, have to get an early night, got to see a friend . . . the usual stuff."

Her words were like an ice pick to the heart. Did she really think he was going to run out on her now? After all they'd done together? It showed not only how little she trusted him, but how badly she'd been treated in the past. He uncoiled himself from the warmth and comfort of his chair and walked over to where she sat. He took her by the hand and urged her out of her chair, sat in it, and drew her down onto his lap. After brief resistance, she complied.

He wrapped both his arms around her and pulled her back against his chest. Their position meant he couldn't look her in the eye, but he placed his lips at her ear and said, in all seriousness, "Mahalia, listen carefully to what I have to say: I'm not him. Understand?"

"Who?" Her mouth could barely frame the word.

"Whoever did that number on you. I'm guessing it was Will's dad—"

"Don't call him that! He's never been a dad to him, not once, not for even a day. The only thing that ties them together is blood and obligation. That man has seen his own child twice in his life, Darius. Just twice. Once, at the hospital right after I gave birth, when he came to tell me he'd opened an account in Will's name, but that that would clear him of any other liability. The second time, when Will was three, and he'd just been diagnosed with autism. Came to see if Will really was the aberration he thought he was. He stared at him for five minutes, and then he walked away without a word to me.

That's the last I've heard of him. I don't know if I'll ever see him again, and I don't care. That sound like a *dad* to you?"

She was becoming so agitated that he had to tighten his hold around her to prevent her from leaping up. "Honey, sweet, calm down. That's what I mean. This man did something to you. He smashed your life into pieces and walked away. I don't know him, but I hate him for it. I swear to God, if I ever come across him . . ." He was about to promise to champion her cause, to make this shadow-man hurt the way he'd hurt Mahalia, but that was going counter to what he was trying to tell her, so he shut down that avenue of thought and tried again.

"He hurt you, and whoever came later hurt you as well, and made you feel you weren't worth sticking around for. But they're damn fools. They aren't worthy of your grief. But you have to know this: I am not them. I'm me. Darius Grant. I'm your friend. I'm your artist; I share your dream to write the best damn book we can. But if you let me, I'll be your lover, too. And I'll show you all the respect and kindness you're entitled to."

She was rigid in his lap, not soft and pliant against his body as she had been hours before, but he knew that she was listening, and that's all he needed from her right now. He plowed ahead. "All you have to do is let me in. Trust me. Take me at my word. And it's all up to you. You call the shots. I'm not coming up with any excuse to leave, because I haven't got one. I don't want one. I want to be here, with you. If you want me to leave, say the word, and I'll go. But if you want me to stay, I will. Lay your head on my shoulder and I'll stay awake until you fall asleep, and when you get up in the morning, I'll still be there."

She twisted so she could look at him. Her face was the

picture of bemusement. "But why, Darius? You don't even—"

"Know you. You brought that up already. I shot it down. What I know of you, I like. What I don't know, I'll learn, if you stop being so damn self-protective. You've got walls around gates, and gates around fences, and so help me, I'm going to get to the center of you if I have to climb over, tunnel under, or plow through—"

The hammering on the door startled them both. Knocking on doors? At Casuarinas? That was strictly against the rules. The artists were protected by inviolate privacy rules that prohibited disturbances of any kind. Visits to each other's cabins were by invitation only. So who could be kicking up such a racket?

"You expecting someone?" he asked Mahalia, but knew by the surprise on her face that she wasn't. So he helped her up, got to his feet, and answered the door. By the light of the security lamp that hung overhead, he could see the anxious face of the elderly Casuarinas handyman. Jennings, if he remembered correctly. Wiry gray hair poked out from under a battered Padres cap, and red-rimmed eyes, their pupils milk-blue from cataracts, were anxious behind Coke-bottle spectacles. He was as old as the hills, and as tough as dried leather, but still put in a tireless workday. He lived in the main building and not only took care of the grounds, but did just about every odd job that needed doing. "Mr. Jennings?"

The man seemed surprised to see Darius there, and naked to the waist at that. He shifted a little, trying to see beyond him and into the room. Darius was conscious of Mahalia hovering at his back, and spoke for her. "Is there a problem?"

"I got an urgent message for Miss Derwood."

Almost before the man could finish speaking, Mahalia

had squeezed to the front, and was almost shouting, "What? What is it? Did something happen?"

The man shrugged, but his face was sympathetic. "One of the ladies, they take a call for you back at the house a few minutes ago. Somebody say to call home. Urgentlike."

"God," Darius heard her gasp. "Will."

Jennings hovered. "You want me to drive you back to the office, so's you can call?" Cell phones were forbidden at Casuarinas, and the only way to call was from a bank of phones that stood in an alcove back at the main house, over a mile away.

Mahalia was halfway out of the door, barefoot and in her bathrobe, before Darius could restrain her. "No, thanks, I'll drive her over," he said. "We'll be right behind you."

Before Jennings was out of sight, Mahalia was frantically stripping off her robe and hunting for her clothes, but they kept slipping from her numb fingers. "Coretta wouldn't call unless something awful's happened," she panted. "My son . . . my son . . ."

Darius murmured every soothing thing that crossed his mind as he helped her into her clothes, and then into his car, but his words had very little effect. By the time they skated to a stop at the main entrance to the office, she was trembling. She threw open the car door and squirmed out of her seat belt, sprinting up the wide stone stairs into the old building. Darius didn't even bother to park properly; he just shut the engine down and loped after her.

The high-roofed main hall was paneled from floor to ceiling with polished mahogany, and the thump of her footsteps made the handful of other residents look up, startled at the noisy intrusion into the almost monastic atmosphere. Mahalia grabbed the nearest available phone, and before he could say, "I have a phone card," she was cramming coins into the slot.

He came behind her and laid a hand upon her waist, to let her know he was there for her, but even as she pounded at the numbers, she snarled like a dog whose owner was coming a bit too close to its food bowl. "Back off, Darius!"

"But . . ." He was bewildered. Surely, at such a frightening time, she'd want him at her side?

"Just back off. This is my family. It's my problem." She scowled at the digits on the chrome panel, and suddenly he didn't exist.

Stung, he drew away, and plopped heavily onto a low, narrow wooden bench against a nearby wall. He wasn't sure if he was more wounded by her rejection of him than concerned for her plight, whatever it was. He kicked resentfully at the bench's curved legs and tried to focus on the jumble of artwork on the walls, a collection of paintings and drawings left behind by Casuarinas residents over the decades. His anxiety wouldn't let him, however, so he returned his attention to Mahalia's tense form, and wished he'd learned to read lips.

After an agonizing time, she ended the conversation, trying blindly to put the phone back into its cradle, but it slipped from her grasp and hung from its cord, swaying, banging gently against the wall. Darius ran up to her, retrieved it, and set it in its rightful place. Then, he spun her around to face him.

The glow he had put there with his loving had been replaced by an ashen dullness that could only come from shock. Her eyes were stark and fever bright.

"Tell me," he said softly. "Please."

"Will . . ." she began, and then stopped. She tried again. "Will . . ."

"Is he okay?"

She nodded, movements robotlike.

"Thank God," he breathed in relief. At least, there was that. "But what happened, then?"

"My son set my house on fire."

Five

Hailie glanced sideways at Darius as he leaned forward to change CDs. She was surprised to learn that someone as young as he enjoyed the old guard of the jazz movement, the likes of Duke Ellington and Charlie Parker. The music soothed her troubled soul.

He hadn't said a word in the last hour or so, and she wasn't sure whether he was brooding or just giving her her space. He had every right to brood: she'd been pretty mean to him tonight, shoving him away when she went to make that call, and then arguing spiritedly with him over her means of returning to L.A. He'd insisted that he would drive her, although she was perfectly prepared to return the way she had come, by hiring a taxi. Even as he shoved her clothes into bags and threw them into the back of the car with his, she'd contended that she didn't need any help, and she'd find her way home on her own.

But he'd taken her verbal abuse with equanimity, even good humor, calmly settling her into the passenger seat and buckling her in while she railed and threatened to hop out at the first red light they came to. Now, as miles of dark, desolate, ugly highway sped by, she felt ashamed of her behavior, and promised herself that as soon as she had a moment, she would apologize profusely. If she was honest, she'd admit to herself that she was grateful for his help, glad that he was here at a time like this, when everything seemed to be falling down around her ears.

She broke the silence, because the alternative was loss of sanity. "Had you figured for a rap fan." She pointed at the CD player belting out a honeyed sax from the dash.

He looked amused, but whether it was at her awkward attempt at making peace, or her reference—once again!—to his youth, she couldn't tell. "That, too. I'm flexible."

"Evidently." Flexible he was. Why, at a time like this, was her mind being flooded by an image of his arching, supple bare back, and the strength of his legs wrapped around hers?

He relieved her of the need to slap her mind back into focus by asking, "How's the kitty doing?"

Glad for the distraction, Hailie twisted in her seat, craning her neck into the back of the station wagon. The Casuarinas laundry basket was securely wedged between the back of her seat and the floor. The little white bundle, which had up to quite recently been vociferously indignant at having been unceremoniously snatched up and shoved back into the dreaded basket, had fallen silent at last. "Sleeping, looks like," she reported.

In the dimness, she was sure she saw him smile. "About time. My ears were getting quite a workout there. With any luck, she'll shut up the rest of the way."

The cat that had been the trigger of their intense conversation this morning—the conversation that had led inexorably toward its profoundly erotic conclusion—was coming with them. She'd agreed with Darius: there wasn't much choice. Veda Two wasn't well enough to be released. She'd just have to take her chances with Will's reaction, and right now, considering the circumstances, there were more pressing traumas facing him than the arrival of a five-pound, one-eyed cat.

"She'll do all right," Darius comforted. "Cats have a way with children. She'll know when to approach, and when to keep her distance. Don't you worry." He let his hand rest on her knee, comfortingly, not intrusively. She surprised herself by settling her own hand upon his.

"And how're you doing?" he ventured to ask.

"Bearing up."

"Good. I'm glad."

He was so patient with her. She wasn't used to kindness. It made something hard form in her throat, and she knew that if she didn't keep it down, it would continue upward, and liquefy into tears. "Thanks, Darius. For everything."

"Glad I was there to help."

She had to say something about her earlier behavior. "I was so mean to you—"

"Forgotten," he interrupted. "Over."

"No," she persisted. "Not over. You tried to be nice to me, and I slapped you away."

"I'm getting used to it," he said wryly. Then added, "But seriously, Mahalia, try to keep your strength up. Get a little rest. Why don't you take a nap, and I'll wake you up when we get closer, so you can give me directions to your house?"

Sleep? She probably wouldn't be able to do any such thing for quite a while. She shook her head vigorously. "Can't."

He understood. "Then lean back in your seat, and just listen to the music."

She was too much on edge to do that, either. Before the silence could claim them again, she murmured, "The fire started in the east wing, where the bedrooms are. Coretta thinks Will got his hands on some matches."

"Don't you keep them out of his reach?"

"Nothing's out of his reach. He can climb like a monkey. We have no idea where he got them, or how long he's had them. He could have hidden them anywhere in the house. He's a pack rat. Collects things, hides them everywhere."

"How much damage?"

She bit her lip. "Pretty bad. Three bedrooms, two of the bathrooms, and the eastern porch. I'm sure what wasn't burned out is smoke- and water-damaged. It'll take forever to recover."

"Not forever." He squeezed her knee. "It'll take a while, but not forever. You'll do okay. You'll see."

She was afraid to broach the subject, but it was on her mind, so she did so tentatively. "It probably started this afternoon, about the same time we were . . . you and I . . ." She trailed off miserably.

He took his eyes off the road long enough to give her a hard look. "The one had nothing to do with the other, sweet. You didn't do anything wrong. This was an accident, not divine punishment."

She wanted to believe him, but the sequence of events was so uncanny that the possibility of coincidence was hard to swallow. One minute, she was glowing like a new penny at the hands of a young man of whom she knew so little, but who had, from the minute he walked into her life, sent ripples through her like a pebble tossed into a stream. The other, her life was torn apart.

"Don't ruin it," he advised. "Don't turn it into something rotten. I'm begging you. Okay?"

She mulled over his plea for several moments, until she was sure he'd given up on a response from her, and then, reluctantly, she gave in. "Okay." She settled into her seat and resumed staring out into the darkness.

* * *

"There," Mahalia said. She stiffened in her seat and pointed through the window. "Third on the left. Right there."

Darius didn't need to be told which house was hers. The desolation made that self-evident. Half swallowed by the night, it stood in sharp contrast with the others on the street that, even at one in the morning, were brightly lit on the outside by security lamps and external lighting systems. He turned into her short flagstone-paved drive and came to a stop, not bothering to ask if she had the remote for her garage door, or whether there was space inside for him to park. He was too busy trying to think of what to say to her, and forming a plan to stop her from running full tilt into the damaged wing. There was no telling how stable the structure would be, and an ill-placed step might very well bring bricks and mortar crashing down. If she tried to run forward, he was going to have to restrain her, by force if necessary.

He needn't have worried. She sat frozen next to him, unable to shift a limb, peering through the windshield that was streaming with the steady, cold rain that had dogged them since they entered the city limits. He let his eyes follow hers, and his gift for empathy, this curious new ability that he had discovered to see what she saw, and to feel what she felt, let him share in, and, he hoped, halve her anguish.

It was a beautiful house; hardly huge by L.A. standards, but comfortably sized, it sprawled unself-consciously over a well-tended plot of land. The fire had severed the electrical connection, so the entire structure was in darkness, but his headlights were sufficiently bright to reveal broken hedges and trampled flower beds, which had probably fallen victim to the now-absent fire department.

It was a single-story structure, and its open, unassuming layout made him think of one of those desert homes that seemed to blend right into their environment. To the right, the house seemed untouched by the blaze, and the rough stucco walls were a cheery honeysuckle yellow. A wide bay window ran the length of it. The front door was wooden, and brass fixtures dripped rain onto the tiled front steps. The roof was constructed of overlapping red clay tiles that gave it the undulating look of heat rising off hot sand. The red of the tiles was echoed in the paved driveway. Tall yuccas and cacti thrust themselves haphazardly out of oversized clay pots, and a wrought-iron park bench was tucked away under a traveler's palm that waited for someone to sit in its shady comfort with a good book.

The overall effect was cozy and unpretentious, and he didn't have to close his eyes to imagine Mahalia stooped over out front in a straw hat, with yellow rubber gloves on, pulling up stray weeds that dared to poke up among the flagstones between mowings. It was a happy house, warm and homey, and spoke of sanctuary.

The left side, however, was an entirely different story.

The roof was like a thirsty mouth on a tilted-back head, wide open, guzzling rain. He was sure that most of the tiles had held, but their supporting wooden beams had succumbed. Those beams that were left hissed sullenly as the droplets of rain spattered onto their cracked, blackened surface, angry at the change in the weather for having spoilt their party. The yellow paint had given way to a layer of soot that clung to the walls, the nearby paving, and the grass. Scorched bushes cringed, shying away from blown-out windows. The air stank of acrid smoke, charred wood, and melted plastic.

Darius tried to be objective. It looked horrible, frightening, obscene, but from what he could see, the damage was not nearly as bad as he had expected. At least the entire house hadn't been razed. Maybe 20 percent of it, a third at the most, had succumbed, and, come morning, he was sure that the daylight would reveal little structural damage, apart from the roof itself. The walls seemed, for the most part, to be standing strong. The contents of the rooms, of course, would be irretrievable, but there was hope, and lots of it.

But that was easy for him to say. Mahalia, shell-shocked, exhaled the softest of whimpers, and his heart went out to her. He felt ashamed. He'd been studying the problem objectively, like a bystander at the scene of a tragedy, but this was Mahalia's life that had collapsed in cinders. This was her home.

He reached over, and, hindered by the bucket and the emergency brake between their seats, tried to pull her shaking body against his. He wished there was something reassuring he could say, but for the life of him, couldn't think of a thing. So he stroked her hair and let her cry.

In the darkness, Mahalia's front door opened. A figure held a storm lamp aloft, peering out at them. "Coretta," Mahalia said softly. She popped her seat belt, threw open the door, and ran across the driveway in the rain. Darius followed, having missed the chance to make sure she covered her hair from the rain, or to run at her side, using his jacket to shelter her.

In the orange, flickering light of the storm lamp, Coretta's face was ghostly and indistinct. She appeared to be a woman in her late sixties, with skin the color of walnut. The only sign of gray in the thick skein of black hair appeared at her temples in twin stripes, running along the sides of her head and disappearing into the single braid that bristled agitatedly behind her. She was heavyset, but comfortably so, in a way that made Darius think of solidity and capability. She wore a light blue nurse's uniform, with an apron that buttoned on at the bosom, but Darius sensed that she still had it on at this hour not because of a meticulous devotion to duty, but because the chaos of the day had obliterated any impulse to remove it. Her eyes, creased at the corners by time and the onslaught of smoke and ash, were reddened and anxious. The women embraced, clinging to each other in that way women had when both needed to be consoled.

"Hailie, I'm sorry. I'm so sorry. It was awful. It happened so fast—" Coretta's voice was Angelou-deep and powerful, and Darius immediately got wind of a melodious West Indian accent. He wished briefly that he knew more about the islands, so that he could identify which of them she was from.

Mahalia didn't have time for apologies. She leaped to the most important thing on her mind. "Where's Will? Is he okay?"

"Inside. Asleep. He was hysterical, beside himself. I called Dr. Allen; he came right over and gave him a shot. Says he'll sleep until morning. It's best."

"Asleep where?"

Rain was slashing in at them, and the eaves under which they stood were of no use against its insistent campaign to soak them to the skin. Neither woman seemed to notice. "Ladies," Darius began, "maybe we should—"

It was as if he had never spoken.

"In the guest room. The fire never made it that far. It smells a little smoky, like the rest of the house, but it's clean. He probably wouldn't have wanted to sleep there ordinarily, but the shot had him so groggy he didn't have a chance to protest."

Darius decided to be more assertive. He took Mahalia by the elbow, and pushed open her front door. "Inside, Mahalia. Come on, out of the rain."

She was about to obey, but Coretta, who stood between her and the doorway, didn't budge. Instead, she lifted the lamp and shone the light on his face, as if only just realizing that he was there. Her brow furrowed suspiciously, defensively, and she threw Mahalia a questioning glance.

Distractedly, Mahalia made hurried introductions. "Sorry. Darius, this is Coretta, Will's nurse. I told you about her."

"You did."

"Coretta, this is Darius. Darius Grant. My . . . um . . ." She paused for the briefest moment, and then said, "My artist."

My artist. Darius felt his self-esteem slip half a notch. The least he had hoped for was "my friend." It made him feel left in the cold, a little superfluous. The very last ghost of the afternoon's intimacy melted away in the rain, washed down the flagstones like spilled sugar.

Selfish, he chided himself silently. *She's lost her home, and once again all you can think about is you.* He shoved the twinge of hurt into a private, out-of-the-way place, where he would be free to examine it later, after this crisis was over.

"Grant, eh?" Coretta's eyes narrowed briefly, and she peered at him searchingly, making an uncomfortable sensation ripple down his spine. What was she searching for?

"Yes, ma'am." He offered his hand, but she didn't take it. Awkward seconds passed before he withdrew. He had no choice but to put her seeming rudeness down to a combination of stress and the encumbrance of the lamp that she held, because before he could puzzle any further over her question, or her suspicion, she gave him a nod, and relaxed slightly.

He had to insist again that they all go in out of the rain, but Mahalia beat him to it. She'd had enough of the conversation. She put space between herself and them, and they hurried to follow her.

Inside, rows of candles flickered everywhere, from brass candlesticks that stood upon bookshelves to clusters of small tea lights in saucers, placed upon every available surface. There had to be at least thirty lit candles in the entrance hall and living room alone, and the result was a parody of the fire that had gone before.

"Dark was getting to me," Coretta said sheepishly. She gave Darius a half smile, accepting of him now that Mahalia had legitimized his presence.

"It would," he said reassuringly, but he wondered whether the resulting light was any better. At any other time, the rows of dancing flames would have been cheery, even romantic, but the orange glow was tainted by the need to have them, rather than the desire to forgo electricity for something softer. Even with the darkness chased, the effect was eerie.

Mahalia was past the living room and through another doorway, leaving him no more time to further absorb his surroundings. He hurried after her. Beyond the corridor was another room, its door wide open, and therein a single candlestick mocked the dark. She snatched it up from the shelf and approached the bed.

Darius braked at the doorway, unsure of whether to penetrate any further into her private moment. Coretta certainly hadn't; she'd stayed behind in the living area. Should he go further, or give Mahalia her space?

He compromised, standing at the foot of the broad bed, near enough to be available to her if she needed him, but not close enough to make her feel crowded. He wanted to say something; in fact, words were thronging at the tip of his tongue like thoroughbreds at the start of a race, but he held his silence, and simply watched.

She lifted the candle overhead, and the light revealed

a sleeping form. The little boy was small for nine, fine-boned and sharp-faced. Even in chemically induced repose, the face held a spark of warmth, one that Darius recognised immediately as the boy's mother's. He was, in fact, a dead ringer for her. Mahalia's long, black lashes, which Darius had earlier praised, were reproduced in miniature, sweeping Will's cheeks like tiny brushes. He had her cheekbones, her snub nose and full mouth, the last of which quivered from time to time, as though he were mumbling in his sleep. Darius remembered she'd said Will couldn't—or wouldn't—speak much. Maybe in his dreams, he did.

Lightly, she ran her fingertips along his hair, which was as thick and black as hers, and quite long, having been cornrowed closely to his skull and ending in tight braids at the base of his neck. "He hates having his hair cut," she explained. "It used to take half a day, and two pairs of hands. I even used to cut it in his sleep, but he always sleeps on his left side, so the other side of his head stayed long. This was the best solution."

Her face glowed with a mother's indulgent pride, and he watched the heartache and tension that had been etched upon it since their departure from Casuarinas drain away, like the tide receding on sped-up film.

"He's a beautiful child." He meant that sincerely. Darius wasn't what anyone would call a fan of children; as a matter of fact, he wasn't sure he knew what to say to one if he was pressed into it, but the boy was special because he was hers.

She didn't acknowledge the compliment; her attention was no longer directed at him. The bed sank under her weight as she sat next to her son. The small hand was clutching something that gleamed in the candlelight, and she gently pried it from his fingers and examined it. Darius could swear it was a black patent leather shoe.

She turned it over in her hand as if she had never seen it before, and then let it fall to the floor. "Pack rat," she murmured indulgently. "You've got to stop doing that."

Then there were no more words, at least none that were spoken. Instead, she began to sing an old lullaby, one Darius remembered from his boyhood. His mother had sung it to him. She'd sung it to all of her brood.

> *"Hush, little baby, don't say a word,*
> *Mama's gonna buy you a mockingbird."*

Darius sensed that the lullaby was meant more for Mahalia's comfort than for Will's, as, already being asleep, he didn't need one. Darius listened, feeling like an intruder, yet still riveted, as she went through it from beginning to end, three times. The third time, the lyrics had devolved into a soft but melodious hum, and he realized that she had lulled herself half to sleep.

Gently, he took the candle from her and set it down. He eased the covers aside just so that she could slip in beside the boy. "Are you warm enough?" He had reason for concern: with the power down, there was no heating, and it *was* January. She'd suffered quite a sprinkling in the rain, and he was sure her clothes were still damp.

"Mmm," was her only reply.

He managed to get her boots off, but when he reached for her jeans, she brushed his hands away. "I'll be fine, Darius, stop fussing! Leave us alone."

She couldn't have been clearer. He felt like an intruder because he was one. Between the two of them, mother and son, they formed a tight little circle. For all the concern he felt, and for all that had passed between himself and Mahalia earlier, this was somewhere that he didn't belong. He was totally blindsided by the urge to stay and protect them both—he wasn't even sure why he wanted to—but his hovering was both unwanted and unnecessary.

Resignedly, he blew out the candle, and felt his way out of the room in the dark.

Six

Hailie's hand was beginning to sweat. Will hadn't let her go all morning, not even to eat his breakfast of cereal and milk, and now, as they walked through the damaged wing of her house, he was clutching her hand so tightly that his fingernails were making little indentations in her palm. The strangeness of the smell left behind by the fire, and the blackened walls and furniture, scared him badly, and each time she glanced down at him to catch his dark eyes saucer-wide and fixed on some ugly, melted lump that once formed part of her home, her heart went out to him. While most outsiders would be stumped if they tried to read his otherwise closed-off, stoic little face, she felt with her mother's heart every twinge of emotion that rippled through him. He was terrified.

"How's he doing?" Darius broke into her thoughts, almost taking her by surprise. He walked alongside them on their morbid early-morning tour, keeping pace, and saying very little. Like Will's, his eyes darted here and there, taking in every charred rafter, every ashen streak. Unlike Will, though, his face reflected his horror. She even caught his occasional sideways glances at her, and knew he was trying to read her, perhaps even bracing himself for more tears.

He'd be disappointed. She was done crying. She'd

awoken before dawn, and for the few brief moments before consciousness had returned, relished the sheer warmth and comfort of her son's still-sleeping form against hers. She'd even allowed the memory of Darius's loving to flit over her, kissing her skin like a passing cloud of butterflies. But the luxury of that remembered sensation had been dashed aside by the cold water of reality. She'd woken up next to Will, she remembered, not because he'd had one of his frequent nightmares and she'd gone to comfort him. They were sharing a bed because it was the only one left standing. That realization had brought with it fresh tears, tears that dripped down her son's neck until he muttered in complaint and wiped them irritably away. As he opened his eyes, she'd hastily dried the last smear of dampness, unwilling to let him see them.

So now she returned Darius's anxious look with a determinedly dry eye, and answered his question with a level voice, even as her life's possessions lay blackened at her feet. "He's scared. He's trying to figure out what's happened, why a place that used to be so familiar to him doesn't look the same anymore."

"Does he understand what happened? Do you think he remembers starting the fire?" Darius asked these questions without a hint of the malice and unkindness that Hailie was used to, coming from people who didn't know Will or understand anything about his condition. There was no disdain in his voice or on his face, nothing that told her he thought that Will couldn't feel fear, or pain, or sadness, or, worse, that he was less than a person, period.

She was touched by his concern, and managed a smile. "I'm sure he remembers. He's a smart kid. I'm just not sure he can link the scary light of the fire, and the heat of last night, to the coldness and wetness, and the dark of this morning. I don't know if he can see that the one is a consequence of the other."

"Maybe it would be better if he didn't, so he wouldn't have to suffer guilt. It would be hard on him, having to deal with the fact that he started it. He must know you're hurting, and I know he wouldn't want you to hurt, especially not if it's his fault."

Again, that kindness. That perceptive inner eye. Hailie felt a constriction in her chest, much like the sensation that had overwhelmed her a million light-years away in the woods at Casuarinas, when she realized that Darius was being nice to her, for no reason at all, and that she was liking it. She watched him covertly, taking in the rumpled clothes he'd slept in: yesterday's checked shirt and jeans. His hair, as usual, was tousled, his cheek creased from an uncomfortable night in the armchair in her den, the only viable sleeping place left after he'd ceded the living room sofa to Coretta. He looked sweet and boyish. Too damn concerned. Too damn gorgeous. She wasn't ready or willing to handle any of the above.

Flustered, she stepped through a doorway, pushing her braids out of her eyes with her free hand. "This is Will's room. Mine's on the other side, through the bathroom. It's all connected, so I can keep an eye on him at night. He has nightmares. Actually, he keeps an eye on me, more often than not, because I have nightmares, too. It's a little worse here than in the hallway or the bathroom, see?" She was babbling. She was rattling off at the mouth. She knew it, but she couldn't stop. "But it's not as bad as I thought it would be. I mean, it's bad, but I thought everything would have been totally wiped out, sucked into some sort of black hole, and nothing left but ashes, you know? I didn't think there'd be anything left." She stopped, not because the need to talk in order to put more space between her and her thoughts had diminished, but because she'd run out of air. She took two hurried gasps. *Relax*, she chided herself. *Relax*.

"Fire works in mysterious ways," Darius agreed gravely. His eyes had left Will's face, and were now fixed upon hers, with the same perceptive, armor-piercing look. And yet, she sensed that he was humoring her, picking up the garbled thread of her conversation with ease. "Sometimes, it cuts paths through a house, touching one thing and leaving the next. It's like a live thing, like a hungry animal. It can go on a rampage and eat everything in sight, or it can pick and choose what it pleases."

"Like a werewolf." A nervous giggle popped from her mouth like a bubble.

"Like a werewolf."

She turned from him and tried to absorb the extent of her loss. Her initial prattled observation was right: not everything had been consumed. While a large wooden dresser was miraculously untouched, Will's toy box had been reduced to rubble, and his bed—Hailie flinched at the thought of how easily this all could have started while he was lying on it, or how often children in danger ran to their beds to hide—was another story altogether. Though the iron frame had resolutely resisted the heat of the blaze, allowing only its fire-engine-red paint to be licked off by the eager flames, the box spring had succumbed. It sank toward the floor, wire coils a tangle of Medusa's hair, contorted, jumbled. The only evidence of the existence of a mattress was an oblong heap of ash, more metal, and melted foam that had hardened on the hardwood floor in great, smelly globs. It was a tiny cataclysm, crammed into a space just six feet by four.

Will's hand twitched in hers. Hailie look down. His face was unusually animated, as it became only in times of great joy or distress. Under his skin she could see blotches of color. Even his hair seemed charged with a strange electricity. She watched the movement of his head as he turned it slowly, like a flower tracking the movement of the sun across the sky. He examined everything, swallowing it with his eyes, sucking every new image into his secret place, where he would hoard it, save it for later, to examine and reexamine it in that locked room in his mind to which only he had a key.

"Shouldn't have let him come with us," she berated herself, barely loud enough to be heard. Darius, and the awkwardness brought on by his proximity, took a backseat to this heightened concern. "It's scaring him even worse, being in here. Having to face all this."

Darius put his hands on his hips and expelled a long, thoughtful breath. "Maybe. But there's more than fear."

"What, more than fear?" Hailie tried to push aside a twinge of irritation. Half an hour in the boy's company, and he thought he could tell what Will was feeling? There were professionals who trained all their lives to be able to do that! She was the one who knew him better than anyone. And she was the one whose palm was being torn to shreds right now by small, sharp, agitated fingernails. "I should send him to the kitchen, back to Coretta. He doesn't have to see all this. He hates change. He likes everything to be the same, always. This is all so different. Confusing. I should—"

"Exactly. It's different. And he's just trying to figure out the connection between the house he knew yesterday and the house he's seeing today. He's looking for a link, something that'll prove to him that he's in the same place, which just *looks* different, and not in a different place altogether."

Hailie stood stock-still and stared at Darius. Could he be right? What made him the expert? "You think?" Maybe there was a little sarcasm in her voice. Maybe she wanted there to be.

"Yes."

"And how do you know that? Seeing as you've only just met him."

Darius's lips twitched slightly under the assault of the tiny arrows in her voice, but he showed no offense. Instead, he dropped to his haunches, bringing his head down to Will's level, eye to eye. "I don't know how." He sounded as surprised as she. "I just . . . know."

Hailie watched Darius watch Will, and as she did, her breathing slowed. Those toffee eyes, which still sparkled, even in this dismal place, followed Will's gaze as it flitted around the room, and then returned to Will's face, to the small pair of lips that moved mutely but steadily, like lines of poetry being mouthed by a reader trying to amplify the meaning of the written word with his hushed voice.

"Lines," Darius said softly.

"What?" *Too uncanny,* Hailie thought. *Lines. He couldn't be saying what passed through my mind a second ago. Too weird.*

"He's watching the lines. Following them. Like an artist preparing for a sketch. The window's busted, but the lines of the frame are still there, and that's what he's seeing. The closet, the chest. The frame of the door, and the places where the walls meet the floor, and where they meet the ceiling. That's what he's looking at. He's measuring them in his mind. That's his connection. That's how he knows it's the same room he's always slept in."

With his face just inches from Will's, Darius lifted his hand and laid it gently upon the back of the boy's head. *Don't!* she wanted to yell. *He hates being touched by strangers. He'll scream. He'll fight you off. Don't, Darius!* But her lips couldn't form the words, because as they leaped from her mind, her heart saw them to be a lie. As Darius's long fingers lit gently upon Will's fine cornrows, like a dragonfly upon a leaf, Will turned. Surprise reflected in his eyes, like those of a child who, thinking himself alone, turns around to find someone a pace behind. As though he had only just realized that Darius was there.

"Look," Darius said. Without a trace of hesitation, he took Will's hand in his, extended the index finger, and began to make tracings in the air.

Hesitant, Will threw her an inquiring look. "Mommy?"

"No." Darius was firm, but gentle. Insisting on Will's undivided attention. "Look." Then, like sparklers tracing their fleeting orange trails in the night sky, imaginary shapes appeared where the man led the boy's finger. "A square. See it? That's your window. It's the same window that was there yesterday. Yours. See?"

The square in the air faded, but as Hailie watched it imprinted itself upon her son's mind. His lips quivered, faster now, as he committed the shape to memory, writing it down in his own secret, silent language.

"There." Darius made another shape. "Your chest of drawers. That's an oblong, with three more oblongs along one side. Those are the drawers. You've probably got your clothes in there. Right?"

Will's eye moved from the tip of his moving finger to Darius's mouth, reading the shapes made by both.

"That's the same," Darius was saying. "This is the same. And this . . ." He led Will's mind to the agonized tangle of metal in the center of the room, and Hailie cringed, waiting for the fascination to turn to pain, and the pain to turn to anguished howls.

"This," Darius said, "is different. See? The lines are gone. The shapes, not what you remember. But it's the same bed. It's just changed. Nothing to be afraid of."

Everything else disappeared for Will. The walls of sky-blue, with their border of brightly patterned hot-air balloons, the melted model airplane mobiles that hung sadly from the ceiling and in the window, the photographs on the walls, ceased to be. Nothing existed, nothing *was,* but the wreck that he once slept on. That bed had once been covered with superhero bedsheets, topped by four pillows and the firm, springy mattress Hailie had bought him and regretted forever afterward, because he loved nothing more than to bounce up and down on it. He did it for hours, breaking even Hailie's old childhood records, as she herself had been a formidable bed-bouncer in her day. He bounced so high that, fearing for his neck, she often begged fruitlessly for him to stop and get down, play something safer, less likely to instill a maternal heart attack.

She remembered. So, clearly, did Will.

"Come, Will." Darius, still holding him, led him nearer to the bed. Will's small hand all but disappeared in Darius's huge one, except for that one finger, which protruded between Darius's forefinger and thumb like a stylus. The pair bent forward, nearer to one of the blackened heaps.

He's not doing what I think he's doing, was the first thing that flashed through Hailie's mind.

He is, was the second.

Black soot was knuckle-deep on Will's finger. He stared at it, looked long and inquiringly at Darius, and then looked at his finger again. What new game is this? he seemed to be wondering. His look held more anticipation than affront. Darius guided him to a bare patch of floor and squatted. Under Darius's hand, the fire-tracings that he had begun in the air were underscored on the hardwood floor in black. A square. An oblong. An oval. A series of parallel lines. A round, smiling face, just two dots and a curve enclosed within a circle.

"Now you try," he urged. "On your own."

Will plunged his hand into a pile of soot, like a painter loading up his brush, and, pink tongue poking from between determined lips, he copied each drawing, frowning hard in his attempt to mimic their exact size and shape. All the while, Darius encouraged him, murmuring softly into his ear. When he ran out of the room, Will shifted to one side and cleared himself a new space, wiping away grime from the floor with a shred of blanket, and using the floor as a huge canvas.

Crawling on his hands and knees, he took his ash-drawings farther, up one side of the wall, tracing over the ghosts left behind on the scorched wallpaper. Then, he stopped imitating. The simple shapes that Darius had drawn for him quickly forgotten, Will became ambitious. The little round faces sprouted emotions. Frowns, and openmouthed laughs. Shapes that had no name in geometry grew under his tireless finger.

Hailie had no idea how long she watched them, and what she felt as she watched them she could not identify. Pleasure, surely, at her son's own pleasure. Surprise at the ease with which Will had allowed Darius to enter his personal bubble. Relief that the trauma she had expected would have seized him this morning had not materialized.

But something else: a feeling of being an outsider, looking in through a window at two people in a private moment. She had the urge to join them, to plunge her own hands into the soot and take part in the game, but something stayed her. It didn't feel right. It would be like cutting in on a dance.

So she watched, forgotten by the two males before her, as Darius became bolder in his strokes, not wanting to be outshone by Will. His drawings grew more elaborate. Suns, moons, stars, animal shapes: cows, gazelles, snakes, spiders, and, yes, wolves. Like two cavemen, they drew a story in words, greedily using up every bare spot untouched by the flames, until the space ran out.

They'll be done now, she thought. The room looked like an archaeological dig: covered in hieroglyphics and wall paintings, evidence of some ancient male ritual. But they weren't done. Darius took one final swipe at his makeshift paint and, with three fingers, drew a row of parallel lines down Will's cheek. "African tribal war paint," Darius said. "For a hero. For an artist."

"Darius!" Hailie began. She braced herself. If Will had one obsession, it was his meticulous cleanliness. He never wore the same clothes two days running, and needed his hair washed twice a week. He was a boy who could stand under the shower for an hour, if you'd let him. It was strange enough, bad enough, that Darius had egged him into getting his hands and knees all covered with soot, but his face . . . ! Darius was pushing it. He meant well, but this just wouldn't—

"Mommy?" Round-eyed surprise from Will, and puzzlement. Again, he turned to her, his mouth as round as a fish's.

"It's okay, it's okay." She rushed forward, insinuating herself between Darius and her son.

Will slapped his hand to his cheek, not believing what he thought he'd seen. Taking his hand away, and looking at the three stripes printed out on his palm, he opened his mouth—wide.

"Look what you've done, Darius!" Hailie shrieked at him, snatching her son up into her arms.

Darius's face was a picture of puzzlement. "What? I was only trying to make him feel less scared. Make him know that what he was seeing wasn't scary."

Will's chest expanded against hers. The screams were building, gathering strength like a far-off storm. She knew it. She felt them against her breasts. When they burst, they'd go on and on. Will was a peaceable child, slow to anger, but when his ire was aroused, his tantrums could go on for hours, and it was all Hailie could do to prevent him from hurting himself, as in his rage he would hurl himself against the walls, banging his head against any hard surface, trying to overwrite his anguish with physical pain. Darius didn't know. He couldn't know. "I understand what you were trying to do," she snapped. "But you don't know what you're dealing with. You have no experience in these matters—"

Darius protested. "He's a child. A frightened one. I thought if I helped him face what he's afraid of, and make it feel normal, even fun—"

"He's a *special* child, and this isn't about fun! You're messing with things you don't understand—" She was running from the room, Will in her arms, as heavy as he was, trying to put space between him and the source of the disturbance. She scrubbed at his cheek with one hand, even as she ran clumsily, trying to wipe away the evidence of Darius's intrusion.

She didn't get very far. Like a leopard after fleeing game, Darius was upon her. He grabbed her by the arm, halting her flight. "What? What did I—"

She would never know what Darius was about to say next, because at that moment, Will's silent screams found their sound, piercing her ears, and filling her head. His mouth was just inches from her ear; she reeled from the proximity of his shrieks, and set him down on his feet.

"See?" she began. "See?" She raised an accusing finger to Darius's face, but halfway up, it stalled. That scream, that high-pitched noise, held none of the anguish and affront that she had anticipated. None of the bottled-up rage that spilled from her son on those rare occasions when his inner dam burst and his howls went on forever.

Will was shrieking, yes, but in laughter. Peals of unchecked, unabashed delight rolled out of him in waves, like the gonging of church bells. Where most people, even those as young as Will, had been schooled by convention and Miss Manners into laughing discreetly so as not to intrude upon the peace and space of others, Will had no such compunction. He held on to his thin sides as though they hurt, throwing himself against a wall for support as the guffaws robbed him of his balance.

This was her son? Covered in black and laughing like a maniac? Hailie wasn't sure whether she should believe it. As perplexed as she was, as astounded as she was, she found his laughter infectious, and a smile ambushed her lips. She glanced up at Darius, to find that he was smiling too, looking both amused and relieved.

"He's okay," he mouthed.

Will was more than okay. He slapped his dirty hands to his cheeks again, smearing the stripes across his face, adding to them with his own black-stained fingers, transforming himself into a tiger. Dodging them both, he ran, not away from his bedroom, as Hailie had been taking him, but through it and into the bathroom beyond. The damage here was greater, with the porcelain fittings cracked and yellowed from the heat, but Will didn't seem to notice or to care.

He stood before the mirror, and in its fire-frosted surface he was but a ghost. A ghost with sooty stripes up to the eyeballs. "Oh!" he yelped. He could barely form words, his mouth and lungs were so busy laughing. "Oh, oh, oh!" He brought his hand up to his cheek, fingers tracing the stripes in wonderment. Then his hands moved swiftly, back and forth, smearing the soot across his cheeks and nose, and into his hair. When there was little left to spread, he stole more from the bathroom walls, dragging it into his hair, tracing the furrows between his cornrows, down the back of his neck, and around to the front. When he was satisfied with his efforts, he turned from the mirror to her and threw his arms open in triumph. "Mommy! Mommy! Look!"

"You . . . clown!" Hailie gave up all attempts to keep her own laughter at bay. Her son looked like a chimney sweep. The only things visible on him were the whites of his eyes and his broad, gleaming grin. He was as proud of himself as if he had produced a work to rival the Sistine Chapel.

When his laughter wound down, like an engine running out of gas, he fell into her arms and covered her with grubby kisses. Hailie brought her arms up around him and clutched him tight. "Oh, I love you, Will. You little rascal."

"Uh-huh," Will agreed. He held her tight and sighed, struggling to breathe normally once again. Then he pulled away and turned to Darius, giving him a delighted look, waiting for his praise, too.

"You look terrific," Darius said obligingly. He bent nearer and pretended to examine Will's living masterpiece. "I couldn't have done any better myself."

Without a word, but with smile spilling upon smile, Will lifted his right hand, extended three fingers, and carefully, with great precision, drew three parallel stripes down Darius's cheek. The African warrior ritual was complete. The initiate had become the initiator, and Darius was now a member of Will's exclusive club.

Darius touched his cheek and brought it away in wonder, and something told Hailie that he understood how precious and rare this welcoming gesture was. The sparkle in those beautiful eyes mellowed to a warm, tender glow. "Thank you, Will." His voice was treacle-thick. He made as if to hug him, but instead, just laid his marked cheek upon Will's grubby one, and held it there, for several long seconds.

"Time to take a shower, kid," Hailie said briskly. Her intervention surprised even herself.

The man and boy pulled reluctantly apart, and stared solemnly at each other.

"Go on, shower time. You've got to, or you'll get all itchy. Do you want to be all itchy?"

Will pouted, and eyed Darius like a child being told he couldn't have dessert, when there was a huge double-fudge chocolate cake on the table right before him.

"Go on, Will. Listen to your mama. Get yourself cleaned up, and we'll play again later. Okay?"

Will nodded, and, without further resistance, made to leave.

"Want me to help you?" Hailie asked before he disappeared.

His only response was a negative grunt. Then he was gone.

Now, why had she done that? Her son rarely bonded. She could count on one hand the people outside of her blood family with whom Will had ever formed any sort of relationship, or whom he even seemed to like, and yet he and Darius were forging the beginnings of a tiny, two-person circle, artist to apprentice, warrior to initiate, man to boy, and she'd cut in. Sent Will off packing with a flimsy excuse. Why?

Why?

If her puzzlement at her impulsive action brought her discomfort, there was another disturbance that made her feel even more awkward, but this one was more immediate, more pressing. As Will's peals of delighted laughter died in the air, she realized that she was alone with Darius, for the first time since that long, silent drive down to L.A. in the rain. Was that good or bad? Was that something she wanted, or something she'd rather avoid?

Hailie squirmed and tried not to look at him, but even

so she had the distinct impression that he was looking at her. Intently. Her skin prickled, and she folded her arms across her breasts in an unconscious, self-protective gesture.

"I'm sorry." His voice was soft, low, and contrite, like that of a penitent whispering at a confessional window.

She wasn't sure what he was sorry for. She was the one who should be feeling abashed. Rushing in on the moment between him and her son, wedging herself in like a jealous woman. Only she couldn't have been jealous. That wasn't her nature.

"For upsetting you. For making you so mad. I was trying to help, honest. . . ."

Oh, God, and then there was that. She'd screamed at him, berated him for not knowing what he was doing. She'd snatched up her son and run, when *she* had been the one who didn't quite understand. She'd expected tears from Will, when all Darius's actions had produced in him was laughter.

She tried to wave away his apology, a little embarrassed. "No, Darius. Don't apologize. I'm the one who needs to. I shouted at you. I yelled at you for no reason. I thought Will would be upset. I didn't know . . . I didn't expect him to enjoy it so much, getting messy."

"He's a little boy. Little boys like getting messy. The messier the better, actually. Trust me. I was a little boy once myself."

"But he's different. He's . . ." She floundered.

"Not that different, obviously. Don't sell him short; he's very perceptive. Very smart. We were playing, and he could see that. He knew I wasn't trying to hurt him. He knew it was a game."

Don't tell me what my son is or isn't, she could have told him. Would have told him, if she hadn't been so rattled by the fact that he was right. She had expected less of

Will than he'd displayed. She'd been wrong about him, and, uncannily, Darius had been right. Guiltily, she hung her head.

Instead of saying anything more, he walked past her and through the bathroom's other door, into her bedroom. She followed several moments later, and came to find him standing at the birthplace of the inferno.

Even though all the other rooms had prepared her for what to expect, she was still shocked. Whereas the fire-creature had amused itself in all the other rooms, choosing to snack upon this while ignoring that, here it had grown greedy. It had gone on a rampage, wolfing down anything in its path, tearing paintings from walls, pouncing roaring upon her antique dresser and chair, and completely consuming the king-sized bed that had been her sanctuary on many a lonely night. Unlike Will's, her bed had been made of polished teak, and thus had fared much worse. There was nothing left.

Darius walked up to the heap of wet rubble and stood where the foot of the bed had been. He stared hard, for far too long, and then closed his eyes, in a gesture she'd come to recognize as his creative retreat, a transition wherein he shut himself off from the earthbound vision of his physical eyes, so that the single inner eye with which he saw beyond light and shadow could prevail. He seemed to be trying to reconstruct the bed in his mind, maybe even place her upon it, supine . . .

Warmth flickered against Hailie's skin, as if the flames, murdered the day before by firemen's hoses, were leaping to life again. She wasn't in the habit of inviting men into her bedroom; this was her sanctuary, her private place. Although it wasn't even a bedroom anymore, lacking any of her personal touches, no nightgown casually draped over a chair, no hairbrush or makeup on her dresser, it still felt deeply intimate. It was intimate, she sensed, because Darius was seeing the unseen, replacing what was lost with figments of his own imagination. She was even sure that what he was creating for himself would be far more delicate, more feminine than her boring reality. Satin where there had actually been cotton, fur slippers replacing her canvas sneakers with the stomped-down heels.

"Maybe we should go back out to the others," she began weakly.

Darius didn't open his eyes. Instead, he held out his hand, unerringly aiming in the right direction, and beckoned her to get closer. "Come."

Unwillingness to comply proved an ineffective weapon against his desire for her to approach. When he felt her near, he opened his eyes, and instead of taking the hand that she extended to meet his, he turned to her, and cradled her face in both his hands.

"My hands aren't clean," he warned her. "Your face'll be a mess."

"Yeah, I know," she responded dryly.

"You can get washed up soon. There's no power yet, but there's still lots of water."

"*Cold* water," she tried to joke. His hands were big, warm, soothing. And oh, he was close . . .

"We'll get this all fixed up in no time. I promise."

We?

He ignored, or didn't see, the puzzled frown that touched her brow. "It's not as bad as it looks. A week or two, a little work, and a lick of paint, and even the smell will be gone. I'll help you. We can have a work crew in here tomorrow."

Now she had to say something. "*We*, Darius?"

Now the puzzled frown was his. "What?"

"What do you mean, *we*? This is my home. It's my problem. I can make those calls. I can hire the crew. Why do you think I need help?"

His hands fell away, and the chill on her face as her cheeks protested his abandonment almost made her wish she hadn't spoken.

"Everybody needs help sometime," he told her. "This is your time. You've lost half your home, a chunk of your life." He indicated the walls with a sweep of his arm. "Your art, gone, your clothes, your *bed* . . . gone. You can't do this on your own."

"You just said it won't take more than a lick of paint!" she retorted.

"Damn it, Mahalia, I was trying to make you feel better!"

"By patronizing me? By saying *we*?"

"What makes you think I was being patronizing? What's wrong with what I said?"

"And what makes you think that you've got the right to say it?"

"Yesterday does," he bellowed. Then, realizing that he was shouting, he lowered his voice, striving for a neutral tone, and failing, as his voice thickened. "Yesterday does," he repeated. "We made love, you and I. Less than twenty-four hours ago. The fact that so much has taken place between then and now doesn't change that."

She wasn't sure she believed him. She wanted to, but experience had taught her that men often said things that sounded good, but which they didn't necessarily mean. She wasn't blind: she'd seen him throw her inquiring glances all day, asking without speaking if she remembered what had passed between them the day before, and if it had left its mark on her.

How could it not? She hadn't been expecting it, hadn't done anything to deliberately trigger it off, but they'd taken that step from a casual business relationship to an intimate, physical one, and from there, there was no turning back. Sure, they could agree to pretend that it had all been a figment of their joint imagination.

They could even decide to declare it a mistake, move on from there, and ensure that such weakness would not engulf them again. But it had left its mark on her, and she was sure that it was a mark that would be impossible to wipe out.

She tried to feel him out. Test the waters. "I thought you said it was supposed to be just one of those things to ease the loneliness. I fill your aching space, and you fill mine. Just two people, holding on, feeling less alone, even if it was just for a little while."

To his credit, he didn't try to deny it. "I was lonely, yes, and I sensed you were. It happens to the best of us. But there was more, Mahalia, and it didn't start last night. I felt it since day one, and if you'd be honest with yourself, and with me, you'd admit that you felt it, too. What we had in bed was good, fantastic. But what we felt out of bed was even better. The way we could share our ideas for your book, and understand each other's point of view, even when we didn't agree with it. The way you looked at me from across the table while we were working, as if you were remembering that kiss, on our first night, and wondering if I'd kiss you again. Know what I mean?"

He was asking her to admit her desire for him, which, she had convinced herself, she'd kept well hidden. He wanted her to confess that over the many days they'd spent working together, arguing over what Veda did next, she'd harbored a secret hankering for this too-young, completely inappropriate man. The very thought of it made her natural instinct for self-preservation begin throwing up its shields, like an embattled fort.

To lie would be easy. To play it cool, shove him back at arm's length where he belonged, would make her feel a whole lot safer. She could even pretend that their love-making had been a purely physical thing, a remedy for what ailed her, an over-the-counter cure for loneliness.

But that lie would have been grievous, an insult to the tenderness he'd showed her, and the utter unselfishness with which he'd given of himself. It would have been a sacrilege.

"I . . ." she began, but her tongue stuck to the roof of her mouth and she could go no further.

"No shame in it," he told her. "Just say it. I need to hear you." His eyes nailed her to the spot. "I wanted you. Tell me you wanted me."

He waited for an age, while the silence of the room grew to a shout, and eventually she slumped forward against his chest, body tired, mind drained, and yet unable to let go long enough to tell him what he wanted to hear. "I can't."

"Why not?" His voice was in her hair.

"Because it'll . . . hurt."

"I wouldn't hurt you."

"I might hurt myself."

"I won't let you."

She might have been able to hold off against his verbal suasion, but she was powerless against his kiss. It was only when his mouth lit upon hers like a bird returning to its nest that she became aware of how badly she had needed it, and how long it seemed since they'd lain with their legs entwined, bodies sated to near exhaustion, but mouths still yearning for more. She caved in like a wave-slammed sand castle, becoming so pliant in his arms that, if he hadn't been holding her securely, she would have slumped to the floor.

His kiss felt so good! Bringing her assurance, soothing her distress. Behind it, like a comet's tail, came desire, an ember from yesterday's fire puffed back into life. For far too long, her body had been on starvation rations, deprived of the nourishment of touch and sexual satisfaction. She was shocked to notice that even though she'd fed lustily on the banquet he'd laid out before her yesterday, she was hungry again. She pressed against him, trying to consume him, wishing she could draw him through the layers of clothes that were their only barriers, and inhale him through her pores.

He sensed the need that had suddenly ignited, and strove to feed it as best as their physical limitations would allow. One large hand slid down to cup the roundness of her bottom and press her harder against him, while the other, around her back, pressed her breasts flat against his chest. The roughness of his shirt against the thinner fabric of hers was torture.

After the longest time, he lifted his head just enough to make his words audible. "It's all right. You don't have to say anything. Just let me be here with you. For you. Just hold that thought until we get this mess sorted out, get your home back to the way it should be, and then we'll see where this goes. Okay?"

When he was holding her like that, touching her like that, she would agree to anything. Would her acquiescence be born out of the drunken sensation that left her as giddy as would a half bottle of Cabernet? Or was she capable of going past the shrilling of her body, to listen to the small, quiet voice that whispered deep inside her that just maybe she could put her faith in this man she barely knew, but who set off every alarm in her body just by smiling? And if she did surrender her faith, that most valuable asset, worth more to her than a king's ransom, would it be torn to shreds? Would Darius leave her broken and bleeding inside, heart crushed, belief shattered, just like the last man she had trusted?

He was waiting. The choice was hers. Give in, take it slowly, and see where it led them, or retreat like a perpetually wounded animal, crawl back into her sanctuary, and condemn herself to being afraid forever?

She swallowed hard and opened her mouth. To her surprise, her voice was loud and clear, not cowed and cowardly. "Okay."

The stars came out in his eyes.

Seven

The cleanup operations were backbreaking, and it looked like they were going to take several days longer than Darius had thought, but he was glad to help. Every morning he showed up early from the small hotel he'd found near Mahalia's home—he certainly wasn't entertaining the idea of another night trying to fold his long body into an armchair in her den!—to have breakfast with her little family. When the electricity was restored, their cold cereal breakfasts were transformed into something more substantial: eggs and sausages, toast, and sometimes ham or good old home-style BLTs. After having been on his own for so long, he enjoyed the opportunity to share his morning meal with a family. If he really tried, he could almost imagine himself being part of it. He even volunteered once to take over breakfast duties from Coretta, but her blank stare put him nicely back into his place. Not everybody in Mahalia's home was as thrilled by his presence as Will was.

After breakfast, it was always up with the shirtsleeves and heavy on the elbow grease, as he pitched in with the half dozen burly workmen who set about tearing down burned-out infrastructure and hauling it away, cleaning up debris and blackened residue, and then carefully rebuilding. He had to admire Mahalia: she didn't shirk hard work. In fact, she was stubbornly insistent that she could lift just about anything he could, and their labors were often interrupted by good-natured arguments wherein he would insist that she *put that table or window frame or chest down,* and she would retort that hell would just have to freeze over first.

Even dressed for rough work, she was sexy. She seemed to have an unending supply of too-large, ragged shirts with sleeves that hung past her fingers, which she had to roll up to the elbow, or risk dragging through her paint. Her jeans, on the other hand, were consistently tight; well worn, washed out, and soft as pajama-bottom flannel, and even though the tails of her shirts often hung down well past her hips, some sort of built-in X-ray vision always allowed him to follow her curves through them. She kept her hair out of the mess with a contraption that looked like a bandana held closed with an incredibly large and ugly brooch that, if he didn't know better, he'd swear she'd swiped from the dollar table at a garage sale, and her feet, which he remembered to be slender, smooth, and sensitive to the touch of tongue or fingertips, were shoved into flat-soled sneakers without socks, even in such cool weather. She shuffled around her house with buckets full of cleaning implements, looking like a dark-skinned version of Carol Burnett's cleaning-lady character, but to him, she was sexy.

She was funny, too. Even in the face of her own small tragedy, she made him laugh, and this set off a warm tingle in him that rivaled the ones that zipped through his veins whenever he caught her staring at him, with a bemused expression on her face, as if she was trying to read his mind and find out for sure what his real motivation was for sticking around, when they certainly weren't doing anything remotely resembling what she'd hired him for. Whenever he surprised her with her eyes on him, she scrambled to cover up with some clownish pantomime—eyes crossed, tongue sticking out, thumbs in her ears—and he always laughed and turned away. He was pleased that she was watching, but sad to think that she found him so puzzling.

He tried to tell her that his only motivation was that he liked her—a lot—but whatever life experience she'd endured, the one that had left her with a deep scar as though her heart and mind had been furrowed with a rusty blade, whispered to her otherwise. They were far too busy, and the house far too crowded, to find many moments when they could be alone, but when they did, she was always cautious, skittish, and not entirely trusting.

He was going to have to change that.

"The new window frames are beautiful!" Mahalia approached from behind, taking him by surprise and causing him to drop the screwdriver he was holding. Flustered by her arrival just as he was thinking of her—either she had developed a habit of doing that, or he'd begun to think of her far too often—he bent over to pick it up, and slammed his forehead into the selfsame window frame.

"Ouch," he grunted, more out of embarrassment than pain.

"Ouch!" At his side, Will mimicked him, rubbing his own forehead vigorously, looking like a miniature reflection of Darius in a funhouse mirror. The little boy had become his shadow, refusing to stay with Coretta, and instead following Darius about, keeping no more than two steps behind. In fact, he'd begun to stick so close that Darius had to make a conscious effort not to stop or turn around too abruptly, to avoid a collision.

"You okay?" Mahalia approached Darius with concern, passing her hand over what could very soon become a bump on his forehead.

"Fine," he said gruffly. Her fingers were cool and soft against his skin, but she was cooing at him as she would her son, and he couldn't have that. "I'm okay."

She let her hand fall away, and as she did so, Will shrieked with the laughter that seemed to come so easily to him whenever he was near Darius.

"What?" Darius asked, even though the boy probably wouldn't answer. "What's so funny?" When a response was unsurprisingly not forthcoming, he turned to Mahalia, puzzled. "Come on, tell me. What's cracking the kid up?"

Her response was a chuckle, and she slapped her hand over her mouth with an "Oooh!"

Was everybody freaking out on him? Was he perhaps gushing blood from the head, and looking like an unknowing Freddy Krueger victim? He put his hand to his head instinctively—and it came away Summer Sky Blue, not coincidentally the same color that dripped from the brush that Mahalia held in her hand.

"Sorry," she said. She didn't look sorry at all.

He grunted. Instead of asking her, he addressed Will. "My face is blue, right? Your mother painted me, didn't she?"

Will grinned broadly, hugely amused.

Mahalia put her brush down and examined her blue hands, her own grin a reflection of her son's. "Sorry," she said again.

"You look it," he retorted grouchily.

Instead of denying her mirth, she grabbed him by the sleeve, getting that blue as well, he couldn't help noticing, and dragged him in the direction of the bathroom. "Come on, let's get you cleaned up before it starts to dry. You don't strike me as the blue-haired punk-rocker type."

Uncomplaining, he let her tow him along, glad for the break, and even happier to see her. She stood him before the newly installed bathroom mirror so he could see for himself the mess she'd made of his face. Even he had to admit he looked pretty ridiculous. "Could you be more clumsy with a paintbrush?" he teased.

"Could you be more clumsy with a window frame?" she volleyed back, without missing a beat.

"Well, at least I'm not covered head to toe in window frame." He pointed at her reflection in the mirror. "Did you get any paint at all on the walls?"

"Some," she said, and then, distracted from attending to him by her own absurd reflection, peered at herself. "Jeez, I look like a Smurf."

"You do," he agreed. "But a cute one."

"Step aside, Smurfette!" She laughed. When she was through cracking herself up, she returned to her original mission of getting the streak of paint off the front of his hair. She wet a washcloth and began scrubbing away. He had to admit that he was enjoying her attention, even though her touch was more maternal than intimate. He was thrown back twenty years to the memory of his mother wetting her hankie on the tip of her tongue and then scouring away at imaginary spots on his face as they stood just outside the church doors.

Mahalia hadn't touched him in many days, not since she'd given up that reluctant kiss in her bedroom on his first day here. He was putting an end to that, he decided. As soon as possible.

"Better?" she asked softly. The smear was gone, but she was still making light, rhythmic strokes at his hairline. His usually obstreperous hair lay meekly under her hand. She had the power to charm his most unruly of body parts!

"Better," he agreed. He took the washcloth away from her, but then put her hand back where it had been. As he did so, her mood changed, and her impish spirit was replaced by something more serious. Her fingers penetrated the tangled mess of his hair and tugged lightly, causing a mild pain that was nothing short of erotic. It set off a heat that raced backward down his scalp and forward down his face. He clamped his lower lip between his teeth to quell the tingling there.

He was that close to forgetting that they were far from alone, that heavy-booted workmen clomped around the house, one or two of them even in the next room. He almost didn't give a damn. All he wanted to do was to kiss her, right here, right now, and if they were offended, well, they'd just have to look away.

What he did care about, though, was Will. The small, reflected face hovered behind them in the mirror, tilting from Darius to Mahalia and back again, intent and inscrutable. Public displays of affection in front of a general audience were one thing; doing the same in front of Will was another. He knew the kid adored him; that much was plain. What he couldn't predict was Will's reaction if he were to see him kissing his mother.

Control, he told himself. *We'll be alone soon.* But as the reins tightened on his physical impulses, they slackened on his tongue, and before he could halt himself, he blurted out the question that had been hovering at the forefront of his mind for days. "Tell me about Will's father, Mahalia."

The last ember of amusement flickered and died. Her self-protective seriousness slammed into place like prison gates. "You asked me that once before."

"I know. You didn't answer me that time, either."

"You didn't have the right to ask."

"I've got more of a right now than I did then." He tried to keep his tone on an even keel, so that Will wouldn't have to suffer the distress of watching their tensions rise.

"Yeah?"

"Yeah. Because you shared your bed with me, and you will again," he replied.

The stunned look on her face would have been comical if their situation hadn't been so serious. "What did you just tell me?"

He put his hands on both her shoulders to help prevent her defenses from completely encasing her. "Honey, honey, don't be upset. I don't mean it in a bad way—"

She sputtered. "Exactly what way did you mean it? Could your ego get any bigger? You think I'm just hanging around, *dying* to go to bed with you again? You think . . ." She swallowed hard and turned to her son, who was eying them solemnly. There was no way of knowing how much of their conversation he could absorb or understand. "Will, sweetheart," she said softly, and her voice held no trace of the acid she had hurled at him a second before. "Go back outside and find Coretta. It's lunchtime. Go let her give you something to eat."

Usually quite compliant, Will picked a fine time to put up a show of resistance. He folded his arms and looked mulish. "No."

Surprise registered on Mahalia's face, and grew even more when Will slipped his hand into Darius's, and pressed closer. He barely came up to Darius's elbow, and the small body was warm against his side.

"Go on now, Will." Mahalia's voice took on that barely perceptible maternal edge that Darius remembered so well in his own mother, the kind that said that obedience right now could allay a heap of trouble later.

Will looked even more resistant. Darius looked down to see the small mouth quiver, even though it was pursed into a stubborn little knot. "No," he repeated, and buried his face in Darius's cotton shirt. The little fingers clenched tightly around his hand. Sensing that troubled waters were about to brew, Darius threw himself down like a bridge. He dropped onto his haunches and gently dislodged the child's death grip on his hand. Holding on to both bony arms, he looked Will in the eye and said, "Son, listen. Your mama wants you to go outside for a while. She says it's time for your lunch. And look . . ." He held up his wristwatch and pointed at the luminous face. "It's way past one, and you were supposed to have your lunch an hour ago."

"Help you," Will said. He looked about to cry.

"You helped me a lot with the window," Darius agreed. "I couldn't have done it without you. And you can help me later, after you eat something, and maybe have a nap. And if by then I'm done with the window, maybe we can take out my pencils and do some more drawing. I'd like that. Wouldn't you?" He and Will had gotten into the habit of spending an hour or two in the evenings, before he retired to his hotel, spreading art pencils and heavy paper out on the table in the kitchen, and making rapid-fire sketches of just about anything that came into their minds. Will had proven himself to be a dab hand at drawing, a true natural talent. He was a fast learner, and a pleasure to teach.

His question elicited a hesitant nod, and Darius went on. "But right now, you do as your mother says and scoot, okay? We'll be right behind you. Promise."

Will glanced from his mother to Darius, hesitated, and then, with a martyred sigh, dislodged himself from his grip, and without a word to his mother, left the room. When the sound of little sneakered feet dragging reluctantly along the floor subsided, Darius stood again, and turned to Mahalia, smiling.

The look she gave him could curdle milk. "Don't you ever do that again," she hissed.

Knock me over with a feather, Darius thought. "Do what? What have I done?"

She stabbed her finger in the direction of the bathroom door through which Will had passed. "You undermined my authority with my son."

"Say that again?" He wasn't sure he'd heard her right. He almost laughed in incredulity.

"I gave him an instruction. It's up to me to ensure that he complies with that instruction. You can't just come along and change it—"

"I didn't change it, I repeated it. I just sweetened the deal a little, made it easier for him to leave. I told him that if he left now, we could spend some time drawing together later."

"That's another thing!" Her voice was growing louder with each emphatic sentence. "Just how much is there to draw? You two spend hours huddling together, drawing apples and oranges and monkeys and cats. And don't even get me started on the cats! We're ankle high in cat drawings."

"Veda Two makes a very good artist's model," he interjected. "And the fact that Will likes to draw her should be proof enough that he's not afraid of her, as you had expected. He likes her. I've seen him pet her once or twice. Lord knows, she could use the affection."

Mahalia went on as if she hadn't heard him. "And he follows you around. Everywhere you go. And when you're not here, he wishes you were. This morning, he spent an hour standing in the drive waiting for you to turn up." She glared at him as she would at a convicted kidnapper. "He won't spend three minutes with me all day, because he can't tear himself away from you for a second. And now, I tell him to do something, and he refuses, and then you tell him, and he just skips away!" She waved her hands in the air, emphasizing her frustration.

Ah, he thought, *that's it*. His bewilderment was replaced by understanding. "You don't have to be," he told her comfortingly.

She passed her hand across her forehead and looked at him as if he were speaking a foreign language. "Don't have to be what, Darius?"

"Jealous."

She sputtered. "Me? Jealous? What the hell makes you think—"

"Come on, Mahalia." His tone was not accusing, but he had to make her see the source of her frustration. "You're used to having Will's full attention. Except for Coretta, you're the only person he sees most of the time. He's used to being your universe, and you're used to being his. And then I come along, and he's formed an attachment. It's perfectly normal."

"That doesn't mean I'm jealous," she said, defending herself.

"You sound like it," he countered.

"What I am," she shot back, "is annoyed. Irritated. You're very good at doing that to me."

He stepped closer and put his hands on her hips, pulling her against him. He knew he was risking a kick in the groin, but he was fairly sure that, provided he saw it coming, he'd be able to dodge it well enough. "That's because I've gotten under your skin."

"Here we go again! Playing homage to your huge . . ." She squirmed as he pressed her more firmly against him. "Overblown . . . masculine . . ."

"Yes?" His voice was like a snake: beguiling, and yet slightly dangerous.

"Ego!" she finished. He was glad to see that she made no move to wriggle free, even in the throes of her resentment.

"Calling things as I see them isn't ego," he pointed

out. "It's honesty. A little something you should try yourself, if you don't mind my saying so—"

"I *do* mind—"

"You won't even admit that you're all bent out of shape because Will's got a little crush on me, and all of a sudden you haven't got his undivided attention." He waited for her to protest or to deny his assertion, but she fell into a sheepish silence, so he pressed on. "Will's got true talent. Trust me: I know. I've done a teaching gig or two, and besides, it takes an artist to recognize one. He has a great eye for light and shadow, and his range of expression on paper is awesome in someone his age. He may not be big on words, but his pencil speaks volumes. His autism gives him something lots of artists strive for but never truly achieve. He thinks in terms of space and movement, shapes and form, not words, like you would. Will thinks in pictures. He's been looking for too long for a way to bridge the gap between himself and the world, to express what he's thinking and feeling. And you know what? Art might be that bridge."

"So," she interjected caustically, "with all the money I've spent on experts over the years, trying to come up with ways to help him, you just mosey on into his life and find it in a week. . . ."

"Maybe."

"Huh!"

Her pained look made him wonder if he was pushing her too far, but he had to say what needed to be said. "So please, Mahalia, don't resent the time we spend together. It probably isn't any of my business, and I'm probably way out of line here, but I'm trying to offer him a way out."

Her dark eyes glistened. "I don't mean to be resentful—"

"If you want me to, I'll back off," he said hastily.

"No!" She lifted her hand to halt his thought. "Don't." She hung her head. "You were right, Darius. I am a little jealous. It's just that he's all I've got."

Shifting upward from her hip to her hair, his hand twisted into her braids. "I'm only trying to help."

"I know."

Before she had the time to be drawn in by melancholy thoughts, he said, "Now that we've got that settled, let's get back to my ego."

She scowled, but he wasn't sure if she was being playful or not. "I think I've had just as much of your ego as I can handle for one day."

"Well, I'm not done dealing it out, and believe me, there's much more where that came from. Tell me . . ." He bent forward until his lips all but brushed her ear, and lowered his voice as if sharing a scandalous secret, even though most of the work crew were hammering up a storm on the outside of the house, and thus were well out of earshot. "Are you really going to try to convince me that you don't want more of me? More of this?" His tongue shot out like a dart, striking at the fat vein that ran down the side of her neck.

Her body went rigid at the assault, and she couldn't stop the hiss of air that escaped her surprised lips. He waited for her to protest, argue, and plead her case, but she barely made a whimper. Like any good strategist, he pressed home his advantage. The marauding tongue-tip followed the pulsing vein like a tributary to the valley between her collarbones, and he dipped into it like a thirsty hummingbird. "Or this?"

"Mpff!" Whatever she was saying was muffled against his hair.

"Are you saying you don't want to feel me over you again? That you didn't like it the first time?"

"Course I liked it," she answered irritably.

"So, does that mean once was enough? Am I that good a lover that I can quench the fire of ages in one afternoon? That I can leave you completely satisfied, permanently satisfied, when no man has touched you in . . . what? How long has it been?"

"That's mean!"

He shook his head slowly, brushing against her skin, partly in denial, and partly for the enjoyment of the sheer feel of her. "I'm not being mean. I'm being honest. We agreed on honesty, remember?"

"You're the one who brought up the honesty thing," she reminded him.

"Maybe. But I'm holding you to it all the same. So, when I say that I'll be in your bed again, or, better yet, that you'll come to mine, am I deluded, a visionary, or a bare-faced liar?"

"Wanting doesn't automatically mean doing," she said, resisting.

Music to his ears. He pounced on her admission. "Aha! You admit that you want me, then. I'm halfway home."

"You're no-way home. I've got work to do. My house is a shambles."

"And we'll have it all right as rain in a few days." He dismissed her flimsy excuse for what it was.

She tried again. "In case you haven't noticed, I've got a kid to take care of."

He was armed and ready, having seen that one coming. "A kid with an eight-thirty bedtime and a full-time nurse. And if you're squeamish about us being together under the same roof, my hotel is two miles away. And I can vouch for its privacy *and* its discretion."

She searched for another obstacle to lob at him, found one, and threw it out wildly. "All right, all right. It was good. I enjoyed it." She said that as though it were being torn out of her under torture. "But I don't want it again. We can't do it again. It's only physical, and that's not good enough. Sex for the sake of it just isn't my thing."

His face was the picture of exaggerated surprise. "Was that what it was?"

"You said it was just to feed our needs," she countered accusingly. "You said it was about two lonely people, hanging on to each other for a little while. You said it was all about skin hunger, me feeding you, and you feeding me. No fair, no foul."

They'd been through this before. Why did she need convincing once more? Was it because she already knew the answer, but was too stubborn to admit it, even to herself? He decided to be patient, and humor her in her deliberate blindness. "I did say that," he conceded. "And I was wrong. I touched you, I kissed you, and in ten seconds I knew I was a damn fool who didn't know my elbow from a hole in the ground about anything. I was wrong. It was more than physical from the get-go, Mahalia. That hunger went deeper than our skin. I tried to tell you, didn't you hear?"

She wriggled away from him in frustration. "You didn't say a thing!"

He could have pursued her, cornered her, with no effort at all, but he held back. Instead, he nailed her to the wall with his eyes. "I said it over and over again, with every touch. I told you things with my body. Weren't you listening?"

"Maybe we had a bad connection." She returned his stare with a rebellious one of her own. "What were you saying?"

He played along. "I was saying: 'Mahalia, I'm an idiot. Or I was lying to myself. This isn't a body thing; it's a mind thing. And I want more of you. You got to me

somehow, without even trying, and now I'm hooked.
And I want to take this further.'"

"That's what you were saying?"

"Yes."

"Oh." She looked thoughtful.

"Oh, what?"

"And all this time I thought you were just showing
off!"

Darius bellowed in laughter. Mahalia was a trip. Oh,
the woman could smear an insult with honey and make
him eat it up off the floor. When he was able to speak
evenly again, he said, "I don't show off in bed, honey. I
leave that for my art. And I find it very hard to lie when
I'm naked."

"That puts you in about one percent of the male pop-
ulation!" She was laughing right along with him, not
fighting him, not trying to weasel her way out of a tight
question, and that was promising. That made him feel
that things just might work out okay.

Her relaxed defenses gave him courage. "So, is it a
deal, then?"

"I didn't know there was a deal on the table."

"There is now. I propose we stop lobbing rocks at each
other . . ."

"And?" She was sure of herself, almost coquettish,
knowing what he was going to say, and welcoming it.

Thank you, Lord, he thought.

"And we try to see where this goes. See if we can nudge
it along in the direction I hope it's going. And, to sweeten
the pot, I think I can see my way clear to feeding you
tonight. . . ."

"A bribe!" She clapped her hand over her mouth in
an exaggerated display of surprise.

"Let's just call it an incentive—"

"Spoken like a true politician," she interjected.

"... A gesture of goodwill. I clean up good; you'll see. Let's finish up our work early today, put on the Ritz, and then you can show me where a guy can take a lady out for dinner in this part of town. Then we can talk, really talk. Man to woman. As if we were trying to build something between us. I can tell you stuff about me, anything you want to know, and you can tell me things about you. Even things you don't want to. You can trust me with your secrets. I promise you, there's nothing you can tell me about anything you've done or anywhere you've been that would make me any less interested in you. Or make me like you less. Okay?" He had to stop to catch his breath, because in his eagerness to ensnare her into having dinner with him, and opening up to him, his words had just tumbled out of him like grammar school kids rushing past school gates on the last day of term. He waited.

She seemed to be thinking about it. Summer Sky Blue paint winked as she drew her brows together, and her passing her hand thoughtfully across the bridge of her nose didn't make her face any cleaner.

Gelatinous seconds trickled past. He was about to make some flippant crack about his feelings being permanently wounded if she didn't answer soon, but held back, because he became painfully aware that it wasn't as much of a joke as he had thought. His tongue stuck to the roof of his mouth like a pancake flipped by an inept chef.

"Okay," she said. She was smiling broadly, and the thoughtful blue wrinkles on her forehead smoothed out.

"Okay?" he echoed stupidly.

"Okay, meaning yes. As in, 'Yes, Darius, I'd love to have dinner with you.' Dancing, even."

"Dancing?" He was being a complete idiot, and he knew it, but he couldn't help himself. Not only was this gorgeous woman agreeing to share a meal with him, alone, away from her household demands, but she was willing to risk having her feet squashed by both his left ones.

"You do dance, don't you?" Her tension was replaced by mischief, reflected in a light in her eyes.

"I have." He didn't want to tell her that in at least ten states, his dancing was classified as a threat to public safety. "I'd love to dance with you. Where?"

"Never mind where. Just meet me at eight, and come dressed to trip the light fantastic."

"More likely to trip over my feet and put my own lights out," he predicted under his breath.

"What'd you say?"

"Nothing," he said hastily, and began beating a quick retreat, back through the bathroom door through which he had come. "Nothing at all." He pointed at Will's room, and the window frame that was waiting patiently for his attention. "Back to work. Don't want that window falling out."

She threw him a sly grin, as if she'd suddenly discovered that she had the upper hand. "Eight o'clock, then," she reminded him, and sashayed away. He watched those old blue jeans hugging her bottom as she went, swinging jauntily, swaying in time to music that only she could hear.

Eight

Hailie hated to admit it, even to herself, but she was as excited as a teenager on prom night. The only thing worse than a giggly teenager looking forward to a date with a cute guy, she thought, was a thirty-three-year-old woman who was acting like one. But the heck with it. She deserved a night out, and nothing she could think of would be better than a night out with this impulsively kind, devastatingly sexy young man with melted-sugar eyes and star-spangled skin.

Laden with an armload of shopping bags, she staggered into the guest room and dropped them onto the small bed she was sharing with Will. Coretta followed close behind, clucking about her hurting her back, carrying all that weight around. "It's not good for you to be hauling around all that load, Hailie," she chided like a scandalized grandmother. "Why you keep taking all this onto yourself? Think about your womb, child. Young woman like you, you ain't half done using it. Why you want to stress it carrying all them packages?"

She smiled at the older woman's solicitude. Coretta really could be like a grandmother sometimes—a stern, no-nonsense one, spilling over with good advice, home-grown cures, and an unending internal library of health myths and old wives' tales, in spite of her nursing training. Her Caribbean origins only served to widen her storehouse of truisms and superstitions. Hailie's womb—and her constant abuse of it—came up whenever Hailie tried to lift anything that weighed more than a bag of sugar or a footstool. "It wasn't that heavy," she lied. She brushed away a stray lock of hair from her damp forehead and plopped onto the bed. "It just looks bulky. Lots of shopping bags, not a whole lot inside. Besides, Will helped."

Coretta snorted and folded her arms forbiddingly across her aproned bosom. "Bulky, my foot! You come straining in here like you fixing to give yourself a hernia. And Will helped, eh? There's more stuff here than both of you can carry, and if I know Will, he probably got caught up in some daydream, put his bags down, and wandered over to the toy store. And you gone and buy him some of them new boy-dolls, didn't you?"

"Action figures," she corrected before she could stop herself.

Coretta sniffed. "A dolly is a dolly, whether it dress up like a superhero or not. And you buy them for him, I know. You don't have to say it: I can see it in your eyes. How many toys you think one little boy need to have?"

"Don't forget," she reminded Coretta gently, "he lost most of them in the fire. And his clothes, too. He needs new stuff. Clothes *and* toys. And he didn't wander off. He stuck with me all the way."

As a matter of fact, Will had carried one or two of her bags, a task he always seemed happy to perform, but a risky one, as if anything diverted his attention from his duties, he was prone to plopping them down on the most convenient spot—usually the floor—and trotting off. His notoriety as an escape artist was so great that mall security knew him well, and kept an eye out for him from the moment they saw Hailie pull into the parking lot. But she liked shopping with him: between the two of them, they had developed a good rhythm, and she

found that a vigilant eye and the ability to expect the unexpected helped her ensure that their trips out were safe
for him, and panic-free for her.

But he'd been remarkably good today: the only time
he'd threatened to disappear was when he'd become entranced by a tall figure with extraordinarily long legs
disappear around a corner. She'd had a devil of a time
convincing him that the receding back he'd spotted had
not been Darius, because Darius was, in fact, back at his
hotel getting ready to take Mommy out for dinner.

Her son was really getting obsessed with Darius. Un-
derstandably so, she supposed. There had never been a
male presence in his life, and Darius seemed to have a
special touch with Will that she had never seen in anyone else. When she thought about her flare-up with him
this morning, she was embarrassed. She knew he was
only trying to help, but she couldn't help being protective, could she?

Coretta didn't allow Hailie the luxury of extended in-
trospection. She barreled into her thoughts like a runaway
train, returning unerringly to her favorite bone of con-
tention: Hailie's apparent abuse of her physical well-being.
"How many times I got to tell you, girl, when you go shopping you get yourself one of those motorized whatsits,
those carts, and take a load off your feet? You'll thank me
for that advice when you're older, and I'm giving it to you
for free. Wait till those knees of yours give out. Wait till
your back calls it quits. Wait till your *womb*—"

Hailie interrupted her hastily. "Thanks, Coretta." She
knew the womb lecture by heart: there were a whole lot
of babies in her future, once she stopped dating all those
jokers she seemed to get herself tangled up with and
found the right man and settled down. If she did find
the right man, he was sure as shootin' going to want babies, and what would he say if he landed himself a wife,

only to find out that there was an "out of order" sign hanging on her womb, all because she had been fool enough to act like a man, dragging heavy furniture around, and digging in the garden? What kind of fool woman took risks like that?

So she cut Coretta off before the lecture could reach its histrionic conclusion. "I promise I'll give your electronic buggy idea more thought next time I have really heavy things to tote around. Okay?" But in her mind she was thinking: *Like hell.* It'd be a cold day down below before she found herself scooting along the halls of her local mall in a Rascal, with Will scurrying to catch up. Unless, of course, she could find the pink polyester slacks, cat-eye shades, and blue hair to go with it. The image of herself as an irascible geriatric, trundling around the malls and taking swipes at "those durn kids" with her walking stick made her laugh out loud.

Coretta pursed her lips. "Think it's funny, do you? Well, wait and see, missy. Wait and see."

Hailie was used to Coretta's caustic moods, even enjoyed and appreciated them. The older woman was more than an employee: she was the grandmother Hailie had never known, and she knew that Coretta's tart tongue hid a warm and gentle heart. True caring was hard to come by, so Hailie tolerated the authoritative tongue-lashings with good humor. But she threw up a roadblock anyway, diverting Coretta from her dark and dire predictions. "So, d'you want to see what I bought?"

"Silly question, girl. Scoot over!" Coretta plopped down onto the bed and began peering into the shopping bags.

Hailie started by hauling out several T-shirts and a few pairs of jeans, boys' underwear, and socks. "Got these for Will. Where is he? He was right behind me two minutes ago."

Coretta grinned and extended her arm to show Hailie

her watch. "Don't you remember what time it is? He's gone and planted himself in front the TV, catching up on the soaps. Don't worry, he'll be quiet for at least another hour or two."

She was right. Like any other kid, Will was a TV addict, and could while away an entire afternoon engrossed in his favorite shows. Unlike any other kid, however, his drug of choice was not the cartoon channels or any of the action-adventure drivel the TV stations dished out as child-pacifiers. Will was a hard-core soap addict, and could easily watch two or three in succession. Hailie couldn't fathom it, as she hated them herself: they were just too hard to keep up with, and were made up of too many interwoven threads. But Will drank it all in, sitting so close to the screen that Hailie had to constantly tell him to move back a few feet. She surmised that his fascination came from the endless interplay of pathos and melodrama, the parade of emotions that were splashed across the small screen in all their overacted glory. His limited capacity for displaying emotions in no way meant that he was incapable of feeling them. He felt them, very deeply, and loved seeing them played out on the faces of others.

"Forget the boy's clothes, Hailie." Coretta folded away the shopping bags containing Will's things and pushed them aside. Her black eyes were gleaming. "Show me the good stuff. What did you get for yourself?"

Now Hailie smiled, too. She wasn't one for splashing out on clothes for herself; as far as she was concerned, clothes were generally made for covering her body, for the sake of modesty rather than adornment. But she wouldn't have been female if she hadn't felt that spark of excitement that came with building an entire new wardrobe practically from scratch. Eagerly, she began pulling garment by garment from her shopping bags, revealing new jeans, T-shirts, shorts, and dresses. They'd

cost her a bomb, but she'd been psychologically prepared for the impact, and besides, her insurance would
cover most of it. As for the rest, well, she was overdue for
a wardrobe upgrade anyway.

Coretta was suitably enthused over her purchases,
oohing and aahing whenever Hailie whipped a new garment out of her seemingly bottomless bags. "And this,"
she said with a flourish, "is what I'm wearing tonight!"

Coretta's eyes narrowed. "Where you going tonight?"

Hailie felt her face flood with heat. The dress she held
in her hand was of a soft, fine cashmere, in a deep wine
color that leaned to just this side of ruby. Its sleeves were
long, and the hemline dropped to the knee, in deference
to the cooler winter air, but the fabric was so thin she was
sure that the entire dress could be drawn through the eye
of a needle. She'd known it was hers even before she'd
tried it on, and after buying it she'd rushed into the next
store to find herself the perfect pair of wine-colored
pumps and silk stockings—stay-ups, of course, not panty
hose—with just a hint of shimmer.

Dressing up for this gorgeous man was tantamount
to admitting to him just how eager she was to be in his
company. Going out with him, however, was bringing
something very private out into the open. "Well," she
began. "Um . . ."

Coretta wasn't a woman who allowed much to escape
her notice. She snapped her fingers in triumph. "I knew
it! I knew it! You're going out with that young man,
aren't you! I knew it! I saw it coming a mile off!"

She began to protest. "It's just—"

"Don't 'It's just' me! I saw you two. He's been making
goo-goo eyes at you since he's been here. Or at least, making goo-goo eyes at your butt! Can't seem to drag his eyes
up past your waist. I know his type. And you, bending over
all the time, lifting this and that, giving him the perfect op-

portunity to stare you down, *and* doing yourself harm into the bargain!"

"Coretta!" Hailie was half amused, half scandalized. She was sure that Darius was not staring her butt down half the day . . . well, pretty sure, at least. "He has not been staring at my . . . my . . ."

"You don't know, because you don't have eyes in the back of your head. I know, because I can see everything." Coretta's ship was in full sail, and she wasn't slowing down any time soon. "And don't talk about you, young lady. Leaping half out of your skin every time he sets his little toe inside the room. You like him right back, and don't deny it. I may be old, but I'm not stupid!"

"You're not old, Coretta," Hailie hastened to reassure her, while hoping to throw a red herring into the fray at the same time. "You're one of those people who never gets—"

"Don't change the subject on me, young lady. And flattery won't get you nowhere, either. You like this young fella." The last was not a question: it was an incontrovertible statement of fact.

Hailie's cheeks grew several shades deeper, and she concentrated hard on folding away the dress. She stroked it as she would a kitten, enjoying the texture of it against her fingers. Right now, "like" was beginning to seem a bit of an understatement. What would Coretta say if Hailie told her that it had progressed way past the attraction stage, and that this date was, in fact, a bit like putting the cart before the horse? She and Darius had been in circumstances far more intimate than a night out on the town. She tried to keep her words cautious and unrevealing. "Yes, I do like him. He thought . . . we thought we'd go out to the Speakeasy; have dinner and a few drinks." She shut up, because if she said any more, she knew she would reveal too much.

But Coretta had been right: very little slipped past her. Instead of her usual acid, her tone was gentle, motherly. "Hailie, you sure you know what you're doing?"

"Will likes him," she said defensively.

"I know Will likes him," Coretta countered. "He's not the one I'm worried about. You like him a whole lot more than Will does. And that's saying something."

Embarrassment made her squirm, but the warmth that coursed through her when she thought about Darius, and dressing up for him tonight, was pleasurable, too. It was silly. She was a grown woman with a fair share of experience under her belt. This *wasn't* prom night, and Darius wasn't the cutest boy on the track team . . . even though she was sure that there was a time when he was. So she squared her shoulders, reminded herself to act like a grown-up, and asserted, "Yes, Coretta, I like him. A lot." As Coretta's lips thinned just slightly, she rushed on. "I know you have your reservations. You haven't said anything, but I see you looking at him, and I know there's something going on in your mind. And you're never rude to him or anything, but I know you don't like him. Not really."

Coretta hastened to correct her. "It ain't that I don't like him, honey-child. I like him just fine. It's just something in my stomach that just don't sit right over him. It's just too strange. Like one of them karma things. I mean, twice in your life—"

Hailie understood just what Coretta meant, and she agreed. It was a little weird, she had to admit. She nodded vigorously. "I know. . . ."

"That out of all the men you could find yourself—"

"I know," she said again, "but it doesn't mean anything. It's a coincidence, not an omen—"

"You wind up falling for *two* men—"

"No connection," Hailie said. "None whatsoever."

"More than a decade apart—"

"There's a world of difference between the two. Chalk and cheese. No connection. If there was, I'd have known—"

"And both of them named Grant?"

There. It was out in the open. The spoken word. The thought that had been niggling at her all along, ever since she had met Darius, but which had become more intense from the moment it had dawned that her attraction for Darius was more than a cursory, pleasant thought. It was weird, but not that unheard of. Grant was a common name. She'd met a few people who had it. Didn't mean it was a bad omen. Didn't mean there was any connection between the two.

One was tall, lanky and bright-skinned, and boyish. The other was dark, hard and compact, and mature, even a dozen years ago when she had met him and fallen in love so hard and fast. One was impish, funny, generous, and kind to a fault. The other suave, accomplished, charming when he wanted to be, or needed to be, but inherently selfish, and equipped with an astounding capacity for cruelty. One was talented but virtually flying by the seat of his pants, struggling for recognition in his field and the chance to make a decent living through his art. The other was a Brother with a business of his own and more money than he knew what to do with.

The two men were miles apart in nature and in spirit, and much more so in plain geography. One had blown in on a chill wind from the Midwest, the other, even though he had refused to see her or speak to her for years, lived right here in California, perhaps two hours' drive away, if she chose to put God out of her thoughts and actually go looking for him.

So, no. As much as Coretta chose to read dire things into what was merely a small coincidence, easily overlooked, she was wrong. There was nothing weird about it. The Darius Grant on the brink of her trembling present and the Phillip Grant of her shattered past had nothing to do with each other. Nothing whatsoever. Of that, she could be sure.

"Phil!"

"Hey, bro!" Phillip's urbane voice was as mellow as barrel-aged scotch, and full of pleasant surprise. Darius had been meaning to call him all week, but things had just gotten out of hand. But, as always, he was happy to connect with his older brother. Somehow, no matter what was going on in his life, Phillip always made him feel grounded.

"How you doing, man?" Darius hooked the phone between his ear and shoulder, and tossed his shopping bags across the small hotel room. Usually, he hated shopping: he was the kind of man who spent fifteen hasty minutes at the nearest store tossing a few things into a basket before making his way to the counter, hoping that what he'd settled on would last long enough to spare him the pain in the tail of having to venture back into a mall for another few months. But this time, he'd stunned himself by spending two hours combing gentlemen's stores, spending money he probably he could not afford on some really fancy duds. He was taking Mahalia out tonight. He had to dress the part.

"So, my man, what you been doing? How're things up there in Big Sur? Any snakebites yet?"

Darius smiled. Phillip always seemed to come up with a worst-case scenario. "No, no snakes. Didn't get much of a chance to interact with the wildlife, actually. . . ."

"Not even a lil' old black widow spider crawling in through a crack in one of those drafty old cabins?" Phillip laughed, deep and rich. "Cabins. Imagine that.

Shoot me dead, that's the last place you'd find me. I haven't done the summer camp thing since grade school, and you can bet the farm I'm not going to start again. Hook me up with a nice comfortable hotel, shampoos in the shower, and young maids in sexy little outfits turning down my sheets at bedtime. . . ."

Typical of Phillip, Darius thought to himself. When it came to accommodation, his brother never settled for anything less than four stars, and even then he thought himself slumming. Darius considered coming to the defense of Casuarinas, describing the coziness of the nostalgic little cabins he and Mahalia had shared, and the splendor of the silent, living forest, but that would have been like describing a symphony to a deaf man, so instead, he simply said, "No, no spiders, and it wasn't summer camp. And we're not there anymore."

"What?"

"I'm not in Casuarinas. I'm in L.A."

The pleasure in Phillip's voice hardened a little. "That dame fired you? That Isis woman?"

"Circe," Darius corrected patiently. "Wrong goddess. And no, she didn't fire me. I'm here with her. She had a problem, and she had to leave, so I drove her down to L.A."

"What kind of problem could be so big that she had to drag you away from the gig of a lifetime? She one of those hysterical, dependent broads who haven't got the good sense to solve their problems on their own? And what's her problem got to do with you? What'd she do? Spot a wrinkle that needs expert attention on the double?"

Dependent? Mahalia? That was laughable. "No, Phil. It's nothing like that. As a matter of fact, she's just about the most independent woman I've ever met." *Stubbornly so*, he thought, but didn't say. *Frustratingly so.*

"So," Phillip persisted. "What happened?"

"Her house caught fire."

"All on its own?"

Even though Phillip couldn't see him, Darius shook his head. "No, her son was playing with matches, we think." He could have explained further, but he was reluctant to reveal more of Mahalia's affairs than she would have, under those circumstances. She was stringently private about her family, which, given her status as a writer, he could understand. So he wrapped it up lamely. "It's a long story."

Phillip snorted. "It probably is. So what about the book?"

"The book was coming along just fine. We work well together." They did more than that well together, even though Mahalia was shy about admitting it. Maybe later, tonight, he would be able to convince her that it was worth more than just considering.

"*Was* coming along? What about now?"

"It's on hold," Darius explained patiently to his impatient brother. "I'm helping her get her house repairs done. The fire damage wasn't all that bad; in a few days it should all be back to normal."

"Why're you doing that? Hasn't she got a contractor?"

"Yes, but—"

"So leave him to do his job, and come on over, man. Get into your car and come give your brother a visit. We could hit the town, have a few drinks. I know a few ladies I could set you up with. We could double-date. Or tripledate, if you're into that." Phillip's laugh rumbled, pleased as he was with his little joke.

It sounded tempting, Darius had to admit. Not necessarily the double date part, but the idea of spending time with Phillip. When he was a teenager and Phillip was already a grown man, they used to go out riding in Phillip's first sports car, a banana-yellow number with leather seats and a sunroof. It cornered like a roller coaster. Even though Darius was well below the drinking age, Phillip would buy beers for both of them and cigars for himself, and they would sail down Sunset Boulevard taking in the twinkling lights and the teeming life around them. Phillip would regale him with dirty stories, some of them made up, some anecdotal, some of them his real life adventures, and he told them all with such aplomb that young Darius had always been at a loss to discern one from the other. To young Darius, nothing was more enthralling than the real life adventures of his hero-brother, and when their jaunt was over, he was filled with anticipation for the next time his brother would turn up and throw open the door on the passenger side for him.

He was a grown man in his own right now; he could buy his own beers, and the last thing he needed was to hang on to every scurrilous word that fell from his big brother's lips, but he did miss him, and he would like to see him. Yes, a visit would be nice, and maybe they could go driving—sans dates, of course—laughing, talking about old times and times to come . . . but there was Mahalia. She needed him.

"Oh . . ." he began.

"Tell me you're coming," Phillip insisted. He wasn't used to being denied what he wanted, so there was just the finest edge to his voice.

"Well, I'd like to. . . ."

"So come." That imperative held a note of satisfied finality. As far as Phillip was concerned, the matter was settled.

"But I promised I'd stay and help."

"She paying you for that?"

"Don't be ridiculous!" The idea was absurd. He did what he did for Mahalia out of a caring that was growing stronger every day, not because she had to make it worth his while. "I'm not going to expect payment for doing the right thing. She needs help, and right now I'm it."

"She at least paying you for your book while you're not working on it?"

"I'm being paid a specific rate for the book; I told you that already. I got half of the advance up front, and when we're done, I get the other half. A week's delay isn't going to make a difference." A filament of irritation ran through Darius. Phillip might know his way around a stock report, but when it came to human interaction— at least, the kind that didn't require both parties being prostrate—he was clueless.

Phillip proved him right. "So why are you going through all this?"

"I'm doing this because I want to." There was heat building up at the back of his neck, and it spilled over into his voice. "Why is that so hard for you to understand?"

"I understand fine." Phillip didn't even bristle at his brother's irritation. Instead, he was amused, indulgent, almost paternalistic. "That's just like you. Always stopping to take care of stray kittens and lame ducks. You can't help it."

"She's far from a lame duck," Darius retorted. "She's a brilliant, beautiful woman who just happens to need my help. So I'm sticking around to do what I can." Why was it always like this with Phillip?

"Oh," Phillip said. The single word weighed a ton.

"'Oh' what?"

"You like her."

"Yes, I do." Darius stated it boldly, even though he knew that his brother had a way of taking anything that he valued and belittling it, as he did with his taste in art and his choice of career. But he did like Mahalia: liked her, wanted her, wanted to be close to her, and wanted to help. That was one thing he wasn't letting Phillip trample on.

"She worth it?"

"Worth what?" he asked, although instinct gave him a hint of what was coming next.

"She worth giving up a chance to spend time with your family? Your blood? I ask you over to see me, but you have to hang around and help some chick put the pieces of her life back together. I was hoping we could chill out, and chew the fat. I haven't seen you in ages. . . ."

"I saw you the week before."

"At an airport, for like two hours. Oh, yeah, that was lots of time!"

"Don't do this, Phil," Darius pleaded. The last thing he wanted to do was offend his brother, make him feel rejected. "It's not about giving you up for her. Don't turn this into something about blood and water. I want to see you. I'll see you soon, but right now—"

"Okay, okay." Phillip was soothing, placatory. "Don't kick me for making an observation. I was just calling it like I saw it; don't think I'm being mean or anything. I'm on your side. You're my baby brother: I'm always on your side."

"This 'baby' thing's got to stop," Darius began. The only person he ever needed to prove his adulthood with was Phillip, and this he seemed to need to do every time they interacted. It was getting fatiguing. Would it ever end?

"But let me tell you this: there are big shots all over the state who pay me big time for my financial advice. I may be an expert at that, but I'm no moron when it comes to sex, either. And this advice, you get for free. Never let a woman tie up your head. Never let a woman get the upper hand, make you choose between her and what's important in your life—like family. You sound like you're half in love with her—"

"I'm *not* in love . . ." Darius was quick to cut in, and

then stopped. He took a breath to speak further, but found that his throat had run dry. He wasn't . . . was he?

"Oh," Phillip said again as the pause drew out longer. "Aha." He sounded satisfied, as though he'd predicted a long-shot stock deal and been proven right. When Darius didn't say anything, he repeated himself. "Like I said, never let a woman get the upper hand. You've gone and fallen off the deep end for this woman, and that's bad. Downright stupid, I'd say."

This time, he didn't deny it. "So I have. What's so stupid about that?"

"For starters, she's your boss—"

"Technically, her agent is, but it doesn't matter anyway."

"And furthermore, she's a lot older. Isn't she?"

"Six years. We're hardly a generation apart. And it makes no difference to me."

Phillip barreled on like a runaway train. "And she's got a kid, you said? That's a red flag, if I ever saw one. There's nothing more dangerous than a woman with a child in tow. They're always on the lookout for some sucker they can saddle with the responsibility some other dude didn't want to take. To them, a single, childless man is like gold. Don't get confused. Women like that are lethal. They look into your eyes, all soft and romantic, and you think they're looking at *you*, but they're not. They're looking at a concept they made up for themselves. An ideal. So tell me, this woman, she got daddy-stars in her eyes? And if she does, you think you got what it takes to be able to tell?"

Mahalia? Daddy-stars? Not likely. If anything, she was passionately against the idea of sharing Will with anyone; he'd learned that the hard way. She was almost jealously protective, and as maternally aggressive as a she-bear. He wasn't sure what the type of woman Phillip was interested in was like when it came to the subject, but he was willing to put his neck on a block that Mahalia was not the sort that set out to ensnare a man in order to have a ready-made father for her child. It was not in her nature, and even if it were, she didn't need to. Materially, she and Will had everything they needed.

He leaped to her defense. "Look, Phil, that's enough. I don't want to hear another word against her. I called you up because I wanted to chat with my brother, not get a lecture about my private life. So I want the subject dropped. You got that?"

"Whatever, Dar. But she's got you in a tangle, that's for sure. And you shouldn't have let that happen. You're the man; you're the one to remain in control. A woman is nothing more than a rag, a bone, and a hank of hair. Remember that."

How did his brother manage to evolve into such a blatant misogynist? How did Estelle Grant contrive to raise two boys who were so radically different? A rag, a bone, and a hank of hair. The image was appalling. To hear Mahalia so described—to hear any woman so described— sent a wave of nausea rolling through Darius. He suddenly realized that the hand that clutched the phone receiver was slick with the cold sweat of anger. "Where the hell did you learn to talk like that? I know our father never taught you any of that. And what about Mama? If she heard you saying that garbage, it'd kill her."

Phillip's voice was a verbal shrug. "You going to tell her?"

"No. Of course not. I wouldn't hurt her like that. But sometimes, I don't understand you. You grew up in the same home I did. What happened to you?"

"I left home a long time ago."

"I know, but home should never leave you."

Phillip exhaled heavily, tired of the conversation. "Look, Dar, tell you what. You get back to hauling bricks or baby-sitting or whatever you're doing for this woman, and when you have some free time to spare me—when you don't feel like jumping down my *throat*—you give me a buzz, okay? But right now, I don't need this . . ."

Darius felt a momentary twinge of panic. He and Phillip never argued—or at least, the flow of recriminations was usually from Phillip to him, and not the other way around. He wasn't used to speaking out against his hero: it was against the natural order of things. But for once, his anger outweighed his need to placate Phillip. "I'll do that," he answered tightly.

"Fine," Phillip said. "Tell Aphrodite I said hi."

"Circe," Darius said automatically, but this time he knew Phillip was only trying to get his goat. "Mahalia," he added. But Phillip never heard him: the line was already dead.

"You look fine, Hailie," she muttered to herself in the mirror, but in the same heartbeat ignored her own assessment and scrubbed off her lipstick. It was too scarlet. Too flashy, too sexy. That wasn't her style. She couldn't for the life of her remember why she'd bought it in the first place. It was part of the grab bag of cosmetics she'd compiled for herself this afternoon, to replace all that she had lost in the fire. She had to admit she'd gone overboard somewhat. She'd actually bought more than she'd lost. They'd probably sit around and get all moldy, she chided herself. She didn't wear the stuff that often.

She rummaged through her new black and red satin makeup kit and withdrew something more low-key, almost nondescript. It was the type of color she wore to meetings with her editor, when she wanted to be taken seriously.

"Ugh," she said. That was too serious. Too dull. She didn't want to come across like a vamp with an "open for business" sign flashing on her forehead, but she still wanted him to look. She scrubbed her mouth clean and started again, searching even more hastily through the confusing jumble of tubes and pots. Makeup wasn't her thing. It made her nervous: when she wore it, she just didn't feel like herself. She had half a mind to go without any at all. That was the way Darius knew her: she was sure she had never worn any in his presence before. Maybe she should just give up, wash this gunk off her face, and he'd just have to take her as he got her. She had precious little time to decide, anyway. He'd be here any minute now.

Ah, a nice warm burgundy. That would be perfect. It suited the deep liquid red of the dress that now clung to her upper body and swirled around her hips. She popped off the cap and began applying.

"Mommy." Will rushed into the room she was still sharing with him, tripping over his feet. Under one arm, he clutched a baseball cap that Darius had given him several days ago, and which he preferred to carry around rather than wear on his head.

"What, sweetie?"

"Ooooh," Will said, his eyebrows lifting as he took in the sight of her.

Hailie laughed as she zipped the makeup case shut and put it down. "I'll take that as a compliment." She did a turn in front of the mirror and struck a pose. "Looks good, huh?"

Will nodded, his face split with a smile.

She had to admit, she did look good. She'd spent the better part of an hour loosening her braids, and then even more time washing and drying the thick black hair that fell between her shoulder blades in tight curls. She'd fussed nervously over whether she should pin it up, but Darius had never seen her with her hair loose, so she left it down. Then she tried to rationalize that she wasn't doing it entirely for his benefit. It would, after all, be a little chilly tonight. It was best to keep the back of her neck warm. . . .

The wool of her dress was as soft and as fine as a baby's first sweater, and the color reflected a warm light into her eyes. Where the dress left off, sheer stockings began, hugging the curves of her long legs. Her new leather pumps completed the look. She hoped they wouldn't squeak!

"Mommy!" Will said again. He grasped her hand and began tugging her in the direction of the door.

"What, sweetie?" Will could be impatient when he wanted to.

"Darius!" He pointed through the open doorway.

Hailie felt her mouth go dry. He was here, dead on time, and they were going on a date. Their first date. The irony of it did not escape her. They'd made love, shared their bodies with each other, and now he was taking her out. Usually, by rights, it should have been the other way around, and in a way, that made her feel somewhat awkward. But she was an adult, and had made that decision responsibly. She hadn't been catapulted into intimacy with him against her will. They'd both needed each other at the time, and she was not making any apologies for that, not even to herself.

She searched for and found her bag, took her son by the hand, and said, "Come, Will. Let's go out and meet him."

Darius was standing in the living room with his back to them, trying to make pleasant conversation with Coretta, who, as she would have expected, didn't seem all that interested in being pleasant back. "Don't you be keeping her out all night, now," Coretta was saying, sounding like a crotchety, overprotective grandmother. "And don't drive too fast. Y'all young men, you got lead feet. Lead feet, I tell you. Slamming down on that accelerator like you got Satan on your tail. Don't think I haven't been there. I've been out with boys like you in my time. One of them damned near killed me, driving like a maniac. If you ask me," and she threw a meaningful look in Hailie's direction, "*older* men know how to drive. They done got the devil out of their system. If you ask me, older men are a safer bet."

Darius took the dig at his age with good humor. "I promise, Coretta. The last thing I'd do is let Mahalia get hurt. I'll bring her back home in one piece. You have my word on that."

"Early!" Coretta insisted.

"Soon as she wants to come in," he responded.

Coretta twisted her lips in disbelief, folded her arms, and deemed the conversation over.

Thus dismissed, Darius turned around to face Hailie, and as he did so, each one got a good look at the other.

"Oh," Darius gasped.

She would have done the same, but she was bereft of speech. He looked good. He looked incredibly good. His thick sweater was the color of camel hair, and the broad stitches and knobby appearance of the wool just begged to be touched. He'd shed his jeans for slacks the color of bitter chocolate, and even though she'd grown accustomed to the suggestion of every curve and angle of his body through the worn denim that he favored, this new, streamlined configuration made his legs look even longer, if such a thing were possible.

But the clincher . . . the clincher was the jacket. It was the exact same shade of chocolate as his trousers— how'd he manage that? Generously cut, its broad, open lapels drew her eyes to his chest and then led them down, and down.

The overall impact of chocolate and beige, and the bright tan of his skin, made him look like a Reese's peanut butter cup. Unconsciously, she flicked her tongue over her lips, suddenly becoming aware that she was salivating. "You look . . . yummy," she managed, and he cut her off with a burst of laughter.

"Thanks. I think."

She dragged her eyes back upward, away from the tantalizing package that he had transformed himself into, back to the bright face and sparkly eyes . . . and almost choked. "Darius!"

He flushed self-consciously. "Yeah?"

She ran to him, needing to touch him to ensure that what she had seen was real. She brought her hand up to his hair, which was now, miracle of miracles, shorn to within a quarter of an inch of his scalp. The tangled, unkempt mess into which she'd lost her fingers during their afternoon at the cabin, and which had silently begged for her touch ever since, had been shorn off. He'd laid down a bundle for an expert cut; the crop was perfectly level and meticulously done, the edges razor-marked with the angular precision along forehead, temples, and . . . yes, she examined him more closely, drawn into twin points at the nape.

"Ohmigod," she breathed. "You cut it!"

He chuckled again, a little embarrassed at her reaction, and passed his hand over his smooth hair. "Well, uh. Yeah. I thought . . . well . . . thought it was time for a change."

"Darius!" Her fingers followed her eyes, their tips tracing the shape of his skull. Smooth on top where the hair was slightly longer, and then gradually fading into soft, fine prickles at the back. It felt good, and in a flash she wondered what those prickles would feel like rubbed slowly against her bare skin.

"Me!" Will hopped about, both arms outstretched, clamoring to touch, as well, so Darius dropped to one knee to allow him access. "Vroom! Vroom!" Will drove his fingers along Darius's head, starting at the forehead and slamming on the brakes at the nape, turned a sharp corner near his left ear, and proceeded to do another lap.

"Looks like my cut's a hit." Darius laughed. Then his gaze rose to her astounded face, and he amended his statement. "At least, with one of you. You look shell-shocked. I've had haircuts before, you know. This isn't a sign that Armageddon's about to begin."

She grinned. "Don't be silly. I like it just fine." And she was speaking the truth, although, if he'd dragged it out of her, she'd have to admit that she wasn't sure if she liked it as much as the tangled mess that had gone before. It had lent such a boyishly appealing cast to his face. Now, neatly groomed and stripped of his omnipresent denim, he looked older, harder, smoother, and more serious. She repeated, just in case he hadn't believed her the first time, "I like it, Darius. A lot." And to prove it, she let her lips brush against the razor's edge where his hairline met his temple.

His eyes sparkled. Coretta snorted derisively. They'd all but forgotten her presence. Darius coughed and straightened guiltily, depriving Will of the Indy 500 race-track for his fingers. "Maybe we should hit the road."

Hailie threw a glance at Coretta's stony face and tried to swallow a smile before it was born. "Maybe we should."

She found her jacket and slung it over her shoulders, and then took Darius's proffered arm. Then, as they were about to broach the doorway, he stopped absent-mindedly and patted himself down. "Almost forgot," he mumbled. He buried his hand in his cavernous jacket pocket and withdrew a brown paper parcel. He called Will over and presented it to him with aplomb. "Here you go, son. The start of an awesome collection. Enjoy."

Curiosity got the better of Hailie. She leaned forward,

still holding on to Darius's arm, but eager to see what he could possibly have bought her son.

Will tore the paper off without ceremony and stared at his gift. There were two—no, three—glossy comic books in the boy's hands, their covers bursting with Lycra-clad, dark-skinned superheroes. Sleek, impossibly muscle-bound bodies contorted into positions that defied the laws of human dynamics. Will's eyes popped.

"Now, these guys," Darius explained reverently, "are the best three black comic book artists around today—"

"Bar you," Hailie interrupted.

"Too kind," he responded, and threw in a modest bow, but Hailie could tell he was pleased by her endorsement. Then he continued rhapsodizing to Will. "Black comic art is hard to come by, but take it from me, there's a revolution under way, and there are more of us rising up and making our names known. Your mama's a part of that, and so am I. Maybe by the time you're a grown man, things will be different, and you won't have to bounce from comic store to comic store to find heroes that look like us. In the meantime, though, you enjoy your books. Okay?"

Will stared at the books for several long moments, struggling to flip through the pages while still trying to keep his pet baseball cap firmly tucked into his armpit.

"One more thing for my little pack rat to walk around with," Hailie joked, but she was shocked by the extent to which Darius's gesture touched her. It was as if the stars in Darius's eyes had come out in Will's, too. She blinked rapidly in an effort to maintain control, and all but lost it when her son threw himself around Darius's arms and clung there like a limpet.

It was a long while before Darius could ease himself free. He kissed Will on the forehead, with infinite tenderness, and then rubbed his hair affectionately. "Time for your dinner, Will," he told him, and showed him his watch to prove it. Will nodded solemnly, but although he usually insisted upon his meals at specific times, he looked rather reluctant to leave. "Go on," Darius coaxed. "Go have dinner with Coretta. You won't be up when I bring your mama home. . . ." He paused to smile at Hailie, who was doing her best to get a grip on her emotions. Darius had such a way with Will, it was almost scary. She'd never seen her son so bowled over by anyone. It almost hurt to watch. "But you'll definitely see me first thing in the morning. I'll be here in time to have breakfast with you. Okay?"

Appeased, Will nodded, and, managing to carry his comics in both hands while not releasing his underarm grip on his cap, he allowed Coretta to lead him away to the kitchen. Hailie watched him go, struggling against the impulse to let go of Darius, run after Will, and give him one final hug, just for being such an amazing human being.

Seeming to sense her dilemma, Darius gave her hand a kind squeeze. "Great boy," he said.

"Yes," she agreed fervently. "Thank you for thinking of him. With the present, I mean."

"No problem. My pleasure."

"He can't read, you know," she added unnecessarily.

"I know." Darius led her through the door and shut it firmly behind him. "Do you want to lock up?" He gestured at the door. "Or . . ."

"Coretta'll do it."

"Okay." As they walked to the car, he continued their initial conversation as if it had never been interrupted. "Will can't read the words, but he can understand the story. Like I said before—"

"Will thinks in pictures."

He nodded gravely and opened the car door to let her in. "Correct."

She waited until he was seated beside her, and then

asked, "You sure?" She still marveled at his confidence in his diagnosis. He'd found a way to tap into the workings of her son's brain that she, his own mother, never had. It was almost too uncanny to be real.

"Positive. I know it. I sense it. I see it in his eyes. I look at him and I know that that's the way he processes his information. It's the way he understands his world. And I'm sure because . . ." He trailed off and seemed to become lost in his thoughts.

"Yes?" she prodded.

"Because I do, too. When I see him look at things, and file them away under colors and shapes, rather than items with names attached, I see me. I see the way my own mind worked, at that age. There are things you don't know . . ."

"Tell me," she said at once.

The engine was running, but he hadn't pulled onto the road. Hailie felt the warmth of the car heater as it clicked on, puffing air onto her hands and face, but a chill still went through her as she prepared herself for what Darius would say.

He took a deep breath and began. "I didn't start reading until I was about nine. Letters just didn't make sense to me. I wasn't dyslexic; they tested me for that. So they assumed I was a slow learner, and the school system treated me as such. I got kept back, year after year, and wound up being kicked into a special class, which wasn't special at all. Most of the teachers there just didn't give enough of a damn to make an effort. My classroom was more of a holding bay where we were stored until we were too old to hang around anymore, and then we got kicked into another class, where we had to suffer more of the same."

Darius? A slow learner? Impossible. He was one of the most imaginative, incisive, visionary people she knew.

"That's wrong," she began to protest. "They were wrong about you."

"Yes, they were, and my mother knew it. She fought them every step of the way. She fought them when they told her I'd never learn to read better than a five-year-old could. They advised her to hang on with me until I was twelve or fourteen, and then see if she could find work for me as a shop apprentice, or with a builder. Because a scholar I'd never be."

"You weren't handicapped."

"No."

"And there was nothing wrong with your eyes."

"Twenty-twenty, all my life."

"So what was the problem?"

"I couldn't grasp the concept of the word as symbol. I couldn't understand that an apple and the letters A-P-P-L-E were linked in some way. When I thought 'apple,' all I had in my head were images of red, waxy skin, white, textured flesh. I could tell you exactly how the shape of an apple changed when the light hit it from an angle, and how the red turned to black if it was hidden in the shadows. But I couldn't form the image of a written word. I could never do that.

"I could see the letters on the page fine, but all they translated to me were shapes, curves, and lines. Dashes and dots. I looked at a word and couldn't recognize it as such. I got sucked down into the millions of little dots that made up the printed words, not the words themselves. And when I tried to write, instead of making letters, and writing rows and rows of words, I'd go into some sort of trance and fill page after page with whorls and squiggles. I was more interested in the thickness of the lines, the color of the ink, and the difference between the mark I could make with a 2B pencil and a 4B pencil. What would smudge under my thumb, and what

wouldn't. I was in a world of my own, and words didn't
have any place there."

Hailie found her breath bated, waiting to see how this
story of despair and repeated failure translated into the
confident, well-read, articulate man seated beside her.
"And what happened?"

"My mother happened. She refused to give up. My
teachers told her to, the child education experts told her
to, and she called them fools. She'd sit and watch me
struggle with my work, and watch my eyes dart across the
page. And then she figured it out. I remember the night
she had her 'eureka' moment with me. We were sitting at
the kitchen table, my siblings and I. Everyone was doing
their homework. They all got by without her help, except
me. She sat with me for two hours every night, trying to
hammer concepts into my head that just wouldn't stick.

"But that night, something clicked. She brought her
face level with mine, and instead of looking down at the
page, tearing her heart out at all the words I couldn't recognize, and couldn't remember, she looked at my eyes,
and watched their movement. And then she whispered,
'Shapes.' She threw her arms around me and started
laughing like a madwoman, as if she'd received the punch
line for a joke several years too late. 'Shapes!' she started
crying, and called my father. Then she hugged *him*, and
danced the poor, confused man around the room. 'Pictures, Lonnie, pictures! That's the answer!'"

His description was so vivid, Hailie could see the mad,
joyful scene in the cozy little kitchen. "And?" she asked
eagerly, leaning forward in her seat to catch the look
on his face as he told his story.

"And then my mother made sure I never saw a word
that didn't have a picture attached, or an item that
didn't have a name on it. She taped words to every stick
of furniture in the house. My bed had a label with B-E-D

written on it in Magic Marker. She labeled the inside of all my clothes, not with my name, as other mothers did, but my shirt was labeled S-H-I-R-T and my pants labeled P-A-N-T-S. My brown paper lunch bag had the word *lunch* written on it. She scratched the words *banana, pear,* and *apple* into my fruit with a needle. She iced the word *cake* onto my Twinkies and painted *cheese* or *tuna* onto my sandwiches with food coloring and a small brush."

"And then came comic books," Hailie intuited.

"Yep." His eyes held a nostalgic, faraway look. "Then came comic books. That was my big brother's idea. He figured that if Mama's method helped me understand nouns, comics would help me understand action and emotions. Human interaction, logic, drama. He bought me a handful, and I practically inhaled them. Sucked them up. He sat with me and I read them aloud to him every night. I fell for them, so hard and so fast, it was like being shanghaied. I started racing through my homework so I could spend more time reading my comics. I got sucked so deeply into the world of fiction, I almost never found my way back out. I started hiding comics under my pillow, rolling them down the legs of my jeans so I could sneak them into class. I stored them in apple crates in my room, and when that got filled I packed them in the garage. My father used to toss them out by the box because he said I didn't leave him any room for his car."

"How did you afford all those comics?"

"My brother kept me bankrolled. He was much older; by then he had his first part-time job while he was working his way through college. At the time, I didn't think much of what a sacrifice it must have been for him, but I was typically selfish for my age. He slipped me a few bills every Friday, regular as clockwork, and on Saturday morning I blew them all at the comics store. Don't know if I ever remembered to thank him."

"Great brother to have."

He looked pensive, frowning a little, and Hailie wondered if her remark had picked at the scab of some private family issue. After a while, though, he said slowly, "Yes. He *is* a great brother. I talked to him this evening, couple of hours ago, before I came over. We . . ."

"You what?"

"Oh . . ." He waved it away. "Nothing." But his brows were still drawn together at the center by some dark, uncomfortable thought.

She rushed to interrupt it before it put a damper on his spirits. "And your mother? What did she have to say about this comic book invasion?"

"Well, she used to threaten to call the FBI and report that I'd been kidnapped and replaced by an alien clone. I'd gone from hiding in the backyard to avoid reading lessons, to hiding away to win myself more time to read."

Hailie felt a smile dancing around her lips. "So it worked."

"Like a charm. I was out of special ed by the next term, and back with kids my own age in two years. I entered junior high on par with everyone else, and made it into college on a scholarship."

She pried his hand from its grip on the steering wheel and squeezed it. "I'm proud of you."

The bones in his hand flexed as he returned the squeeze, and then he set the car into motion before he answered. "Thank you." His voice was thick.

They descended into comfortable silence for several moments before she spoke again. "So, you think the same method can work for Will?"

He glanced sideways at her, eyes for once somber. "I don't know. I'm not a specialist, and I don't know squat about autism. I have no way of judging his capabilities. But he has a therapist, you said . . ."

"Yes."

"So ask her. See what she says."

Silence again, but a less comfortable one. Why, she asked herself, why did this link between her son and this man scare her so? Throughout his life, she'd been resentful and contemptuous of men who flitted into and out of her life, coming on to her with the intensity of an avalanche but turning tail and running scared when they became fully aware of the enormity of Will's problem and the impact it could have on their lives if they remained as interested in Hailie as they initially were.

But now, here was Darius, and he was not only unafraid and unrepulsed, but concerned, actively interested, caring . . . even fatherly. More disturbingly, his interest was genuine, part of the relationship that had formed between man and boy, and distinct from what she had with him. That alone was worth more than gold.

And she'd fought him at every turn, bristling every time Darius made a move toward Will, clawing him away like an angry mama bear. How foolish she felt now!

She had to swallow the lump in her throat before she could speak again. "I'm sorry, Darius. I owe you an apology."

His look was a mixture of surprise and bemusement. "You do? Why?"

"I was a real pain in the tail with you when you first got here. Over Will, I mean. You were trying to be nice to him. . . ." That's what he always was. Nice. Generous. Kind if it killed him. Her chest was suffused with warmth. How could she have been so dumb? Could there be room enough in that big heart of his for both of them? And was there room enough in hers, constricted as it had been by mistrust and hurt, for him? "And all I did was hiss and spit at you, like a female cobra with a clutch of eggs. Warned you off him." She covered her face with her hands, hoping he wouldn't see the flush of embarrassment there.

His hand moved from the wheel to her thigh, and she could feel the warmth of it through her skirt. "You looked mighty sexy when you were hissing and spitting, I have to tell you. Not snakelike at all. And if there was anything serpentine going on, you were the charmer, not the charmed."

He wasn't even letting her apologize properly. His light touch and good humor were both too distracting. "Darius!" she protested.

"Honey?" he replied innocently.

"I'm trying to say I'm sorry!"

"I know. I heard you."

"Well, could you please stop seducing me while I do so?"

"Am I?"

"Are you . . . ?"

"Seducing you."

Was he kidding? The touch of one hand, which wasn't even *moving*, was leaving her pretty near incapable of finishing a thought. It would have killed her to admit it, though, so she stubbornly pressed her lips together.

He laughed mockingly, but let it go. Instead of pressing home his advantage, he said, "Look, Mahalia, you don't owe me an apology over Will. The two of you have your own closed circle, and your special way of doing things. I'm an interloper. And there are things you know about him that I never will. So you were a little protective—"

"*Over*-protective."

"Whatever. It's only because you love him. And my ego hasn't been permanently damaged. So forget it, and let's enjoy this time together. Okay? No more 'I'm sorrys' from you tonight, young lady." His smile was indulgent, but brooked no opposition.

"Okay," she agreed finally. Tonight, there would be no need to say "I'm sorry" again. Tonight, there would be dinner and dancing, and the opportunity to be truly alone with him after so long. She'd promised to share her secrets with him, the ones he'd been probing after since their time together at Casuarinas. Tonight, with two glasses of wine in her to prop up her courage, she would tell him all about a man named Phillip Grant, who shared his last name but nothing else. Phillip, dark, hard, sexually lethal, and cruel even in love, hardened by a lifetime in L.A., who was as different from kind, forthright, and gentle Darius as it was possible to get. She was ready now. She would tell him everything.

"Where to, then, sweet?"

"Hmmm?" His voice sounded distant, like someone calling her name on the outer fringes of a dream.

"You're navigating, remember? You promised to take me to your favorite watering hole. So which way do we go?"

"Left at the next light," she told him.

His hand remained on her thigh as he drove.

Nine

Darius felt a buzz run through him, up his spine, tingling at the back of his neck, and running along the tips of his freshly mowed hair. Sheer adrenaline, sending his heart rate jumping, making electricity crackle in the air around him. By the time they pulled into the parking lot of the Speakeasy, he'd made up his mind not to order anything stronger than a glass of wine. He was drunk enough on an overdose of Mahalia.

He helped her out of the car, taking advantage of the fact that she was distracted—having to smooth down her skirt and get her bag and jacket—in order to stare at her, drinking her in. She was stunning. He remembered the feel of her thick braids under his fingers: even thus confined, her hair had been vibrant, thick, and strong. Now, unbound and left to spring free around her shoulders, it gleamed, practically yelling at him to bury his face in it.

And that dress! It looked like burgundy, poured over her, trickling down over her breasts, and pooling around her hips. He could almost smell the intoxicating scent of fine wine. If her stockings were any more sheer, they wouldn't be there at all. He recalled the thrill that had shot through him like a silver bullet when, on letting his hand fall onto her thigh, he had discovered that she was, in fact, wearing stockings and not panty hose, because he could feel the light ridge of her stocking-tops through the fabric of her skirt. His mind was inundated with images of her posing for him in the half-light of a quiet room, in nothing *but* those stockings, and his groin constricted painfully. He thanked God and all the angels for the camouflage of his new leather jacket, and surreptitiously pulled it closer around him to avoid any embarrassment.

"My favorite, favorite place," Mahalia was saying, and he struggled to drag his mind out of a very inviting gutter, to focus on her words. "But I haven't been here in ages. I hope it hasn't changed." She was smiling—no, she was glowing. Her glow was contagious, he was sure, because he felt his own skin grow hot and prickly. He took her arm and led her in, past an accommodating doorman, and into another era.

The Speakeasy had the rich, decadent air of an underground Prohibition-era hideaway. The colors on the walls, the extravagant draperies and thick-piled carpet washed over each other, wine and roses, old gold and deep, patina green. A coat-check girl in a too-short skirt took their jackets, but not before Darius rescued a rolled-up package from his inner pocket. Mahalia gave him a curious glance, but said nothing.

An usher dressed like someone out of a Walter Mosley novel led them into the dining area, where tables were surrounded by softly lit, semiprivate booths where small tables were embraced by padded leather banquettes that sighed under their weight and smelled of walnut oil and old brass.

"Incredible," Darius breathed.

"Tell me about it."

"I keep expecting gangsters with fedoras pulled over their eyes to bust into the joint and riddle us all with tommy guns!"

"Well, at least the booze is legal. We won't be doing time

in the pokey for *that*." She ordered wine for herself, and, after lifting an inquiring eyebrow to him and receiving a nod in response, requested one for him, too. Then she leaned back, sighing as she sank into the upholstery. "I think I'll let this seat just eat me up."

"Don't let it," he said at once. "That's my job." He could have accompanied the statement with a comical leer, turning it all into a joke, but he was dead serious, and wanted her to know it.

Her lashes lifted as she looked at him, eyes liquid brown, contemplating, evaluating. Thinking. He tensed a little, waiting for her to warn him off, as she usually did, or, if the heavens smiled on him, to respond in some way that would let him know that he had the all-clear to turn the heat up, begin his seduction. She did neither. "You going to show me what you got there?" She pointed with one burgundy-tipped finger at the small package he had rescued from his pocket.

He looked down at the parcel he was still clutching in one hand, slightly surprised at finding it there. Forgetful of him, considering he had picked it up only moments before. But then, that was to be expected. When he got close to Mahalia, he became befuddled. If it weren't for gravity, she'd make him forget which way was up. He turned the parcel over in his hand, examining it as if he wasn't the one who had wrapped it in the first place. "Oh," he said. "This?"

"Yeah, that." She was grinning like an imp, while trying her best to maintain an innocent air. It wasn't working.

"You know it's for you," he countered. "So don't try to play innocent. It doesn't wash."

"For *me*?" She pretended to be bowled over by surprise. "You sure?"

"Yeah," he said. "Pretty sure." He turned it over again,

noticing for the first time how badly wrapped it was. The paper was crooked, and the tape was peeling off in one place and bunched up and stuck to everything in another. He was an artist, he chided himself. He was used to working with paper, even took a three-month mini-course in origami and papier-mâché during his first year at art school. So why couldn't he wrap a present without it looking like a rock wrapped in newsprint by a three-year-old? Once again, it was probably all her fault. When he had her on his brain, he just couldn't seem to keep his hands steady.

"Well . . . ?" The cheeky grin was growing more impudent.

"Well, what?"

"If it's for me, aren't you supposed to hand it over? Or is it going to be a table decoration for the rest of the night?"

He looked around them. "No, no table decoration. There are enough flowers on it already." He handed the parcel over, resisting the urge to kiss her, even lightly, as he did so. "You're just going to have to open it."

"I'll see what I can do." As it turned out, she was one of those annoying people who unwrapped presents carefully, peeling the tape away without damaging the paper underneath, and rolling up each piece of tape into a sticky ball and depositing it in the ashtray, instead of going about it the way he would have, which is to say, tearing off the paper without ceremony. Before she could finish, their drinks came, and she paused, took a sip, and went back to her task, her brows drawn in concentration, and the tip of her pink tongue peeking out between her distressingly beautiful lips.

"You're doing this to torture me, aren't you?" he inquired with a martyred air.

"Hmmm?" She was all innocence.

"You're going to take all night to open it?"

"The suspense is half the fun," she countered tartly, and returned to her project. Half a drink later, the wrapping was finally off, and she held the banded scroll of heavy art paper in one hand. She seemed unsure as to whether she should go any further and actually unroll it.

"You've got to take the band off," he said helpfully. "Would you like me to do it?" He held his hand out over the table, but she didn't pass it over. He was shocked to notice that his feet were literally cold. He wasn't used to making presents, especially not for women. With women, you could usually get away with flowers or a trinket from a store. The last time he'd made something to offer as a gift, he'd probably been about twelve, patting together some clay monstrosity for his mother at summer camp. Right now, he *felt* about that age, and if he didn't look sharp, would probably wind up being tongue-tied in the bargain.

He watched as she popped the thick rubber band off with her thumbs, laid the scroll on the table, and unrolled it. She gasped.

"You like it?" he asked aloud. *You overeager fool,* he told himself silently, *couldn't you give her at least thirty seconds to decide for herself whether she likes it or not?*

She was silent, eyes popping as they roved over the full-color drawing, so he forced himself to remain quiet, watching her watch it. The background of the drawing was lush, a palette of deep midnight blues and purples, silver and black, as an entire landscape was thrown into drama by the light of a full moon. In the midground, a man-creature stood, his dark skin gleaming in the pale light. He was tall, and lean, lighter-skinned than the Romulus that Darius had been used to sketching, hair overlong and a bit tangled, body and face tensed by the rigors that only a lycanthropic transformation could bring. The man-wolf, in fact, had features that closely resembled Darius himself, or as he would have looked if his blood were seething with an ancient virus that made him powerless under the metabolism-altering light of the full moon.

But the man did not seem in any way disturbed by the agony that such change might have brought. His star-filled eyes were riveted on the other person in the drawing, the one who filled the foreground, glorious, warm, and almost alive.

It was Veda, powerful as she always was, breathtakingly beautiful as she always was. Her face lifted to the moon, eyes closed, drawing in its rays as another person would the rays of the sun. But no, it wasn't Veda. It was Mahalia. Mahalia charged and altered by a supernatural force, as strong as he always saw her to be, and as beautiful.

Darius waited to hear her say something, and when she didn't, he filled the quiet. "It's dumb," he said. "Just a doodle. You don't have to actually stick it up on your wall, just to make me feel good." Right about now, he was pretty sure it had been a laughable idea from the get-go. What the hell had possessed him in the first place? Had he really imagined she'd find it interesting, or even vaguely amusing? Had he been armed, this would have been an appropriate time to excuse himself, proceed to a dark alley, and put himself out of his misery with a bullet.

"It's . . . amazing!" she breathed.

"It's stupid," he said automatically. She couldn't possibly like it. She was just being nice.

"No, no!" She tore her eyes away from the page long enough for them to hold his. "It's gorgeous! I don't think anybody has ever done anything like this for me before!"

Probably because nobody's quite that lame, he thought, but then the suspicion penetrated his mind that she might actually be telling the truth. "You really like it?" He was half prepared to hear her say, "Well, not really. I was just trying to make you feel good."

Instead, her gaze dropped to the drawing again, and her fingertips glided over the form of the Veda-Mahalia creature who so enraptured the Romulus-Darius nearby. "I do. I can't tell you how much I do. And I *am* going to hang it on my wall. You couldn't stop me if you tried! You've made me look . . . so beautiful. Out of the ordinary. I almost don't recognize myself."

"I've made you look exactly as I see you," he said immediately. There was no way he was going to allow her to dismiss her own true beauty, as though it didn't exist.

She smiled. "What, all hair, fangs, and nails?"

"All beauty, strength, and courage," he responded. "All sex and power. All grace and wit. Look at me. . . ." He leaned forward in his seat and lightly tapped the image of the smitten he-creature in the drawing. "I'm in the agony of transformation, and yet all I can see is you. You've taken up my whole range of vision; I can't focus on anything else. Even in my own pain, nothing matters in my eyes but you."

Quiet descended upon them, even as the jazz piano that trickled down like water filled their ears. She let her gaze flit across the drawing, intensely, as though she were committing it to memory to be quizzed about it later; but Darius knew her mind was on his words, and that they had taken her by surprise as much as they had taken him. Unawares, he'd made a declaration of his affections, and now she was digesting this. When the time for her to respond elapsed, and still there was no word from her, he grasped her hand and squeezed it lightly. It was cold.

"Come on, Hailie. . . ."

"You've never called me that before!" Her eyes were pools of surprise. "You always call me Mahalia. You're the only person who calls me Mahalia."

"Just trying to get your attention," he said dryly, trying to make a joke of it, but the pit of his stomach was filled with crawly things. "Did you hear what I said . . . Hailie?" His gaze nailed hers down like a specimen butterfly in a display case.

"Yes."

"And what do you think?"

She tried to concentrate, but nothing seemed to come to her. "I don't know."

"What do you feel, then? That's a more appropriate question."

"I don't know that, either." She gnawed away the lipstick on her lower lip as her brows drew together, but under his hand, hers grew warm again. "Scared," she acknowledged finally. "Surprised too, I guess."

Well, at least she was feeling *something*. As a matter of fact, scared was good, because knowing her, she was scared because her world was changing. If there was one thing to put this stubbornly independent woman into a tailspin, it was that.

"Anything good you can add to that list?" he asked gently, trying to ease her tension away.

It worked. Her lips curved slightly. "A few," she confessed.

"Name one," he challenged.

She thought hard. "Warm."

"Warm is good," he allowed. "Shoot again."

"Safe—"

"You know that," he interrupted fervently. "There's never any question about that. You're safe from me, because I'll never hurt you. And I promise you this. If you give me half a chance, I'll keep you safe from anything that would ever threaten to harm you."

Her throat bobbed as she swallowed hard.

"And do you feel anything else? For me?" He knew

he was pushing, but he had to know. Things had gone on long enough. It was time to know where he stood.

She drew in a lungful of air in preparation for a response, but seemed to lose her courage, and let it out heavily. "It's so hard, Darius."

Frustration gnawed at him. He needed so badly to know if what he felt for her was matched by what she felt for him, but he sensed that bullying the information out of her would be like tramping through a flower bed. Instead, he stood, and urged her to stand as well. "Come. Let's not waste this great music. Dance with me. That way, if you have anything you want to say, you can just whisper it in my ear. Tap it onto my shoulder in Morse code. Whatever you like."

To his surprise and delight, she complied without protest, pausing only to return the scroll of paper to the protection of its rubber band and wrapping. She laid it down carefully beside her place setting, and allowed him to lead her to the dance floor.

She was a solid woman, hardly tiny, but in his arms she felt light, almost childlike. Paradoxically, she filled his arms, but felt like a puff of air that could slip through them at any moment. Her steps were hesitant, slightly out of time with his, and it took a lot of gentling and half a song for them to fall into sync. But when they finally did, he closed his eyes and just let the burbling, bluesy strains of the music guide his feet. He felt one of her hands fall from his shoulder to the small of his back, and in response the nerves twitched erratically, sending shock waves up his spine.

There was so much he wanted to tell her, but he didn't dare speak. It was like standing at a closed window and watching a bird land in your garden, and knowing that you'd almost be able to reach out and touch it if you opened the window and leaned out, but to do so would scare the little creature into flight. So he focused on the sensations that her hand on his body was arousing in him, and made do with stroking her thick, crinkly curls with his chin.

She broke the silence first. "Mmmm. . . ." She sounded like a woman settling into a warm bath, or under the covers of a huge comfortable bed.

He murmured his agreement into her hair.

"Darius . . . ?"

"Yes, sweet?"

"Is this for real?"

His heart skipped, but he forced moderation into his voice. "Do you want it to be?"

Her hesitation went on a little longer than he cared, but eventually she answered. Nothing more than a muffled "Yes" that was all but lost under the music that drizzled around them, and the folds of his shirt, but that was enough to send his heart soaring to ridiculous heights. His immediate, ludicrous response was to laugh, exultant, joyous, triumphant.

Immediately, she stiffened against him and stopped dancing, jerking her face out of the warm nest of his shoulder, and staring up at him, wide-eyed and suspicious, searching his face for signs of ridicule. He hastened to reassure her. "No, honey. Mahalia, please, don't take that the wrong way." He squeezed her against him again to cut off any notions of flight. "I wasn't laughing at you. Believe me. You should know that. I was laughing for joy. And surprise. You've been so prickly with me, and hard to read. I was half expecting you to back away. Reject me. So when you didn't, I just . . . you know. Felt like doing a victory lap." Then, he added contritely, "I didn't mean to make you feel bad. I'm sorry."

To his relief, she laughed, too, forgiving him easily. "Well, I guess laughter would be better than an actual victory lap around the dance floor. That would have been a tad embarrassing."

"The last thing I'd ever want to do is embarrass you. If I do anything, anything at all, to do so, let me know right away. Kick me under the table if you have to."

She reached up and caressed his newly cropped hair. "Well, you've taken care of one thing already."

He took her playful dig at his former tangle with good humor. "I thought you liked it messy. All part of my boyish charm."

"Nice, this way, too," she said immediately.

"I can shave it *all* off, if you'd like," he offered. "Or dye it. Or let it grow back and get braids put in, Milli Vanilli style."

She shuddered. "Ugh. Don't even!"

"Anything to please you. Anything at all, beautiful." He realized that what had started as banter had grown dead serious. He was speaking the truth. He *would* do whatever it took to please her. Anything at all.

She read the sudden seriousness in his face and grew serious, too. Around them, a handful of couples danced, but he couldn't hear the music. She probably couldn't, either, because she stood stock-still, her eyes locked into his. When he kissed her, the other couples faded away to the same distant place the music had gone, and they were alone, the only two people alive on earth, and everything in it was theirs and theirs alone.

There was the faintest taste of wine on her lips, and again, he was damned if he didn't taste those mystery strawberries, the same ones he'd savored on her mouth back at the cabin at Casuarinas, that first night he'd met her and had been unable to keep from kissing her. They weren't a part of his imagination, he acknowledged, and had nothing to do with what she had or hadn't eaten.

Everyone, he supposed, had a scent or feel or taste that defined them. Hers was strawberries.

There was a world of promise in their kiss, and a world of surrender. The prickly pear he'd fallen half in love with had become a softer, sweeter fruit. Her mouth opened under his insistence, just as another, equally delicious part of her had for him once, and did for him every night in his fevered memory. Her teeth were a row of smooth, shiny miniature carvings, each perfect, each done by hand. Her tongue was a tiny bird, alternately shy and daring.

Now he could hear music again, but not the seductive jazz that probably still played around them. His was the rambunctious pounding of a waterfall against stone, relentless as a watercourse the day after a storm. His blood flowed through him, keeping pace with the river in his ears, making him ache all over, desire driving away hunger. He began to wonder what she would say if he dared suggest that they skip the dinner they'd come for, and find their way back to his hotel, pronto. There'd always be room service, after they'd slaked another, more urgent appetite.

But that would be rude. Mahalia wasn't a woman you rushed. He'd sit her down, and feed her properly like a gentleman should . . . and *then* he'd race her across town like a madman. He broke their kiss, half reluctant, half in a bid for survival, because if he didn't breathe soon, his brain was going to shut down. When he lifted his head and looked down at her, her eyes were dreamily shut, and a smile danced around her lips, which were now devoid of the lipstick she'd left home wearing.

"Feel good?"

"Mmm . . . yes."

"Want me?"

"You know I do." She didn't even flush at the admission.

"Trust me?" This time, his voice was more serious.

She swallowed hard, and ran her tongue along her lips, causing him to cringe a little inside, and hope against hope that after all this, her response was not going to be in the negative. "Yes, I do. I trust you, Darius."

"Good. That's the one guarantee I'll always give you. You can always trust me, no matter what."

Her eyes were luminous. "Thank you."

"Well then, tell you what. Since we seemed to have stopped dancing . . ."

She looked around them at the other couples, who still seemed capable of hearing the music, and were still swaying rhythmically, wrapped in each other's arms. "Yeah," she said slowly, as though the realization had only just hit, "we've stopped, haven't we?"

"We have," he concurred in all seriousness. "And since that's the case, maybe we should just head on back to our seats and have dinner. You're hungry, aren't you?" And as he said the words, he became aware that, whereas a few seconds ago he was devilishly contemplating skipping dinner and whisking her away to enjoy another kind of delicacy, he could, in fact, do with a bite himself.

So he was glad when she said, "Starving!" and then added, with a wicked, very Veda-like grin, "but the food will just be the first course!"

He couldn't get her off the dance floor fast enough. The crowd was thickening slightly, so negotiating their way back to their table involved a little maneuvering to avoid colliding with one romantically entwined couple or other. They had almost made it when a heavy hand dropped onto Darius's shoulder, almost causing him to jump out of his skin.

"Grant!"

Both he and Mahalia spun around. In the dim light Darius could make out the silhouette of a giant, a man

taller even than Darius himself, and that was saying
something. He was built like a butcher, almost half as
wide across the shoulders as he was tall, with shadow-
dark skin and a Don King thatch of graying hair that
gave off a halo's glow under the light of the wall lamps.
The hand upon his shoulder weighed as much as a clod
of beef, and the grip was powerful. Darius was sure he
knew the voice, but his mind flailed about for several
seconds, trying to place the face.

A second after the name clicked into place, the giant
was elbowed aside by one of the world's tiniest women,
who threw her arms around Darius's waist before yank-
ing him down by the lapels—showing surprising
strength for one so small—to plant a kiss on his cheek.
"Darius, how are you!" the little woman enthused, and
patted his cheek, refusing to release her grip on his
lapel. She was a fine-boned woman in her sixties with
peanut-butter skin and dark eyes. Her hair was completely white, well coiffed, and adorned with a sprinkling
of pearl-tipped pins. Her emerald dress shrieked money
and taste. She had been a beauty in her youth, Darius
recollected, and she was still.

A genuine smile of pleasure spread across his face as
he returned the kiss and gently disentangled himself in
order to offer his hand in welcome to the huge man who
was standing beaming behind his wife. The man's grip
nearly broke his fingers. "Charles! Angela! Nice to see
you!"

Immediately, he caught Mahalia's slightly bemused
smile, and pulled her to him possessively, thrilling in the
feel of her body pressed against him. "Mahalia, these are
Charles and Angela Portman, old friends of my parents.
And this"—there was pride spilling over in his voice—"is
Mahalia Derwood." He was this close to adding, *She's a
best-selling author,* but he remembered her zealously

guarded anonymity, so instead he buttoned his lip while greetings and handshakes were exchanged.

Then, he clarified the relationship for Mahalia's sake. "Charles and my father grew up together. They even spent a few years in the army together."

"'Nam," Charles added gravely. "We covered each other's butts a thousand times over. Hell out there. *Hell* out there. One place you really needed a friend you could depend on. And Lonnie was that man. Wouldn't have made it back without Darius's dad, I can tell you that much, missy." He grunted, and looked thoughtful for a moment. "Hell," he said again, but this time, to himself.

Mahalia nodded soberly.

"Fixed his parents up, too. Not that it was my intention. As a matter of fact, I sort of had sweet little Estelle all lined up for myself—" He winced as his wife gave him a playful but effective punch on the arm, but that didn't stop him from going on, his black eyes gleaming behind oversized metal glasses. His face was animated by the relish of a storyteller who loved to talk, and found himself fortunate enough to have a captive audience at his mercy. "But then I made the mistake of introducing her to him on our third date. Sneaky mongrel charmed her right from my side. Should have rolled up my sleeves and invited him out back, right off, but my daddy didn't raise his boys to be anything other than gentlemen, so I stepped down."

"Good thing you did, too," Angela said meaningfully, but with the patience of a wife who had heard her husband tell the same story once too often.

Darius explained to Mahalia, "When I was still living at home, I saw Charles and Angela all the time, but I haven't seen them in—"

"Ten years, feels like," Charles interrupted. He laughed like a lion with a chest cold. "I wouldn't have recognized you, if it hadn't been for those eyes. You've got your mother's eyes. Can spot them clear across the room, even in this light. Your mother had eyes like the northern lights, she did. Could turn night into day. I remember that very clearly."

"Oh, you can stop with the eyes, now, Charles," Angela warned, and, suitably chastened, Charles fell silent.

They were standing at the edge of the dance floor, and beginning to cause an obstruction, so Darius tried to take his leave gracefully. He offered his hand to Charles again. "Well, it was great to see you both again, but Mahalia and I were just about to have some dinner."

Charles didn't accept the hand. Instead, he slapped him on the back again with his beef-clod mitt and boomed, "Well, you're having dinner with us, and I won't take no for an answer."

Immediately, Angela clapped her hands in delight, like a child at a party being told that it was time to cut the cake. "Yes! Yes! What a lovely idea! That would be absolutely perfect!" Without waiting for them to accept or decline, she grabbed Darius by one arm and Mahalia by the other, and began leading them to the dining area. "Come, children, you're eating with us."

Darius felt his heart sink. This wasn't how he had planned it. He loved the old couple dearly, and he had indeed not seen them for years, and if it were any other night, he'd have been delighted to spend some time with them, chewing the fat and catching up on lost time. But not tonight. Oh, not tonight!

Tonight was for him and Mahalia. Tonight, he was sitting her down to dinner, feeding her shrimp from his own fork and mellow red wine from his glass while his eyes made promises his body would be fulfilling, over and over again, in his hotel room later. Tonight he was setting the scene, conducting his foreplay in words, glances, and light touches on her arms, thus making love to her in full view of everyone else before he spirited her away to make love to her some more in private.

Oh, not tonight.

He quickly found words to excuse them. "We'd love to, but—"

"Nonsense," Angela interrupted. Her grip on his arm tightened. "Whatever you're going to say, I don't want to hear it. Come along, no weaseling out of this one. We insist."

Over Angela's head, he caught Mahalia's eye, and his thoughts and hers were one. She wanted to be alone with him as much as he did. He tried again. "Charles, maybe we could make a date to meet again, soon. Over the weekend. We could catch up then—"

Charles brushed away his protests congenially. "Don't be ridiculous! I insist. Come on, boy. For your father's sake. Sit with us." Then a shadow of something else passed across the old man's face, and Darius recognized the bonhomie for what it was: loneliness. As in love as the two of them obviously were after all these years, they still craved the company of others.

Darius was sure that his shoulders drooped an inch. He glanced over at Mahalia once more, and saw his own defeat reflected in her. There was nothing left to do but comply; to further protest would have been boorish— and unkind.

Delayed, not denied, she telegraphed, and he understood her message clearly. What would it cost them? An hour, maybe a little more. And then they would scoop up their things and race out of there like bats out of damnation, and then they would be alone, alone, alone. Small sacrifice to make, he conceded, to make an old couple happy.

The smile that he gave them was real. "Mahalia and I would love to," he assured Charles. "Just let me get our things from our table." Mahalia beamed at him for his graceful acceptance, making him sure he had done the right thing.

He hurried over to their table, gathered up Mahalia's bag and drawing, and let their waitress know that they would be moving to another table. By the time he joined the others, Mahalia was sandwiched in between the couple, and they were peppering her with so many questions about her personal life that it was all she could do to field as many as she could, and let the others fall to the floor.

"Yes, it's all mine," she was saying good-humoredly to Angela as Darius dropped into the only vacant seat, across the table from her. She pulled at a lock of black curls, stretching it out and then letting it spring tightly back into place.

"Good." Angela patted the back of Mahalia's hand. "I can't understand what young ladies are doing to themselves these days. Stitching horse's tails into their hair! I mean, really! As if the hair God gave them isn't enough!" She pursed her lips, leaving no one at the table in any doubt as to what she thought of the practice.

Darius could see the muscles in Mahalia's jaw working frantically to prevent a burst of laughter. Quickly, he changed the subject, swinging it around to neutral topics: the news and current affairs. After about ten minutes of idle chatter, Charles twisted in his seat, looking for a waitress.

"I don't know about you," he grunted, "but if I don't get something to stick to my ribs soon, they'll have to call the meat wagon to haul away my starved carcass."

"There's little danger of that happening, dear," Angela retorted, but with more amusement than censure. She turned to Mahalia and added, "Still thinks he can eat the way he did when he was twenty-five, that man. I must have told him a thousand times, if and when the meat wagon does come looking for him, it'll probably be because of cholesterol overload. Certainly not because of starvation!"

As the waitress approached, Charles grunted at Darius and said, in a low *this is just between us men* voice, "You just wait, young man. Just wait. Your young lady here will feed you up all through your youth, as if she's fattening a bull for the slaughter. Then, when you get to my age, she'll be tripping over herself to make you unlearn all the bad habits she taught you in the first place."

"I think I met you with all your bad habits intact, dear," Angela shot back without missing a beat, but Darius could barely hear her. Mahalia was grinning at him, and by that he knew she'd heard what he had. Charles and Angela were seeing them as a couple. Not just a dating couple, but a couple who would likely be together long enough to benefit from long-term advice from an older pair about what to expect in their old age.

That felt good.

Dinner was ordered, and arrived in due course, but for the life of him Darius had only the barest sense of what he was eating. It could have been coq au vin, it could have been boiled chicken feet; he wouldn't have been able to tell the difference. All he could think about was Mahalia, and about what would come later as soon as dinner was over.

Oblivious of the fact that his audience of two seemed barely capable of concentrating on the meal, far less on the conversation, Charles prattled on, regaling Mahalia with stories Darius had heard a thousand times before, about all the youthful high-jinks two young men with a thirst for life could possibly get up to. Eventually, Darius forgot his food completely and was happy to watch Mahalia from across the table, experiencing the merest shred of jealousy as her attention gradually shifted away from him, and she became engrossed in Charles's stories.

Charles, too, seemed pleased by her response; a seasoned storyteller gratified by an entranced listener. He stopped in midtale to slap Darius on the back with a hearty blow that would have sent a smaller man sprawling face-first into his plate. "You picked yourself a fine one, here, Darius. A fine one. She's a lil' darlin', I'm telling you. Take my word for it. I know the special ones when I see 'em."

"Charles!" Angela exclaimed.

"Oh." Mahalia blushed.

"Thanks." Darius smiled broadly, first at Charles, and then over at Mahalia, who was getting prettier by the second, as the color flooded upward into her face.

"You take her home to meet the folks yet?" Charles wanted to know.

Darius shook his head. Until now, the thought hadn't even entered his mind, so busy had he been simply striving to win Mahalia over in the first place. He wasn't even sure the deal was sealed. They'd need to spend quite a bit of time together, getting to know each other, before he even tried to cajole her down that road. But, in order to avoid a lengthy and extremely personal explanation, he simply responded, "Not yet. Soon, maybe. I'd love nothing better." He discovered that this last statement was the truth.

Charles grunted his approval. "That's the way to do it, son. I have to tell you, family approval is the way to go. Without that, you've barely got anything at all." He beamed at Mahalia. "Not that you have anything to worry about. Not with this little charmer over here. As a matter of fact . . ." He leaned in closer to Darius and confided in him in a stage whisper loud enough to be heard on the other side of the room, even with the band playing. "As a matter of fact, you'd better watch your back, I'll tell you that right now."

Darius knitted his brows slightly, unsure of what Charles was getting at. "I don't follow . . ." he began.

"Your brother, son! You'd better watch your brother! Don't think I'm too old and too cold to know what *that* boy's been getting up to. You watch him near your girl, let me warn you." He laughed, big booms rolling out of him.

Mahalia smiled. "Oh, really? Two charmers in one family?"

Darius felt his face go numb. He tried to nudge his mouth into a smile but it stubbornly refused. The argument he had had with his brother before he'd left to go pick up Mahalia still rankled, and not even her kiss had completely wiped the bitter taste of it away. Lame duck, Phil had called her. Insulted the woman he . . . loved. Mocked him for his faith in her. He squirmed in his seat.

"Got that right," Charles barreled on, fanning the flames of the conversation like a mischievous Puck. "And if you haven't met his brother yet, it's probably because he's afraid of what would happen if he ever laid eyes on you. He's a walking threat to anything female, that Phillip. A danger to everyone, including himself, since he was what, sixteen?" Charles's grin betrayed his masculine approval of Phillip's shenanigans.

Darius lifted his shoulders, throwing a wry look across at Mahalia. *He's right,* he telegraphed over at her. *Phil's a lady-killer, all right. Tell you all about it sometime.* His message was never received. Darius watched, confused, as the lovely flush that had infused Mahalia's face only moments before drained away, leaving her skin sallow, even under her makeup. Her head dipped as if she'd been sucker punched to the solar plexus, and her meat-laden fork, its journey to her mouth aborted, fell from her hand and bounced off her plate, whereupon rich sauce smeared the tablecloth.

She seemed to be struggling for air. "Your brother . . ." She couldn't finish.

Darius half rose in his seat, scared out of his mind, but for the life of him he couldn't tell why. "Mahalia?" He stretched his hand across the table to touch hers, and it was as cold as dead flesh. He tried again. "Hailie?"

"Your brother . . ." Her breathing was labored, as if her chest hurt.

Angela looked deeply concerned, throwing her eyes around for help, although where it would come from was unclear. "Dear? Are you choking?"

As always blithely oblivious, Charles charged on like a loose bull. "Left more casualties in his wake than the A-bomb. Darius had better watch out Phil doesn't do to you what his dad did to me."

A flash of anger crashed into Darius's concern, like two bolts of lightning colliding in midair. Whatever was wrong with Mahalia, Charles was the cause of it, and he didn't seem to know or care. It was only respect for his elder, and for his father's friendship with the man, that prevented him from grasping him by the jacket and physically making him shut up. A dagger glare did the trick. Stunned into silence, Charles deflated into his seat like a blimp with a puncture.

Darius tried to wedge his way around Angela's chair to get at Mahalia, wanting to lift her in his arms and take her out into the fresh evening air, away from this place and whatever had made her look as if the denizens of hell had risen up and confronted her.

"Hailie . . ." *Think, think,* he chided himself. What had scared her so badly? What had upset her so much? Was it the crack about Phil? "He was only kidding," he tried to assure her. As correct as Charles had been about his brother's reputation, there was no way that Phil would overstep filial bounds and do anything inappropriate. "Phil's not . . . he wouldn't . . ." He wished he knew what to say. "He's my *brother!*" was all he could manage.

Was it shock, or disbelief, or fear, or anger that he saw on her face, or a mixture of all? She was shaking like someone with the ague, but her voice was brittle and frighteningly steady. "Your brother is Phillip Grant?"

What kind of question was that? "Yes . . ." he answered slowly.

"From L.A.?"

"Yes!" He managed to get past Angela and was now close enough to Mahalia to pull her to him. "But what—"

"Don't touch me!"

Her shout was like a lance thrown from a great distance, impaling him against an invisible wall, preventing him from moving. He was only inches from her, near enough to pull her to him, but as much as he yearned to, he was immobile. All he could do was beg her to help him understand. "Tell me," he pleaded. Charles and Angela were staring, both goggle-eyed, but he was unembarrassed. "Please, Hailie, tell me. I can't help you if you don't—"

"Help me?" She laughed like one deranged, but he wasn't sure if she was losing her mind, or if he was. "You arrogant, deceitful son of a—" She choked on the next word, and a tremor ran through her. She screwed her fists up tightly before her face, but whether in a stance of attack or defense, he couldn't tell. "Go away! Go away!"

"Sweetheart . . ."

"Is this amusing to you? This, this, all of this . . ." She waved her arm to encompass the restaurant, and the turned heads of the diners around them who had by now become aware that a delicious drama was being played out within earshot. "Taking me out, making me presents . . ." She pointed at the rolled-up drawing that now lay on the table looking piteously lonely and bereft. "Is all this your idea of a joke?"

Deceitful? A joke? What was she talking about? Before movement could return to his limbs, Mahalia sprang into action. Lithe and sinuous as a fish, she twisted, scooped up her bag in a single, fluid motion, and leaped free of their table. Being much larger than she, and wedged in by the chairs around him, he was delayed by several seconds, even when Angela got up and shoved her chair against the table to allow him to get around.

He caught a glimpse of her skirt near the exit, and he tilted his body into a run, muscles bunched, thrusting him forward—only to screech to a halt at the appearance of a pastry cart, laden with sinful riches. He cursed more viciously than he had in a long time, but space constraints lost him several seconds as he stood aside to let the waiter ease the cart past him. Then, he was off and running again, past the coat-check, not caring that he'd left his new coat behind. Before the doorman could open the doors for him, he exploded through them, evading an incoming couple like a quarterback sidestepping a tackle, and found himself in the parking lot, frantic, his heart and lungs screaming more from panic than the exertion, looking desperately around him. Where was she? Where was she?

At the curb, traffic whooshed by in both directions, ignoring him. Mahalia wasn't there.

Ten

"Look, miss, I gotta know. You getting out or not? Because if you ain't getting out, I'm gonna have to turn the meter back on again."

Hailie lifted her head from its resting position against the back of the cab's front seat, feeling her skin peel wetly away from the vinyl. She peered confusedly through the car window. It was dark, and her vision was blurred by a veil of tears, but from what she could tell she was parked in front of her house, and probably had been for at least five minutes.

Her head reeled from shock, rage, and pain that curled down upon her like breakers on a hurricane-slammed shore. The blood in her temples all but drowned out thought. Phillip Grant. Darius Grant. Brothers. Kin. Of all the sick, ugly . . .

"Babe, I ain't gonna ask you again. You gonna get out? I'm a busy man. Gimme a break. Why'nt you just pay me, get out of the cab, and go sober up somewhere else, huh?"

Just her luck. She'd somehow found herself the rudest, most impatient cabbie in town. Things were *really* going her way tonight. Plus, he thought she was drunk. Not that she could blame him. Her limbs felt like straw, and she wasn't too sure she could successfully stand if she tried. She had half a mind to tell him to go ahead, turn the meter back on again if he wanted to, and at least buy herself another few minutes in which to pull herself together before she got out and had to face her own home, with all the many questions awaiting her inside. Coretta would still be up, and she would be curious about her early return and disheveled appearance. Could she really face that now?

But this was ridiculous. She couldn't cower in the back of a cab forever. *Find your spine,* she told herself. *Get out of the cab, and get inside.* Besides, if she knew Darius, he'd be over here as soon as he realized she'd left the parking lot. She'd need as much time as she could muster to lock her doors, batten down the hatches, and keep him from getting in.

Knew Darius. Ha. Whatever she thought she knew about him, it obviously wasn't enough. At least, she'd been missing one critical piece of information that would certainly not have allowed her to let things get this far! To think that tonight she'd made up her mind that she was going back to his room with him after dinner! It was all too ghastly to contemplate. She was prepared to give herself up to him, heart and soul, having deluded herself into thinking that she actually loved him. And, so help her, she'd been well on her way to telling him so—

"Lady!"

"I know, I know!" Time to get a move on. Her hand roamed blindly for the door handle, but her numb fingers couldn't find it. With an irritable grunt, the huge man leaned over and popped the door open for her, and then sat back down again, giving her a baleful, meaningful stare.

For a few seconds, she wasn't sure what he wanted, but it came back to her. Money. Of course. Only a Grant man could leave her so traumatized that she'd lost her grip on the simplest of mental functions. Too upset to count out what she owed him, she shoved her purse at him over the seat. "Just count out what I owe you, and give yourself a tip. Then I'll get out of your car. Okay?"

The cabbie's eyes bugged in surprise, and then narrowed. "You're kidding, right?" He held her bag as if it were a live snake. "You want me to open your *purse?*" His wary gaze moved from her purse to her face, as if he'd decided not only that she was bombed out of her mind, but that she was not exactly conversant with sanity in the first place.

The pounding in her temples was louder now, drowning out thought, and overwhelming sensation. If she had to spend one more second in this unpleasant man's company . . . Her voice was sharp. "If you want me out of your cab, you're going to have to pay yourself. Just take what I owe you, add a little for your time that I've wasted, give me my purse back, and we'll both be on our separate ways, okay?"

Apparently, those terms were acceptable. The man opened her purse with the tips of his fingers, doing his best not to allow the live scorpions or virulent radiation that he was sure was in there to come streaming out and harm him. He extracted a few bills and jiggled them before her face, allowing her to determine their value. She nodded, retrieved her purse, and stepped out of the car.

Immediately, she remembered her jacket. The air had turned quite chilly, and the thin fabric of her dress, which had thrilled her with its sexiness when she had put it on earlier, left her shivering now. She clutched her purse to her chest and rubbed her arms. The cabbie switched the engine on, but didn't peel off as she expected him to. Instead, he dipped his head and stared at her out of the window, his face showing concern for the first time. Probably wondering if she was about to collapse on the sidewalk, she thought with grim amusement.

"You gonna be okay?"

She nodded mutely.

He indicated her house with his chin. "You live here?"

She nodded again.

The man shrugged and slipped the cab into gear. She turned to walk away, but the man had one last thing to say to her. He called her back. "Lady?"

Exhaustion made her patience as thin as his. "What?" She made no attempt to hide her exasperation.

"Next time, remember: no matter how hard you try, you can't drink it all. Okay?"

Mahalia fled, but was unable to shake off her embarrassment and leave it at the curb. The cab disappeared with the stench of peeling rubber.

At her door, she fumbled for her keys, but her fingers were cold and clumsy, and she knew she'd never manage to slip a key into anything as small as a keyhole. So she pounded on the door, hard, half as a summons, and half as an outlet for her frustration.

The door flew open, almost causing her to catapult inside. A strong, dark arm grabbed her by the shoulder and pulled her in. She heard the door slam behind her.

"What in the name of the good, sweet Lord happen to you, child?" Coretta shrieked. The large, black eyes bugged behind her thick glasses, and the gold chains on which they hung swayed around her neck. "Come, come here, let me take a good look at you."

Hailie felt herself being dragged into the living room and shoved under a light, where Coretta examined her minutely, like a trauma nurse assessing an accident victim.

"Where your jacket? What you gone and done with it? You lost it?"

Hailie shook her head vehemently. She hadn't lost it; she knew exactly where it was: hanging in the coat-check closet at the Speakeasy. "Didn't lose it," she mumbled.

"What then? Somebody take it off you?"

She shook her head again. "No, no, Coretta. Nobody took it. I forgot it. That's all. It's not a problem." She rubbed her arms, trying to get the circulation back into them.

"What you mean it's not a problem? Obviously it's a problem, because you shivering." Anxiety was raising Coretta's voice to a higher and higher pitch at every second, and deepening her West Indian accent until it emerged pure and broad, untempered by the twenty years the woman had spent on U.S. soil. "And it was a nice jacket to boot. Nice, nice, nice. Y'all young people, y'all too careless with your belongings. If it hada been me, I woulda never lose a nice jacket like that." She sucked her teeth and sighed heavily at the tragedy.

Hailie tried to edge past her. If Coretta got all worked up, she'd be lecturing her all night. "I'm tired," she murmured.

Something else struck Coretta, shoving aside all thoughts of the jacket for good. "And where that Darius boy?"

"I don't know," Hailie said, but she did know. Darius was on his way over here, and would be arriving any second. The thought of it sent a tremor of anxiety through her. Her glance flew to the main door to make sure it was securely locked. Even the cat seemed to know he was coming: she faced the door, her one-eyed gaze fixed intently upon it as though she expected it to be thrown open at any time now.

Coretta persisted. "Where the boy? Why he didn't walk you to the door? You mean to tell me he drop you off at the curb like a sack of potatoes? Where his manners?"

"He didn't bring me back. I . . ." Oh, she was so embarrassed, even discussing the evening's devastating closure with someone she knew and trusted. "I took a cab," she finished staunchly.

Coretta gasped. "What you mean, he make you take a cab? He didn't even bring you back here himself? What kind of halfway, no-account man is that? In my day, that woulda never happen. No man ever take me out and didn't bring me back home."

Hailie wanted nothing more than the sanctuary of her room. "Coretta . . ." She held up a hand, trying to stem the flow of loyal indignation.

"Mommy!"

Both women stopped and turned to the sound of the voice. Will was standing there, in his pajamas, smiling at them both. He was still clutching to his chest the comics Darius had bought him.

Hailie looked at her watch. It was way past Will's bedtime. "What are you doing up, son?" she asked, but gently rather than reprovingly. She stooped to hug him, and he felt good in her arms. The glossy paper of the comic books crinkled between them.

"Girl, I've had a devil of a time trying to get this one into bed tonight. I keep putting him in, and he keep jumping out again. He say he want to wait for you and Darius to come back."

"But he always—"

"Not tonight." Coretta shook her head.

Will slipped from her grasp—she would never have let him go voluntarily—and looked around, worry invading his normally expressionless face. "Where's Darius?"

Coretta snorted. "Hmff! I was just asking your mama that same question. I still waiting for an answer."

"He's not . . ." Hailie paused, but pressed on. "He's not here, son."

"He coming?" Will turned to stare expectantly at the door.

Any second now, Hailie thought, but instead, she said, "No, not tonight." *And not ever again, if I have my way,* she added silently.

"But why?" Will looked confused. His hero, not coming? That wouldn't do!

"Because he . . . can't make it."

"But *why?*" Will insisted.

"Go to bed, son," Hailie insisted gently. She pressed a kiss against his forehead. "Coretta, please."

Her voice becoming slightly softer, Coretta ushered Will back into his room, and in moments, emerged, smiling triumphantly.

"Did he get into bed?"

"Yes. I tell him if he go to sleep now, he gonna get cookies and ice cream for breakfast. That always do the trick."

Well, at least that was settled. There would be only one more problem to deal with . . .

Brakes squealed outside, sending the gravel in her driveway flying. Her problem had arrived. Her head snapped in the direction of the sound, and she went rigid, like a startled deer on the first day of hunting season. Veda Two bristled, anticipatory electricity making her fur move down her back in ripples.

"That him?" Coretta asked, as if she needed to.

"Yes," she managed weakly. "Don't let him in."

"You bet your boots I'm not letting him in." Coretta looked all too happy to be given the mission.

A car door slammed, and Hailie darted from the living room, with Coretta close on her heels. She headed for her own bedroom, the cat an excited stumbling block between her feet.

The smell of paint assailed her, but she was damned if she was opening a window to let any air in. Work was only half done, and her bed was not yet mounted, but the floor and a few blankets would suit her just fine. Refusing to turn on the lights, Hailie braced her back against the wall, head turned in the direction of the driveway.

The doorbell pealed.

"Don't let him in," she warned again.

"I hear you the first time, honey. And don't worry. If he coming in, it's gonna be over my dead body he have to crawl."

The doorbell rang again.

"Tell him to go away!"

"First, tell me what he do to you. When you leave here tonight, you was all rosy and smiling, like God open up the sky and this man fall out. What he do to you?" Her face grew sharp, shrewd. "He advantage you?"

Darius? Hardly. That wasn't his style—although she had to admit that she'd learned less than an hour ago she wasn't too sure what his style was, apart from lying and being sneaky and underhanded, that is. She shook her head vehemently, although she couldn't understand why she was still prepared to defend him. "No, he didn't. He didn't do any such thing."

"He better not, because I can tell you, where I come from, we got ways of dealing with men who think they can force themselves on a woman and get away with it. When we done with them, they won't be thinking about nothing like that for a long time!"

"He didn't touch me, Coretta." Not without her permission, at least. And if Charles and Angela hadn't turned up and blurted out the truth, there would have been a whole lot more touching going on again, and she would have welcomed it. Her stomach churned violently at the thought.

"Well, whatever it is he do, I'm gonna deal with him for you." She swiveled her eyes toward the ceiling. "Lord, You my witness; I never did like the boy. Not from the start."

Out of the darkness, a voice. "Mahalia!" Darius had abandoned the doorbell and was working his way around the house.

"Coretta, please," Hailie pleaded. "Please, just get him to leave."

She expected the older woman to make her way out to the front door and dispatch Darius from there, but with the vengeance of Nemesis glowing in her eyes, Coretta hitched up her breasts with both hands, prepared for battle, stomped over to the window, and threw it open. If Hailie hadn't been so upset, she would have laughed out loud at the gesture.

"You! Boy! What you doing making all kinds of racket outside decent people house at this time of night? Your mama never teach you better manners than that?"

Hailie could hear Darius's response clearly. "I'm sorry, Coretta, but I really have to speak to Mahalia."

"Ringing that doorbell! Ringing it and ringing it! At this godless hour! Making all that noise! You ain't worried you wake up the boy?" Coretta's voice was now much louder than the doorbell had ever been.

"You can't hear the doorbell from the guest room," Darius responded reasonably. Hailie could tell he was hanging on to his patience by a tight but thin rein.

"That don't matter. It's late, and you need to go home. You can't see the girl don't want to talk to you?"

"I gathered that. I just want her to tell me why."

"Why? Why? You do something to send her flying home like a pigeon outta hell and you want to know why?"

Darius gave up on trying to reason with Coretta. There was movement, and Hailie could hear him right under her window. "Mahalia, I know you're there."

"She not here!"

"Hailie, sweetheart, please. You owe me an explanation."

She owed *him* an explanation? She wasn't the one that cooked up whatever malicious, vicious scheme he had with his brother. For the life of her, she couldn't understand what it was, and what his purpose had been in infiltrating her life for Phillip's sake, but whatever it was, it was ugly and deceitful, and she would never forgive him.

She ran to the window, edging Coretta out of the way. "I don't owe you anything, Darius."

"You hear that?" Coretta shrieked. "She don't owe you—"

Hailie lifted her hand. "Coretta, please . . ."

"Please what?" Coretta goggled at her, startled by the interruption in her righteous tirade.

"I'll deal with it." She'd been wrong. Sending Coretta out to fight her battles was weak and cowardly, and she was ashamed. "Just leave us alone, please."

"What, so he can sweet-talk you like he always do? Not while I—"

"Coretta, I'll handle it." This time, Hailie's voice was firm, and not even Coretta could oppose her. With a nasty look out the window and a snort of contempt, Coretta swept out of the room and slammed the door.

Darius let a gust of air out between his teeth. "Thank you."

You're not welcome, she wanted to say. *I didn't do it for you.* Instead, she told him firmly, "I want you to leave, too!"

Darius lifted his head to look up at her. From where she stood, his head came only to her waist, just level with the windowsill, and she was glad for the slight advantage this provided her. But he was as determined as she. "I'm not going anywhere until you tell me what happened."

She curled her lip. "Like you don't know!"

"I *don't* know!" His eyes were lifted to hers, bright, almost sincere. He was such a good faker. "We were having such a wonderful time. We were dancing together. We were laughing. I was touching you, and you were touching me back. And then all hell broke loose. Mahalia, I swear to you, I have no idea what spooked you, but I'd give anything to find out."

It was ridiculous, this charade. Why was he going on like this? Why didn't he just confess that he'd been caught in a lie, and be done with it? "I didn't get spooked," she retorted. "And you know it. All I got was the scales torn from my eyes, and now I see who you really are. . . ."

"Who I am is the same Darius you left home with this evening. I'm the same man who stuck by your side all week, helping you get back on your feet after the fire. I'm the same man you . . ." Something caught in his throat. "I'm the same man you made love with that afternoon back at your cabin. We shared something then, and I'm not going to forget that. Neither should you." This last was said with a mixture of bewilderment, accusation, and hurt.

Hailie felt her stomach churn, and a wave of nausea almost brought her to her knees. There it was, the thought she had been shunting to the back of her mind all this time, refusing to acknowledge. Sucked in by want, need, and loneliness, she'd given herself to a man who was little more than a stranger. A charming one, yes, a devastatingly attractive one, who seemed caring and gentle. Honest. And one who, through some prank of the gods, turned out to be the brother of the one man who had seduced her, used her, lied to her, and then crushed her heart like an empty beer can.

Phillip Grant: user, liar, false lover—and the father of her son. And she'd slept with—fooled herself into thinking she was actually in love with!—his brother. It was repugnant, too grotesque to voice openly. Not incest, but something close. Something made all the worse because of Darius's refusal to come clean from the beginning.

When she didn't answer, he tried again. "You were willing to go back to my room with me tonight. Don't deny it. You told me so with your body and you told me with your mouth. You said you trusted me. What happened to that trust?"

"I should have known better than to trust a *Grant*," she bit out. The humiliating knowledge that what he had said was true, that she had been willing to go home with him—more than willing: eager—and that up to then, she had trusted him, rankled. *Fool, fool, fool.*

"Trust a . . . What has my family ever done to you? Was it all those stories Charles was telling? That's just the way he is. He talks all the time; there's no stopping him. Don't take him seriously. All those stories about him and my dad, getting into trouble, half of them probably aren't true. The other half, well, that's just young men being young men."

"It's not your *dad* I'm worried about!" she volleyed back.

He snapped his fingers. "It was what he said about my brother, wasn't it? I knew it! I just knew it!" Darius reached up to the window and held out his hand, palm up. "Touch me, Hailie."

Stubbornly, she removed both hands from their position on the sill and shoved them behind her back. "Why?"

"I just want to touch you. To feel your flesh. I want to reassure you. Don't let what Charles said about Phil worry you. He's a womanizer and a bit of a cad, but he's still my brother, and he'd never try to importune you or embarrass you in any way."

At least, never again. Not if I have anything to say about it. She glared at him, mute but resolute, still refusing to take his hand.

After several long moments, he gave an impatient grunt. Something came sailing through the window, and before it hit the floor she realized it was her jacket. He'd probably gone back to get it before leaving the restaurant. His hands now free, he grasped the windowsill and with a mighty heave, hauled himself inside. The sound of his feet thudding on the floor made Veda Two scurry off to one side. Even she could tell that something was wrong. The room was filled with tension, and she didn't like it.

"You can't do that!" Hailie screeched, but he already had. She put a few steps between them and glared at him. "I didn't invite you in!"

He bent over, picked up her jacket, and held it out to her. She refused to take it. He walked over to her bathroom and draped it over the doorknob, and then, with a sweep of his arm, flicked on the lights.

They'd been in darkness so long that the light slashed at her eyes like blades. She squinted and held up her hand against it.

"I'm in anyway. And I'm staying here until you spill it."

His voice was no longer pleading. Her resistance had made him angry, and she knew he was speaking the truth. She would have no peace until she stopped fighting. He returned to face her, standing so close that all she could see when she looked up was his looming face, and the determination had dimmed the stars in his eyes, like gray clouds being blown across them in a gale. "Okay, Mahalia. Twenty questions are over. You ran out of there like a frightened rabbit. You embarrassed me, and you embarrassed my friends. You owe me an explanation. Now, I know that it was something that Charles said that spooked you, but I can't for the life of me understand, so it's up to you to rectify that. Start talking."

She scanned his face for evidence of pretense, some proof that he had been caught out in whatever scheme he had cooked up with his brother, whether it was for some need to humiliate her, or some boyish game of hand-me-down, with one brother passing on his castoffs like an old pair of sneakers.

But there was none.

Darius Grant honestly, simply, wanted to know the truth. Laughter slipped past her before she could stop it. "You don't know," she marveled. "My God, Darius, you really don't know."

"No, I don't," he whispered. "You have to tell me. Please."

Tell him? How was she supposed to tell him? *What* was she supposed to tell him? That a decade ago she'd been young and foolish and vulnerable and simply too damn stupid not to recognize a shark when she saw one, and that she'd gone and fallen crazy in love with his brother, the big man on campus, the stud, the star, who was old enough to know better, and certainly old enough to know exactly which of her buttons to press? That Phillip Grant had used her up, sucked her dry, and abandoned her without a second glance when she found herself pregnant?

She didn't know where to find the words.

He held his arms out, as he had earlier, but didn't advance. "I'll hold you while you tell me, if you like. You don't even have to look at me, if you don't want to. Just bury your face right here. . . ." He touched the left side of his chest, lightly, just over his heart. He waited for her to step into their circle.

Her nerveless feet would not have responded, even if she had ordered them to step forward. "I don't know how," she breathed.

"Try," was all he said.

Ages crept past and died before she spoke again. "Phillip . . ."

"Yes?"

"I knew him. A long time ago."

"Knew him . . . how?" But his voice told her he had an inkling. His arms fell to his sides.

"UCLA. I was young, a freshman, and he was a grad student. He was older and smarter, and everybody loved him. He was a genius and a football hero, and every man wanted to be him. Every woman wanted to be with him. Me too. He was interested in me, and I was flattered. He could have had any woman he wanted, and I'm nothing much to look at—"

"You're beautiful," he interrupted reverently.

She waved away his words, because they weren't true. "I was just so damned grateful for his interest. I'd have done anything he asked."

"And did you?"

"Yes." Her response was laced with self-disgust.

"So you slept with him. My brother." He rubbed his temple as if his head hurt.

"Yes."

"How long?"

"Not long. A few months. A semester, maybe." She laughed self-deprecatingly. "I didn't exactly have what it took to hold the attention of the great Phillip Grant much longer than that!"

"He hurt you." He wasn't asking, he was stating. He seemed to know exactly what his brother was capable of.

He gouged me, she wanted to say. *Turned me inside out.* But instead, she simply said, "Yes."

"I'm sorry, Mahalia. I'm sorry he did that to you. But I'm not Phillip. I'm Darius. We're two different people. I had no idea. I never set out to hurt you."

She was willing to concede that. Maybe he hadn't known. But he'd never gone out of his way to leave her any clues as to his identity, either. "How could you let this happen? You told me you were from Detroit!"

"I *live* in Detroit! I'm *from* L.A.!"

"You made love to me!"

"We made love to each other!" he countered. "We shared something, and that had nothing to do with anyone but us. We didn't know. We needed each other, and we took what we needed."

"Doesn't it make you sick?"

"What?"

"Knocking me back and forth, brother to brother, like a badminton shuttlecock, that's what! It's wrong."

This time, he didn't await her permission to touch her. Her grasped her by the arms, fingers buried deep into her flesh. "It's not wrong, Mahalia! You and I aren't kin. It's not illegal, it's not immoral. It just happened. It was a million-to-one shot that we'd meet. A *hundred* million to one. But it's happened. And I for one am glad it did. Ten years is a long time. Can't you just put Phillip out of your mind? Can't you forget him?"

He grasped her chin and forced her to focus on him. "Look at me. Who do you see? Me, not Phillip. I'm not going to hurt you like he did. I'm not going to use you like he did. I'll never hurt you. I promise. You said you trusted me. Trust me now. I want you. Forget Phillip, and be with me."

She raised her leaden hand to clutch his wrist, and twisted her chin from his grasp. "I can't," she mumbled, and her heart weighed more than the earth itself. "I can never forget him."

"Why not?"

"He left me something. He gave me something. And so I remember him, every day of my life."

"What did my brother give you?" he asked, but in his voice there was a growing understanding. He repeated the question hoarsely.

In response, her head turned, and his turned with

hers, until they faced the door behind them. Beyond that door was a corridor, and a series of other doors, the last of which led to a guest room with a single bed. And in that bed, a little boy slept.

Eleven

Will, Darius thought.

"Oh, my God," he said. His legs suddenly couldn't hold him. If he didn't find a wall against which he could brace himself, he'd keel over for sure. He found the nearest one, the one that separated Mahalia's bedroom from her bathroom, and backed up against it.

"Yes," Mahalia said. "Exactly."

Shock and confusion made him stupid. "But, how?"

"The usual way," she responded dryly.

"You know that's not what I meant," he responded tiredly. His strength, his vitality, were slowly draining from him, down his legs and out through the bottom of his feet, until his legs couldn't support him anymore, and he found himself sliding into a squatting position. He let his head fall into his hands.

Will, the sweet child who had stolen his heart from that first night, even faster than his mother had, was his nephew. Phillip's son. The information left him strangely elated, as if he'd found concrete proof of something his heart had been whispering to him all along. His blood had found its own, like a dowsing rod seeking out and finding a deep underground stream.

As blood always stood up for blood, he'd stand up for the boy, just as his instinct had urged him to from day one. There was no doubt that he'd always be a part of Will's life. Will wanted it, he knew . . . and so did he.

But . . . then there was Mahalia.

There was more between her, him, and Phillip than the faded memory of a bitter sexual encounter. That little, sleeping boy was a length of genetic rope that bound them all, and with that, a dozen nameless taboos reared their heads. *You and I aren't kin,* he'd just said to her, and they still weren't. Not in any real sense. But kinship required more than flesh. It was tribal, and in his African ancestry, the extended family was as real as any clinically defined one.

He and Mahalia had been lovers, once, briefly, on an evening that suddenly seemed far away. They'd yearned to renew that relationship, and almost did tonight, had not fate, with its sick sense of humor, intervened in the form of a garrulous old man and his wife, thus throwing a spanner into works that had promised to flow so smoothly. Changing everything for good.

Somewhere, the word *sister* had become blurred into the concept of her as a lover. And with sister came another word: *forbidden.*

He lifted his gaze to her face, which was pinched, agitated. "It shouldn't matter," he tried to tell her, and himself.

"It *does* matter," she insisted.

"But it *shouldn't!* There's no law against this, against us. Not God's law, and not man's. We don't share a drop of blood—"

"I know!" She was wringing her hands and pacing the floor, like a cat in a too-small cage, while the real cat sat nearby, her body tensed with caution, her single eye a mere slit under the bright bedroom lights, following them back and forth as each spoke. "I know that, Darius! But inside, in my gut, where it counts—"

"Cast your mind back," he pleaded. "Think back three hours, to the time we were alone together. Think about what you wanted, and what I wanted. It was clean and honest then, and it's clean and honest now. What we felt then hasn't changed!"

Instead of arguing his point, she stopped abruptly in front of him and pointed an accusing finger. "You! You could have said something! You could have given me a clue!"

"I didn't know!"

"I understand that, but you could have let something drop about you, your family. About growing up in L.A. About who your parents were, and your siblings . . ."

He struggled to his feet, unwilling to fend off her accusations sitting down. "It never came up! We talked for hours, you and I, but who I am and where I come from just never seemed important. We talked about Romulus and Veda, and about art, and books, and about . . . Will. Nothing else seemed important."

"You don't even look like him! There isn't even a clue . . ."

He had to agree with her there. Not only did he and Phillip not share the slightest physical characteristic, but neither did Phillip and Will. His nephew was Mahalia in print. Strong women must run in the family. "I look like my mother," he agreed, "and Phil looks like our dad. That, and there's fifteen years between us. If you don't actually know, there's no way to tell."

Her hands flew to her face, and to his horror he realized that her gesture served to catch her tears. "A Grant," she wept. "Of all the men in the world. Another Grant. How? How?"

He tried to brush away her tears, but she wrenched away from him. He didn't insist. Inwardly, he cursed his brother. As much as he loved him, he was far from blind to his ways with women, and, alarmingly, Phillip had actually *mellowed* over the years. Ten years ago, the grad student with all his future ahead of him and the world at his feet was brasher, bolder, greedier, and far more callous. Phillip had brought pleasure and suffering to a great many women, and the one Darius loved was one of them.

That grieved him, slashed him to the quick, but he refused to be tarred with the same brush. "I told you: I'm not my brother," he insisted. He tried to sound reasonable, rather than defensive. "I don't look like him, I don't sound like him, and I don't think like him. We're two separate people. I'm not going to do to you what he did."

"How would I know?" she shot back. "I don't know anything about you!"

"A few hours ago you were willing to learn!"

"A few hours ago, things were different!"

"Yes, but we're two adaptable, intelligent adults. We can adjust to anything!"

Her shoulders sagged, as though the life were draining out of her through the fingertips that dangled at her side. Her head drooped, and when she refused to look him in the eye, he knew the battle was lost. "Not anything." Her voice was pained, hoarse, but held a frightening finality. "Not this."

He shivered, and the chill that coursed through his blood had nothing to do with the weather. "What're you saying?"

"You know what I'm saying." She was still ashamed to lift her head and look at him. "I think . . . maybe . . . you should leave."

"No," he rasped. He planted his feet firmly, well apart, and folded his arms. "No."

"Get out, *Grant.*" She spat his name out like a piece of poisoned apple. "Let it die."

She might be willing to give up on what they had—or could have had—but he wasn't. That wasn't the way he chose to live his life. "It won't die! Not if I have anything to say about it!"

"It's already dead, it's just refusing to lie down. Your *family* killed it."

The gibe about his family could have prodded him into anger, but he resisted the impulse, and instead struggled to sound calm and rational. "Mahalia, look. My brother broke your trust. I can help you build it up again—"

"I don't want your help. I don't want anything from a Grant! As a matter of fact . . ." The thought seemed to have only just struck her, but when it did, it was solid and immutable. "As a matter of fact, I don't think I want you working on my book anymore."

She couldn't really mean that. Whatever their personal problems, they were a world-class team. Between her words and his art, *Romulus* was destined to become a blockbuster. He knew it in his heart. A sudden wave of nausea put his dinner in jeopardy. Could he really be losing both the only woman he wanted *and* his only shot at success in one night? His life, his career, had been built upon sand, and now the storm breakers were crashing down upon it, sucking it out from under his feet.

"You're firing me?" was his incredulous croak.

"No, I'm not." This time, she did lift her eyes to him, but when she did, he almost wished she hadn't, because they scared him. They were as dark as the night sky would be, if the moon were to fall out of orbit, and they were as hard and cold as the ammunition her words had become. Silver bullets slammed into his chest—*thunk, thunk, thunk*—and the man-wolf was vanquished. "I'm not firing you. But my agent will. He'll call you. Soon." *Thunk, thunk, thunk.* Inside him, Romulus howled in agony as his flesh was rent.

"Don't do this," was all he could manage.

She was already turning away. "You'll be well taken care of, financially. We had a contract, and I'll uphold my end of it."

"Don't do this," he repeated, but this time he was speaking to her back. A tingle at his ankle told him that Veda Two was extending her sympathy, bidding him a silent farewell with the brush of her tail.

"Good-bye." Mahalia echoed what the cat had left unsaid.

Darius took several long moments to reassure himself that his heart was still beating, and his lungs still functioning, before he commanded his legs to move. He knew a tactical retreat when he saw one, and that was all it was, he reminded himself. A retreat, not an admission of defeat. He'd be back. He refused to mouth the word in return. Instead, he returned to the window through which he had entered, sat on the sill, and threw over a leg.

Mahalia paused and turned, and his ribs contracted. She was changing her mind! But all she said was, "Can't you leave through the door, like normal people?"

"Leaving the way I came," he muttered, sorely disappointed.

She shrugged. "Suit yourself. Hope the neighbors don't call the cops."

As he continued his descent, something crackled. He reached into his breast pocket to retrieve an item that had been forgotten in the heat of the moment. "Hailie," he called, praying that she didn't ignore him.

"What?" she asked tightly.

He extended his rolled-up offering, the drawing that had so pleased her earlier, but of which he was now almost ashamed. "You left this on the table."

Even from the other end of the room, she spotted it for what it was. "Keep it. I don't want it."

"I made it for you," he coaxed. "Keep this, at least. A souvenir—"

"I don't need to be reminded of anything, least of all you!" Her passion startled him. Her voice was loud enough to cut through the still night. "How much clearer do you need me to make it? I don't want it! I don't want to remember. All I want to do, if you want the truth, is forget. And get a good night's sleep, if that's still possible. Good-bye, Darius."

Wordlessly, he slipped the drawing back into his jacket pocket, extended his long legs, and fell silently to the soft earth below. In the window above him, the light went out.

Darius expected his brain to be teeming with scrambled thoughts, but his focus surprised him. He had the mind of a man who had been tossed into an iced-over river, and had emerged energized, startled by the extreme cold into pure mental clarity. He could think only of one thing, and he was on his way to dealing with that one thing right now.

It was well after midnight, but even so the freeway was busy. Phillip made his home in west L.A., over an hour away yet, especially considering that if Darius wanted to avoid the humiliation of being hauled over to the side by the highway patrol, it would be in his interest to keep his foot light. But head there he would, right now. This couldn't wait for tomorrow.

He was in pain: heat tore through his viscera and spread malignantly outward, shredding and scorching, until not an inch of him was left unscathed. His pain was fueled by loss, but also by anger. He was mad at Mahalia for her stubborn refusal to hear him out, give him the chance he felt he deserved, but madder still at his brother, who was, he knew, the source of the problem.

Mahalia had never talked much about Will's father, at least not to him. His earlier probing had caused her to withdraw into her little shell of hurt like a snail tormented by a schoolboy. But if there was one thing he remembered of their conversations, it was her declaration that she was both mother and father to her son, and it didn't have to be that way. It was that way because Phillip had defaulted. What Phillip had done was shameful and inexcusable, and, younger brother or not, it was up to Darius to tell him so.

He changed CDs deftly with one hand, and the mellow sounds of jazz sax filled the car. It was one of the discs he had listened to during his late night run down from Casuarinas with Mahalia, and the sound alone was enough to fill his nostrils with the memory of her scent. He murmured her name, his tongue heavy with regret. He missed her already.

When he eventually drew up to Phillip's tall, black wrought-iron gates, his anger had not subsided. In fact, at the sight of the sprawling home, with its well-appointed, well-lit grounds and general glow of wealth and taste, his bile rose. Mahalia was hardly suffering for money; in fact, her writing had made her quite comfortable. But the idea of Phillip ensconced in his mansion, sealed off from the world and its cares, angered Darius. Phillip paid child support; that much Darius knew, and Phil had never been tightfisted, so he assumed that the sum was adequate. But that was not all a child needed. A child needed a father, and the knowledge that that father respected his mother enough to share in the cares of child rearing. Neither Mahalia nor Will had received that respect, and that, above all things, enraged Darius. No woman should be obliged to raise a child, especially a special-needs child, alone.

Darius levered himself out of the car and hammered on the intercom button, sending, he knew, a peal of bells throughout the large house. He pounded again, and then settled for keeping his thumb pressed against it. If that didn't get Phillip up, nothing would.

There was a crackle of static, and an irritated voice barked, "What?"

"Get up, Phillip."

Like a jungle animal roused from deep sleep, Phillip grunted again, his irritation level rising. "Who is this? Do you have any idea what time it is?"

Darius glanced at his watch. "It's twenty to two, and it's Darius. Get up, Phillip, and open the gate. Now."

The tone of Phillip's voice became slightly less aggressive, and a little concerned. "Dar? Is it really you? Is something wrong?"

"Yes, on both counts. You opening or not?"

There was a creaking sound, and the huge, heavy gates began to swing open. Darius had to sidestep them as they moved. Not bothering to drive through, or even to lock his car, he stomped along the long driveway that led to his brother's house. Around him, large cacti loomed, and yucca plants cast long shadows. Bleached gravel crunched underfoot, and somewhere nearby, water tinkled gently in one of Phillip's artificial water features. It was like stepping into a desert scene—if nature had had the presence of mind to have its deserts laid out with mathematical precision, perfect balance, and flawless landscaping.

At the top of the drive, the house sprawled lazily, like a fat, pampered, nonchalant dog. The entire thing was surrounded by a wraparound deck of aged, rough-hewn wood that was so expertly laid that it made not a sound as he stepped onto it. Huge baskets of ferns hung from the rafters, and overstuffed loungers competed with swaying Mexican hammocks over which looked more comfortable.

The heavy wooden door swung open, and in the half-light Darius could see the broad shape of his brother, dressed in a maroon terry robe. Even roused from bed, Phillip looked well groomed, urbane, and handsome. "Dar?"

Darius shoved his way past Phillip, into the foyer, and turned to face his brother.

Phillip let the door swing silently closed and peered at him, his mind still half groggy with sleep, brows drawn together with concern. "Did something happen to Mama?"

"No."

"Dad?"

"No. The family's fine." Darius folded his arms across his chest in a self-protective gesture, trying to steel his nerves. Anger had fueled his flight over here, but now, face-to-face, he remembered the fifteen years that separated his brother and himself, and the lifetime of hero worship that had characterized their relationship. Phil had always been his god, his alpha-dog. When they did things, they did things his way. Could Darius really chew him out?

Phillip's voice was strained, but patient. "If nothing's wrong with the family, then what brought you here? Not even *God's* up at this hour." He squinted into his younger brother's face. "You drunk?"

Darius dismissed the idea with a snort. "You know I don't do that."

"Then, I presume you have a damn good excuse." Phillip's patience was beginning to ebb. He folded his arms as well, mimicking Darius's stance. "Let me ask you again. What brings you here?"

Mahalia, his brain shouted. *Mahalia, Mahalia, Mahalia.* And her son, his nephew. "Mahalia Derwood," he answered shortly, and waited for a reaction.

He got one. Phillip's jaw dropped. "You know Mahalia Derwood? How?" He floundered, trying to figure things out. Then, his jaw set on edge, and he spoke through gritted teeth. "What, did she track you down? Did she get to you? What does she want? More money? She come to you with some sad story—"

Darius cut him off. "No, Phil, she didn't 'get to me.' At least—" At least, not in the way Phillip meant. He replaced that thought with, "She didn't track me down."

"So, then, how did you meet her?"

"She is . . . she was my employer."

Phillip was incredulous. "Her? She's the werewolf woman? *Mahalia's* your writer?"

"Yes, she is." Then, he added sarcastically, "Small world, isn't it?"

Phillip scratched his head, looking mildly amused. "I can't believe it. That little mouse, a hotshot writer. I mean, it's true she was a fine arts major, when I knew her." He looked like an old man trying to dredge up half-forgotten memories from the dark recesses of his mind. "Did okay, too. But I never figured her for the kind of woman who'd have the drive to make something of herself. Who'd have thought it?"

Darius leaped to her defense. "She's extremely talented—"

Phillip lifted his hands as if to shield himself from his protests. "All right, all right. I get you. She's Pulitzer material. And she's your boss. But what does that have to do with—"

"You have a son with her!"

Phillip waved dismissively. "Correction. She had a baby. It turned out to be mine. There's a difference."

"I *know* there's a difference. That's why I'm here. What I want to know is: do *you* know the difference?"

Phillip looked resigned to a prolonged conversation, and sidestepped Darius, heading into the expansive living room. He threw open the doors of a paneled cabinet and brought out two shot glasses. "Scotch? It's good stuff."

"You know I don't drink hard."

Phillip shrugged, and his smile held a hint of malice. "Soda pop, then?"

"Nothing," Darius responded tightly. "I'm fine."

Phillip poured his scotch neat, drank half, and set his glass down. "Okay, so tell me now—"

A noise from above made them both turn. At the top of the stairs that led to the bedrooms stood a tiny, exquisite Chinese woman. From where Darius stood, she couldn't have been more than five feet tall, if that much. Her heart-shaped face glowed in the dim light, the color of a peeled almond. She was wearing a maroon robe, identical to Phillip's. Darius wondered fleetingly if his brother had an entire collection of them, in a variety of sizes, to offer to any one of his many female visitors.

"Phillip? What's going on? You coming back to bed soon?"

"Soon enough," he answered dismissively, and then remembered his manners. He indicated Darius. "This is my baby brother, Darius."

The "baby" thing rankled, but Darius said nothing. He nodded politely.

"And this beauty here, is . . ." Phillip hesitated for a millisecond, fishing for a name, but recovered gracefully. ". . . is Kim. Kim, Darius."

Kim didn't look too pleased at the interruption. Instead of acknowledging Darius's presence, she tilted her pretty head in Phillip's direction. "Bed's cold."

"There's an electric blanket in the closet next to the bathroom. Second shelf. Get under it and wait." Then, he softened his command. "I'll be up soon, kitten. Keep things warm there for me. All right?"

The tiny woman pouted, but returned resignedly the way she had come. As though they had never been interrupted, Phillip asked him again, "So, let me ask you again. What brings you here, and why couldn't it wait until morning?"

Darius recovered from his discomfiture at discovering that he had interrupted his brother with a woman, enough to retort, "I want to know why you haven't done more for her, and for the child. My *nephew.*"

Phillip's laugh was mocking. "Your *nephew?* Oh, come on. Give me a break. Blood ties don't translate into a relationship."

"Will and I *have* a relationship. And we had it long before I discovered who he really was."

"Good for you. Enjoy. But don't come here telling me I have to have one with him, too."

"Phillip, think of our father. Think of the kind of man he is. He never raised us to treat a woman like that! And what about Mama? She taught us that women need respect!"

"I left home a long time ago." Phillip finished his drink and poured himself another, this time not bothering to make even a symbolic offer to Darius.

"And you left behind everything our parents ever taught us about decency?"

"And I became a man. An example you might do well to follow. This isn't Sugar-Candy Mountain. This is the real world. Things don't always go the way you want them to."

"There's common decency in the real world, too. And responsibility."

Phillip gave a pained sigh, like an irritated parent fatigued by the nagging of a child. "What exactly would you have wanted me to do, Darius? Marry her? I don't think so. I did what needed to be done. I did what thousands of men wouldn't. I acknowledged my responsibility, set up an account, and made sure that a nice fat check would turn up in it, on the first of every month, just like clockwork.

She didn't tell you about *that* when she sent you over here to whine on her behalf, did she?"

Mahalia, send him over here? Hardly. She didn't even want to see him again. But he didn't tell his brother this. "I came over here on my own. She had nothing to do with it."

"So, what did you come for?"

"To tell you that money isn't enough. Not to a child."

"It's as far as I'm prepared to go." Phillip had that obstinate, self-righteous look that some people got when they felt they had the power of their convictions on their side, even in the face of all evidence that they were in the wrong. His bearded chin jutted, a wall of determination between himself and further persuasion.

"Go further."

"And do *what?*"

"Be a father. Even if it's not full-time. You've never even met him. Not in any real sense. Why can't you spend time with him? Take him to the circus. Take him to the zoo. Be there for him. Be a man, for God's sake!"

Incredibly, his brother's shoulders began to shake. Darius stared, not sure if Phillip had taken leave of his senses. An obscenity sprang to his lips, but it was quickly overtaken by derisive laughter. "Darius, Darius, Darius. Kid brother—"

"Don't call me that!"

It was as if he had never even protested. "Let me explain something to you." Phillip set his glass down again, carefully, so as not to spill a drop. Then, in a single, swift movement, he kicked at the densely woven rug at his feet. "See this?"

Darius wasn't in the mood for games. "What of it?" he grunted.

"Iranian. Had it smuggled into the country in 1997. Cost a bundle, I can tell you. And it's flawless." He lifted his arm, throwing it up and away from him in a commanding gesture. "Look. See that painting?" He didn't wait for acknowledgement from Darius. "Barcelona, 1999. A little imitative; there's an element of Picasso about it. But by the time I'm fifty, I'll be able to sell it for three times what I paid for it, and in the meantime it looks just fine, hanging where it is. And it's also flawless."

He seized a small, black carved statuette from an end table, closed the space between them, and thrust it under Darius's nose. "Rhino horn. Kenya, 2002. Customs agents would wet themselves if they even knew I'd brought it across the border. And it's perfect."

"Get to the point," Darius ground out, repulsed by the objet d'art of which his brother was so proud, and which had cost an endangered animal its life. But deep in his gut, he knew what the point was, and that repulsed him even more.

Phillip evidently preferred to drag it out; a natural-born braggart, he was enjoying himself. He expanded his arms to embrace the whole world, his broad chest heaving. "This house: bought it for a mint, and spent another mint tailoring it to my specifications. I've got two men spending three days a week in the grounds, going over it with nail scissors and a fine-toothed comb. The room I sleep in, the food I put in my mouth, the clothes on my back: all perfect. Flawless in every way."

"Don't say it, Phil," Darius pleaded. It was bad enough to know his brother thought it, but he couldn't bear to hear it said.

Phillip was in no mood to be kind. "Given all this, given the man you know me to be, what in the world makes you think I'm willing to be father to Mahalia Derwood's *im*-perfect, flawed, mentally defective little boy?"

Darius had the brief sensation of being airborne, and before he could bring a halt to the madness, his long, lean body collided with the wall of muscle that was his brother. It was like a thrown spear making contact with a water buffalo's thick hide. Phillip, not expecting the attack, staggered slightly, but was strong enough to maintain his balance even under the force of the blow. Darius felt the thick pile of Phillip's bathrobe crumple under his fingers, and realized that his other arm was raised above his head, poised to strike.

Phillip's black eyes were holes filled with a hellish fire. "What are you going to do, Dar? Hit me?"

He wanted to. He dearly wanted to. The face of the little boy, who had muscled his way into his heart without any warning, loomed before his eyes. It was immediately replaced by his mother's. Phil's taunt made his fist itch, but fraternal love stayed it like the hand of God descending between them, forcing it back down to his side. He released his grip on Phillip's lapel, but his brother was unrepentant. The mocking twist of his lips branded Darius a coward for not seeing it through, but he said nothing.

Darius filled the stifling silence. "He's a child!"

"He's a mistake." Phillip was matter-of-fact, as though he were discussing an architectural flaw, rather than a human being who shared his genes. "He's a freak of nature. Kids like that, they don't know a thing. They just lock themselves up in their own little world, and refuse to come out. It's sick. He probably doesn't speak."

"He speaks just fine," Darius defended.

Phillip shrugged. It was all the same to him. "Whatever. If his mother had listened to me, she wouldn't have had that burden to bear today. I tried to reason with her, get her to do the intelligent thing and solve the problem from the get-go. While she still had the chance. I offered to pay for it. She decided to be a martyr. She wouldn't hear of it." He held his hands out to Darius, palms up, in a gesture that said, *What else do you want me to say?*

"So, you've washed your hands of him."

"I told you, I haven't washed anything. I pay my dues. Just don't expect me to be his daddy."

Darius felt heartsick and disheartened. He felt slightly foolish for having stormed over here, as though he honestly thought he could have done something. Been an advocate for Will, defended Mahalia's honor. What had he expected? He tasted failure, and it was bitter and rank. *Leave,* he said to himself. *Just go. You've wasted your time, embarrassed yourself, and damn near hit your own brother.* His entire body went slack with defeat.

But before Darius could murmur his good-byes, the Devil himself flitted across Phillip's handsome face, bringing his hobgoblin, Malice, with him. "Although, Dar," Phillip said casually, "from the sound of our conversation on the phone earlier this evening, you look as though you're fixing to fulfill that role yourself. A little taken with her, aren't you?"

The searing pain of Mahalia's dismissal was still fresh and sore, not having benefited from the curative effects of time. He winced. "Phillip, it's over. Let it rest. I'm sorry I stormed in here, and I'm sorry I disturbed you. Forgive me. But leave Mahalia alone."

Phillip was not in a forgiving mood. He pressed on relentlessly. "You sleeping with her?"

A muscle in Darius's jaw spasmed.

Phillip tilted his head back and closed his eyes, dredging up memories that had been buried under rubble for a decade. "Ah, little Hailie Derwood. Needy little thing, isn't she? But sweet, sweet . . ."

Darius could barely force the words from his paper-dry throat. "Stop. Stop."

Phillip hadn't heard him—or chose not to. "Didn't know a damn thing. Green as a Granny Smith apple, and just as fresh. She came to me all shrink-wrapped in plastic, and I had to bust the seal to get at the toy inside. Know what I mean? Unlearned, but bright and willing. Not all that pretty, but sweet enough to make what could have been a tiresome task a really delightful challenge. For a time."

Darius glanced around the room before letting his eyes flicker back to his brother's spite-distorted face. Was the house on fire? His skin was burning. His feet were blistering, as if the leather of his shoes was searing and sticking to his skin. Surely, if there was no fire, then he had a fever.

He'd scarcely come to grips with the knowledge that Mahalia and his brother had once been lovers. His knee-jerk instinct toward revulsion had been replaced by his rational acceptance that every woman came to a man, and every man came to a woman, with some sort of past. That was the way it was. Nobody was a clean slate. The fact that there were indelible markings scratched upon her slate by a familial hand shouldn't make any difference. He was a rational man, and he cared deeply enough for this woman to get past that.

But this ugly mockery was something he wasn't prepared for. Phillip, speaking about Mahalia as he did about any casual encounter, any insignificant woman who was willing to be blinded by his charms and allow herself to be used and disposed of at his whim. An arrow of boiling rage shot upward from Darius's stomach, until he could taste it at the back of his mouth. Again, he begged his brother to have mercy, and hold his tongue. "Phil, you don't understand. I'm in love with this woman. I'm asking you, brother to brother, please—"

Phillip barreled on, and each word was a rock, hurled at Darius's head. "At least I hope I taught her something, for your benefit. Hope you're able to reap the rewards of the lessons I took the time to—"

"That's enough!" Darius found himself close enough to feel Phillip's whiskey-tainted breath on his face, and he had no idea how he had gotten there.

"Brother to brother? That's appropriate. Big brother to little brother. From me to you—just like everything else you've ever had in your life. The first pair of jeans you ever wore were mine first. You didn't get them until I was too big to have any use for them anymore. By the time your textbooks got to you, my name was scrawled all over them. Your first car was an old heap I didn't have any more use for. And now you're doing it again: scrounging for my leftovers. My hand-me-downs—"

A knuckle-crunching blow hurled Phillip clear across the room, sending him crashing into the drinks cabinet. The door flew open on impact, and the fine crystal scotch decanter smashed to the floor, along with several heavy glasses. Unprepared, Phillip was unable to defend himself, and before he could get up, or even raise his arms, Darius pounded his fist down several more times, feeling skin split and warm blood flow. His rage fed off the smell of the blood, growing larger and more deadly.

But Phillip was fit, hard, and strong, and outweighed Darius by an easy forty pounds. He recovered in time to wrap his arms around his brother and slam him down onto his back like an ancient Greco-Roman wrestler, and then brought the full brunt of his weight down upon him.

Grasping each other, locked in a furious embrace, the men rolled across Phillip's prized Iranian rug, knocking down anything in their way. The coffee table tipped over, sending the rhino-horn carving skittering across the parquet like a fallen chess piece. Punches were blocked and traded. They were boys again, scrabbling in the dirt of their parents' backyard, but this time they weren't fighting over marbles. Darius found his blows propelled by years of sibling rivalry and frustration at the belittlement and dismissal that had always tempered his brother's love for him. Hailie might have been the catalyst for the first punch, but there was more at stake now: his manhood, and his independence.

Phillip pinned him onto his back, straddling his chest. One hand was encircled around his neck, bringing pressure onto his Adam's apple. The other was raised, ready to strike. "Say you've had enough!" he grunted.

Darius reached up and caught the fist, twisting it painfully, feeling tendons stretch, buying himself enough time to heave his brother off of him. He wriggled out from underneath and got to his feet. There was a loud clanging of bells in one ear, and he wondered if his hearing would ever be the same. His eye hurt, as did the cheekbone directly below it. Salty liquid smeared his lips.

Phillip was crouched again in a fighter's stance, inviting another attack. "Come on! Come on!" He didn't look much better than Darius felt. Welts and bruises marred his handsome face, and the dark maroon of his robe was a deeper red in places.

Darius spat the blood out, disgusted with both of them. "I'm not going to hit you again."

"Coward!" Phillip taunted.

"No. I'm done. It's finished. I'm not hitting you again." He found the door, a difficult task with his eye rapidly swelling shut. As he threw it open, the chilly air was like a dose of smelling salts, clearing his head, bringing a semblance of sanity.

But Phillip, drunkened by the brawl, wouldn't let it rest. "Don't turn your back on me!" He followed Darius outside into his perfect garden, unfazed by the cold night air. "You were always the baby! Mama spoiled you! *I* spoiled you! I gave you everything you ever had. I made you what you are!"

Darius stopped before the car, and fished for and found his keys. He opened the door and, without getting in, started the engine before he answered. When he did, his own calm surprised him. "*I* made me what I am. Nobody else." He lifted his arm and pointed it at Phillip in command, and his voice was like gravel and steel. "And don't you ever, ever speak that way about Mahalia, or Will, again. Do you hear me, *brother?*"

Phillip gnawed at his ravaged lower lip and looked about to speak. Then, thinking better of it, he dropped his eyes, did an about-turn, and made his way back into his house, leaving Darius standing alone under the clear, crisp, starry sky.

Twelve

Hailie groaned and turned over. The floor under her was hard, and even the thick blanket that she had tossed onto it proved not to be adequate compensation for that. Her head ached, and her limbs felt sore, stiff, and bruised, but she knew that it was better that she spend the night in her room, bed or no bed, than share the guest room with her son and subject him to her tossing and turning. Just because she couldn't sleep didn't mean he should be deprived of his.

She lay on her back and drew her knees up to her chest, trying in vain to stretch the kinks out of her spine. She should never have given up yoga. She brought her feet back to the floor and took three deep breaths. Would she ever have the strength to get up?

"Oh, Darius," she murmured. "Why've you done this to me?"

She wasn't sure if she was more angered or saddened by the way things had gone last night. Her initial reaction had been that Darius had known right from the start who she was and what role she had played in his brother's life. They must have cooked up some kind of bizarre scheme between them, for whatever reason and to whatever end, to infiltrate her life and cause her more pain.

But that was ludicrous. If Phillip Grant had wanted to

confront her, he was more than capable of doing so in person, or even of siccing his lawyers on her; after all, paying someone else to do his dirty work wasn't beyond the man. Why bring his kid brother in on whatever nebulous scheme he had in mind? Even Phillip wouldn't torture her that way, not because he was too kind, but because he simply couldn't be bothered.

Besides, Darius's surprise had been genuine. As little as she now trusted him, she could see that. He had honestly not known that the man who had devastated her young life, wreaked havoc on her emotions, and left her with a permanent reminder of his presence, had been his own brother.

Hailie laughed softly, surprising herself, even though the laugh was mirthless and flat. She rolled her eyes upward, looking past the ceiling that covered her and into the heavens beyond. "You guys have a great sense of humor," she said to all the gods of the pantheon. "Funny. Very funny."

Of all the men in the world she could have chosen to fall for, she had to go falling for two from the same litter. It was as unlikely as swimming in the ocean and being bitten by the same shark—twice.

Admittedly, the Grant name had thrown her, but it hadn't made her cautious. Grant was a common name, after all, and she had believed that Darius was Detroit born and bred. Physically, two brothers couldn't have been less alike. As far as personality was concerned, Darius had been as kind as Phillip hadn't. He had been a generous and comforting lover, where Phillip had been demanding, even derisive of her ignorance and inexperience.

Darius had taken to Will instantly, and Will had taken to him, as though the bonds of blood had cried out to each other, and been heard. He'd spent more time with him, and showed him more respect in a few short days, than his own father had in a lifetime.

Hailie snorted again, her laugh transforming into something more contemptuous. The attraction between man and boy had had nothing to do with blood. If that had been so, then surely his own father would have felt the same tug on his heartstrings! They'd just been two strangers, enjoying each other's company, and sharing a love for art, color, form, and line.

But that didn't mean she could trust Darius. He was, after all, a Grant, and Grant was spelled t-r-o-u-b-l-e. One of them had hurt her badly enough for her to know that she had no business trusting her heart to another. She'd sooner welcome the plague into her own home than let Darius near her again.

"Never," she vowed, and her vehemence gave her enough energy to propel herself into a standing position. Immediately, she howled, as a cramp seized her calf muscle and wrenched it. She hobbled around the room, placing one hand along the wall for support as she tried to walk it off, cursing aloud. Damn the man for making her sleep on the floor, and making her feel so lousy in the first place. Damn him for being so nice to her, making her stupid enough to think she could try again. Damn him for making her love him, and then turning out to be the one thing she couldn't and shouldn't have.

She stopped short, forgetting the pain that twisted her calf like a wet rag in a wringer. Love. Darius. In the same sentence. What a load of rubbish. She'd been willing to believe it last night, but that had been the wine talking. Daylight and sobriety changed one's perspective, made the vision clearer. It was no more than a crush, fueled by loneliness. She'd fallen into . . . something. Something warm and twinkling, his eyes reflected somewhere inside her. Something sensual, sexy, drawing her to him like a silky thread tugging at her from deep inside.

She dismissed it with a twist of her lips. Lust. Hunger, need, desire, attraction, hormones, want. Not love. Surely, if they had not run into those two characters, Charles and Angela, she'd be waking up in Darius's arms in his hotel room, somewhere across town, her hunger slaked, her need fulfilled. She'd tasted what he had to offer once, and she knew it was good—very good. She was almost resentful of the other couple's intrusion, because with their news they had robbed her of what she wanted, and the opportunity to return home sated, drunk with good loving, able to put the ache of physical hunger behind her, and get on with the business of setting her house back to rights.

Darius would have given her that, at least, and she was sorry he hadn't.

But that didn't mean what she felt for him was love.

She'd loved Phillip, with every ounce of her uninitiated young heart. She'd loved him totally and completely, although everyone had warned her not to. Even though half the girls in her dorm had already slept with him and the other half wanted to, they all knew the score. They'd tried to tell her that Phillip Grant was not that kind of animal, and that she was authoring her own destruction by loving him so hard. But she hadn't listened. Too young to take control of her emotions, to learn to feel with her head rather than her heart, she'd let herself love him, wholeheartedly, completely, and foolishly, even when he had tired of her and become cruel, doing his best to make her leave. She'd loved once, and once was just about as much as a body could take.

"Not again." She spoke aloud, even though she was unaware of it. "Never again." Determination and the need for self-preservation put steel in her spine.

Outside, she could smell bacon, and heard Coretta

humming as she moved noisily about in the kitchen. Hailie realized she was hungry. She hadn't eaten much last night, not after the bombshell had fallen. She sat down at the breakfast nook, and was pleased to feel Veda Two's welcoming brush against her ankles.

"Morning, Coretta." Hailie sniffed the air hard, drawing in the scent of breakfast sizzling on the stove, overlaid with coffee perking.

Coretta gave her a dark look, proving in that one simple gesture that she hadn't forgiven her for depriving her of the opportunity to tear a strip off of Darius's hide last night. "You almost mean 'good afternoon'! You got any idea what time it is? I waiting on you whole morning to get breakfast started. I decide I better go ahead anyway, before the rest of us starve."

Hailie took her chastisement in stride. "Smells good," she said, in an attempt to mollify her offended housekeeper.

Coretta shrugged. "Bacon always smell like bacon. Nothing different about this particular set."

Hailie poured herself a cup of coffee, resisting the urge to tip a dash of something stronger in there while she was at it, and then took a plate off the rack and set it down upon the counter in readiness. Coretta laid out the crisp strips of bacon onto paper napkins, turned off the stove with a loud click, and then surveyed her gravely.

"I'm starved," Hailie hinted broadly, and held her plate up.

"You going to keep on being starved, if you think you gonna be eating in that getup." She pointed at Hailie. "You look like the cat drag you in, beat you up, and toss you in the litter box."

It was only then that Hailie became aware that she had slept in last night's dress. She was a mess. The soft, clingy dress that had made her feel so sexy, so female, so alive as she swung out of the house on Darius's arm last night was now a creased, crumpled rag that sagged and bagged in all the wrong places. She wondered if she would ever be able to wear it again—or if, for that matter, she would want to.

"Oh." Her laugh was the first genuine one of the morning. "I forgot. I think I'd better take a shower and clean up."

"I think you better, too," Coretta agreed caustically.

Sighing like a martyr, Hailie relinquished her plate, but held on to her coffee. "Okay, I'll be back out in ten minutes. You can go ahead and feed Will, if you like. He must be wondering why he hasn't eaten yet."

"Hmmph!" Coretta twisted her nose as though she smelled something bad. "He don't want to eat anything. You think I'd have let him go so long without his breakfast? You know he like to eat on time. This morning he inform me he don't want to eat nothing yet."

Will? Not eat? Worry assailed Hailie. That never happened. Will had an appetite, and he loved bacon. "Is he sick?"

"Lovesick, if you ask me. He been sitting on the floor right in front the door, ever since he get up this morning. He say he not eating anything until Darius get here. You try to talk some sense into him, if you like, because I try and I try, and I ain't trying no more." Coretta tossed her towel in the sink in disgust at having to mention the dreaded name, and then set about serving her own breakfast. Hailie knew the older woman long enough to know that their conversation was over.

She went to find Will. He was exactly where Coretta had said he would be: seated on the floor, arms wrapped around his knees, mere inches from the front door, staring intently at it like an expectant dog waiting for his master's return. In his folded arms, he clutched something close to his bony chest. Hailie peered down to see what it was.

The comics Darius had given him yesterday. Damn the man; he'd provided the boy with just one more thing to obsess about. She wondered if Will had read any of them, or even opened one. He was probably just going to cling to them as he did to many other objects that took his fancy, like her shoes or articles of clothing. Maybe this new prize would remain the object of his desire until something else came along and replaced it. Or maybe, she groaned to herself, he was just waiting on Darius to turn up so they could read them together. Oh, God.

She squeezed between him and the door, and hunkered down. "Honey?"

Will lifted his eyes to her, and they were clear and bright. "Mommy!"

"What are you doing, sweetie?" she asked, although she already knew.

He looked at her as though that were the world's most inane question. "Darius is coming," he said.

"No," she told him gently. "He isn't." Not ever, she wanted to tell him, but she chickened out and said, "Not today. So why don't you come into the kitchen and have breakfast with Coretta and Mommy?"

"Darius is coming," he repeated, and held up his wristwatch to show her the time. If Darius had indeed been coming, he was long past due. For Will, time was a rule that shouldn't be broken. To his mind, Darius was late, and every minute that ticked by would make him more agitated.

"Well, you can eat something in the meantime, can't you?" She tried to keep her tone light, struggling to prevent her own anxiety from penetrating.

"I'll eat with Darius."

"I could bring it out here for you, and then you can eat while you wait," she cajoled.

"I'll eat with Darius."

Hailie recognized the stubborn, cautionary cast to Will's face. He was perfectly capable of throwing a tantrum if he didn't get his way, and she was treading a fine line between peace in her home and chaos.

But she ached inside. Which would be the greater evil? Letting him hope and wait in vain, or telling him, and risking one of Will's specialty tantrums, the kind that could last for days? And if she did tell him, what could she say?

She opted for the middle road. "Honey," she began timidly, "I don't think Darius is coming today."

Will's head snapped around. "Why?"

"I . . . I don't know. But he . . . he told me he wasn't coming. He said to tell you he'd miss you, but that we should go on and eat without him. Do stuff without him." She was a lousy liar. Will would sniff her out like a bloodhound would a dead rat.

Will's brows lifted in alarm. "Sick?"

She hastened to reassure him. "No, no, he's fine! He just—"

"Sick?" The voice was higher now, anxious, demanding. "Sick?"

"He's not sick, Will!" Her traumatic evening and lousy night had stretched her nerves to the snapping point, and her response was a little harsher than she had intended it to be. "Listen to me!"

"Darius!" Will leaped to his feet in alarm. "Darius! Darius!"

"Will, please," she pleaded.

She rose, too, but he eluded her and wrenched open the door. With his prized comics tucked under one arm, he pelted outside, barefoot, not even aware of the hard flagstones under his feet, and raced to the bottom of the drive, screaming the beloved name over and over. Panicked, Hailie pursued him, anxious to divert him before he hit the road.

But to her relief, he had more sense than to run out into the morning traffic. Instead, he stood at the curb, peering frantically in the direction from which Darius usually arrived. She threw her arms around him, almost sobbing, partly with relief that he had not put himself in danger, but partly, too, at the depth of the pain she had caused him.

"Come," she urged. "Come inside."

And then, the screaming began. When Will was much younger, these tantrums had occurred almost daily, for the most trivial of causes. He'd screamed because he was hungry, or because she'd taken away his favorite toy. He'd screamed when she left the house, and, according to Coretta, the keening had continued without letup until she returned. But recently, these spells had become rare, as Will developed a greater awareness of the world around him, and more self-control. He'd learned there were more ways, better ways, to get what he wanted.

Today, though, it would not be the case. The wail was high-pitched and piercing, like that of an agitated banshee, shattering the quiet of the street. She knew from experience that begging or demanding that he stop would be of no use. Will, once he began, was a runaway train. He'd wind down in his own time, and after his own fashion. It remained only for her to get him back inside again, before he caught himself a cold, barefoot as he was.

She tried to lead him, but he was immovable, rooted to the spot by sheer determination. She tried lifting him, but didn't make it very far. He'd grown somewhat since she'd last carried him. Winded, she set him down again, still a great distance from the door.

"What is all this godforsaken racket about?"

Hailie had never been so happy to hear the crotchety voice. Coretta was stomping down the path, her breakfast fork still clutched in one hand, glasses slipping off her face in indignation. She confronted Will, arms akimbo. "What all these good people on the street gonna say, when you start up with this racket? You sound like you calling up the dead, boy."

"Coretta," Hailie begged, "just help me get him inside." Her eyes held Coretta's buggy ones over the top of Will's head. "Please."

Coretta sucked her teeth long and hard, and then handed Hailie her fork. "Hold this."

Before Hailie could get over her surprise, Coretta lifted Will in a single, sweeping motion and made for the front door. It was all Hailie could do to keep up. Coretta carried him as far as the back room, and deposited him, still screaming a single, penetrating note, onto his bed. Will didn't seem aware of their presence, or of his change of location. He pressed his comic books to his chest, like flotation devices in wild waters, and bawled.

He had to be left alone until he calmed down. There was little else Hailie could do to help, and certainly nothing she could do to interrupt the tirade. Meekly, heart aching, she followed Coretta back outside and handed her breakfast fork back. "Thanks, Coretta," she said. Her body weighed a ton. She wondered if she'd make it as far as the couch before she crashed.

"That's what you get," Coretta said in response. It was a wonder she could get a word out: her lips were pressed together in a taut, disapproving line.

"Excuse me?"

"That's what you get for bringing people into your home, letting the boy make friends with them like that. You should just let him stick to your family. Family never leave you. Family always stick by you. But men, they come and go, and if you let the boy love them, all he gonna get is heartbreak."

He's not the only one suffering heartbreak, Hailie could have said, but the prospect of suffering Coretta's further derision halted her. She didn't even bother to counter the comment: Coretta was right: in fact, never bringing a man home was a rule she had set herself, for the very same reason. It wasn't right for Will to become attached to people, when there was no way of telling how long they would be in his life. Her desire for Darius had caused her to make an error in judgment. It was an error she would soon rectify.

A shower and a meal did nothing to improve her mood. When she was done forcing down what tasted like toasted cardboard and deep-fried leather, she looked in on her son. He was lying in bed, face to the wall. His persistent screams had abated somewhat, leaving in their wake a high-pitched keening that tugged on her heartstrings as strongly as the crying had. Will would continue crying until an exhausted, uneasy sleep claimed him.

She longed to run over to him and gather him in her arms, but experience had taught her that such a loving, impulsive maternal action was likely to bring on the screams again, so she shut the door quietly, cursing Darius for the hundredth time that day. He still managed to do damage to her family, even though he was not physically here.

As a matter of fact, she fully expected him to turn up at her doorstep, if not today, then sometime soon. He was, if nothing else, a determined man. His youthful impetuousness and self-assurance would not allow him to let things rest, even though she had been very clear in her dismissal of him, on both personal and professional levels, last night.

Yes, he would come again, cropping up unwanted like a case of the flu, with an armful of flowers or some such nonsense, hoping to charm her back, and when he did turn up—

"You got mail, Hailie. Hand-delivered special, it seems." Coretta's voice told her there was nothing special about whatever it was.

Hailie spun around, her back to Will's door. She recognized the proffered object at once, and practically snatched the rolled-up paper scroll from Coretta's hands. "Where did you find this?"

Coretta looked as though the paper smelled bad. "In your mailbox. I didn't see anybody pull up to the house today, so maybe he put it in there last night. If you'da listened to me last night, and give me half a minute more with him, he woulda never had the *chance* to put nothing in your box. The scoundrel."

Hailie didn't need to unroll the paper in her hand to know that it was the drawing of her and Darius, as Veda and Romulus, that had so charmed her last night. At the table, flushed with excitement and half drunk on Darius's mere presence, she had felt the drawing to be at once funny and sincere, sweet and tender. Now, it itched in the palm of her hand.

"Did you see what was inside?"

"Yes, I see what inside. How else I woulda know it was for you?" Coretta pursed her lips. "Nonsense. Some boys, they like Peter Pan. They never grow up. Wooing a lady with a comic book drawing. He couldn't bring you a bracelet or a nice bouquet like other men?"

He's not like other men, she wanted to protest, *and he is all grown up, more than most men I've found myself entangled with,* but then chided herself. Darius Grant could stick up for himself, even in the face of Coretta's fearsome wrath. He didn't need Hailie to do it for him, and furthermore, she didn't *want* to do it for him.

"That does it," she muttered through teeth so tightly gritted that her temples hurt.

"What?"

"Nothing." Abruptly, she walked away from the conversation, throwing over her shoulder, "I've got a call to make."

Once in her study, she shut the door, closed her eyes, and inhaled. The smell of polished wood and old books invaded her nostrils. Wall-to-wall bookshelves groaned under the combined weight of hundreds of books on every imaginable subject—although a significant proportion of them dealt with mythical creatures in general, and werewolves in particular. Her desk was flush against a wall, and above her computer monitor, framed covers of each of her books took pride of place, reminding her, each time she sat at her computer, of all that she had achieved as a writer.

She hadn't spent much time in here since her return home. It was her sanctuary, the quiet space where her muse waited for her each day when she logged on to begin work. This was the room she and Darius would have occupied, if they had ever managed to take a moment away from their home repair duties to actually *do* any work. Instead of spending his time fulfilling the contract he had undertaken, he had volunteered to oversee the builders, haggle with suppliers, and put more than his fair share of elbow grease into getting her home back into a livable state. Guilt at what she was about to do tugged at her, but she put it out of her mind as one would the chirping of an annoying insect. She picked up her phone and dialed.

The other side answered on the third ring, and a familiar male voice said crisply, "Yes?"

Her heart was thumping in her throat, adding its protest to that of the conscience insect that was determined to derail her intentions. "Tony?"

"Hailie!" As always, her agent sounded glad to hear from her—but then again, he was the consummate salesman. He was very good at sounding glad to hear from people. "How are you doing? How's the house coming along? Got it all fixed up yet? And how's your son? And dear Coretta—"

"Tony." She cut him off before he could entrench himself knee-deep into his schmoozing routine.

"Tell me." Tony, bless him, had sensed the note of urgency in her voice and immediately become all business.

"I need you to call your lawyers."

"And . . . ?"

"And have Darius Grant's contract terminated." She could all but hear Tony's jaw drop. Guilt writhed through her like a live wire. She'd thought about this all night, and by morning had been determined that this was the right thing, the only thing, to do. Darius was a dangerous man. He made her feel things she wasn't prepared to feel, and she wasn't stupid enough to ignore the fact that, despite her resolve last night, what they had—what little they had—was damned, and she knew in her heart that if he was near her again, working closely with her every day, her rickety resolve would slip. It was a mean thing to do, firing him for personal rather than professional reasons, but it all boiled down to a matter of survival—hers. She had to protect herself and her son from further hurt, dig a moat around the castle of her life, and fill it with all manner of vicious creatures. Pull up the drawbridge and hide, even though she knew it was the coward's way out. It was necessary, and had to be done. But why did it make her feel so bad?

Tony floundered on the other end of the line, his notorious composure slipping a little. "You want to . . . to fire Grant? But why?"

Why? What reason could she possibly give him? Certainly not a professional one. Darius had gone above and beyond his contract. He'd given more than any employee would be expected to, sticking by her even when half her home lay in ashes. What could she say?

"Is his work unsatisfactory? I don't understand. He came so highly recommended. And from what I've seen, he's brilliant. Don't you like his work?"

Hailie realized she was flicking the rolled-up drawing against her thigh, like the tail of an agitated cat. The deeply etched planes of Romulus's face came immediately to her mind. Under Darius's hand, her characters had taken on a life of their own: breathing, feeling, wanting, loving. Through his love of her work and his art, Darius had made her vision his. "His work is fine," she had to admit.

"Then what's the problem?" Tony's voice was becoming a little irritated. He wasn't a man who tolerated being denied information. Then he asked shrewdly, "So, if there's nothing wrong with his work, is it his . . . conduct?"

She knew what he was asking, and choked out her denial. "No. No, Tony, there's nothing wrong with his conduct. He's never been anything but a gentleman."

"Well, I hope so. Because I know how these young men can get a little out of line sometimes. If that's the problem, I can deal with it, you know. There are ways."

She shuddered to imagine what a man like Tony's "ways" could be. Hastily, she said, "No. He hasn't gotten out of line."

"Then why the hell are you throwing your best book down the toilet?" Tony exploded in exasperation. "Because that's exactly what you're doing. Do you have any idea how hard it will be to replace him? Do you know what goes into setting an artist search in motion? It takes months, Hailie. Months. And that's time you don't have. You're under contract, remember? And a sizable contract at that. You've already received your advance. First of all, if you fail to hold up your end of the bargain, your publisher will come down on you like a pile of bricks to return what you've been paid, and I don't think you can afford to give up that kind of money. I certainly can't. Second, you've already paid Grant *his* advance. If you fire him for no earthly reason—and if you actually have a reason, Lord knows, I can't fathom what it could possibly be—getting that back won't be a walk in the park."

"He can keep it," she said promptly.

"What?" Tony sounded as though she had begun to babble in a foreign language.

"Darius can keep his advance. I don't want it."

"You don't want your own money back? How could anybody not want money?" Tony was half a tick away from an apoplectic fit. Any trace of his urbane, jaded pleasantness was gone.

"Because all this isn't his fault. Because it's the least I can do." *Because he doesn't deserve this*, her little voice said, and this time it was hard to ignore.

"Mighty nice of you," Tony griped. "If you're going to toss away your career, you might as well toss away your hard-earned money, too. But don't say I didn't warn you. You're committing professional suicide—the slow way."

Hailie was growing tired, both of having to confront her own meanness and of the conversation. She rubbed her hand across her eyes. "Just do it for me, okay, Tony? Call him up, and explain to him what I've decided. I've already pretty much told him, so he won't be surprised. Tell him he'll be hearing from your lawyers, but in the meantime the termination is verbal, and binding. In case he's worried, tell him he can keep his advance—"

"Suicide," Tony muttered. "Suicide, I'm telling you."

"Just do it, Tony," she said firmly. She had to remind herself that *she* had engaged Tony to perform services for *her*, and not the other away around. In the end, the final decision was always hers.

"I will," he answered sourly, well aware that there was nothing he could do. But he wasn't rolling over without getting the last word in. As he hung up, she was sure she heard him mutter, "It's your funeral."

Hailie set her phone down, feeling cold, bereft, and guilty as sin. Perhaps she would manage to snatch her career out of the jaws of failure by finding someone else, someone competent, and fast. Her name was big enough in the industry to draw at least a few contenders. The career that was about to suffer would be Darius's, not hers.

She'd been his big break, a chance to make a splash in the one domain he'd always ached to be a part of. And in her cowardice, she'd scuttled that for him. She hoped he would forgive her. Pinpricks tingled at the back of her eyes, and acid stung her lashes.

It's your funeral. Even as the tears threatened to spill, she had an image, ludicrous under the circumstances, of Darius telling her, in expansive detail, all about his prize-winning cockroach funeral art campaign. It elicited a painful grin that was more of a rueful grimace. As serious as he was, as intense as he could be, he was funny too, and rarely failed to make her laugh.

She became aware that she was crushing the scroll of paper in her hand, and looked down at it. She spread it out on her desk, smoothing out the wrinkles, and cocked her head on one side to look at it. Romulus and Veda. Darius and her. The lines between the real and the imaginary had become blurred, and that was what had made him dangerous.

She sucked her teeth, a habit she'd picked up from Coretta at her most irascible, crushed the paper into a ball, and threw it into the wastepaper basket with an emphatic *thud*. Without a backward glance, she exited her study and shut the door.

Moments later, the door flew open again, and, like a puppet on a string, she found herself being impelled toward the basket. She withdrew the now sad and crumpled drawing and smoothed it out a second time, and then, unable to bear looking at it, buried it under a pile of rubble at the back of a drawer, slamming it shut.

Thirteen

Detroit, in the dead of winter, was a far cry from California. The sky seemed to have difficulty deciding whether to rain or snow, and by the time Darius made it to his apartment door he was covered in sludge. Kid gloves made it difficult for him to find and select the right keys, which hung from a large brass ring with a miscellany of others, most of which he no longer had any use for, much less remembered what they had opened in the first place.

Finally, the lock gave, and the door creaked open. Stale air, the kind that said that nobody had lived here in weeks, greeted him as he tossed his bags onto the floor. Even in the face of biting cold, the place cried out for an open window, just to let a fresh breath in.

"Already froze my butt off," he reasoned. "Can't get any colder than this." He lifted the latches and threw up the sashes on the three living room windows that faced the street, immediately filling the room not only with a fresh, crisp wind, but also with the impatient sounds of traffic teeming in the street several floors below.

The tranquillity of Casuarinas, and the sedate peace of Mahalia's home, had spoiled him. The irritable honks and beeps that normally were for him an urban lullaby, now grated on his already fragile nerves. He was tired. Bad weather had delayed his flight, and what would have been a four-thirty homecoming had stretched into an eight o'clock arrival. He looked at his watch. Nine-thirty. Even the ride from the airport had taken longer than it should have. He was damp, tired, miserable, and upset . . . and he knew that he'd never be able to fall asleep.

Without even removing his jacket, shoes, or gloves, he paced the small apartment, moving from living room to kitchen, throwing open the cupboards and rummaging around inside like a bored bear. He was hungry, but there was nothing there that could even tease his appetite. He circled the apartment again, motion offering distraction to his teeming mind.

Mahalia. Phillip. His thoughts veered from one to the other, skating back and forth at the speed of light. He would be hard-pressed to decide which of them had caused him the most anguish. It was now three long days since Mahalia's agent had turned up at his doorstep with a lawyer in tow and a briefcase of papers for him to sign, papers that effectively relieved him of any legal obligations to her, or vice versa. That alone had been as bad a shock as he had ever suffered. True, she had told him vehemently, that last night at her house, that she thought their business relationship would be better off ended, but part of him had been convinced that she had only been speaking in the heat of the moment, and that a day's cooling off would bring the realization that professionally, at least, they had been made for each other. Maybe, he had rationalized, when he arrived at her place again, ready to work, he would have been able to try, albeit slowly, to rebuild . . . something.

But she'd cut to the chase and sent a mouthpiece, too cowardly to come on her own. He was both disappointed and wounded. As promised, she'd let him keep the advance she'd paid, and he could fathom no reason for this other than that she knew he needed it. That cut into his pride more deeply than the presence of the lawyer had. That she was a woman of means had never presented any problem for his self-esteem, but the knowledge that she felt he needed her charity did.

He cursed, and looked around him for something to do. He was too restless to read or to sit and watch TV, and his mind was whirring much too fast to allow him to draw, if there was anything he wanted to draw in the first place. In desperation, he did what most people did when returning home after time away: he checked his voice mail.

It was the usual stuff: calls from friends and acquaintances he'd neglected to remind that he would be away for a while, calls from his bank, telemarketers, and a handful of miscellaneous nuisances that he wouldn't have to deal with until the next morning.

And then there was a call from Mama. "Darius, it's your mother. Now you listen to me. I know you're headed back to Detroit, because your hotel says you've left. I don't care what time you get in, you call me as soon as you get this message. I mean that, boy. Wake me up if you have to. You've got some explaining to do." The message clicked off, but not before the phone slammed down in his ears, the recorded anger as evident as it would have been in real time.

Darius groaned. Mama was mad, and it didn't take a genius to guess why. Somehow, she'd gotten wind of his fight with Phillip, and he knew Estelle Grant well enough to know that waiting her out would be akin to trying to wait out a pit bull with blood in its nostrils. He checked his watch again, but it wasn't a whole lot later than it had been the last time he looked. Might as well face the music now, rather than let it sit there and grow inside Mama like a tumor. Reluctantly, he dialed.

The phone picked up, and a man's voice, much like Phil's but more mellow, with a greater maturity to it, answered. "Hello?"

"Dad?"

"Darius? Oh, son, it's you. I had a mind you'd be calling."

Darius wasn't sure he liked how that sounded. "Why?"

"Because your mother has been storming around the kitchen all day, banging on pots and pans, slamming the fridge door, and calling your name. Calling you a whole bunch of things I don't think you want to hear. And I think you can guess who didn't get any lunch today, even with all the noise she was making in here."

So he was right. Mama had found out about the altercation he'd had with Phillip, and she wasn't happy. He resigned himself to his fate. "Yes, well, whatever she's been saying *about* me, I guess now she can say them directly *to* me. You want to pass the phone over to her?"

"All right. But if you need help, just holler. And if you need a body bag, I'm sure that can be arranged." With that, he gave a sympathetic chuckle, and then the line was silent for a while. Darius heard the further rumble of his father's voice, and a brief, muted conversation followed.

"That him?" he heard his mother say, in the kind of voice she used to assume when they were boys, and somebody had a good hiding coming to them. "Took him long enough. Keeping me sitting here waiting. Hand him over. I'll deal with this."

His father handed the phone over with very little reluctance, and the last thing Darius heard his mother say was, "All right, Lonnie, go read your paper or something. Let me talk to my son alone."

His father didn't answer: he knew his wife better than to argue. A few seconds later, when Darius presumed his mother was alone, the storm cloud broke. "Darius? Is that you?"

"Yes," he confirmed unnecessarily, and steeled himself for the assault.

He didn't have long to wait. "What's all this nonsense

about you and Phillip brawling like two wild animals?
What's this I hear about the two of you rolling around on
the floor, punching each other's lights out, like you grew
up in the gutter? Like you aren't blood relations? Huh?
Like I didn't make the two of you get dressed every Sun-
day morning of your lives, and hike your little tails off to
church? Didn't you grow up in a Christian family? Didn't
you? Did your father and I raise you to be heathens? Did
we raise you to be animals? Answer me! Your sisters
wouldn't have behaved like that, scratching each other's
eyes out. Oh, no, your sisters would have sorted it out
like adults, with breeding. Whatever it was, they'd have
talked about it, at the very least. How come the two of
you grew up in the same house with them, and you can't
settle your differences like they would?"

Darius waited until Mama ran out of breath, but for a
slender woman she had a powerful set of lungs on her,
and it was a long while coming. When he finally heard
the sharp, indrawn breath that signaled a pause, he
stepped in. "How did you know about it, anyway?" Phillip
might have been many things, but he wasn't the sort of
man who went running to his mother.

"How do I know? How do I know? I'm your mother,
that's how I know. I went over there today after church,
looking to have lunch with my son, hoping my *other* son
would turn up, since he was in California and all, and
never even bothered to drop by all the time he was
there. And I find Phillip there with a black eye like he's
been in the ring with George Foreman. And bruises all
over. Your brother's got a lip like he caught it in a door!
Are you proud of yourself?"

You should see my *face,* he could have said, but refrained.
"Mama, it was just one of those things. It happened. It was
wrong, and I'm sorry for it, but it happened, and there's
nothing I can do to change that."

"Just happened? Things like that don't 'just happen.' Somebody's got to make it happen. He's your big brother! Your only brother, who loves you so much. Who never did you wrong. After all he's done for you! After all he's given you! Where would you be, Darius, if it weren't for Phillip?"

Darius felt his stomach wrench. That had been the final, cruel taunt that Phillip had thrown in his face. Everything he was, he was because his brother had made him so. His successes would not have been his, if it had not been for the influence, the guidance, and, he had to face it, the money that Phillip had provided over the years. It was then that he became aware that his humiliation had followed him home from California.

"What was it all about anyway?" Mama demanded.

Mahalia's face loomed before him, even when he shut his eyes to keep her out. Her scent filled his nostrils. *It was all about a woman,* he wanted to say, *a very special woman I fell in love with when I least expected it. When I wasn't looking. It was about a woman who had a child by my brother, only I just found out about* that *part, and now everything we had, or I thought we had, has suddenly gotten too complex.*

But he couldn't say it, not only because the truth about Phillip's progeny, and the existence of a grandchild that Mama didn't even know she had, was Phillip's story, and not his, to tell. He didn't say it because the knot in his belly told him that this wasn't true. He'd gone over to Phillip's house because of Mahalia; that was true. He'd turned up at two in the morning full of righteous indignation, ready to defend a lady's honor. But when had he really hit Phillip? When Phil had taunted him, not about his relationship with Mahalia, but about the fact that Phillip had done everything, everything, first. Left home. Made a fortune. Made love to Mahalia. And that everything that Darius ever had was seconds.

That had been the cause of the fight. *That* had been what had hurt most.

It was too ugly to admit, even to his mother. He had fooled himself into thinking, over the past few days, that he'd fought for love. For honor. But now it was real and clear to him that he'd fought for ego. He'd left California, and Mahalia, over wounded pride, and nothing else. There was no nobility here. Knowing this, though, didn't make things any better.

"I'm waiting, boy," Mama demanded, impatiently slicing through his inner debate. "What sent the two of you swinging at each other like drunks out back of a bar?"

Commingled shame and discretion made him refuse. "I'd rather not say, Mama."

Mama snorted. "Hmpff! That's what your brother said. Can't say I agree. Better to have everything laid out in the open, and dealt with, than let it fester under the surface." She sighed heavily, and Darius could just see her, seated at the kitchen table, her usually neat gray hair electrified with indignation, but in spite of all her tartness, deeply concerned for her two boys.

"Mama?" he ventured.

"What, boy?"

"Can I ask you a question?"

"Go ahead. I'll answer it, if I can." After venting her spleen, her tongue was less acid, and her voice a little closer to the gentle one he knew so well.

He squeezed his eyes shut and tried to cast his mind back to his childhood, to dredge up a picture of himself as a young boy. In most of the images churned up from the ocean bed of his memory, he wasn't alone. His brother was usually there with him, playing, joking, pulling pranks, coaching, mentoring. "Do you remember my first pair of jeans?"

"What?" The question seemed to throw her, as absurd as it was.

"I know, I know. It sounds ridiculous. But do you remember the first pair of jeans I wore? Did you buy them, or did they belong to Phillip?"

Mama, God bless her, didn't even ask why he'd needed to know. She hemmed and hawed for several moments, trying her best to remember, but finally said, "I don't know, son. You're asking me to throw my mind back more than twenty years. But what I can tell you is this: up in the attic, there's a big old hardwood trunk. Used to be my hope chest. . . ."

"I know that trunk." It was bigger than a coffin, at least a hundred years old, handed down through three generations. When he was a boy, it had made hide-and-seek quite interesting.

"Uh-huh." Mama's voice was a little distant now, as she drifted into memories. "My hope chest, that's what it was. I used to keep lots of things belonging to you children in there. Clothes, too. Lots of room in there for clothes."

"I remember, Mama."

"I can't tell you anything about your jeans, son, first or otherwise, and I can't say I know why you're asking. But what I can tell you is this: there are so many years between you and your brother, with all those girls in between, that everything your brother ever outgrew ended up in that box, biding its time until you were big enough for it. We didn't have much money then, not for too many new clothes, so everything Phillip didn't need anymore wound up in that box, wrapped up in brown paper and lavender leaves, waiting for you to get big enough to wear them. Your first pair of jeans? I can't rightly remember. Probably. Your jeans, your sneakers, your shirts, your schoolbags . . . whatever. Just sat there until you were ready for them."

"I see."

"That help?"

It did, he supposed, but not in a good way. Mama's words were like waterproofing tar, sealing closed any cracks in his resolve to let what he had with Mahalia lie down and stay dead. Hailie had insisted that it was over; he was the one to resist. Now he knew that she had been right. If he ever was to be a man, separate and distinct from his brother, no longer dependent on his brother for seconds, castoffs, leftovers, or anything else, this was where he had to start. He couldn't go on like this, wanting Hailie, craving her, fooling himself into believing that he needed her. This had to stop. He'd find a way to end the aching. It was the only way he could be free.

"Darius?" Mama probed, and it was then that he realized that he hadn't answered.

"Yes, Mama, you've helped." But his words, like his heart, weighed a ton.

"You don't sound like it. You sound like you need *more* help."

"I'm fine, Mama," he insisted, although he was anything but.

"Son?"

"Yes?"

"Anything more you need to know?"

"No, Mama. Thanks." He knew all he needed to. Anything else would only bring more pain, like sharp nails picking away at an unhealed wound.

Mama, her ire cooled and replaced by loving concern, was persistent. "Anything you think you need to tell me?"

Any more words would have to be torn from his mouth, dragged from his tongue with hot pincers. "No, Mama. Nothing." Then, feeling bad because her offer had been born out of kindness, he added, "Thank you."

"All right." She was reluctant to give up, her mother's

instinct telling her that something was wrong, but she knew she would get no further with him. "Sleep well, then, boy."

"I will, Mama," he lied, and set the phone down. Sleep. What a joke. There would be no sleep for him tonight.

"Mission accomplished," Tony informed Hailie acidly. "I've visited your artist, and I've got him to sign off. Contract's terminated. Thought you'd be happy to know." He sounded like she would be the only person happy about the whole deal.

Happy? She was anything but. Mahalia felt the slow sensation of being cut adrift, like a crippled boat having its towline severed from the ship that was leading it to shore. "It's done, then," she said hollowly.

"Yes. I'll pass by later, if you like, and drop off your copy of the contract."

She didn't exactly feel like company. "Mail it, Tony. That'll be fine."

His voice was a shrug. "Whatever."

She hesitated, and then ventured to ask, "Did he say anything?"

"Not much. But he didn't look too happy about it. Poleaxed, practically. Like he never saw it coming. Although, considering the mess his face was in, I was hard-pressed to say I recognized any emotion on it whatsoever."

"What do you mean?" she demanded instantly. "What was wrong with his face?"

"Looked like a piece of meat. Like he tangled with the wrong end of a steamroller."

Concern prompted her to ask, "Car accident?"

"I dunno, Hailie, it wasn't my business to ask, you

know? But I wouldn't say so. I'd say it was more like he took a few punches. He a boxer?"

"Somebody beat him up?" she shrieked. It was too bizarre to be believed.

"I don't know if I'd rightly say he got beat up, Hailie. From the look of those bruises on his knuckles, I'd wager it was a pretty two-sided fight."

Darius? In a fight? With whom? "And he didn't say anything?" she asked again. "At all?"

"For someone who wanted this man out of her life pronto, you sure sound worried about him. You sweet on him?" Tony asked shrewdly.

"No," she hastened to assure him. "Just concerned."

"Very concerned, looks like," Tony observed dryly. Then he was all business again. "Look, sweetheart, it's none of my affair, okay? I'm just telling you what I saw. Your contract's signed, and I'll send you a copy, just like you asked. Okay? Now, if you'll excuse me . . ."

Hailie knew Tony's signals well. He was still upset with her over breaking her deal, and when he was upset he could be short. She knew, too, that it didn't make any sense trying to persuade him to linger. So she allowed him to end the conversation, wished him good-bye, and hung up. Then she plopped back down into her desk chair in a daze.

Somebody had hit Darius. And he'd hit back. Who? And why? It boggled the mind; he was so easygoing, so peace-loving. He'd never struck her as a fighter. Yet, somehow, within the few short days since she'd last seen him, he'd managed to find himself a shiner or two, and some bruised knuckles.

"Why?" she asked Veda Two, but the cat, sprawled out on its belly in the center of her desk, lifted her one good eyelid, gave her a baleful glare for having disturbed her sleep, and then shut it.

She shouldn't be concerned, she reminded herself. She'd cut him loose, legally and emotionally; it was the only thing she could do. And yet the thought of that kind, beautiful face marred by bruises brought her nothing but anxiety. Had he been mugged? Had he gone out after their argument, gotten drunk, and . . .

No, Darius wasn't much of a drinker. So what had happened? He'd left her upset, that was true, in the early hours of the morning, but he wasn't the type of man who'd go drown his sorrows in the nearest bar. So where had he gone, and who had he encountered?

The answer hit her like a lead pipe to the stomach.

Phillip.

Darius wasn't the kind of man who bellied up to a bar and made himself miserable over strong spirits and ice. He was the kind of man who had very strong ideas about what was right and what was wrong, and when he saw something wrong he went crusading off to try to set things right again.

Darius had gone off to Phillip to defend her honor. It would have made her laugh, so old-fashioned it was, but this wasn't a laughing matter. She shot to her feet. "Phillip, Veda. Phillip hit him." The cat ignored her.

She was angry, defensive, and curious. What had the two men said to each other? What had triggered the punches? And where the heck did Phillip Grant get off, hitting the man that she . . .

. . . loved?

She sat again—no, she fell heavily into her chair, weakened by the idea, the knowledge, that what she had been shoving to the back of her mind, telling herself it wasn't real, actually did exist. Now that she had distanced herself from him, his beautiful, sculpted body, star-studded eyes, and that bright, clear skin speckled with constellations that led downward to a maddeningly erotic place, now that she

was far from his sonorous voice, quick humor, and unending patience, she could see clearly. Think clearly,
unclouded by what she thought was longing, loneliness,
need, and lust. Now she knew that everything she had told
herself in an attempt to steer herself away from the truth
meant nothing. What she felt for him was none of the
above, all of the above, and more.

Love.

Love, love, love.

And she'd thrown it all away. Shoved him from her
windowsill like an errant Romeo, signed him out of her
life with a lawyer's bloodless words on white paper, and
a stroke of the pen.

This man loved her son, even before he'd discovered
that he was Will's uncle, before the bond of flesh had
made itself known. This man had been willing to give her
everything: his time, his patience, and his body, even *after*
he'd discovered that his own brother had used her up and
tossed her away. He'd been kinder to her than Phillip had
ever been, made love to her with more tenderness and
honor and respect in one afternoon than Phillip had
done throughout their entire, painful, humiliating affair.
Been willing to wait her out, help her recover from
wounds inflicted upon her heart and self-esteem more
than a decade ago.

And she'd sent him away.

She shot to her feet again, this time with a purpose.
She'd made a mistake: she wasn't afraid to admit that.
Now she had to fix it, as fast as possible, and the way to
start was by finding Darius.

"Checked out?" Hailie asked the desk clerk for the
second time.

Although the hotel was quite small, it was busy, and

the lobby thronged with middle-aged men, all dressed rather peculiarly in ruby-red jackets with broad yellow sashes, topped off by even more peculiar-looking, squashed yellow pillbox hats with red trim. They were everywhere, hollering across the floor to draw each other's attention, and climbing over carelessly dumped luggage to embrace each other like old friends and long-lost brothers. Obviously a convention of some sort was in town: what kind of convention, she didn't dare guess.

It was probably the frenetic pace of the morning's activities, compounded by the length of the check-in line, that caused the clerk she was talking to to be a little less helpful than he would have been otherwise—or so Hailie would prefer to believe. The little man, who appeared short enough to have to stand on some sort of stool in order to reach the counter, glared up at her over the tops of his bifocals. "As I just said, madam, Mr. Grant has checked out." His tone could corrode metal.

Hailie shrank a little, partly in the face of the man's impatience, partly in despair. Darius was gone. She was too late. But she straightened her spine, and asked another question. "Please, I know you're busy—"

"Evidently," the man cut in.

"But could you tell me when he checked out? What day?"

"That would definitely be in our records," said the snippy clerk, and he patted the computer terminal before him like a spy-thriller villain stroking a cliché cat.

"Yes?" Hope glowed a little, and then was dashed out.

"But as you can see, things are rather hectic this morning. I hardly have time to go rummaging through old files, not when I have *paying clients* waiting for service." His tone blatantly excluded her from the category of the worthy.

She glanced over her shoulder. Even more yellow-and-red-clad conventioneers had poured into the lobby, and the hubbub had become even louder. It was no use. She'd have to think of something else. "I'm sorry to have disturbed you," she said humbly.

The chill of the man's stare was undiminished, but he clicked his heels together—almost drawing a puff of incredulous laughter from her lips—and gave her the briefest, stiffest of bows. "Madam." And with that, she was dismissed.

Dazed, she made her way through the sea of older men, who, as she passed, tipped their ugly yellow hats at her, smiling broadly at their own chivalry, fancying themselves debonair. She gave them grateful smiles; at least somebody here was being nice to her. Then, finding herself back outdoors in the pale, watery light, she sat in her car and wondered: what next?

What she did next took even her by surprise. By rights, she should have retrieved Darius's Detroit number—for she had no doubt that that was where he'd gone—and found a phone, just to make contact. Just to hear his voice. To tell him she was sorry, and beg him to come back. *Tear up those papers I made you sign*, she wanted to tell him, *and come back. Let's give Romulus and Veda a second chance. Let's give* us *a second chance*.

Instead, her car, of its own volition, pointed itself in the opposite direction from her home, finding the smog-filled, traffic-clogged highway all on its own, heading toward a house she'd never visited, and a man she hadn't spoken to in more years than she cared to think about.

Finding it was easy. Each month, money turned up in a special account set aside for her son, and each month, her accountant sent off a receipt. It was all neat, all sanitized. She never even signed the receipts; those were signed for her. Lord knew, she never touched the money, or, at least, not since she'd found her own success. That money was Will's, his to do what he pleased with once he came of age. But she'd seen that small white envelope once or twice, as it left her accountant's office, and once or twice was all she'd needed for the address to be branded onto her memory. She found Phillip's home as effortlessly as if she'd driven to it all her life.

She stared at the house through heavy metal gates that dwarfed her, making her look like a street urchin peering longingly at the hugest house on the block. It was a splendid house, by any standards, and she was surprised to discover that she didn't resent Phillip for having done well. He'd always held that promise; for all his flaws, he was a brilliant man, marked for success from birth, propelled toward it by a synergy of ruthlessness and destiny.

Not allowing herself to lose her nerve, she practically ran to the gatepost and thrust her thumb into the doorbell. She kept it there, listening for a voice on the intercom, afraid to remove her hand from the buzzer because, if there was no initial response, she might not be able to dredge up the courage to ring it again.

There was an electronic blip in her ear, and the intercom buzzed to life. "Yes?"

She could have been a woman of eighty, with her youth and most of her memories fogged by time, and yet she would have recognized that voice with all the clarity and immediacy of her foolish youth. Phillip. Oh, God. There was a time when she spent her hours, her days, within earshot of the phone, hoping he would call her. It hadn't mattered what he said to her: all that had mattered was that he was speaking *to her*, and not to any other woman. That voice, crisp, commanding, as different from his brother's as the sound of lightning smashing into a tall pine was from the gentle, sonorous shushing of the wind coming down over the mountains. That voice had made her give up her body and her heart. That voice had made her lose her mind.

"Hello?" Slight impatience now. Phillip wasn't a man who liked to be kept waiting.

"Phillip?" she asked, irrationally, because she already knew.

"Yes. Who is this?"

Run, run, run, her instincts told her. *It's not too late. He'll never know you've come.* But she shut her instincts up and said, "It's Mahalia."

There was a stunned silence on the other side, so she clarified, "Derwood."

There was a trace of ironic humor in his reply. "I only know one Mahalia."

"Oh." Now she felt like an idiot.

"Hailie?"

"Yes?"

"Take your finger off the buzzer, for Pete's sake. You're giving me a migraine."

"Oh, sorry," she apologized. Doubly idiotic.

"You coming inside?" He sounded resigned to the fact that she probably was.

"May I?"

There was a click, and a creak, and the broad gates began to swing open. "Drive up to the top," was the last thing she heard. "I'll meet you there."

She drove in as instructed, only vaguely aware of the beauty of the landscaping that flanked her, and the scent of desert flowers that hung in the air like an enchantment. She parked near a moat of sorts, which led to rough wooden steps. At the top of those stairs, Phillip stood.

She left her car door ajar, either too numb to shut it, or subconsciously providing herself with a fast means of escape. She stood at the bottom of the steps, hands folded before her like a child approaching a formidable grown-up, staring at the face she'd seen just twice in the last ten years.

Phillip looked . . . good. Good, that is, if she discounted the blue-black bruises that were still quite evident against the dark skin, even after several days, and the red-purple cut that marred his almost too full, sensuous mouth. She believed—knew—that Darius had done that damage, and that their altercation had had something to do with her. The bud of guilt that she had been nurturing inside her grew into full blossom.

Nervousness left her unable to move, capable only of staring, her eyes taking in every detail. He looked better than she remembered him: the years had refined him, mellowed him, given him a smooth patina of sophistication. Even at home, he was wearing finely tailored pants and a linen shirt that would have stood its own in any semiformal setting. Gold glinted discreetly at his wrist, and on one finger. She might have been crazy, but she was almost sure she could smell his cologne: dark and musky, just like he was.

But even now, confronted by this ghost from her past, breaker of her heart, destroyer of her self-esteem, this man who had become her personal benchmark for every man she had ever met thereafter, all she could do was search in his face and demeanor for signs of his younger brother.

She could find none. Phillip's head was carefully shaved, giving him a smooth, yet slightly dangerous air, whereas up until Darius's recent haircut, which she guessed now was an attempt to please her, his had been wilder. Careless, squirrel-brown, and unkempt. The kind of hair you got your fingers well and truly tangled in, when you slid them through it in the heat of lovemaking.

Phillip had grown a beard, meticulously trimmed, dark even against his dark skin. Darius had shaved when he felt like it, and his smooth cheeks and nonchalant shadow had been more charming than debonair.

Phillip was not very tall, but compact, hard, dangerously muscled, like a bricklayer disguised as a stockbroker. Phillip's presence was immediately replaced in her mind by a vision of Darius, poised above her, smooth body naked, taut, slender but defined, rock hard under her fingertips, his scorpion's tail of moles descending his throat and chest to encircle one nipple . . .

"Are you going to say anything, or did you drive all the way over here just to gape at my battle scars?" Phillip interrupted. He sounded edgy, cautious, as though all she could possibly be bringing was bad news. And yet his caution was tinged with his customary dismissive humor. Ten years ago, he had seen her as a silly little girl, to be humored. Little had changed *there*.

Say anything? What could she say? She glanced around her, and then up at the sky, waiting for inspiration to strike. Why had she come? She'd been propelled by some unrecognizable force, whim, or lunatic impulse through hours of dense L.A. traffic to arrive at Phillip's door. What had she really intended to do once she'd arrived?

Phillip's soot-black brows, thick but fastidiously trimmed, drew together slightly. "Is the boy sick?"

So, she thought sourly, *he remembers he has a son. Seems to have forgotten his name, though.* "He's fine," she assured him, and then, unable to keep the vitriol from dripping off her tongue, added, "And he has a name. It's Will."

"Willard. Yes, I remember." He looked briefly thoughtful, but then dismissed with a slight shrug whatever had disturbed his complacency. He waited again for her to speak, and then, when she didn't, asked, "Do you need more money?"

I'm a writer, she wanted to tell him, *and a popular one, too. People line up to buy my books.* But she resisted the need to prove herself to him, because that would have thrown her back too many years, to the stupid young woman that she had been, eager for his approval, needing him to tell her she was okay. She didn't need that anymore. She knew what she was worth. That was enough. So she simply snapped, "Hardly." In any case, if she did, he would be the last person she'd ask. "Will and I are doing just fine on our own."

"So I've heard," he said gravely, and she struggled to detect any trace of irony in his response. She could find none.

Hailie could hear birds singing as they darted in and out of the shrubs and cacti that surrounded them. She could smell the sweetness of desert flowers, and their heady scent was like a drug, numbing her against the discomfort of the long silence that followed. Phillip didn't invite her in, nor did he volunteer to take a third guess at the reason for her surprise arrival. He simply clasped his huge hands before him and waited.

When Hailie could take it no more, she opened her mouth, and out tumbled the question that had been on her mind all along. "Did Darius do that to your face?" She clapped her hand over her mouth to prevent the words from taking shape, but it was too late.

To her astonishment, Phillip roared with laughter, not unkind, not dismissive, but full of mirth, as though the question genuinely amused him. He unclasped his hands and rubbed his cheek thoughtfully, running his thumb along the seam that marred his lower lip. "Yes, he did. He did indeed. But I can assure you, Hailie, my sweet, that I managed to throw in a few punches of my own. It's almost funny, in retrospect. We always used to scrap a bit, and I usually won, being older. But we were boys, then, and now we're men. I don't think there was anything like a clear winner. I may be heavy, but he's fast."

Hailie didn't think it was funny at all, in retrospect or otherwise. Two grown men, taking swings at each other. Rolling on the floor like cattle wranglers . . . "Why?" she managed to ask.

"Why what?"

He knew why what, she was sure of it, but it amused him to make her say, "Why did he hit you? He hit you first, didn't he?"

"Yes, my dear." Phillip was still unable to kill his smile. "He certainly did. Should have seen it coming, but I guess it was late, and I was sleepy. Plus it's just not like him to strike out first. If there's a fire-starter in the family, it's probably me."

This was all a joke to him. He was enjoying her discomfort. She tried to retain her equilibrium. She repeated each word slowly, carefully, letting him know with each syllable that she was far from joking, and that she wanted an answer now. "Why did Darius hit you, Phillip? Tell me, or, God help me . . ."

The amusement on Phillip's face drained away, as it would on the face of a man who had suddenly become tired of cocktail party banter, and was ready to get down to brass tacks. He descended the short flight of stairs that led to the patio where he had been standing, and walked forward until he was close enough for her to feel his breath on her face. "I think you already know."

His proximity made her skin prickle. It remembered his touch. It remembered his devastating, self-assured caresses, the way he used to stroke her like an animal soothing its prey, lulling it out of its terror, fooling it into ignoring its instinct to preserve itself. It was ridiculous, she scolded herself. This man may have touched her body, but he no longer held her heart in his mean, unrelenting grip. Darius had changed that. In loving him, she had been released. By force of will she stilled her quickened pulse, and stepped back, letting air in between them. And then, like the shackles of their ancestors falling away for the last time, his hold on her was no more.

She was free.

She found new courage, and there was a new glint in her eye as her gaze met and held Phillip's. "It was because of me."

"Yes."

"What did he say?"

"Plenty. But I doubt the problem lay in what he said. Almost certainly, it lay in what *I* said."

"And what did you say?"

"Plenty," he repeated. As if hearing the death knell of her feelings for him, Phillip switched off the aura of sex appeal that hung around him, like a man switching off the lights for the night. That indefinable connection between them was severed forever, and they could have been little more than strangers. "What part of it would you like to hear?"

"You told him that you and I had . . . you know . . . slept together."

"I think that once he became aware of Willard's paternity, that much would have been evident," he answered dryly.

"What I mean is, you told him that you were my . . ." Even now, it was something she was reluctant to say.

"First," he supplied helpfully. "Yes, I did."

Oh, God. "And he took it badly."

"Pretty much. He's a proud kid—"

"He's not a kid!"

Phillip looked thoughtful for several seconds, and then nodded slowly in agreement. "You're right. I keep forgetting. Man, then. He's a proud man."

"And you hit him where it hurts." She couldn't disguise her disgust. What kind of person would do something like that to his own brother? Slash him in a soft spot, and then rub salt into the raw flesh. Her history was her history, of course. Darius had one, and so did she. But still, brother to brother . . . oh, that must have stung.

"I did," Phillip agreed, and, to her surprise, looked rueful. "And more besides, I'm sorry to say."

"What else?"

He shook his head. "It doesn't matter, Hailie. Saying it once was bad enough. I don't have much of an excuse. I was tired and angry, and not used to him questioning my authority. I saw him as a man for the first time—"

"Many years too late!" she interjected.

"Yes." He accepted this without trying to shirk the blame. "I realized for the first time that he was a grown man and didn't need me. He was talking back to me, calling me on my behavior with you. He was enraged at the way I had treated you and Will, and that made me mad."

"So you took the biggest weapon you had—me—and lashed out."

"Yes."

Hailie put her hands up over her hot face, rubbing her eyes to keep them from stinging. Poor Darius. She'd gone and hurt him, and then his brother had hurt him worse. No wonder he'd left town.

Phillip cut into her thoughts. "In retrospect, I shouldn't have, especially knowing . . ."

"Knowing what?"

"How he felt about you."

Hailie could swear that, at that very second, her heart stopped. Her mouth was drier than the faux desert at her feet. "And how . . . does he feel?" she managed to ask.

"He's mad about you. He came here, wild with anger, ready to haul me over the coals for you. Willing to storm the ramparts in your defense, that sort of thing. And every time he pushed, I pushed back harder. I pushed him too hard, and we fought. I said too much, and he left. Crazy with pain."

There was quite a bit that she would have liked to tell Phillip, at this point, but she decided to save her energy for what really mattered: finding Darius, and setting things right. So instead of unleashing a hail of arrows, she simply said, "You pig."

Phillip couldn't answer.

She turned without saying good-bye, and climbed into her car. She sat down, buckled up, and started the engine, quite convinced that Phillip would have nothing further to do or say, but as she slid the gear into reverse, he approached her and tapped on the window. Reluctantly, she wound it down.

"You going to see him?"

"I will," she vowed. "He's gone back home, probably, but I'll find him, whatever it takes."

"When you see him, tell him something for me."

She waited without making any promises.

Phillip struggled with what he was about to say next, as though it killed him to be so weak. "Tell him I'm sorry."

Hailie hit the button on her window, and it began its ascent. Before it was all the way up, cutting him off from the sound of her voice, she answered, "You're his brother, Phillip. Tell him that yourself."

Gravel spewed out under her wheels.

Fourteen

Darius looked down at his uneaten TV dinner and made a face. He wasn't the world's best cook, but he did make the occasional incursion into the kitchen, and even the slapped-together meals he was able to forage for himself when he was thus inclined were far better than this swill. He gathered it all up, tossed the barely used knife and fork into the sink, and dumped the dinner in the trash. He wasn't hungry, anyway.

It pained him to waste food like that, and he briefly wished he had, at the very least, an animal that would have been grateful for it. But if he had a pet, it probably wouldn't have touched it, either. The word *pet* made him think of Veda Two, who, although not a particularly fussy cat, was still a cat, and he could easily imagine her giving him an affronted glare for having the temerity to offer her anything less than premium cat food. In spite of his foul mood, he chuckled at the thought of her, but his chuckle died deep in his throat.

Thinking of Veda Two made him think of Mahalia.

He cursed, and stomped through the living room and back into the second bedroom of his apartment, which he had converted into his studio. Normally, he kept it in meticulous order, with all his paints, pencils, crayons, papers, and an inexhaustible miscellany of paraphernalia properly ranged so that he could find what he needed, the moment he needed it.

The studio was in an uproar. A sea of wadded paper lay on the floor, as thick as the carpet of snow on the sidewalk outside, having spilled up and over the rim of the full wastebasket. Open bottles of ink congealed, pencil shavings flecked his desk, untended sable brushes hardened nearby. On the drawing table, sheets of art paper lay covered with sketches. He picked up a few, and shuffled distractedly through them.

Romulus and Veda lived on every page. Scene after scene from Mahalia's draft emerged; oftentimes, the same scene was interpreted repeatedly, from different points of view and angles, with different tones and moods. The thick sheaf of drawings, and the many others shoved into his desk drawers, represented the almost uninterrupted stretch of time he'd spent at his table this past week. Sometimes, he'd work up to eighteen hours at a single sitting, looking up in surprise to find that the entire night had passed, and the first gleam of daylight was staining his walls with its irritatingly cheerful glow. When he did try to sleep, it was fitful at best, and, at worst, fractured and populated by people who looked like wolves, and wolves that looked like people.

"Fool," he chided himself. "Working pro bono for someone who doesn't even want to see your stuff. Or need it. Don't you know you're out of a job?" Not that his need was all that pressing; the advance he'd been paid through his canceled contract would see him through for quite some time, even if accepting it had rankled. Mahalia had let him keep it out of the same kind of patronizing charity that had so often prompted his own brother to send him money for no reason. There had been quite a few times this past week when he had been so rattled by this knowledge that he was willing to get up on his high horse and send it back, but good sense and his survival instinct had always prevailed. He knew what his bank balance had been before he'd accepted the job, and wasn't that inclined to watch it return there. The concept of the starving artist was, to him, not a cliché but an ever-present threat.

But the money wasn't half of it. His obsession with a project on which he no longer belonged was not only motivated by an almost puritanical conviction that he should do the work he had been paid for, whether it was welcome or not. Romulus and Veda kept that link between him and Mahalia alive. If he let them die, then Mahalia died in his mind, too.

Bzzz. . . .

Confusedly, he looked around. The phone seemed to be ringing, but when he picked it up, it was silent.

Bzzz. . . .

Alarm clock? No; door buzzer. That was it. "You need to get some sleep, Grant," he chastised himself irritably. Fatigue was turning his brain into pap. But who could it be? He'd barely told a soul he was back, and hadn't been out much, except to slouch around the grocery store with an empty shopping basket like a big bear that was hungry enough to leave its lair in daylight, but not hungry enough to find that anything seemed appetizing.

Still puzzled, he hit the intercom. "Yes?"

Then came the voice he knew so well, clear as stream water, even over the intercom system that was older than dirt and needed replacing. "It's me."

His hand released the button as though he'd touched something hot.

Mahalia.

How?

The buzzer sounded again, probably several moments later, but time had collapsed upon itself and he had no way of knowing just how long it had been. Cautiously, he pressed the button, which was as cool to the touch as it should have been, anywhere outside of his frenzied imagination. "Yes?" he asked again.

"Darius, it's me." She sounded less confident now, cautious.

"Hailie." His mind was a blur. Mahalia was here, in Detroit, downstairs, in the snow outside his apartment. Why had she come? What did she want?

"Can you let me in? It's sort of cold . . ." Less self-assured still, as though her confidence were draining out through her feet with every second that he left her standing out there on the icy sidewalk.

"Rude of me," he mumbled. "Sorry." He let her in.

Ninety seconds. That was about as long as it took someone to make it to his door from downstairs. He glanced around wildly. He had ninety seconds and his place looked as though a family of pigs had moved in and refused to be evicted. He looked down at himself. He was wearing crumpled gray sweats and little else. Had he had a shower today? Yesterday? He was tempted to give himself a surreptitious sniff, but was half afraid he'd knock himself out.

He hopped into the bathroom and splashed some water on his face, peering blearily into his mirror. His bruises embarrassed him; they made him feel naked, all his foolishness exposed. Before he could do any more, think of a way to hide them, disguise them, or cover them up, there was a knock on his door. His time was up. He went back out and opened it. Cautiously.

She was a vision. Travel-worn, bundled up against the cold, her face framed by the curls that escaped the hat that she had unceremoniously dragged down over her ears, tired, and taut with nervousness, but a vision all the same.

"Hailie," he breathed. He itched to touch her, but was afraid that if he did, she'd disappear with a *poof*, and then he'd shoot upright in his own bed, sweating with disappointment at the discovery that he'd finally given in to his fatigue, and that her presence here was simply a manifestation of some deeply rooted desire.

"Darius," she replied, and then *she* touched *him*, and that dispelled any doubts as to her tangibility. She seemed to be waiting.

For what? She'd flown in unannounced, halfway across the country in foul weather, to turn up at his door, and now she just stood there, her eyes fixed on his face. The long silence rattled him, gave his doubts time to take root again. Like a chilly wind blowing in over mountaintops, hurt blew away his initial happy surprise, leaving defensiveness and suspicion in its wake. She'd hurt him—badly. Dismissed him without the benefit of a trial. He'd pleaded with her for the opportunity to prove to her that although he and the man who had devastated her life had emerged from the same womb, and grown up in the same house, they were not the same man. He'd asked her for that one small favor, and she'd refused him it.

Instead of the warm, delighted welcome that would have spilled from his lips but moments earlier, his next question was short, to the point, and left no leeway for misinterpretation. "What do you want, Hailie?"

Her mouth fell open slightly, and she shrank visibly at his abruptness. "Umm," she began, but then could go no further. Her eyes darted along the hallway, as though she was considering beating a hasty retreat.

Instantly, he was ashamed of himself. This wasn't like him, this callousness, but he was like a man attacked from behind, searching in the dark for a means of defending himself. Had she warned him, e-mailed or called to let him know she was coming, he would have been prepared, and had ample time to arm himself more appropriately. As it was, he'd been denied the luxury of notice. Thus unprepared, keeping his distance was the only answer; in his condition, further hurt would certainly lead to madness. He repeated his question baldly, resisting any temptation to temper it by tone or demeanor.

She stuttered, but was finally able to ask, "May I come in?"

He hesitated, but not for long. Self-protection was one thing: rudeness was another. His mother had never raised him to leave visitors standing out in the hall like brush salesmen. He stepped aside, and with the anxious look that she might have given to a jack-in-the-box that threatened to pop out at her any second, she darted past him and into his living room.

This wasn't good. Mahalia had made the decision to come here, and had acted on that decision almost immediately, allowing herself very little time to question her impulse, for fear that common sense would have warned her that it was not a very wise idea. So now here she was, dropping with the exhaustion brought on by lack of sleep and her son's increasing fractiousness over the past few days, standing in Darius's living room, on some half-baked mission to win him back, and he was looking at her, his battered face schooled into a mask that told her nothing, invited nothing.

What an awful mistake. To hide her confusion, she busied herself fussing with her hat and coat, even though Darius's expression made the interior much colder than the exterior of the building. Darius took her things from her, carefully avoiding contact with her skin. "Your coat's wet," he observed.

"Snowing out," she said unnecessarily.

He gave her something that was pretty near to a half smile. "I noticed."

She felt the flush sweep up her face. Stupid thing to say.

"Do you want me to put it in the dryer for you?"

She nodded. It would have dried off on its own in time, but she had a deep, cold suspicion that if she didn't play her cards right, she'd be needing it again soon. So she simply thanked him, and he left the room.

Hailie put her hands on her hips and looked around herself, curiosity displacing her nervousness for just a moment. All she'd ever seen of Darius had been in her own setting, on her own territory. Now she had the chance to see what his environment was like, maybe learn a little more about him.

For starters, he wasn't much of a housekeeper. A few cushions were tossed about on the furniture, and a jacket lay here, and the odd sneaker there. There were stacks of newspapers on the coffee table, in pristine condition, making her think that he'd collected them from the hallway every morning, laid them meticulously in a pile, and then forgotten about them. But the room smelled of him; the air in it had a signature scent that nobody could copy. She tilted her head back a little, closed her eyes, and inhaled.

Directly behind her, he cleared his throat, and she jumped, guilty in spite of herself.

"I'm back," he said, pointing out the obvious.

"So I see." He was still waiting on an answer to his initial question; she wasn't sure she would be able to give him an honest one. To play for time, and motivated by genuine curiosity, she crossed the floor and examined the framed pictures that adorned the walls. They were almost all original art: vintage comic book covers with scrawled signatures in the bottom right-hand corner, and, in some cases, miniature cells from cartoon shows that were no longer even on the air. In one large frame, taking pride of place in the middle of his display, was the original artwork from one of her very own books, signed in quick, black strokes by the artist.

"I searched long and hard to get my hands on that." He had come to stand at her elbow, and seemed willing to allow her to stall for as long as she pleased. She was grateful for this small concession.

"It's beautiful," she said.

"Yes. It is."

When it became obvious that neither could remain silent any longer, words spilled from her like water from a glass that had been teetering on edge for a time, and had finally tipped over. "Come back, Darius."

His face registered neither surprise nor any other emotion that she would have expected. "Why?" was all he asked.

"Because I was wrong. We worked well together before. We started something, and we should finish it. I fired you for all the wrong reasons. . . ."

He winced at the word *fired*, but she pressed on determinedly.

". . . I shouldn't have. There's nothing wrong with your work."

"Thank you," he said dryly.

That went over badly. She tried again. "I mean, your work is wonderful. It's like nothing I've ever seen before. I couldn't imagine myself working with anyone else but you. Darius, please . . ."

He was still just inches from her, arms folded, regarding her impassively, as though her words made no impact on him whatsoever, whether positive or negative. He just wasn't making this any easier. She forged ahead, in spite of her dwindling confidence. "Let's finish the book, Darius. Please. I'll call Tony, and he'll call his lawyers, and we'll scrap all this nasty business with the . . . uh . . . termination." She fished in her shoulder bag and withdrew the vile document that she, through Tony, had bullied him into signing. "Here. Here's my copy. You take it. Tear it up. Burn it. I don't care. Do the same with yours, and Tony can make sure the other copy goes away. And then it will be like it never happened. Things would go back to the way they were."

Only that wasn't true. Things couldn't go back to the way they were, because she was in love with him now. He wasn't just the cute, disheveled, talented kid that had turned up at her cabin at Casuarinas, willing to crawl into a dark space on his belly to rescue kittens. He was no longer the visionary artist who left her in awe of his bottomless well of ideas. He was different. He was the man who had penetrated her mind, pierced her soul, and wrought havoc on her heart. And she'd hurt him, rejected him, so badly that she doubted he would easily yield to her what he had been so willing to give her before.

But if only she could get him to go back with her, if she had him beside her every day, his head close to hers as they pored over their work, arguing over silly things like point of view and character motivation, then maybe things would get better. Maybe she could find ways to show him that she still wanted him, now more than ever, in fact. Maybe she could teach him to trust her again.

"So you want me back . . . for work. Is that it?"

Oh, that frightening, unreadable face. Not a hint. Not a clue. So unlike the Darius she knew!

"Yes. That, and . . ."

"And?"

"And Will misses you." She couldn't believe she'd actually said that!

"*Will* misses me?" This time, a slight flicker at the corner of his mouth; amusement, perhaps, but if it was that, it was cynical amusement indeed.

And so do I, she wanted to confess. *Terribly. Awfully.* But the ego is a fragile thing, and she protected hers by holding her son up like a shield. "Ever since the morning when you didn't turn up for breakfast, he's been waiting for you. Sometimes he waits down by the gate, with Veda Two sitting next to him. Sometimes he sits right in front of the door, so close that if anybody really opened it they'd trip right over him. Sometimes he cries . . ."

For the first time, his face truly softened. He bit his lip, and then said, "I'm sorry to hear that."

He could have added *but that's all your fault,* but he was enough of a gentleman to refrain. She kept on going, pressing gently on what appeared to be his only soft spot. "And those comic books you gave him, he doesn't put them down. He sleeps with them, with his arms wrapped around them like a pillow. He eats with them in his lap. I don't think he's read any of them. Don't think he's even opened them to peek inside. He just carries them around, like a charm. As if he thinks they'll bring you back."

His guard slipped just long enough for her to see the love this man held for her son, and it made her chest hurt. In part, it made her happy. Will had so few people in his life who loved him, and this one did, accepting him without effort for who he was. Maybe that love didn't extend to her, or maybe if it had been just uncurling like the new tendril of a fern, and she'd crushed it under her boot, she could nurture it again, if only she had the time. He might come back for Will, but if he did, she would make every effort to ensure that he stayed for her.

"I'm sorry he's hurting," Darius said.

"My fault." She finally stated the obvious. "It wasn't you, it was me. I sent you away."

He didn't bother to acknowledge her statement. Although his eyes and face had softened, his arms were still folded. He leaned a little closer—much too close for comfort—and asked, "Is it only Will who misses me?"

Panic! This was too direct. Too pointed. There was only one answer she could honestly give, but it was an answer that would leave her wide open to the searing agony of his rejection. Why did he ask? Why did he want to know? Was it for the satisfaction of seeing her hurt, like she had hurt him, a valuable weapon with which to stock his arsenal? Was he enjoying seeing her squirm, waiting for a confession, so that when he turned her down, the sting of rejection would be all the more painful? Or did he need to know because he missed her too?

She floundered like a fish on deck. "I . . . I . . ." *Courage, Hailie. Courage. Tell him. Love is risk. Love is worth the risk.* "He's not the only one," she finally managed to confess, but it was a halfway confession, barely one at all.

"He's not?" He wasn't making this easy.

She shook her head vehemently, but was unable to go any further.

"Who else?"

She stared down at her feet like a naughty girl hauled into the principal's office, struck dumb by the prospect of punishment.

"Hailie? Who misses me?"

I do. I do. Every hour of the day. Every night. I miss you, miss you, miss you, and I'd do anything to make you come back. Please, Darius, please. But her mouth and lungs refused to give breath to the words her mind was screaming.

He took pity on her, unexpectedly injecting humor into a situation so taut it was about to snap. "I know it isn't dear old Coretta."

In spite of the sensation that she was standing in a

field of hot glass shards, she almost smiled. "She's just protecting me," she said, defending her helper.

"From me?"

"From all comers."

"I'm different."

"I know."

"I told you I wouldn't hurt you." He looked as though the mere idea that she thought he was capable of that hurt *him*. "I told you that more than once."

"I remember." He had, and she'd allowed herself to forget.

"And you never defended me to her. You never stood up for me."

She felt rotten. Coretta's behavior was her version of kindness, like a cantankerous old hen protecting her brood, but still, Mahalia could have said something. Guilt made her skin hot. "I'm sorry."

He could have left her dangling on the hook, but his mercy was boundless. He drew her back to their original line of conversation, but this time his question was not a gimlet, boring into her, but a gentle probe. "Who else misses me, Hailie?" He extended a single finger and tilted her chin upward, forcing her to lift her stare from the point on the floor on which it had been fixed.

The soft, light touch, and the unexpected gentleness of the question, were all it took. The heat and ferocity of her tears surprised her as they spilled down her cheeks and onto his hand. They came without a warning sob or tingle at the back of her throat. Not even a moan of pain escaped her, so that when he felt the moisture on his fingers, he was as shocked as she.

Then, sound followed, in great spasms that rocked her body so hard he had to hold out his arms to support her. Agony twisted her face and made her knees buckle, and to save her from falling he held her gently and brought her to the floor, where he knelt before her, not pulling her close or trying to stop her from crying, but just waiting out the storm.

When it finally passed, his arms tightened around her shoulders, and one hand came up to stroke her hair. It was damp from melted snow, and matted from hours of travel, but he slipped his fingers through it anyway, moving down to the base of her skull and stroking the tense ridges of muscle there. He whispered soft, soothing things against her temple, but then after a while he stopped talking, and let his lips speak another language.

They slid across her forehead, down past her ear to her cheek, soft, in spite of the stubble of several days that covered his jaw. They roamed across her cheek, as lightly as a baby's hand, or a butterfly. Then to her chin, and her throat, all the way down to the hollow that lay between the two small bumps at the point where her neck began. Each time they swept past her lips, she turned her head, trying to trap his with hers, but he deftly avoided her.

After two or three games of catch-me-if-you-can with his mouth, and losing at every turn, she whimpered, "Darius, please. . . ."

He was resolute in his resistance. "Who else missed me, Hailie?"

Did he really have to insist? Did he really have to make her say it? She tried to hedge. "You know."

"I don't. Tell me."

"You do," she insisted. She tried to take the lead, grasping his head and forcing him to hold it steady, pressing her mouth against his firmly closed one. No deal. He stood his ground.

"I don't." He pulled away from her, and feeling him wrest himself from her arms was like clinging to a rock face and hearing her safety cord snap.

"Darius!"

"I don't know anything, unless you tell me." He folded his arms, effectively creating a barrier between them. His eyes were still warm, still star-filled, but focused, steady, waiting.

She hung her head, feeling both shy and guilty. Confession may be good for the soul, but it is a darn hard thing to do, anyway you slice it. But the space between them was killing her, and she knew that speaking up, telling the truth, would hurt less than not having him pressed against her again, so she gave up the battle. "I did." Her voice was so low that only someone who was trying, really trying, could hear her.

He did, apparently, because he pressed her further. "You did what?"

She groaned and held out her arms to him, hoping he would give up on all this foolishness and just fall into them. "You know! You know! Why do you need to make me tell you?"

"Because I have to hear you say it. It's not worth anything, unless you say it." The line of his mouth was firm, inviting no opposition, but not unkind.

When she finally gave in, there was no stopping her. "I missed you! I missed you! I missed you! It was awful. Every day, I listened out for you, hoping you'd come back, even though I'd treated you so badly. I knew you wouldn't, but I hoped—"

He never let her finish. He fell so heavily into her still-open arms that she tipped over backward, landing hard against the carpeted floor, with the full weight of his body on top of her, but she felt no pain from the jarring impact. If there would be bruises later, she didn't care. Because he was kissing her, hard, over and over, and even with the wind knocked out of her body, she responded with equal ardor.

When he lifted his upper body a little, so that she

could finally breathe again, a gust of laughter escaped
him. "I'm sorry, honey. I'm *sorry!*"

"For what?" The impatience in her voice was impossible to conceal. He wanted to *talk* now? All she wanted
to do was touch him, strip him down so she could spread
her hands across that magnificent chest, inhale him,
take him in through every pore. She needed this. Her
mind ached for him, her heart ached for him, and her
body, well, her body was ravenous, stark, raving, crazy
hungry for him.

"For holding you back like that. I had to hear it from
you. I had to know."

"Isn't it enough that I flew all the way here?"

"Your book could have brought you here."

"It didn't. It was just a convenient excuse." She tried
pulling his sweatshirt up over his head, but he was much
too big to be manipulated easily, and being flat on her
back didn't exactly give her much leverage. Her arms
flopped back down to her sides.

He was grinning broadly. "I was hoping . . ."

"I came here for you."

"Good." He was propped up on one arm, staring
down into her face as though searching for something.
"Because if you hadn't, I'd have had to come back for
you! I missed you, Hailie. You got on my very last nerve,
but I missed you. I didn't know how much longer—"

"Oh, for the love of—" Enough was enough! She
wanted him, now, now, now. They could talk later. They
could say everything that needed to be said later. She'd
spill out all the words of love then, when her mind was
cleared, uncluttered by the overwhelming, urgent demands of her body. Right now, she was hungry, and she
needed to be fed. Since he was proving so difficult to un-
dress, she grabbed at her own shirt and opened that
instead.

It worked. Whatever he was about to say next died still-born on his lips, as her breasts came into view, separated from him only by a thin barrier of sensible cotton. *Should have worn silk,* she admonished herself, *something more alluring, more captivating.* But she needn't have worried. His eyes rounded slightly, and then darkened noticeably, and his next action was to free her breasts from their offending restraints. He stared, speechless, until she squirmed. Her rapidly hardening nipples hurt like pebbles pressing up under her skin.

"It feels like a million years ago," he murmured, "since I saw you like this. Touched you . . ."

"Just weeks," she reminded him.

"Long weeks," he agreed. "Long, never-ending . . ."

"They're over now," she reminded him, and shut him up for good by pulling his head down to her left breast, where his tongue could torture her flesh, and his lips feel her heartbeat.

The room fell quiet, except for the soft rustle of clothes as they were shed, one by one, and her sharp gasps of delight as he nipped, licked, and sucked every body part as it came into view.

When she couldn't stand the heat that he had ignited in her now slippery, supersensitive body, she fought back, pushing him down against the floor, and in turn stripping him down. He went limp, allowing her total dominance, and that thrilled her. She rued the fact that he no longer sported his long hair, as that would have allowed her to grasp his head securely as she darted her tongue past his lips. His hot breath mingled with hers, and it was with great regret that she eventually left his mouth to explore further. Her only consolation was that there were many more delights yet undiscovered, and, so help her, she was woman enough to seek out and claim every one of them.

Like a traveler of old, she let the constellation on his skin be her guide, following the scorpion's tail of moles down his jaw to his neck, and farther still, over the hillocks of his bones, along the golden sand dunes of his chest, which rose and fell rapidly under her ministrations. The skin around each mole reddened slightly as she inflicted tiny, cruel bites, exacting her revenge for the torture *he* had just inflicted upon *her*. His only protest was a series of muffled groans, but the idea of holding such power over him, even though he had relinquished his control gladly, delighted her. The tip of her tongue circled his nipple like a space capsule seeking a place to land.

This time, he was the one to protest her stalling. "Bed's better," he gasped.

"Floor's nice," she said in mock resistance.

"Bed's better," he insisted. "Trust me."

She did. She did trust him, and it was amazing and scary at the same time. Without any further opposition, she allowed him to help her to her feet. He moved to take her into his arms, to carry her inside, but she demurred. "I'm heavy," she reminded him.

"Don't make me laugh," he countered immediately, but to avoid any further delay, he allowed her to walk next to him, linking his fingers with hers. They were very naked, very much aroused, and absolutely unabashed about both conditions.

The room was untidy, but smelled of him, and as soon as he tossed aside a few stray articles of clothing from the bed, she lay down, anticipation driving her to the edge of sanity. He joined her, and as he did so, the huge, old metal bed creaked in protest.

"At least the floor didn't creak," she couldn't resist pointing out.

"I like the sound of the creaks." He was smiling hugely

as he lowered his body upon hers. "Sounds like cheering. It's encouraging."

"You need to be encouraged?" she teased back.

"Doesn't hurt."

His hand snaked down her belly, over her soft, furry mound, and then a little farther south, and her vision was besieged with colors, like flashbulbs going off in her face. "Go, team!" she managed to joke before the shudders claimed her.

He continued his coaxing, warming her up like a fine engine in an expensive Italian car, but she was all warmed up already, and she wanted him, now, deep inside, so she could wrap her legs around him and lock her ankles across his back, so that he would never get up and leave her again. "Darius! Darius! What are you doing? Please, please, I want you *now!*"

He lifted his head, but his fingers never stopped their expert movements. "Ready?"

"Yes! Yes! Hurry!" If he didn't cover her now, bury himself deep inside her, she would die, right this very second. Her nails raking along the bare, marble-hard flesh of his flanks underlined her distress.

"My pleasure." He was smiling like an angel, glowing like the sun, and withdrew his fingers. Pausing only to let his damp, perfumed fingers trace the line of her lips, he leaned forward and rummaged around in his bedside drawer until he found what he was looking for. There was a rustle of foil.

"Let me," she said, and took it from him.

He leaned back and submitted to her willingly, and under her light, sensual touch a necessary precaution became an experience in eroticism.

They delayed no longer.

It was a long time before they could catch their breath. Darius's head lay heavily on her breast, bobbing gently like an abandoned rowboat on the ocean as she struggled to bring her respiration back to normal. "Your heartbeat sounds like a runaway horse, galloping on cobblestones."

"Is that a good thing?"

"It's a very good thing." He laughed softly. "It means yours is beating at least as fast as mine. I'd hate to think I'm the only one on the verge of a heart attack."

"Maybe if we stay really still for a while, neither of us will have to suffer one."

"Let's try that, then." He reluctantly lifted his head from her breast and slid up a little, so that they were now face-to-face, but did so without releasing her from his embrace. To prevent her breast from getting lonely, he cupped it, brushing her still-erect nipple with his thumb as he did so.

She shivered.

"Cold?"

"Are you kidding?" After what he'd done to her, her skin was giving off more heat than a bed of hot coals. She was quite sure that if she ran outside into the snow right now, naked as she was, it would melt even before it hit her.

"Well, if you get cold, let me know. I'll put things right in a jiffy." He gave her a leer that was meant to be menacing, but which only served to make her laugh out loud.

"I look forward to that."

Silence fell, and their lighthearted mood gave way to sober intensity. Darius held her even closer than he had before, if such a thing were possible. "You ran me through a wringer, girl." His voice caught in his throat.

"I'm sorry."

"I couldn't eat; everything tasted like packing foam. I couldn't sleep. My mind never let up; thoughts just kept whizzing around and around. Half the time I told myself

I hated you, and that you were just a chapter in my life, and all I needed to do to get over you was turn the page. The other half, all I could think about was what I had to do to get back to you, and what it would take for you to see things my way."

"I'm sorry, Darius. If it helps any, I felt the same way. It was awful. It was torture. Between Will and myself, I don't know which of us went more crazy." She drew her brows together, straining to think. "I don't understand. How could this all happen so fast? I fought you and fought you, but it was like trying to fight gravity. I felt you under my skin. And then you were gone, because I sent you away, and suddenly there was this great big hole in me, and nothing could fill it. And even now, I can't understand how . . . or why. . . ."

"It's not up to us to try to understand. Love has its ways."

The word, so small and yet so huge, ran through her. Four letters. Four small arrows, slamming into her chest. L-o-v-e. Was this an admission? She wasn't sure she dared ask him to say it again. He was beaming at her, looking into her face, waiting for her to say something, but her mouth was too parched to form a reply.

When he became aware that she couldn't say a word in response, he said with great compassion, "You don't have to say anything yet. If it hasn't come for you yet, I'll wait. I'll wait as long as it takes, and do everything in my power to prove it."

He didn't understand! Love *had* come to her. It had a long while ago, only she was too busy struggling for her own self-protection to recognize it for what it was. But try as she might, the confession refused to take shape on her lips. So, instead, she ran the tips of her fingers along the fine scar on his lower lip, the painful testimony to his altercation with his brother, and assured him, "You don't have to prove it. You already have."

His face was the picture of perplexity. "What do you mean?"

"This, silly. I know how you got it. I know why you went over there—"

"How could you know?"

"I had a hunch. Tony told me you'd been in a fight, and I put two and two together."

"And . . . ?"

If she had been on her feet, and dressed perhaps, she would have been more wary, more alert to the slightest change in his intonation, to the tensing of his body against hers. But she was drunk with lovemaking, intoxicated by his proximity and his scent, so she rushed blithely on where an angel would have feared to tread. "And I went over there." Then she clarified unnecessarily, "To see Phillip."

His body blew backward from hers, thrown out of her arms with the force of a shotgun blast. "You went to see him?" He was aghast, rigid with shock, and that scared her.

"Yes, I . . ." She was still dazed by his reaction, too confused to try to soothe him.

"Why? Why in God's name would you . . ."

Danger! Danger! Something scary was happening and it was getting out of control way too fast for her. "I don't know. I have no idea. I just started driving, and found myself outside his gate. Darius, you have to understand, I was looking for you, and you'd already left your hotel, and I didn't know where else to go. So I got in my car, and the next thing I knew—"

"What did he tell you?"

"Nothing happened," she hastened to assure him. Being prone put her at a great disadvantage, so she sat up, but her nakedness still left her feeling vulnerable. And now, with all the warmth sucked out of the room, she *was* feeling cold. She tugged at the covers, but he was sitting on most of them, so she made do with a corner of one blanket, and held it up against her breasts. "Nothing," she emphasized. "I swear."

"I didn't think it did," he said caustically. "My brother never goes back to graze in the same field twice, once he's past it."

She flinched at the analogy, as though she were nothing more than something passive, sitting there waiting to fulfill her role in life as a source of pleasure for men who deigned to choose her. "That was mean, Darius!"

"What did he tell you?" he insisted. He didn't seem to see her shivering, or hear the pain in her voice.

"Nothing! We talked, five minutes, tops. He asked about Will—"

"And?"

"And he was sorry for the things he said to you."

"He can tell me that himself, if he has a mind to."

"That's what I said!"

"What else, Hailie?" His eyes were a color she had never seen before, not even on that night when she had asked him to go. If the clouds had blown in front of the stars then, right now they had completely fallen out of the sky, leaving a lonely moon to be eclipsed by his anger.

"He told me that you . . ." She didn't dare use the "L" word right now, not when he was looking at her like that. Her courage failed her before she even tried. "That you cared for me. And I knew I had to find you."

"Phillip told you to come look for me?"

"Not in so many words. . . ."

He catapulted off the bed and slammed his fist into the wall beside him, his face not registering anything close to pain at the action. "So you're here because of him."

"No," she said slowly. "I'm here because of you."

"If you hadn't seen him, or spoken to him, would you have come?"

"Yes!"

"I don't believe you! He sent you!"

"No!"

"He's thousands of miles away, and still he sent you over to me, gave you to me as a gift. Just another example of Phillip Grant's generosity. Doling out his largesse to those in need."

This had gone so bad, so fast! Now she was off the bed, on the opposite side, and her anger was rising to meet his. "I am not his to give away! I don't belong to your brother!"

"You could have fooled me. Every step I made toward you, you pulled back two. Every time I tried to approach you, you made it very clear to me that there was another man who'd come before me, and who'd taken up so much space inside you, there was no room left for me."

"That was *then!* Things have changed!"

"What's changed?"

She was far too naked. She ran past him into the living room and searched among their jumbled clothing for hers. He was right behind her, watching her as she dressed.

"Everything's changed," she insisted, but was sure he wouldn't believe her.

"Why?"

"Because of you. It's over. That stupid torch I was carrying for him blew out when I met you. I saw him, and he looks good. He looks rich and happy and I'm glad for him. But I don't want him anymore. There's nothing I can do to sever the tie between him and Will, because it will always be there. But what there was between him and me, it's over. It's dead. I looked at him and didn't feel a thing."

He was standing in the doorway, not saying anything more, his stony face registering nothing. She could have pleaded her case more, but suddenly she was tired. Not just physically exhausted, but tired of this nonsense. This thing between brothers, it was bigger than she, and there was nothing she could do to fix it. They'd have to do it themselves. She pulled her boots on, found her coat, and headed for the front door.

"Where are you going?"

"As far as I can get from you," she spat. "I'm not going to stand here while you two big dogs have a long-distance spat over me, like I'm some kind of bone you both think you have dibs on. You think Phillip's got *me* in his thrall? Think again. *You're* the one who can't move forward with your life until you get him out of your system, not me. You're the one who can't distinguish between the love you have for him and the hate."

"I love *you*," he said quietly.

"I don't want to hear that! That's not enough now. What do you think we'll do? You come home with me, and we start working together again. Sharing an office, and sharing a bed. And maybe we'll take it further one day. But if you think I'm going to live my life with you on tenterhooks, you're wrong. If you think I'm going to sit around, waiting for you to fly off the handle next time I say Phillip's name, or the next time you catch Will at an angle, and see some of your brother in him, you're wrong. I don't want you with all those demons on your back. If you straighten up, give me a call." Her shaking fingers found their way around the tricky door lock, and she wrenched it open. She stepped into the hall.

He immediately followed her. "Don't."

"I have to."

"We can work on this."

"*You* work on it." She was running for the elevator, and

he was only a step behind her, naked as a jaybird. She punched the call button and turned to face him. "You going to follow me all the way out like that?" She pointed out his nakedness with a thrust of her chin.

He looked down at himself, seeming surprised, and then flushed slightly. "Let me get dressed. Ten seconds, Hailie. Give me ten seconds. I'll be right out."

"You'll need a lot more time than that," she informed him, "before you get any more time out of me. Set things straight, or forget it." The elevator door opened, and mercifully for Darius, it was empty. She stepped inside and punched the button for the ground floor, turning her back on him as the door closed. Even if he dared go back inside, dress, and come after her, she'd be long gone by the time she hit the sidewalk.

Fifteen

Was it really possible to go from pure bliss to desolation in such a short space of time? Darius dressed, but he knew that he was doing so more perfunctorily than anything else. It was no use. He knew that Mahalia wouldn't be there by the time he got downstairs, but he raced out anyway, coatless, into the cold, and then after a few moments of futile searching, trudged back upstairs, disheartened.

He was a fool, and he deserved this. Opening his mouth like that, saying stupid things, asking stupid questions, at a time when she was most vulnerable: naked, pressed against him, and emotionally wrought by the searing love they'd made. Of all the damn-fool things he could have done! The one woman he wanted had turned up—had come to him instead of him having to go hunting for her—and he'd sent her storming into the night.

And he knew she wasn't coming back.

"You blew gold dust into the wind," he told himself aloud. "The gods smiled on you, and you snarled back. You stupid, stupid . . ."

He had to find her. There was no doubt about that. He wanted her, needed her, and a quick look around himself at the desolate mess his room had become in the last week told him that he couldn't live without her. He was finding her, no matter what it took, and getting her back.

But where to start?

It was late. He and Mahalia had spent a long time savoring each other's bodies. She was no fool; it was dark and cold, and as mad as she was, she would go to no other place than her hotel room. Where that was, he would have to find out—tomorrow. Tonight, he had another, equally hard task at hand.

Mahalia had been right: if he was to win her over, he'd have to get those demons off his back, and there was only one way to do it. With a quick glance at the clock, he picked up the phone and dialed a number, knowing full well that with the lateness of the hour he was violating every rule of telephone etiquette, but what needed to be done needed to be done now. His restless spirit wouldn't let him wait.

The phone barely rang twice before it was snatched up on the other end. "What?"

The sound of his brother's voice set his heart thumping in his chest, like the crash of a hammer against an anvil. "Phil, it's me."

There was the briefest of pauses, and then, "You're making a habit of waking me up." His tone was dry, but there was almost a note of humor in it.

"I'm sorry." He remembered what he had interrupted the last time. "You alone?"

"That I am. A man must get some rest—at least occasionally."

Phillip sounded as if he was smiling, and that surprised Darius, considering the acrimony with which they had last parted. He went quiet for a while, wondering what to say next. He'd expected at least a barrier of belligerence to overcome before he could get down to the meat of the conversation. But maybe brotherhood was like that. One moment, they could be rolling on the floor, brawling like grade-schoolers, and the next the anger was all gone.

The silence on the other end was patient. He couldn't even hear the sound of his brother's breathing. He floundered a bit, but then tried, "Mahalia was just here."

"I sort of figured she might turn up. She came to see me. Did she tell you that?"

"Yes." Shame made him squeeze his eyes shut.

"She's crazy over you. Did she tell you that, too?"

"Not in so many words." She hadn't needed so many words. He remembered the heat of her skin against his. And then thought about how cold he was, now that she was gone.

"Take it from me," Phillip confirmed, "she is."

And I sent her running, Darius thought, *over you.* "She left," he confessed.

"It didn't go well?"

It went well for the first few hours, he could have said, *and then I opened my big mouth and proved conclusively what an ass I am.* Instead, he only said, "No."

"Why not?"

"I lost it."

"Why?"

Frustration made Darius more honest than he would have been otherwise. "Over you, okay? She mentioned your name. She said she'd been to see you, and the next thing I knew there was this red veil over my eyes, and I started saying things."

Phillip groaned. "Oh, God, Dar, that was a long time ago."

"I know."

"She came over and stood in my garden, and there were just three feet between us; she looked at me, and I looked at her, and there was nothing there. It's long gone."

"Not for her. She's carried you around in her heart all these years, nursing you like an open wound. . . ."

"I'm sorry. I was a bastard to her. She never had any closure. I knew she wanted it, especially considering . . ."

"Will."

"Yes."

"She's still in love with you, at least a little." It hurt Darius to think it, and it hurt him to say it out loud. Mahalia had told him otherwise, right here in this same room, and as much as he wanted to, he wasn't sure he believed her, not 100 percent. He wanted to, but Phil had this all-consuming magnetic power over women that Darius could never dream to emulate. If there was a contest between them, then surely he would lose.

"*Was,* Darius, *was.* Maybe she carried this little flicker around, long after it was over between us—"

"She carried this whole ball of hurt around, you mean," he accused.

"I know. My fault. I told her I was sorry. Now I'm telling *you.* I did some things I shouldn't have done. I could have been kinder, especially considering . . . the circumstances. But that's all gone now. There's nothing left in there. Not for me."

"That's what she said."

"So why's she gone?"

Darius sighed. What could he say next? Embarrassment, and his jumbled feelings for his brother, hindered him from going any further. He tried hard, but eventually the best he could come up with was, "She said I've got to get you out of my system." Then he added miserably, "And she's right."

"And how am I in your system?" Phillip asked softly.

When he began to explain, it all came out in a rush, pent up over all those years and eager for an outlet. "I'm sick of it, Phillip. I'm sick of being treated like a child. I may be the youngest, but I'm a man, not a boy. I'm sick of your patronizing me, giving me things, offering me money. I earn my own keep. I may not be in your league yet—"

"You will be, one day. You're talented and brilliant, and there's a fortune waiting for you—"

He rushed on, unimpeded by his brother's encouragement. "Every time we get together, you try to force me ten years, fifteen years back into the past, when I *was* a kid, and when I *did* need you. When you were my hero. It's as if you need it."

"Need what?"

"To be a hero to . . . somebody."

Phillip inhaled sharply on the other end. Darius expected irritable denials. Phillip hated chinks in his armor to be pointed out. But the protests didn't come. "Maybe I do."

"But there's a little boy out there, who spent almost ten years searching for one, and you've done nothing."

"I know. I was wrong. But you're his hero now."

He was right. Darius was, in Will's eyes, the same thing that Phillip had always been in his. It felt good. He understood why Phillip would want it to drag on. But that was okay when he was a boy. He was an adult now, and he demanded to be treated like one. "It's different between you and me. There's no kid brother and big brother anymore. We'll always be siblings, but we're both men. I don't want any more of your patronizing attitude."

"Agreed."

"Or your money."

"Agreed."

"Or your hand-me-downs."

"Hailie isn't a hand-me-down."

"I didn't think she was!" Darius said hotly.

"Didn't you?"

"Well . . ." To be honest, that *had* been part of the problem. A huge part. "If I did, I had help."

"I'm sorry for what I said. We were fighting, and I was hopping mad. I wanted to hurt you—"

"You succeeded."

"I'm sorry. It wasn't true. Hailie isn't an old car, or a pair of jeans. She's a good woman, and if you love her—"

"I do."

"Then let it go. Forget about her and me—"

"Not possible. You left behind a little souvenir, remember?"

"That souvenir is a living child. I failed him, but then, like I said, I'm a bastard. You've always had a bigger heart than I. Don't fail him, too, because of me."

"I won't fail him. I love him. And blood's got nothing to do with it."

"Good. Because they're a package deal, him and her."

"I know. I don't have a problem with that. I *want* the whole package."

"So what are you waiting for? Set it down. Forget what there was between me and her. That's a long-dead corpse, crumbling in a graveyard. And forget what happened between you and me. I'll throw down my weapons, if you'll throw down yours, and let's swear a truce."

It sounded so good. He could have Mahalia's love, if it was still available, Will's trust, and his brother's friendship, all at the same time. All he had to do was throw off the mantle of angst he'd been wearing like a martyr. A hard, bitter ball formed deep in his throat, preventing him from getting a word out.

Phillip, unable to see him, persisted, still trying to convince him when he was already convinced. "You can do it. You're bigger than I am. Stronger. Just let it go. You remember that song Mama used to sing?"

Darius knew exactly which song Phillip was referring to.

It was an old Negro spiritual, passed on to their mother by an aunt who had come from the islands. Mama used to sing it when trouble lay on her heart, encouraging herself to set her problems down for the Lord to shoulder on her behalf.

Phillip began in his deep, perfect baritone:

> *"Leave your burdens,*
> *down by the riverside,*
> *down by the riverside,*
> *Leave your burdens,*
> *down by the riverside. . . ."*

"Carry them no more," Darius whispered. In all the hurt of the past week or so, he was sure that tears had never come to him, but right now his eyes were damp. He passed the back of his hand across them and swallowed hard, forcing down the lump.

"You remembered."

"Who could forget?" He closed his stinging eyes, and pictured himself walking alongside the banks of a broad river, shoulders bent under the weight of sibling rivalry and jealousy, of frustration and hurt, and then, kneeling, he set the huge bundle of emotions down. He felt physically lighter, as though his feet were about to leave the floor.

He would have remained in a trance with the phone pressed to his ear, had his brother not eventually said, "You okay?"

"Fine," he said, with perfect honesty.

"Good. So you'll go find her?"

A smile played about his mouth. "At first light."

"Good," Phillip said again. "And no more fighting between us, right? I'm a little too old for that."

"No more fighting," Darius agreed. "I'd probably kick your butt again, if we did."

Phillip laughed outright, some of his old arrogance flooding back into his voice. "You wish! You didn't kick it the last time. If I remember correctly, it took some effort to get your bloodstains out of my rug."

Darius rubbed his chin, clearly feeling the souvenir of *that* altercation. "Call it even, then. No more fighting."

"Fine with me, bro. If we were in the same room, we could shake on it."

"Your word's good enough for me." He felt warm all over, glowing, glad that things were all right once again between himself and one of the most important people in his world.

But Phillip had had enough, and put an end to the conversation with, "Hey, I don't know about you, but *I* need my sleep. I'm calling it a day."

Darius was exhausted, he realized, from the physical exertions of the evening and the emotional battering that he'd taken afterward. "I think I'll turn in myself."

"You do that. You've got a big day ahead of you. And good luck."

"I'll need it."

"You won't. What's destined to be yours will be yours. And trust me, Hailie's your destiny."

Oh, he sincerely hoped so. "Thank you."

"S'nothing." Phillip yawned. "And when you come down from cloud nine, y'all come and look me up, okay?"

Before Darius could accept or decline, the line went dead.

In the morning, Darius made a second phone call, one that was perhaps not as hard as the one he'd made the night before, but which took almost as much courage. The phone seemed to ring endlessly, and he came pretty close to hanging up in utter frustration, but just as his hand moved to do so, there was the softest of beeps, and then a voice.

"Coretta!" he said anxiously.

"Who's this?" The voice was cautious, suspicious, as though she already knew the answer to her question.

"It's Darius. Darius Grant."

"I knew it was you! Don't ask me how, boy, but I knew it was you. You have any idea what time it is? What's the matter, you think you God? Because He the only person I know who don't sleep."

Darius slapped his forehead. He'd forgotten the time difference between them. Coretta was right; it was very early. He'd probably woken her up. He apologized sincerely. "I'm sorry, Coretta. I realize it's early. I know you were probably sleeping. But please, it's an emergency."

"Somebody dead?" was her caustic rejoinder.

Darius tried to be patient. He struggled to remind himself that it wasn't so much that Coretta disliked him, but that she was trying, in her own ham-handed way, to protect her employer, whom she loved like a daughter. With this in mind, he kept his frustration out of his voice. "No, nothing like that. I just need to find Mahalia."

"She not here."

"I know that. She was here last night—"

"I tell her not to come, but she too hard-ears. You young people never want to listen to reason. I tell her she was wasting her time, but no, she leave here all hot and sweaty, saying she got to find you. . . ."

That made Darius feel good . . . sort of. At least she had been anxious to see him. He tried again. "Like I said, she found me, but then she left again, and now I have to find her. Please. It's important. What hotel is she staying in?"

"If she wanted you to know that, you don't think she woulda tell you?"

It embarrassed him to confess, "She left . . . uh . . . in a hurry. We had an argument . . ."

"Glory be!" was the sarcastic reply.

He felt heat rise to his face, but for the sake of the information he needed, he swallowed his pride and went on. "I made a mistake."

"You *did?*"

That did it. He was getting nowhere. His only hope was to be straight with the dragon-lady. "Look, Coretta, I know you don't like me—"

"That ain't true, boy. It ain't true one bit. I don't care about you one way or 'nother. I'm sure you could be a very nice boy if you really try. . . ."

In any other situation, that would have been funny. "Thank you."

She didn't even seem to have heard him. "But you know what? I'm only interested in that poor boy sleeping in his room, and that overburdened girl I got to take care of. I tired seeing her dragging around that burden of hurt, and I'm not about to let any man add to it."

"I'm not trying to add to it. All I want to do is take it away."

"Why? Why I should believe you, and why you want to do that?"

"There's only one answer to those questions." He bit down on his lip, reluctant to expose his heart to her ridicule, but it was the only way to get her to believe him, and thus trust him. "I love her. That's all I can tell you. I love her, and the last thing I want is to see her keep on hurting."

She snorted. "Boys your age, they only love with what they got in their pants."

That did it. He was tired of pleading, tired of throwing

himself upon her mercy. He squared his shoulders and put more authority into his voice. "I'm not a boy, Coretta, and frankly, I don't care if you like me or not, but respect me. Now, I need to see Mahalia—today. Tell me what hotel she's in."

She was quiet on the other end for so long that he was sure that the next sound he would hear would be the crash of her receiver in its cradle, but finally, she said, "She ain't in no hotel."

Well, at least they were getting somewhere. "So she's staying with a friend?"

"Nope. She ain't in no hotel because she done check out already."

Darius almost dropped the phone. "What?"

"She call me. She say she change her flight, and she coming home early. She probably in the air by now. You too late."

Arrows shot through him. Couldn't she have said that in the first place? "What airline? What flight?"

There was hesitation, and a deep sigh.

"Coretta. . . ." The single word held an implicit threat.

She caved in, reluctantly. "You got a pen and paper?"

"Just tell me." There was nothing that would dislodge that data from his mind. As she read off the flight information from whatever she'd jotted it down on, he was already hopping around the room, dragging his shoes on and scrambling around for his coat. He might just make it to the airport in time, if the foul weather, which had worsened significantly overnight, would cut him some slack on the expressway. He was halfway out the door with the phone still pressed to his ear. "Thank you, Coretta. Thank you. God bless you for this."

"Humph," was all she replied.

* * *

Detroit Metropolitan Airport was in chaos, and in compliance with chaos theory, things were getting worse by the minute. To say that Hailie wasn't happy would be an understatement. She had had to haul her weary, aching body out of bed at the crack of dawn after a horrid, restless night wherein the few distracted moments of sleep that she had managed to grab were plagued by images of Darius. Then, after finding a taxi willing to brave the sleet-stricken roads, she had sat restlessly in the back-seat staring at the howling sheet of whiteness outside her window as the driver struggled to get them safely through weather that was becoming increasingly foul.

Now she stood in line, her lone traveling bag sitting between her boots, in exactly the same spot that it had been for the last ten minutes. The disorderly line of disgruntled travelers certainly wasn't moving anywhere. She craned her neck to see what was going on up ahead, but all she could see were the dark shapes of other heads doing the same. Even in her bleary just-got-up-after-a-lousy-night mental state, it was obvious: something was wrong.

"Just what I need," she grunted. She looked at her watch. By rights, they should have been boarding by now, and yet it looked like half the passengers on the flight hadn't even checked in. She rubbed her forehead with her gloved hand. This could not get any worse.

And then, it did. A collective groan rose from her fellow sufferers, one that began at the front and rolled down to her, and beyond her, like a wave, bringing with it unwelcome information. Their flight was delayed—for an unknown length of time. As though sensing their parents' frustration, the babies and infants, who had been up to this time dozing in exhausted heaps on shoulders and in carriers, began wailing, and the wails grew into a chorus as child after child took a cue from the others.

After the usual protests were made and rebuffed up front, the line dispersed dejectedly.

"Great." Hailie stood there for several moments, something inside her half hoping that the customer representatives who had delivered the unwelcome information would laugh, call them all back with a wave of the hand, and explain that they had only been joking, that the flight was in fact leaving in twenty minutes, and would they all step this way?

Obviously, it was not to be. She gave in to the inevitable, grasped the handle of her bag, and dragged it over to the nearest passenger lounge. By the time she arrived, all of the seats had been taken, and she had to make do with a standing position by one of the huge windows. She pressed her face against the icy glass, hoping that the coolness would at least help her raging headache.

The world outside was a silent, swirling mass of white. Snow wasn't falling down: it pelted in at an angle, but before hitting the ground it was snatched up by the wind and hurled about in flurries, spinning and twirling like mad dervishes. It was obvious: she and the others on her flight weren't the only ones stranded. There wasn't an airplane on the ground that was leaving any time soon.

What to do, then? Hang around in the discomfort of the lounge, suffering alongside the others, like souls in limbo waiting on the next boat to Hades? Or go outside and see if there was a taxi driver lunatic enough to drive back to the hotel? Either way, she would be miserable.

She exhaled in a gust. "Back to the hotel, I think." She grasped her bag again, but was assailed by another thought. If she returned to the city, she could be making herself a sitting target. If Darius came looking for her, she would be easier to find there. She dismissed the idea. That was stupid. There had to be a thousand hotels in

Detroit. She hardly imagined that Darius, if in fact he even wanted to find her, would sit with a phone book on his lap, calling each one until he hit the jackpot.

Besides, he probably wasn't going to come looking for her anyway. She'd made it abundantly clear last night that she'd had enough of his nonsense. She could go back, and take a nap in peace, or find somewhere closer and more accessible, and do the same. Darius wouldn't be bothering her any time soon. She spun around to head for the nearest exit, not allowing herself time to wonder whether she in fact really wished the solitude she was seeking, or whether deep in her heart she longed for him to charge up on a white steed—or at least ride up on the hotel elevator—and bang on the door, demanding to have her back.

For her own self-preservation, she shoved any and all such thoughts of weakening from her mind, and took a hurried step forward—careening straight into a hard, living obstacle. "Oh, I'm . . ." she began, but before she could say, "sorry," a pair of arms came up and locked around her.

"Mahalia."

Darius? Here? Nah: she was losing her mind. A hundred flights came and left this airport at any given time. Even if he had assumed that she would be leaving this morning, finding her among this vast network of terminals and concourses was like finding *a specific strand of hay* in a haystack. Surely it couldn't really be he!

"Baby, love, you haven't left." He squeezed her bewildered and pliant form against his chest. "Thank God!"

She stared up into his face, struggling to reconcile her logical denial of his presence with the physical proof of it. "Is it really you?"

His laugh rumbled against her chest. "It's me, love. Are you glad to see me?"

Glad to see him? She wasn't going near that question with the proverbial pole. "How did you get here? How did you know I was here?"

"First question: I got here by the grace of God. I nearly killed myself a dozen times on the way over." He jerked his chin toward the white-blanketed window behind her. "If hell froze over, that's what it would look like."

"And . . . ?"

"Second question: Coretta told me where you'd be. I called, and she gave me your flight number—"

Her eyes widened. "Coretta told you . . ." Incredulity prevented her from finishing.

"I know. I almost can't believe it myself."

She glanced toward the window again and murmured, "Maybe hell really has frozen over. . . ." Then, realizing that they were straying from the point, she squirmed, trying to wriggle from his grasp. He resisted, and held her fast.

Maybe, if she were tortured with red-hot tongs, she'd admit that just seeing him here had lit a fire in her heart, but that didn't mean anything had changed. She considered her options fast, and decided that her best course of action was to play hardball.

She frowned. "That doesn't explain why you're here."

His brows lifted in surprise. "Can't you guess?"

"No, I can't. I don't want to. I told you all I had to tell you last night. Nothing's changed from then to now." She took in his ragged appearance; apart from his boots and insufficiently warm jacket, he was still wearing the same gray sweats she had met him in last evening, and even then they hadn't been fresh as daisies. "Including your clothes," she couldn't stop herself from saying.

He looked down at himself bemusedly, scratching the stubble on his chin that was rapidly heading in the direction of becoming a beard. "Oh, right. I hadn't noticed. I mean, I had noticed, but I needed to get out of there, fast, and come after you. I didn't have time to get too cleaned up. I heard you were leaving and all I could think of was beating you to your flight. I'm sorry. I must look frightful."

You look gorgeous, she wanted to say, but maintained her hard line. "Forget how you look. I asked you a question. . . ."

"I'm here for you." He looked puzzled, as though that much had to be obvious.

"I can see that. But I told you—"

"*That's* changed. I promise you. You were right. It wasn't you putting Phillip between us. It was me. But that's over now. I got it out of my sys—"

"*Overnight?*" She was incredulous.

He nodded, face solemn. "Overnight. I know it sounds—"

She struggled once more to free herself from his grasp, and this time he let her go. "It sounds like a load of—"

"It's the truth. It's the *truth,* Mahalia. I was peeved and jealous and distrustful, but that was all my problem. It never had anything to do with you. I came to you with that chip on my shoulder. You didn't put it there."

"And you knocked it off in one night?" she asked disbelievingly.

"No, but in one night I made a commitment to knock it off. I called Phil—"

"You called him?" Unbelievable, she thought. A week ago, they were bloodying up each other's faces.

"Yes. He's still my brother. Nothing's going to change that."

There, he had a point.

Before she could say anything more, he rushed on. "But that has to do with him and me. It's separate. What I'm concerned about now is me and you."

Like a dog with a smelly bone, she still wasn't willing to let the issue of Phillip rest just yet. "And you're willing to forget everything else. All that happened between him and me. Him being my ... uh ... first, and all." She cringed a little, and waited.

"I don't care. It doesn't matter. All that matters is that I be your next, and your next, and your next ..." She moved a little out of his range, unable to bear his proximity, but instead of pulling her back to him, he stepped toward her. "I love you. That's bigger than everything else. It's more important than everything else."

The din around them, children crying, people complaining, arguing and jostling to make themselves more comfortable, rose to a roar—or maybe it was simply the sound of blood rushing in her ears. He hadn't said *that* before. Not out loud. Not in so many words. They'd talked about desire, about sexual need, compatibility, and companionship, but not ... this.

She struggled to repeat his words, as though speaking them for the first time herself. "You ... love ..."

He repeated it for her. "I love you." A smile danced on his lips, and even on this frigid white day, his eyes blazed like bright fire. "You, and all that you are. Hailie, soft and funny. Mahalia, smart and hardworking and brilliant. And Veda, hungry and sexy, wonderful and wild—"

"Veda's not me," she protested.

"Oh, yes, she is. How else could you write about her so intimately? She's a primitive soul living deep inside you, and I see her sometimes. . . ." He leaned even closer, so that his body formed a shield between her and the roar of the world outside them, and touched her lightly on the breast. ". . . Every time I touch you. I heard her last night, when you were under me, and you closed your eyes and moaned."

Her coat, which she hadn't bothered to remove

during her frantic race along the concourse, suddenly felt constricting. "Darius, stop. . . ."

"I want to see her again tonight, night after night, full moon or not. . . ."

She was sweating. The several layers of clothes covering her were baking her slowly, like a Dutch oven. With shaking hands, she peeled off the padded jacket and tossed it over the handle of her bag. She tore her gloves off, and let them fall.

"Undressing already?" he murmured.

"Hot in here," she answered. The hair at her nape was damp. "So," she asked, still a little disbelieving, "you think you're Romulus?"

"No, not really. I'm just plain old me . . . until I'm near you. Then, something happens. Then I feel bigger and stronger than I really am . . . and hungry. I want to take long, luscious bites out of you. I want to eat you up. Lick you all over . . ."

She shivered, in spite of her heat.

". . . Take you back to a primitive time, where we don't need to be civilized. Where it can just be us and the elements, thunder and lightning, crashing down on us, arcing between us. Where we can take each other apart and put each other back together again. . . ."

This was too much to handle. She needed to sit down, or she'd fall.

He sensed her need, and slipped an arm around her waist. "I've got you," he assured her. "I won't let you down."

I won't let you down. Was that a promise he could keep? She needed to believe that. She closed her eyes and let him support her weight.

"And Veda?"

"Huh?"

He asked the question as though his life were hanging on her answer. "Does Veda love Romulus?"

She hesitated. Admission meant commitment. After this, there was no turning back. She took a leap of faith into the void. "She does. Very much."

He was persistent. "And Hailie? Does she think Darius stands a chance?"

She swayed on her feet, glad that he was holding her, and then fell forward against his chest, burying her face in his jacket. "Oh, God, Darius, you'll never know how much I . . ." His jacket, already damp from melted snow, rapidly became wetter.

Concerned, he stroked her hair. "I didn't mean to make you cry, sweet."

"It's embarrassing. There are people all over."

"People cry in airports all the time. People meet and part. Relationships end, and begin. . . . Cry if you want to. Nobody cares."

"I care. And I can't stop," she sobbed.

"You don't have to. Let it all out. It's just a period at the end of a sentence. When you're done, we can start our own new paragraph. One that begins with 'we.'"

That almost made her laugh through her tears. "That was corny. You'd make a lousy writer."

"That's okay, love. I make a damn good artist." He waited until she was finished, withdrew a handkerchief from some hidden pocket or the other, and helped her blow her nose as one would a child. Then he held each of her hands in his huge ones. "Come home with me. We can talk. Or *not* talk."

She glanced at the windows. "I doubt you'd even find your car, much less the road. . . ."

He bent over and managed to gather up her things while retaining one of her hands. "Then walk with me. It's a big airport: we're bound to find a seat—in a quiet corner." He walked slowly, allowing her to keep up with him in spite of his long legs.

But there was more on her mind than just her and him. "Darius," she began.

He slowed down even more, but didn't stop walking. "Yes?"

"What about Will?"

Now he stopped, and turned to look down at her. "What *about* Will?"

"He's really your nephew. . . ."

"I know. It doesn't matter. It doesn't change anything. Being his uncle won't stop me from fathering him."

"You'd do that for me?"

He shook his head. "I'd do that for *me*. I love him because he's yours, I love him because he's family, but I love him most because he's a unique little boy who just grabbed on to my heart and won't let go."

The last of her tears were dried up by the warmth of his words. She couldn't think of anything to say other than, "Oh."

"Give me a chance. Believe in me. Let me tie things up here and come back to California with you. Let's finish our book. Let's start something else. Let me be your husband, your man, your lover, your protector, your . . . Romulus. Let me be Will's daddy. There'll be a lot of love in that house, because I have a lot of love to give. For you, and Will, and Coretta—"

"Not Coretta!" Now he was going to make her laugh out loud.

He shrugged. "Why not?"

"She's taken to you like a cat to water."

"Doesn't matter. I can be charming when I want to."

"Coretta doesn't like charming."

"That's because she hasn't tasted my brand of charming." He smiled like a devil in angel's clothing. "When I'm done with her, she'll love me to pieces."

"That I'll have to see."

Still smiling, he tugged on her hand, coaxing her to follow him. "Trust me," he urged.

She did.

ABOUT THE AUTHOR

Roslyn Carrington, who writes romance as Simona Taylor, just can't believe her luck. She was born and raised in the Caribbean twin-island state of Trinidad and Tobago, and if ever there was a setting created for romance, this is it! By day she puts her creativity to work as a public relations officer for a major local company, and by night she encounters the fantastic creations that people her imagination, who come alive on her screen and on these pages as she pounds away at her keyboard.

She regrets to break it to her readers that since the birth of her son, she has been unable to write a single page—at least, nothing that he hasn't torn to tatters and eaten. Judging from this evidence, she is sure that he will grow up to be either a literary critic or one of those circus stuntmen who takes bikes apart and eats them.

You can write to her at:

7260 NW 25th Street

Suite #T-926

Miami, Fl 33122

You can also visit her Web site at www.roslyncarrington.com or e-mail her at simona@roslyncarrington.com